The Lake Trilogy

Safe Harbor

AnnaLisa Grant

For Truman and Claire, my miracles.

In three words I can sum up everything I've learned about life: it goes on.
-Robert Frost

Chapter 1

I know I shouldn't, but I've never wanted someone to die as much as I do Gregory Meyer.

It's been 18 days since Holly Reynolds shot Will's father on the steps of the federal court building. Too many days for whatever is keeping him alive – because it certainly isn't a heart – to stop functioning and rid the earth of the most treacherous man I've ever known.

Of course, even in his final days he has everyone eating out of the palm of his hand. I don't know how, but even in the ICU he's managed to make the entire staff cater to his every unconscious need. Private room, fresh flowers every day, doctors for whom he is their only patient.

My best guess during those first days had been that his minions from Meyer, Fincher, and Marks were seeing who could kiss ass enough to make partner when he woke up, but Luke told me, and I wasn't surprised by it at all, that Meyer knew he would be targeted by those he had *challenged* so he had an extremely detailed living will explaining who was to do what, right down to the fresh peonies.

Luke has been in touch with the hospital administrator, a good friend of his, right from the beginning. Meyer was immediately sent to surgery and his injuries were explored. They cleaned out the wounds, breathing a huge sigh of relief that the bullet lodged close enough to the surface of his head that they could get it out without any problem. He's been on a ventilator since then, intimidating people from his comatose state.

Luke went back to Davidson a few days after the shooting to see Holly. He's representing her, pro bono of course. He kept waiting for Meyer to flat line before he went, but it was taking too long and he wanted to get to Holly before anyone else could. There are enough attorneys in five states who would love to defend the woman who put an end to Meyer's reign of terror, bringing relief to any attorney who had the misfortune to be his opposing counsel, but Luke is adamant that there is no way he's letting any of them near her. Luke has been commuting between Davidson and Tallahassee for weeks now, and I imagine he'll be on the next flight out today.

The poor girl has been waiting for over two weeks to know if she's facing murder charges or not. I suppose she went into this prepared to face murder charges. Nobody would shoot Gregory Meyer just to injure him. The objective would definitely be to kill. To leave him alive would only open the doors to a worse fate than if Satan himself came after you.

I haven't seen a lot of Will since the day of the shooting. During these last 18 days Luke and Will have had at least a dozen closed-door meetings. Day after day Will has walked in the front door of the house, kissed me briefly, and made a beeline to Luke's office. He hasn't even looked back as he's closed the door to the office behind him. We've barely spoken when we are together, both consumed with making sure Eliana is alright, although Wes is doing a great job without us. We haven't had a date in I don't know how long, and I can't remember the last time Will *really* kissed me. I miss Will and the absence of him has me questioning the future of our relationship again.

Everyday new information has come out about what a horrible man Gregory Meyer was. Evidence has been leaked and the news is happy to report it. Some of it is Eli's that had been corroborated by Luke and Wes. Some of it is news to all of us. As new evidence comes to light, more people have been speaking out on Holly's behalf, supporting her for ridding the world of such a tyrant.

I'm happy the truth is finally being revealed. That people who had once lived in fear of Gregory Meyer are now free and making public proclamations of it. All I can think, though, is that I was finally coming into my own and now it's all being overshadowed, once again, by Gregory Meyer. I had just been fitted into my mother's wedding dress when Meyer was shot, and now I'm not even sure if I'm ever going to get to wear it.

It didn't take long for me to start hating Holly for creating such a mess, even though I understand her motive. With jurors conveniently dying and disappearing off the face of the earth, it was starting to look like Meyer would never be made to pay for his transgressions. I think I always knew that I'd live to see the day an attempt on Gregory Meyer's life was made. I just never thought it would be by Holly. But after Meyer drove Marcus to the breaking point, it seems Holly wasn't going to let him get away with it.

As the days have dragged on I've become increasingly frustrated. I've done my best to push aside my growing hatred toward Holly for the upheaval of my life she's inadvertently caused, and tried to be supportive of Will, understanding that despite the turmoil of their relationship, Will watched his father get shot on national television. My overwhelming sense of unfairness has been taking over, though. I thought the days of keeping things from each other, even with the purest intentions of protecting the other one, were over. Will's silent insistence on keeping me out of the loop is devastating.

As understanding as I've tried to be, the fact still remains that I'm Will's fiancée and as such should be privy to Will's meetings with Luke.

When I woke up this morning, I made a decision to do something a little childish, but I have to get my point across. I'm sure I'll regret it later, but not enough to stop me. Enough is enough. I have to get my point across to those men.

"So what are we talking about today, boys?" I ask, sauntering into Luke's office as if I had been given a royal invitation, dropping myself onto the luxurious leather chair next to Will.

"Layla…what are you doing?" Will's face scrunches with confusion.

"I'm tired of being treated like I can't be trusted with information. So…what are we talking about today?"

"I understand your need for information, Layla, but you don't need to concern yourself," Luke says in that protective-father voice he likes to use to calm me down. What he doesn't realize is that I'm perfectly calm and not going anywhere.

"How does what you two have been meeting about *not* concern me? Isn't the idea behind marriage that you become one with the other person?" I say, letting my irritation rise to the top of my voice earlier than I planned.

"Honey, there are a several different scenarios we're trying to work through," Will starts.

"Like what?" I ask in retort.

"Like…" Will begins but hesitates. I stare at him, hoping to convey my deep hurt at having been ignored since his father was shot. That whatever they're trying to figure out *does* concern me because everything about Will's life concerns me. "What if my father dies? How long does he stay on the ventilator? When does the plug get pulled and who has the authority to pull it? What if he makes it through but is a vegetable? Any of these circumstances would mean that we can go back to Davidson. We're just trying to figure out what the plan would be," Will explains.

"So, let me get this straight…you two are in here trying to decide how to ease us back into a life in Davidson should Gregory Meyer die or end up with turnips for brains. This would involve me transferring to another college and moving away from the life I've been building here. Tell me again how I don't need to concern myself."

"There will be questions about where my mother and I have been, and why we left. The press is going to hound us. They'll want answers and I don't want you to worry about that. I'm just trying to protect you," Will says, taking a step toward me. He reaches his hand out to take mine but I step back and pull away.

"No, you're underestimating my ability to handle things like you always do. If this is what our life together is going to be like, maybe this isn't the life I want." I storm out of the office and make my way straight to the dock, not knowing or caring if Will is following.

I sit at the edge of the dock feeling proud for having asserted myself, and embarrassed that I didn't just pull Will aside and have a normal conversation with him. I know I have to apologize to him for how I handled the situation, but I will not apologize for how I feel. Will and I have been through too much for him to still think that he has to protect me from everything. I know he's still shaken from the danger I put myself in when I connected with Marcus behind his and Luke's backs, but when is he going to learn that I'm a big girl? Haven't I proven that I can handle whatever life throws me?

"I'm sorry," Will says as he positioned himself close to me on the dock. "I should have known that you would want to be involved."

"Yes, you should have. I don't understand why everyone thinks I'm some fragile little girl. I've been through so much already. What do I have to do to prove myself?" I say to Will, hoping to communicate my frustration and hurt with one single look.

"That's just it, Layla. You've been through enough already. When will you let go and just allow yourself to be totally taken care of? I spent too long not being able to do that for you. Do you know how hard it was not to be able to protect you, the one person whose job it is for me to defend? I made choices that lead to keeping my hands tied, forcing you into a position of having to take care of more than you should have." Will cups my face and stares into my eyes to drive his own point home. "I'm sorry I didn't include you, but I'm not sorry for my reasons why. I finally have the opportunity to protect you in a way I never could before. *Please* let me do that."

I consider what Will has said, knowing that keeping me out of the loop was rooted in his love for me, his desire to protect me. I imagine he knows better than I do what the press is capable of, but there has to be a happy medium.

"I get it. I do," I sigh. "I feel like we take three steps forward and two steps back. We are never going to survive if we don't stop thinking the other is incapable of handling life. If we don't truly start working as a team…I don't think we're going to make it, Will." I feel defeated, like somehow we should have this down by now but we're failing miserably.

"Don't say that! We *will* make it. We *are* making it. I'm sorry that I didn't involve you. I promise, from this second on, I will not keep anything from you…if *you* promise that you'll let me take care of you. That's all I want to do, Layla. That's all I've ever wanted to do." I smile and nod, and we seal our promise with a sweet kiss. "Did you really mean what you said about not being sure if you want a life with me?"

"No. I'm sorry. I shouldn't have acted the way I did. I was just really frustrated. I kept waiting for you to fill me in, letting me be there for you the way you are for me, but it never happened. Then I felt like it passed the point where I could ask. I guess we're all still in shock and acting a little out of character. How are you doing?"

"Surprisingly well, actually. I think I might feel differently when he dies though." Will shakes his head, seeming to clear that thought from his mind.

"He might pull through, you know," I say in an attempt to comfort him. I don't tell him what I'm really thinking, which is the thought of his father surviving is scarier to me than anything. He'll go after Holly, which I'm sure will somehow send him looking in our direction. Regardless of how cut off he has always been from his father, I don't tell Will that I wish his father would die, and die quickly.

"Layla, he's not going to make it. Luke said the doctors told him Holly would definitely be facing murder charges. It's just a matter of time."

"Oh," I say, not knowing really how to respond, but glad I don't break out into a happy dance because that would be in ridiculously poor taste.

"Listen, I don't want to talk about my father dying. There's more involved to my meeting with Luke. Do you still want me to tell you?"

"Yes, but first, I'm sorry I didn't just pull you aside and talk to you," I tell him.

"It's ok, Layla. I understand why you were upset. I should have kept you in the loop." Will pulls me closer to him, wrapping his arms around me, melting away all of the frustration I had been feeling.

"So what else is going on?" I ask.

"Well…it turns out Dad never changed his will."

"What?" I furrow my brow trying to comprehend how Gregory Meyer could have been so neglectful as to not change his will. "Does that mean what I think it means?"

"Yep."

"Wow. What's your mom going to do with all that money?"

"She's not going to do anything with it. It's not hers," Will says with almost a tone of sadness in his voice.

"If it's not hers, then…"

"He left everything to me. There are even instructions on how I'm to decide how my mother spends the allowance I'm supposed to give her. I guess he assumed by the time he died he would have groomed me into the man he expected me to be. It's so gross."

"Well, then…what are *you* going to do with all that money?" I ask, thinking Will might have some great philanthropic idea. Surely Will has some grand plan to use his father's money for good, even if just to make Meyer turn over in his grave.

"Nothing. I don't want it," he says with disgust.

"What do you mean you don't want it? How could you not want it?" I remember that Will and I had a conversation about his disdain for wealth during our wonderful Day of Nothing. A smile crosses my face as I recall the other activities besides talking that filled that day and have to redirect my thoughts before they get out of hand. Will has never been interested in the monetary legacy that belongs to him. Had his father not been so manically focused on dollar signs, Will may have grown up to feel differently. "Don't you think you deserve it after everything he put you and your mother through?"

"It's blood money, Layla. Not a single dime of it was earned with any legitimacy. The law was broken and lives were destroyed. I can't take that money." Will's face is hard, pained even. Time has not healed the wounds his father using money as a weapon caused.

"How much, Will?" I ask because I want to know how far down the mental list of all the good that could be done with it I can go. I also have a feeling that the *amount* of money Will is set to inherit is playing into the weight he's trying so hard not to carry.

It takes Will almost a whole minute before he answers me, and even then it isn't a complete answer. "Nine figures." He sounds almost ashamed.

I silently gasp. I knew Will's father was insanely wealthy, I just didn't know how insane it was. *Nine figures. Wow.*

"Then do something great with it, Will. Do something your father would have never done. Start a scholarship. Start a hundred scholarships! There are dozens of non-profit organizations that are on the brink of going under because they don't have the funding. Find the families he screwed over and help *them* with it. Keep what you think we need, and give the rest away, or give it all away. I don't care. I just think it would be a waste to let it sit there, or go back into the firm, just because it's dirty. You can make it clean, Will."

"I…I hadn't thought of it that way. I've been so perplexed as to why he wouldn't have changed his will when as far as he knew we were dead. Then it pissed me off that he left it to me and not my mom. He treated her like crap for years and then she doesn't even get anything in the end?" Will sighs, showing his heavy heart. "I don't want to hate him, Layla. It's hard not to, though, when even after he's dead and gone he's still disrespecting my mother."

"I understand. But…you know you have to forgive him. He'll keep you trapped in the hate that filled his heart if you don't forgive him and let it go. I think there might be some extra floating lanterns in the garage." I smile and stroke Will's face thinking about the night I was able to let go of all the pain and unforgivness Gram had planted in me. It was a night of sweet release that Will, Luke, and Claire orchestrated in an act of pure love for me.

"Thanks. That's not a bad idea." Will kisses me and reciprocates the sweet touch on my cheek. "In the meantime, Luke and I were also trying to figure out the best way to explain about mom and me 'dying.' I never thought we'd be going back, so I never thought of having to explain myself to anyone." Will is changing the direction of our conversation as a means of not having to talk about the feelings associated with his father. We process things similarly in that we both have to take some time in our own heads before we can really articulate anything. If we don't take that time, we end up a crumpled mess of tears and unintelligible rants.

"So…we're definitely going back?" I ask. I don't mind going back to Davidson, but no one has asked my opinion and I hate that the decision has been made for me.

"Why wouldn't we?"

"Because we're building a life here? We're getting married in a few months…here. And what about school?"

"We'll finish the semester and then move back. It's only eight weeks," Will answers as if the solution is an obvious one.

"I'm supposed to finish the semester, pack a house, move, and plan a wedding all in a three month time span? Will, honey, you're delusional. There's no way! Something will have to give." I sigh heavily, not knowing just how heavy, and feel the sting of tears starting. I don't want to cry, but the thought of trying to pull everything off is immediately overwhelming.

I don't understand why there is such a sense of immediacy in moving back to Davidson. Will has been gone for over a year, and with Holly's impending trial I don't see the need to add more drama to the situation. We could at least wait until after we get back from our honeymoon, letting Luke handle everything in Davidson between now and then. There will be time to finish the semester, get married, and then move back to Davidson if he really wants.

I ponder this thought and start to see the benefits of moving back to a Davidson as I realize it's no longer silently run by a devious manipulator. I think about how the newspapers might read a little differently now that they're free to print the truth about Meyer, possibly recanting stories and setting them straight. I think about how the air might even smell differently, and the crowd at the Concert on the Green might actually intermingle now that there won't be such heavily drawn lines.

In this moment I feel like I can get on board with moving back to Davidson. That Will and I could go back as husband and wife, a *new* Mr. and Mrs. Meyer. We could work together to build trust in the Meyer name and start a new legacy, eventually starting a family of our own. A smile spreads across my face and I'm about to lay out my thoughts to Will when he bursts every bubble and shoots down every idea I have with one look.

"You're right," he says, hardening his face. "Something *will* have to give…which is why I think we should postpone the wedding."

Chapter 2

"He really said that?" Caroline asks through the phone. Living in California she's lost some of her southern drawl, but when she's mad, it shows up and does double duty for all the time it's been away.

"Yeah," I say sadly after recapping the last 27 days to her. She's gotten snips and pieces via text, but this is the first time we've really talked. She actually called me after her mom called her this afternoon to tell her Will's father finally died.

"What did you say?"

"I didn't know what to say so I just got up and walked away. I *still* don't know what to say. It's been over a week and we've barely spoken. I haven't said anything about it and he hasn't mentioned it again. I'm trying to understand, Caroline. Really, I am. It's not like he thinks we should postpone the wedding on some whim. I get that there's a lot going on. But then I'm kinda pissed. After everything he put me through about me not wanting to set a date, now *he's* the one avoiding getting married? No one has to know he's still alive. I mean, what if Holly hadn't shot his father? There'd still be a trial going on and we'd be going to school and planning our wedding!"

"Do you think he wanted to postpone it until he knew for sure what was happening with his dad? I mean, maybe now that he's dead Will feels differently. I know he hated his dad, but it's still his dad. Now that his father is dead, has he given you any indication that he feels differently about postponing the wedding?" I both love and hate how Caroline can be on my side and still make me think about the other side. I need the logic, but sometimes I just want to be selfish.

"I don't know. I haven't even seen him today. He was already holed up in Luke's office when I came downstairs. I know he said I could be included now, but..."

"You haven't even seen him today? GO IN THERE!" Caroline demands. "Go into that office and talk to him, Layla. You're not some weak little girl. You're his fiancée and he's opened the door for you to be involved. Now, more than ever, you need to be with him. I don't care what the circumstances were around their relationship, and I don't care what you two have left unsaid, his father just died and *you* need to be with him. I'm hanging up now. I love you and I'll talk to you later."

Just like that Caroline is gone and I'm left in the wake of her logical instructions. I don't know why I'm scared to go in there. Yes, I do. Without waiting or even asking for an explanation I walked away from one of the most important conversations Will and I have ever had, and I haven't spoken of it since. It was a conversation that left me reeling, questioning my future. Now I'm supposed to go into that office and console my fiancé over the loss of his father, a man who made our lives as complicated as they are right now.

She's right, though. *She's always right.* I make my way downstairs to Luke's office. The door is still closed so I knock twice before opening it. Will and Luke are seated as I found them the day I pouted my way into their conversation. I don't say anything this time. I just look at Will, watching to see his reaction to me. This is the first time in over a week I've been intentional about seeking him out. Every other day we've just happened to find ourselves in the same room.

"I'll leave you two alone," Luke says, excusing himself and closing the door behind him. Will stands and faces me as the door clicks closed.

It takes me a few minutes to say anything, waiting to see if Will has anything to say first. After walking away as I did that day, I feel like Will should have the chance to express his displeasure with me before I make any attempt at an apology.

"I'm so sorry about your dad, Will," I say, deciding he's probably giving me a chance to speak first since I'm the one who walked away. I rush to him, hoping his arms will receive me. "I'm so sorry about everything!" Will holds me and strokes my hair, his first sign in telling me not to worry.

"It's ok, Layla, it's ok," he says softly.

"It's *not* ok. I've behaved so poorly over the last several weeks, and when we had just agreed to work together *I* left the conversation. I left you to figure things out on your own and that was wrong. I'm sorry. I won't do that again. I promise." I hope he can hear the pleading tone in my voice because that's exactly what I'm doing. I'm pleading with him to believe that I'm not going to shut down again. "We're in this together and I will never let anything come between us again. If you think we should postpone the wedding, then we'll do it."

"It was unfair of me to spring that on you the way I did. If I had let you be a part of the conversations I'd been having with Luke you'd have understood my reasons. *I* shut down. I kept you out and then out of nowhere I suggested changing the biggest day of our lives." Will takes a deep breath of resolve. "What do you say to a *serious* do-over?"

"How far back are we going?" I ask.

"How's 27 days?" he says.

"I can do that." I lay my head on Will's chest, listening to his heartbeat go from pounding to a regulated beat. "I really am sorry about your dad."

"I know. Thanks." Will rubs circles on my back and rests his chin on the top of my head. I feel his breath ruffle my hair and it gives me chill bumps. He smells divine and I realize how much I've missed this over the last weeks. I wrap my arms tighter around Will's middle and he responds with a kiss to the top of my head.

"I'm sorry I didn't come see you as soon as Claire told me," I tell him. Caroline is right. Despite what the relationship was like, Will's father just died. The saddest part is that now that he's gone, the hope that things could ever be different between them is gone, too. I remember feeling so hopeful that one day Will's father would come around. It seems silly now,

15

considering the series of events over the last year and a half, but I was hopeful nonetheless. "How are you?"

"It's ok, Layla. It's been a rough few weeks. I don't know that any of us have been ourselves. I'm ok. I had long enough to prepare for it." Will releases me and guides me to the leather loveseat. "I thought a lot about what you said, about having to forgive him," he says as we sit. Will takes my hand in both of his, lacing his fingers through mine. "I have to forgive him or my life is going to be filled with regret, and I don't want to live like that. My father lived with the regret of his father, and I'm not going to leave that legacy for our children."

Our children. That sounds so wonderful. It's nice to know that even though he thinks we should postpone the wedding he's still thinking about our future like this. This makes me immediately want to talk about why he thinks we need to postpone the wedding, but I hold my tongue and wait for a better moment.

"I'm happy to help you with that, if you want me to," I offer with a sympathetic smile.

"I know you are, and I'm not trying to keep you out of anything…" Will begins. I know what he's trying to say and I don't want him to feel badly about it so I cut him off.

"Don't worry about it, Will. Floating lanterns don't work for everyone. Some people need to forgive in private, processing through it in their own way. I don't think you're shutting me out. If I thought that, this would be a very different conversation right now. As united as we are, there are still things we have to do on our own. The important thing is that we communicate that." I run my fingers through Will's hair, fixing it into a messier state. I love that he's let his hair grow longer. It suites him well. "Can you talk to me about your thoughts on needing to postpone the wedding?" I ask, keeping my heart in check. I'm still hurt by this idea, but have had to give my mind the lead on this so that I can be open to hearing Will's logic on the subject.

"That...well..." Will stumbles a bit in collecting his thoughts.

"Spit it out, Will. We're beyond searching for the perfect phrasing so we don't accidentally hurt the other one's feelings," I tell him. I hold his eyes with mine wanting to convey the finality of my message. I truly am done with the drama of it all. Will and I are forever and nothing is going to change that.

"Ok. Well...I meant it when I said that we should postpone the wedding because of how overwhelming things are right now. We've got school, and packing, and Luke is going to be gone a lot, taking Claire with him at times. Something truly would have to give." Will moves closer to me on the loveseat, twisting his body to face me fully. "Those aren't the most important reasons, though. Right now, Will Meyer is dead. And...I know you were happy that I chose your father's name as my new one, but," Will tucks my hair behind my ear and holds my face in his hand. It's warm and I automatically lean into it, closing my eyes for a moment as I relish his touch. "I want Layla Weston to marry Will Meyer. Unless we go back to Davidson, bring everything out into the open, and resurrect Will Meyer, that can never happen."

"Oh," is all I can manage. I hadn't thought of that, and now I feel foolish for having walked away when the explanation was so sweet and simple. Sometimes I really can be a silly girl.

"If you're worried that we won't get married in the gardens like your parents, don't. I don't care where we live, getting married here in the gardens is important to you and I'm going to make that happen." I can see the worry on Will's face. I haven't responded clearly enough to let him know that his reasoning makes perfect sense. "This is our chance to make things as they should have been. Layla, please say something."

"I'm sorry."

Will brow furrows and that cute little 'v' appears above his nose.

"I'm sorry I didn't give you a chance to explain before. If I had, the last nine days wouldn't have been so heartbreaking. If this is your reason why we should postpone the wedding, then I'm in total agreement. Layla Weston wants to marry Will Meyer."

"It's the most important reason," he says.

"There are more reasons?" Now I'm the one with a little 'v' above my nose, but only in jest.

"Well, sure…I mean…there are a lot of factors…as I said. This is just the one that is the most important to me," Will stumbles. "I'm sticking my foot in my mouth, aren't I?" Will gives a quirky smile and I can't help but laugh.

"Yes, but you make it look cute," I say, letting him off the hook. "I understand there are a lot of good reasons to postpone the wedding. I appreciate that the most important one is also the most romantic. I was meant to be Layla Meyer one day. Now that the reason for our compromise is gone, we can begin to rebuild what we started back in Davidson. So…let's go *home*, Will."

"You are amazing," Will says as his lips reach mine.

At first his kiss is soft and sweet and I'm overcome with the emotions that have been dormant for the past month. Before I know it, though, Will's mouth is crushed against mine and he's kissing me like he hasn't kissed me in forever. It's been since before I was fitted into my mother's wedding dress, which was before Will's father died, so it feels like forever since we've been close like this. He pulls me tighter to him and allows me only a moment to catch my breath before his lips are on mine again.

I reach up and grab the back of Will's head, knotting my fingers through his longer hair, pulling his face closer to mine, as if that were possible. As he eases me backward on the loveseat my free leg wraps around his waist and it occurs to me that we have never been in this position before. Even our Day of Nothing make-out session didn't include me wrapping a leg around him and pulling him to me.

It doesn't take long for both of us to realize that we're treading on dangerous ground. If Luke were to come back now it would be incredibly awkward for all of us. I don't presume that Luke thinks we're as pure as the driven snow, but it's still weird for your father to walk in while you're making out like crazy with your fiancé. More than that, Will and I have come so far, sticking to the boundary that Will set for our physical relationship. It was difficult to understand at first – how a guy could say *no* to the very thing that most men live for – but I learned a long time ago that Will is not like most men. I'll have the greatest love story to tell our children one day about how their father cared more about my innocence than he ever did his own desires.

"So…I've *really* missed you," Will says as he straightens himself on the loveseat. He fixes his shirt and runs his fingers through his hair after he rights me in my seat.

"Yeah…I know the feeling." I take the hair band out of my hair and retie it around my ponytail. "So…have they been able to prove that the home invasion gone wrong was a set-up? What about the other juror who disappeared? Have they found him yet?" I say, changing the subject to something that will most certainly take our minds off of tearing each other's clothes off.

"Good save," Will says with a wink. "No, no news. The first juror's death really could have been from an actual burglary, but it was way too clean. I mean, there has been *zero* evidence. Agent Croft has had his lead forensic guy on it and there has been nothing. According to Croft, Agent Lassiter says they haven't found any hairs, fibers, or DNA that didn't belong to the victim. It's like whoever did it wore a Haz-Mat suit. And then the second juror…I don't know. He just vanished." Will shakes his head at the insanity of it all.

"It just seems so unfair to the second juror's family. I know they'd want to at least have his body to bury…to have closure," I say. I know the pain they're experiencing with not knowing where this man is. It's one of the most terrible feelings in the world and I wouldn't wish it on anyone. "So…what do you know about your dad's death? I mean, I know you said him dying was just a matter of time, but he hung on for so long. I really thought he was going to pull through,"

"Well, from what Luke said the doctor told him, my dad basically died from an infection caused by the shots to his chest. It turns out he was allergic to, like, three of the most common antibiotics used and then his body started rejecting the others."

"Wow. Only your father could get shot in the head and that's not what kills him. Honestly, I thought he would have died when they took the bullet out of his head."

"Yeah, well, you can't be in your 60s and take two bullets to the chest and one to head and live long. Between the medications to keep his blood pressure up and the ones to fight the infection, it was only a matter of time before everything just shut down." Will looks sad, really sad, for the first time since we watched his father get shot. Regret fills his eyes and I know he's reliving all the times he tried to make things right with his father; all the times his father refused to bend and see Will as more than a publicity stunt or an heir.

"You ok?" I ask, rubbing his forearm.

It takes him a moment to answer. I'm not sure if he's deciding how well he's doing, or how honest he's going to be about it. "I'm great as long as you're with me." Will takes me into his arms and I feel warm. I wrap my arms around his middle and lay my head on his chest, hoping, in some small way, to comfort him.

"Have you talked to your mom? How's she doing? Is Wes with her? I can't imagine how she must be feeling right now."

"I spoke with her after Wes told her. She's…she's going to be ok. We've had a while to prepare, and, to be honest, my mom has been killing him off in her heart and mind since we moved here. I don't mean that in some Lifetime movie way. I just mean that she's been separating herself and cutting off her feelings from him. Even if he hadn't died, there was going to come a point when he was dead to her. Otherwise, she'd never be able to move on."

"I get that. I'm glad that she's got Wes. At least she can process through everything with him. If she had met someone down here who obviously wouldn't know anything about her past, she would have suffered in silence," I say moving toward the door. I figure if we don't emerge from the office soon, Luke is going to get suspicious and come in anyway.

"Not completely in silence. She's got me, you know," Will says, slightly offended.

"Of course she has you, but you know she's not the type of mom to dump all her emotions on her son." She's not. She would rather stuff everything down than to have Will worry about her more than he already does. "She needs a partner, Will, and she has that in Wes."

"You're right. I wouldn't dump on her either, so I'm glad I have you." Will grabs behind my neck and pulls me to him to kiss me on the forehead.

"Not that you're dumping any emotions on me…" I say with a slight tone of intentional guilt.

"Babe, there's just not a lot to say. I've been so cut off from my father for so long it was almost like watching a stranger getting shot on TV that day. I don't know him and he certainly never knew me. All I've got linking me to that man is DNA, and that sure as hell doesn't make him a real father. Yeah, I'm sad, but I'm not sad like a guy who just lost his dad. I'm sad because whether Gregory Meyer lived or died, I never had a father." Will's expression is so matter-of-fact. He's been thinking about this for a long time, maybe years before I ever met him, and how cut off he is from his father is apparent.

I'm sad for him. I'm sad that he never knew what the love of a real father feels like. How those strong arms feel while consoling you after you bang your thumb with a hammer when you were just trying to help, or what they look like, pumping in the air as you make it down the sidewalk on your bike all by yourself for the first time. He'll only have memories of inadequacy and failure in the eyes of one of the two people on the planet who are supposed to love and comfort you and cheer you on.

"I'm sorry things weren't different for you, Will. You missed out on having a real father for the first 20 years of your life, but you've got us now, and I'm happy to share Luke with you. Since he's my dad now, and you're going to be my husband, that makes him your father-in-law. So, I know it's not the same thing, but I hope you'll embrace it." My hopeful eyes reach Will's. He's smiling and shaking his head.

"No, it's not the same thing. It's better."

Chapter 3

Will and I walk across the quad and somehow the campus feels a little darker now. Our impending departure ahead of us, I take better note of the placement of trees, how many steps from one building to another, and how the steel handle on the door to the coffee shop feels in my hand. Today that handle is warm as I pull the door open and stroll in to find Finn in his usual place.

He's smiling, as he always is. My stomach flips and my face contorts a little at the thought of not seeing him again.

"What's wrong?" Will asks, noticing the change in my expression.

"I was just thinking how sad it will be to never see Finn again," I tell him.

"Layla, just because we're moving back to Davidson doesn't mean we have to say goodbye to everyone here forever. It won't be like it was when we moved here. Once everything is out in the open, you can tell whomever you want. There won't be any more threat to us. And...since we're still getting married in the gardens, Finn will be there." Will smiles, making my heart swell.

"Thank you. Hmm...I guess I'm going to have to get used to not hiding things from people. Not everyone will understand, but I suppose that's how you weed out the real friends from the superficial ones. To be honest, I was starting to feel pretty sad about Finn not being at our wedding...whenever it is." I've grown to really care about Finn. His friendship reminds me so much of my friendship with Tyler. He's funny and honest and I've always felt safe around him.

"Hey Layla, John! What's up? You look like someone just ran over your cat, Layla." Finn's half-joking, half-serious inquiry into my state of being stings a little. I want to tell him about the drama that has been my existence for the last seven years, and the resolution that seems to be unfolding now, but I can't…not yet at least. For now we'll have to concoct a story that will send John, my parents, and me back to North Carolina. It was one thing to withhold information from Finn, but it feels entirely different to have to lie to him.

"My dad just died," Will tells him. My eyes just about pop out of my head and Will has to squeeze my hand to calm me down. *I suppose that's one way of going about it!* Will was always good about not flat out lying to people about our pasts, but throwing in enough truth to not have to explain the whole thing. I wasn't expecting him to be *so* straightforward with Finn, though.

"Oh my gosh, John! I'm so sorry," Finn says, leaving his mouth agape. "What are you doing here? Shouldn't you already be back home?"

"We weren't close at all, but there are some family issues that have to be settled, so Layla and I will be moving back."

"Wow…well, you gotta do what you gotta do, right?" Finn's response is soft and guarded and I can't help but wonder if he doesn't believe Will.

"I'm just going to run to the bathroom. I'll be right back, babe," Will kisses my cheek and makes his way to the back of the coffee shop.

"Ok, tell me what's *really* going on," Finn demands, drawing my eyes away from watching Will walk away.

"It's true. His dad died." My answer is short, like Wes taught me. Never give more answer than someone else's question.

"But moving back? Back where? And what about the wedding? Doesn't this seem a bit extreme?" Finn's protectiveness is sweet and I almost break down and spill everything to him.

"It's a long story, Finn, one I'll be able to tell you at some point, I promise." Finn spreads a distrusting smirk across his face. "Trust me. There's nothing to worry about with John, ok?"

Finn breathes a heavy sigh of disbelief, but concedes anyway. "Alright, but you have to promise to spill the beans."

"I promise."

"You're making promises to other men?" Will asks teasingly, sliding his arm around my waist.

"I was just promising Finn that I would tell him our whole story one day." Taking a page from Will's book of not-technically-lying feels great. I adore Finn and desperately want to tell him everything I've been through and conquered, and everything Will has done to make it possible for us to be together. If I learned anything during the time I couldn't tell Caroline or Tyler what was going on with us, it's that I've undone the damage Gram did. I don't want to hold my feelings in anymore. I want to share my life with people.

"I think that sounds like a great plan. Maybe I'll tell him at my bachelor party," Will says, smiling his invitation to Finn.

"Really? You want me to come to your bachelor party?" Finn is shocked and I love it! He's the kind of guy that is really hard to surprise. I wish I had known Will was going to invite him. I would have taken my phone out and videoed it.

"Absolutely! Although...I'm not sure if Layla told you, but, with everything going on with my father's death and us moving, we're postponing the wedding. It won't be more than a year, and we're still getting married in the gardens. Are you in?"

This is the first I've heard Will put a time frame on our rescheduled wedding and I'm put at ease. I haven't wanted to bring up setting a new date. It's not because I'm afraid to. We've had enough conversations about being open and honest, especially right now. It's because I didn't want to overwhelm Will. There are a lot of cogs in this machine that we're trying to navigate and I didn't want to throw a wrench in and knock everything out of whack.

As Will and Finn discuss what constitutes a bachelor party, I start running through seasons and dates in my head, wondering when things really will be settled enough for us to have our own little destination wedding. I chuckle to myself thinking of the absurdity of Tallahassee being a *destination wedding* location. Fall will be too busy getting back into the swing of things back in Davidson and with school…a new school at that. Winter is too chilly for an outdoor wedding, even in Tallahassee. That brings us to spring next year at the earliest. Well, at least the weather will be beautiful.

"This is why you need me there!" I hear Finn say as my mind rejoins their conversation. "Neither one of us is interested in seeing some skanky girl grind up on you!"

"Um…I know I spaced out there for a minute, but…I came in at the weirdest part of this conversation." I can feel my face scrunch together in confusion. Will immediately recognizes this expression and rescues me.

"I was just telling Finn about how Tyler has been joking that he's going to hire strippers for my bachelor party," Will explains.

"Oh, really?" I say, pretending to get upset with him. I smile, though, because he knows that I know he would never go for that…which is why Tyler pretends to threaten him with it. Will is literally the most loyal boyfriend out there. Sometimes he even turns his head away during love scenes in movies. One time, we were walking across campus and there was a girl wearing a barely-there bikini top. I said something like, "Whoa! Can you believe that girl?" and Will said, "What girl?" That's my Will.

"Great! When we get the date re-set I'll have Tyler call you and you guys can put it all together. I'm trusting you to keep Tyler in line!" Will and Finn laugh together knowing that there really isn't anything to be worried about. They'll probably go bowling or four-wheeling or do some other manly-type activity. "Oh my gosh! We've got to go, babe," Will says checking his watch.

There's all this urgency now that we're moving back to Davidson and trying to figure out how exactly to do that. Will is worried that the press will dig into my past, working to find out who the girl worth faking your death for really is. There isn't anything juicy to find, but he said he refuses to let them hurt me by bringing up my parents' death or my father's arrest and the details surrounding the explosion that killed three people. He also thinks they'll start speculating about my interest in Will's fortune. Most of the time I'm sure I can handle it, but sometimes my imagination runs wild and I have visions of fainting or going Sean Penn on some photographer.

Finn gives me a wink as we say our goodbyes and I know that Will's candor and invitation to help plan his bachelor party has put him at ease.

"I'm not so worried anymore," I say to Will when we're about halfway across the quad.

"That's good. What were you worried about?" he asks taking my hand in his.

"Well…I was worried our wedding would be postponed indefinitely. To be honest, it was kind of killing me."

"Why didn't you say anything?" Will stops and turns me to him, locking his serious, blue eyes on mine. He takes the level of our honesty with each other very seriously now that we have promised not to hold back anymore.

"I wasn't trying to keep anything from you. I was just trying to give your brain some room to move. You've got so much going on in there. Between school and working with Luke to navigate how we're going to bring you back from the dead, my bridal woes are low on the totem pole. It's ok, Will. It was just nice to hear you tell Finn the new wedding date would be no more than a year away." I smile trying to make Will understand that it really is ok. I'm not upset that we haven't talked about a new wedding date, and I truly have just wanted to give him space to figure all the other complicated details out. I just figured that we wouldn't be able to even approach that subject until everything was under control.

27

Will cocks his head to one side and looks to the sky. I can almost see the wheels turning in his head. "Come on," he says, taking my hand and almost dragging me the rest of the way to the car.

"What are you doing?" I'm trying to keep up with Will's long legs. It's a challenge when he's walking so quickly.

"Just come on," he answers with a smirk.

We get in the car and I barely have my seatbelt on before Will is out of the parking lot and heading for the highway. He hasn't wiped that smile off his face and I know he's got something up his sleeve. It's the same look he had on our first date when he surprised me with a picnic on the dock, and the same one he had the night he walked me along the dock to my proposal. Of course, the night of my proposal the smirk disappeared and was replaced by a look of passion and hope.

About ten minutes down the road Will tells me to close my eyes, still having not told me anything about where we're going or what we're doing.

"We aren't going home? Why am I closing my eyes?" I ask in pouty protest.

"Stop being such a girl and close your eyes!" he says, giving me a quick poke in my side, causing me to flail slightly from how ticklish I am.

"Alright, alright! Geez! You got anything back there I can wrap around my eyes like a blindfold? I don't want to get tickled again for accidentally peeking!"

"Uh, I might…oh wait…all that's back there is my gym bag and you do *not* want any of that on your face. But…if you peek you might suffer the gym sock punishment!"

"Eww, gross! No! I'll keep them closed, I promise!" I reach my body across the console and give Will a quick kiss on the cheek. It's moments like this that I love the most. I feel young and alive and just know that everything is going to work out perfectly.

28

The car stops about ten minutes later and I have no idea where we are. I was obedient to a fault, keeping my eyes closed the entire time. At first I tried to gauge where we were by the turns, but gave up after the first one realizing the only way I'd have a clue is if I had seen which exit we took.

"Keep them closed," Will instructs as he helps me from the car.

I take Will's hand, feeling its strength and the deepest assurance of safety when my hand is enclosed in his. We walk on hard ground for a few minutes, move to softer terrain, and then back to solid ground. I don't open my eyes when we stop since Will hasn't told me to open them yet. When he does, I have to close them again in a vain attempt to stop the tears.

We're standing in the exact spot in the garden where our wedding is to be held. The round courtyard is as beautiful as I remember. The green, leafy plants and flowers explode with color against the red brink, and make visions of my wedding day run through my mind like a film strip.

I can picture Caroline in a strapless, pale yellow dress, and Tyler in a white shirt, grey pants, and a yellow tie that matches Caroline's dress perfectly. Claire is patting tears from her eyes as she watches Luke walk me down the red brick path to Will. My arm is locked with Luke's and he's gripping my hand with his. The huge bouquet of white and yellow tulips I'm carrying is wired so they're all standing at perfect attention as I make my way down the path. When I see Will, dressed so handsomely like Tyler, only with a grey tie, a wave of pure, unadulterated joy washes over me. He smiles at me and I know that despite the tragedy that brought me there, going to live with Luke and Claire was the best decision I ever made.

"Don't cry," Will says as he wipes the tears from my face. I open my eyes, releasing my vision back into my imagination. "I don't think I can wait a year to marry you, Layla."

"It'll go by fast. I mean we've waited this long, right?" I say as I try to fix the mess that I'm sure my eyeliner has made under my lashes. "There's plenty to occupy our time, that's for sure."

"Hmm…" Will's lips form a hard line and I recognize this as his thinking face.

"What's going through that brilliant brain of yours?" I start to take a step back, just so I can give him a suspicious look, but he takes both my hands in his and steadies me back to him, locking his bluer than blue eyes with mine.

"I, Will, take you, Layla, to be my wife," he starts. Tears immediately fill my eyes again as I realize what Will is doing. He's giving us our own private wedding, right here, right now. "I promise to love you every day more than the day before. I will take care of you, and protect you, keeping you safe from anything that would cause you pain. I'll be your best friend as you are mine-encouraging you, supporting you, and sharing my life with you. I will live each day with my only goal being to make you happy. I promise to communicate with you, and never leave you out of any decision because we are one. This is my solemn vow to you, and it will *never* be broken."

Tears are streaming down my face and I don't attempt to stop a single one of them. I am the luckiest girl on the planet. Standing before me is a man who loves me so passionately that he can't stand the thought of waiting any longer to make his vows to me. I feel like being impetuous and taking him to the courthouse to get married right now. I don't care about the flowers or venue or even my mother's wedding dress. I only care about marrying Will and spending the rest of my life as his wife. I'm not impetuous, though, because more than anything I want to be with Will right here, right now, in this moment.

He spoke so eloquently, as he always does, probably having already thought out, and perhaps written out, his vows. I've thought of them some, but not enough to lay them out as well as he just did. I think for a second about not saying anything. That maybe I'll just kiss him and he'll know, but I can't do that. I can't leave his beautiful words of commitment to me hanging out there without reciprocating, so I open my mouth and decide to let whatever is in my heart come out.

"I, Layla, take you, Will, to be my husband. I promise to love you every day with a love you never imagined was possible. I will let you take care of me as I will take care of you. I promise to encourage and support you, to be there, all the time, no matter what. I promise to never be afraid because I know you will always be by my side. I'll be your partner, sharing my life with you, knowing that all my dreams, even the ones I didn't know I had, will come true. And I will spend my life making sure that we not only have the best days to come, but that we have the best string of yesterdays anyone's ever known. This is *my* vow to *you*, and it will *never* be broken."

We stand there briefly, our eyes locked on each other in this beautiful moment, before Will takes my face in his hands and kisses me. The world around us seems to disappear as our lips move together in perfection. It's exactly as I imagined the first kiss after our vows would be. It's beautiful and slow, full of love and every emotion we have for each other. Now I know why the first thing couples do after they say their vows is kiss. It seems to me that there's no way you can start your marriage with a kiss like *this* and ever fall out of love.

Chapter 4

We hold each other there, both amazed at what we've just shared. At this point I almost don't care if we ever have a real wedding. I've been married to Will in my heart since the moment I told him I loved him, and now that I've said my vows to him, that union with him is even more solidified.

Without a word, Will takes my hand and gently tugs, forcing my cemented feet to move. We walk down the brick path that has become my personal cloud nine and don't stop until we reach a clearing along Lake Hall. It's perfect, really. All the plans we had for our wedding day, filled with people and music and dancing and food…they were wonderful plans. They *are* wonderful plans. Standing here with Will right now, though…this couldn't be a more picture-perfect ending to the day I married Will.

"You're not going to apologize now, are you?" I ask. Will has a history of apologizing after we've shared some incredibly beautiful moments and I don't want him to spoil this wonderful memory.

"No, I'm not. I will never apologize for committing my life to you. I'll never apologize for loving you." Will pulls me tighter to him and kisses the top of my head. "I love you so much."

"So when do we leave for our honeymoon?" I ask in jest, thinking it'll be fun to engage Will in some conversation about our future.

"I wish! You have no idea how I wish!" he chuckles.

"Well…can I at least start introducing myself as Layla Meyer? Hi, I'm Layla Meyer, it's nice to meet you? See, doesn't that sound great?"

"It sounds like heaven!" he says, squeezing me tighter to him.

"I guess we better head back. Reality is waiting." I sigh, feeling sadness come over me that our imaginary wedding is over.

"Hey," Will says as he lifts my chin so our eyes meet. "Don't think this didn't mean anything. I meant it when I said I couldn't wait a year to marry you. I love you, Layla, and while I can't wait to make it official, I don't need a piece of paper to commit myself to you. In my heart, you are my wife."

"But it still doesn't change why you won't, you know…" I'm a little embarrassed as the words leave my mouth. So embarrassed that I can't even form the words *sleep with me* or *make love*, but Will knows exactly what I mean.

"There's honor in waiting for something so valuable. I want you, Layla. Believe me. I. Want. You. But I want you to look at me as a man who has character, integrity, and honor more. We'll get to the other, but if I don't have your trust now, I never will."

"I do see you that way, and I trust you more than I've ever trusted anyone. Don't worry. I'm a convert. I'd have a hard time saying no if you wanted to have your way with me right now, but…I'd still say no. I look forward to the perfect day when it's right." I reach behind his head and grab a fist full of his hair. I want him to really hear what I have to say. "What you did today was the most amazing thing anyone has ever done for me. We've been through more than two people should have to just so we can be together. I've worried and struggled and been fearful, and it's been difficult at times. You need to know that you made all of that go away today. Thank you. I love you."

I kiss him. I kiss him with everything in me. I kiss him like our lives depend on it. I kiss him like a wife kisses her husband, because that's what he is to me. No legal documents, preacher, or witnesses necessary. Today we exchanged vows and committed our lives to each other. No matter what happens from this point on, we can do anything.

Will has more than proven his unfailing love for me and I'm going to stand by him and support him as we reclaim the life we were meant to have. I'm an expert at that, actually. I worked hard to take back the life that Gram stole from me, and we'll do the same thing with the life his father took from us.

I struggled for so long with the truth that I have a life with Will because my parents died that horrific night. I thought that I didn't deserve anything good that came to me as a result of my life being turned upside down. I know now that couldn't be farther from the truth. I had everything good and wonderful ripped away from me when I was just a little girl. Was I meant to suffer for the rest of my life because of that? No, and I realize that more than ever as I stand here with the man I was born to love. Life is not perfect. It never will be. If we take the terrible things that happen to us in life as some sign that we're destined to be doomed forever, well, that's not a life at all.

Sometimes life really can be a series of misfortunate events. What we turn those events into is what matters most. I could have lived like the weird, reclusive girl I had initially planned on being when I moved to Davidson, but I'm so glad I didn't. Will and Luke and Claire all looked at me and saw who I *could* be, drawing me out and helping me find myself again. My life and my future are embraced in my arms right now and I wouldn't change a single thing that brought me to him.

Will brushes my cheek with his thumb as we release each other. We seem to let out a simultaneous sigh, both feeling the high of our private wedding of sorts. As we stroll back down along the path to the car, I can't help but think about the next steps. Will and I are solid and nothing is going to change that, but there is still so much to be done, so much to consider.

"What now?" I ask him. "I know we're finishing the semester, but is there a target date for moving back?"

"Well, there's a lot that has to happen first, at least before anyone knows we're there. Luke is working with Holly on preparing her defense. He's bringing in some people who will speak to my father's tactics of coercion and manipulation. He's made the same deal with the prosecuting attorney as he had with Agent Croft and his team. Wes, Taylor, and Cline will testify in exchange for immunity."

"I should hope so. They were all victims of his coercion themselves." I'm relieved. The idea of Wes being punished for what Meyer made him do is infuriating and I think I could actually throw up if I consider it much longer. "But what's the point of having them testify? Holly did it."

"Luke is trying to get her the minimum sentence or a conviction on a lesser charge. He's hoping that if the judge can see the lives my father destroyed, he'll go easy on her. So that means that at some point…"

"You and your mom will have to testify. Wow. How's your mom doing with that?" I can't imagine having to sit up there and tell of all the ways my husband disrespected and abused me. She may have to listen to how Meyer used Wes, too. Her worlds are going to collide and I'm not sure if she's strong enough yet to handle it."

"I haven't told her yet. I think we're going to have to get through the press conference first. Claire suggested having someone from Victim's Assistance help walk her through how to give that kind of testimony, and Luke will help her with what to say to the press if she has to say anything at all." Will's face is somber, thinking about what his mother is about to endure.

"She's going to do great, Will," I say with as much confidence as I can. "This is it. Once she steps down from the stand, she never has to talk or even think about him again. There's finality and closure to this, don't you think?"

"Yeah, there is," Will says. I can tell he wants to end this conversation. His answers usually get short when he's nearing the edge.

"Do you know what you're going to say to the press?" I wonder. Surely he and Luke have discussed what to say, which exact words to use and which ones to avoid. There's a system for speaking to the press. You can't be transparently honest or they'll take things out of context, especially in scenarios like this.

"We're going to be truthful, but protective. The last thing I want is for the press to hound my mom about how awful my dad was to her. And I certainly don't want them coming after you. So, we have to give information without telling them everything. Luke's a master at that, so I feel pretty confident going into it."

"So, I already asked this, but, when? When is all this going down?"

"We don't have a target date, but with the semester ending May tenth, I'm guessing we'll be back in Davidson by Memorial Day."

"And...when will Luke hold the press conference?" I'm just as unsure about this as Will seems. It's all becoming so real.

"I don't know. We're still ironing that out." We stop at the car and Will presses his body to mine as my back leans against the car. "So...do you think today will hold you over for a little while until the real thing?" Will is done talking about the heaviness upon us. He's good at changing the subject abruptly, but always to something I want to talk about so I'm engaged right away.

"Hmmm...maybe," I tease.

"Maybe?" Will says, poking my ribs causing me to twist in tickled agony.

"Yes! Yes! Today held me over! It did! Stop!" I'm laughing and crying all at the same time. Will finally stops and presses his lips against mine in a hard kiss.

"Good! I love you, Layla, so much, and I cannot wait until our real wedding. It's going to be the most amazing day ever. And...I think you're going to be pretty happy with the honeymoon, too!" Will gives me a smoldering look that is so unfair.

"Will Meyer! You better stop with all the honeymoon talk! You finally got me to agree that waiting was the best thing, so don't go mucking it up by making me think about it!"

"Alright, alright. But just so you know..." He tucks my hair behind my ear and moves his mouth to where his lips are touching my ear and whispers, "I think about it all the time."

I feel the blood rush to my cheeks and my body temperature starts to overheat in an instant. Of course he thinks about it. He's a guy! I hadn't really thought about him thinking of me like that until now, but he does. Does he dream of us on our honeymoon the way I do? Does he think about what it will be like, feel like, to be as close as two people can possibly be? Tears fill my eyes as I think about that beautiful moment, and how unconditional it will be.

"Oh, babe, did I say something wrong?" Will wipes my tears and holds my face.

"No, not at all. I'm just really, *really* happy," I say through the tears of joy.

"I'm happy, too. C'mon...let's go be happy at home."

We drive home listening to music, stopping most of the songs halfway through to skip to another favorite. I play my Avett Brothers albums, skipping to some of my favorites like *I and Love and You* and the sentimental version of *Swept Away*.

"Oh, I love this one!" I say excitedly.

"You love the song about chickens and milking cows?" Will teases. He really loves the Avett Brothers, too, but likes to pretend to give me a hard time.

"You're about to introduce a band to me that dresses in leather and huge platform boots, and wears makeup as a part of some weird characters they play on stage. You're really going to give me a hard time about the American heritage of farming?" Will is still giving me music lessons and says next week I'll be learning all about KISS. I'm not sure how I feel about that one but I promised Will at our first lesson that I would always be willing to learn.

We spend the rest of the short drive home laughing and singing and teasing each other when we sing the lyrics we think are right but really aren't. It's a beautiful afternoon of normalcy between two people in love; so normal that I almost forget about the logistical nightmare that lies ahead of us.

*****

We walk into the house and I immediately hear Luke's voice. I never know when he's going to be home from his jaunts to Charlotte to meet with Holly, so I'm pleasantly surprised because this time he was only gone two days.

"Where have you two been? Class let out hours ago," Claire inquires as she unloads the dishwasher. She's wearing running shorts and a t-shirt that I think used to be Luke's, telling by its size. I love watching Claire do mundane things. It's a reminder that it is possible to step aside from the drama that always seems to be unfolding.

"We had to make a little stop," Will tells her. He squeezes my hand and gives me a wink. I think we've both made an unspoken agreement to not tell anyone about our practice wedding today. I'm glad because it's been a long time since I've had something to share with just him. So much has happened that we've had to share almost every detail of our relationship with at least Luke and Claire.

"Oh," Claire says. She looks a little perplexed as to where we could possibly have to go. She doesn't ask and I can only assume it's because we now live in a world where there is no threat to us.

"I'm glad you're back, Will. I've got to lay out some plans for Holly's sentencing hearing. You want to grab something to drink and meet me in the office?" Luke heads for the office but Will stops him.

"We can meet here in the kitchen, unless there are too many files to drag in here." Will gives me a soft smile, letting me know that we are most definitely in this together.

"Sure," Luke says with a nod. He's seen the way Will is looking at me and knows that Will is officially done trying to do this on his own.

Will is taking our vows seriously and my heart fills. It means so much to me that I push to my toes and wrap my arms around Will's neck. "Thank you," I whisper in his ear.

"So what's going on? How's Holly?" Will asks.

My heart sinks for a moment when Will inquires about Holly. I float between feelings of gratitude and hatred for her. I'm grateful that she's rid the world and our lives of the torment of Gregory Meyer, but the wrench she's thrown into us moving forward with our lives is infuriating at times. I also can't rid my mind of the fact that she led Will to believe that she really cared for him when it was really another ploy by her mother to infiltrate the Meyer's lives. Will still thinks that she was as innocent as I was in the attacks his father launched. If I'm honest, *that* is what really makes me hate her.

"She's doing fine. She knew what she was doing and is ready to accept the consequences, although it wasn't as premeditated as it looked. She saw what was unfolding with the delays in the trial and made a snap decision. She didn't even know about juror number four going missing. So, I'm working to get the charges changed from murder to manslaughter, or at least the lowest sentence as possible, which is what I need to talk to you about," Luke tells us. "I'm going to call some witnesses that you and Eliana need to know about ahead of time. These witnesses will speak to the abusive behavior of your father, which will hopefully raise some sympathy in the jury. I've got to paint Holly almost as a hero. "Luke looks at me, seeing the disgust spreading across my face. I turn to get something from the fridge so

Will won't see, but Luke knows exactly what's going through my mind. "It's not going to be pretty."

"I can handle it, Luke," Will says with a stone face.

"I'm going to call your father's ex-wives."

"I kind of figured you would," Will says. "Do you think all three of them will be willing to testify?"

"Actually, all four of them." Luke's delivery is slow.

"Mom isn't his ex, Luke. She's technically his widow," Will says, correcting Luke's mistake.

"I'm not referring to her," Luke says with his own stone face.

"What are you saying, Dad?" I ask. Will seems stunned, his forehead creasing.

"Greg was married for a brief time in college," Luke says.

"I'm not surprised. I guess he began his parade of arm candy earlier than we all thought." Will isn't fazed by this information. At this point, I can't think of much that would be shocking to find out about Will's father. "I am a little surprised that we're just finding this out. Dad never made excuses for any of his womanizing, or *any* of his behavior for that fact."

"This…this was different," Luke begins. He's hesitant. I've never seen Luke hesitant like this. He's usually so confident and I'm slightly worried.

"What do you mean it was different?" Will asks.

"Well, her name is Loretta. Apparently they met their sophomore year and fell in love almost immediately. They dated for two years and got married right before their senior year."

"So you've spoken with her already?" Will asks.

"Yes," Luke answers.

"Why are you telling me this? I'm assuming all his exes share a similar story. He married them, used them, and then threw them away," Will says, still not seeing the pertinence of this conversation.

"Her story is a little different, Will, and you need to know before Eliana does. I'm not sure how she's going to take it."

"What's so different about her story?" I ask. I'm becoming fearful for Will and Eliana. What could possibly be different? Gregory Meyer made it clear that he's a cold-hearted man with no use for women beyond photo ops and personal pleasure.

"The way Loretta describes Greg, it's like she's talking about an entirely different person...at least at the beginning of their story." Luke takes a deep breath. "She told me of a man who brought her flowers, took her on romantic dates, and even asked her father for her hand in marriage."

Will and I stand there, mouths open in astonishment. The man just described is nowhere close to the Gregory Meyer we knew. This man shows signs of having a heart and the ability to love and put someone before himself. I see a look of sadness wash over Will and I know what he's thinking. All this time we thought he wasn't capable of love, but he was. He chose to give love to someone, and then chose to withhold it from everyone else.

"If he was this wonderful person, what happened?" I ask. Will still isn't able to speak.

"Greg was beginning an internship at his first choice firm. They only took a few interns and he, of course, gave a stellar interview and got one of the three open spots. Well...Loretta got pregnant and had some complications. She ended up on bed rest and she needed Greg to be there. At first he was fine with being there. He was concerned for Loretta and their baby. But...he was frequently late or having to leave his internship early. He wasn't burning the midnight oil like the other interns were. Eventually the firm let him go and he was left without an internship for the remainder of the semester. Apparently his advisor gave him hell for getting fired from the internship and promised him that unless he made some serious changes, he'd be lucky to find placement with the public defender's office.

"Something just clicked in him and he became resentful toward Loretta and the baby. He became verbally and sometimes physically abusive. When she was seven months pregnant, Loretta couldn't take any more and she left him. He never went after her," Luke explains.

I remember the day Meyer told us about his father. How he could have been something brilliant...a doctor, I believe...but that he let love get in the way of pursuing his dreams. That he watched his father work his fingers to the bones on his family's farm and never had anything to show for it. It was then that Meyer made it clear it wasn't that Will wanted *me*, it was that Will was pursuing love, and that was going to get in the way of him pursuing and fulfilling his destiny. It sounds like Meyer didn't always believe that. That maybe there was a time when he thought he could have a life of love with Loretta *and* an uninterrupted destiny.

"What...um...what about the baby?" Will stutters. The realization, if all went well with the rest of her pregnancy Will has a sibling, has dawned on him.

"Loretta had a healthy baby girl two months later." Luke's response is slow and guarded, not sure how Will is going to respond.

"I have a sister. So that makes two siblings my father kept from me. I suppose he was secretly supporting them, too," Will says. There's deep disappointment in his voice, mourning the life he could have had if he had been allowed to have his siblings.

"No, actually. Loretta contacted him when Erin was born but Greg wouldn't even come see her. After a year of trying, Loretta sent him the papers and Greg relinquished his parental rights," Luke says.

"Does she know about my father...or me?" Will's voice is still unsteady.

"Yes, and she'd love to meet you," Luke answers. "She'll be at the hearing, but you're under no obligation to meet her if you don't want to, Will. She understands it could be quite difficult for you right now."

"Her name is Erin?" Will asks softly.

"Yes. Erin Morcos Wagner. Loretta remarried when Erin was two and her husband adopted her. Wagner is her married name. And...she has a son, named David. "

Will is silent as he absorbs what Luke has just told him. I can't imagine what he must be feeling right now, but betrayal tops my list of suppositions. Disgust tops the list of my personal feelings. Marcus was so right when he said that Will's father was capable of unimaginable things. First he signs away all but his genetic connection to his first born child, then he sends Marcus' mother to have an abortion. I try but just can't wrap my brain around that kind of rejection. As mean as Gram was to me, she at least admitted I was hers.

It takes a few minutes before Will can even try to speak. He opens his mouth a few times but all that comes out are breathy sounds. When he's finally able to put a coherent statement together all he can say is, "I need some air."

Chapter 5

Will takes my hand and leads me outside. We walk down the dock, pushing aside the branches and Spanish moss until we reach the end. We sit and I rub small circles on Will's back for several minutes before he says anything.

"I don't know what to do, Layla," he says, clearly devastated by this news. "I'm going to have to see my father's ex-wives, people he betrayed, and now, my sister? I can handle all the others, but, Erin… I've already seen what my father's rejection did to Marcus. It's been twice as long with Erin. What's she going to think of me? And what has she told her son? Oh my God, I have a nephew." Will shakes his head in confusion.

"She wants to meet you, Will," I say softly. "If she didn't want to meet you she would have told Luke."

"She's going to hate me," he says.

"Why would she hate you?"

"Because he chose me over her. Look what that did to Marcus." Will puts his head in his hands, his body a crumpled mess of fearful emotions.

"Marcus's mother is a psychopath. *That's* what pushed him over the edge. If his mother hadn't made him go to Meyer all those times and ask to be taken in like some stray kitten, Marcus would still be alive today. It doesn't sound like Loretta damaged Erin like Marcus' mother did him. It sounds like she's had a good life, actually."

"Layla…" Will begins but doesn't say anything else.

"Will…Loretta left *him*. It wasn't like with the others. She made a choice based on what she thought was best for her and her baby. If she hadn't made that choice, your father probably would have made it for her just like he did the others. That's the saddest part really. His other wives didn't have a choice. He kicked three of them to the curb, and he manipulated your mom into staying when she wanted to make a different choice for a better life." I hold Will's hand in both of mine, stroking the back of his hand with my thumb.

"If Loretta had stayed with him, what do you think would have really happened?" Will's voice is tired and sad. He's been thrown a lot of information and gained even more revelations about his father in the last year and a half. He went from knowing that his father was a manipulative tyrant to seeing just how deep his depravity went.

"You can't do that, Will. Trust me. You can't spend your life asking yourself that."

"I live every day knowing that, for whatever reason, he chose me and my mom. He treated us like property to be leveraged, but he chose us nonetheless. He rejected Marcus, and now I find out he rejected Erin, too. We're his children, not some mystery prize at an arcade. *Oh, no, I didn't want that one!* I have to ask…it's a valid question, Layla," he argues.

"Ok, I'll indulge you," I say with just the slightest tone of frustration. Will can be so stubborn sometimes. "Let's just say Loretta stayed with him. Something happened to him, Will. According to what Luke said, it was like something snapped. A switch got flipped. He was angry and resentful toward Loretta and the baby. So, she would have had Erin, he still wouldn't have cared, and in who knows how long he would have divorced her. Then however many years later, he still would have met someone else, married her, and then divorced her…and so on and so forth." I sigh, gaining my composure. I can feel myself getting heated because I hate that Will is taking on and carrying the responsibility of his father's choices. "I spent five years living in *what if* world because I blamed myself for my parents' death. After Gramps died, it took me a long time to stop playing that game. My parents' death was tragic, but the bottom line is if they didn't die that night, I would never have met you. As much as we hate it, if your father hadn't been a self-obsessed megalomaniac he wouldn't have had a string of wives, which means he would never have met Eliana, and you wouldn't be here.

Sometimes a tragedy sends us down the path we're supposed to be on so we can find what we're meant to find. It isn't pretty, but its life.

"There are too many *what ifs* in life to account for them all, Will. Yeah, *what if* Erin hates you? That would be a terrible mistake on her part. But regardless of how she feels about you, you're *still* going to move on with your life. We're *still* going to get married. And we're *still* going to live happily ever after." I've said all I can say. Now I just have to hope that it's made a difference. I want so desperately to reach him. He's spent every moment that we've been together helping me put away my fear and self-doubt. He helped me push aside the pain of my past so I could embrace and move forward into my future.

"Thank you for talking me down off the ledge," he says after a heavy sigh. "I hate all the tragedy and lives torn apart along the way, but…we wouldn't be here right now without them. If I didn't have you, my life would be so incredibly sad and incomplete." Will brushes the hair that the wind has casually blown into my face, and kisses me.

"I will always talk you down off the ledge," I tell him. I smile softly at this man sitting next to me – this man who is capable of amazing strength and yet is also so vulnerable. I am so incredibly blessed to be marrying a man who is the very best of both of my fathers.

When we find Luke and Claire in the kitchen, Luke's first concern is making sure Will is ok, like a father does with a son. He puts an arm around Will in a sign of unity between them. A sign that I hope Will receives.

"You ok?" Luke asks Will.

"Yeah, I'm good. I'd be lost without this girl right here, though," Will says, taking my hand and kissing my knuckles. I just smile at him and let the joy of being there for Will fill me. "I need to know the plan, Luke."

"Of course. I'll continue to commute between here and Charlotte, making sure Holly is properly represented. They haven't set a date for her sentencing hearing yet, but I'm hoping to hear something by the end of June.

I've asked the judge for some time to pull together some people to speak on her behalf. We're also working on getting the charges lowered. In the meantime, we'll move back as a family by Memorial Day weekend." Luke mirrors my smile when he says we're moving back as a family. Since Will and I have resolved some of our issues, and especially since we exchanged vows today, I actually feel good about moving back.

"Where are Will, Eliana, and Wes going to live?" I ask. The thought of them living anywhere but with us is distressing. The potential for press hounding Will and Eliana is pretty high and I don't like the idea of him getting trapped in Will's old house without me.

"We have room at the house. We'll have to set up some parameters for you two, but I think that will be best for everyone," Luke says. He's put on his *dad* voice, the one that asserts parental guidance while letting me know he trusts me at the same time.

"Yay!" I throw my arms around Will's neck and squeeze, practically knocking him down in the process. Will is here every day from when I wake up to when I go to sleep, and Wes and Eliana are inseparable, too. It just makes sense for them to live with us.

"Thanks, Luke. We appreciate it," Will says shaking Luke's hand.

"You're going to be there all the time anyway," Luke laughs. "Wes will still be on with us, and with the way things are going between him and Eliana, we know she'll be there all the time, too. And...I know it's not exactly what every newlywed couple dreams of, but, well, Claire and I were hoping you would live with us...*after* the wedding." Luke's face is soft and hopeful.

"Really?" I ask, matching Luke's soft tone. I haven't thought about where Will and I will live after we get married. To be honest, I still have trouble thinking past the honeymoon.

"You don't have to answer now. We just want you to consider it," Luke says.

"Thank you, Luke. We appreciate the offer, and we'll definitely consider it," Will tells him. "Have you told my mom anything about the exes?"

"Not yet, but Wes knows and he may have mentioned it to her. I didn't tell him not to tell her."

"I'll talk with her this weekend," Will says. "Also in the meantime, we still have school. Let's just get through the rest of the semester and deal with Davidson when we get to Davidson. Sound good?" Will has pulled me into his arms now and I'm looking up into his eyes. Will is saying that we can spend the next several weeks just *being* and that makes me so happy.

"That's the best plan I've ever heard," I tell him.

*****

The weeks that come are spent with going to class, studying and just *being*. Will and I enjoy our final days on campus and continue spending time with our friends as if we weren't coordinating how to bring Will Meyer back from the dead. In addition to Finn, we've told Dana, Jason, and Lisa about Will's father dying and us moving back to Davidson. Dana and Lisa are happy that the wedding won't be postponed indefinitely, and everyone shared their condolences even though Will told them he was never close with his father.

Between school and having fun with our friends, we've fallen behind on packing. Eliana made Will promise that he'd spend the day packing or she was going to throw all of his stuff away. It was an empty threat and Will knew it, but he agreed and I haven't seen him since the steamy kiss he gave me when he left last night.

As I pull boxes from the garage I'm taken back to the day I unpacked Will's ring. A well of feelings springs up in me. I remember how confused, but hopeful, I was. I knew he had given me the ring as a sign of some kind but didn't know what. Later, he told me he gave the ring back to me in case I wanted to move on. That was the farthest thing from my mind. I could never move on from Will. He is my lifeline and best friend. He made it possible for me to finally be set free and walk through the dark tunnel I had been trapped in. He became the light at the end of the dark place I had been hiding, and I am eternally grateful to him for that.

I'm trying to be organized as I pack, but all I can think of is just how much I hate packing. Every time I have packed up my life to move, and move far away at that, it's been under stressful circumstances. The obvious first time being when I moved in with Gram and Gramps after Mom and Dad died. The next time I packed I was headed to a new life with Luke and Claire, followed by packing when we were exiled to Florida by Will's father. And now…now I am packing again to go back to Davidson. I would have thought making that move would be joyful, but it isn't. Like every other time I have packed up my life to move, I am headed into an unknown.

I haven't shared this with Will, but I'm just as nervous, if not more, than he is. The people in Davidson were always so wonderful, but I don't know how they're going to receive us. We deceived them, lied to them about Will and Eliana's deaths. They mourned the loss of two great people, with practically the whole town showing up to the memorial service. I have no idea the impact that made on them and I don't know if it was damaging enough to make us outcasts.

"How's the packing coming along?" Claire asks after giving a light triple-knock on the doorframe of my room.

"It's coming. I've quadrupled my possessions since I came to live with you, and doubled those since we've been in Tallahassee. I'm going to have to do a purge before we get back to Davidson," I say as I contemplate the necessity of three summer scarves in three different shades of the same color.

"Don't say that too loudly or Luke will have me purging, too!" she laughs.

"Mums the word!" I say echoing Claire's laugh. "How about you? I'm sure you're farther along in the process than I am."

"Yeah, but I've got packing down to a science. We moved around a lot when I was a kid," she says. This is the first time she's told me anything about her childhood.

"Oh, yeah? Were your parents in the military or something?" I ask, realizing that I know absolutely nothing about Claire's family.

"No. It was just my mom and me. We were poorer than dirt and were constantly moving around from one free couch to another." Her delivery is so matter-of-fact.

"Where was your dad?" I feel confident that Claire and I have done more than just cross the threshold of being able to speak candidly with each other. We've lived in that candid place for quite some time now.

"Well…when I was eight he came home and told my mom he didn't want to be married to her anymore and that he was going to live with his other family," she tells me. It seems like she's come to terms with this being part of her life story. That the pain of it all doesn't tear her apart anytime she talks about it.

"His *other* family?" *What the?*

"Apparently he had been building a life with this other woman. I don't know how long it had been going on. They had a couple of kids who were younger than me, so I'd like to think he didn't start out his marriage to my mom as a cheating a-hole. But…after he left, he never supported her, and she wasn't the type to fight, so his a-hole status kind of solidified then." Again, her delivery is so straight forward, like she's talking about someone else. It gives me hope that one day I'll be able to talk about my life with Gram without letting the pain of that experience be a constant.

"So I guess you understand a little bit of what Will is feeling about meeting Erin, huh?"

"I do, but more from her side. My dad chose his *other* wife and his *other* kids over us. It's not their fault. I thought about reaching out to them, but had to consider why I would be doing it. I have no idea how they felt about our father. I don't know what kind of a father he was to them. He wasn't around that much for me even *before* he left us. But…if I *were* to meet them, it would be to tell them that I don't blame them for the choices my father made. Things were hard with my mom, but we had a good life. We had each other."

"Do you think that's why Erin wants to meet Will? To maybe let him off the hook?" I ask hopefully. It would mean so much to me if she were coming to relieve Will of the burden he's recently taken on.

"I think so. Luke said she's actually excited about meeting Will," Claire says with a smile.

"That's good. Where are your parents now?"

"My mom passed away ten years ago from breast cancer. And apparently my father died six years ago, but his wife didn't feel the need to tell me until four years ago. I suppose it doesn't matter since I hadn't seen him since I was ten, and that was just because we ran into him in the grocery store. I became just as cut off from my father as Erin, or even Will, became from Greg. The thing that made me sad about my father's death was that *I wasn't sad about his death*." Claire takes the scarves I was holding and puts them in the box. "You need all three of these," she smiles.

"Thanks, Mom," I tell her.

"You're welcome, sweetheart. Find a good stopping place soon. Will and Eliana will be here for dinner in about an hour." With that, Claire exits my room having bestowed on me some life-experience wisdom that I'm going to write on my heart and carry with me always.

That was by far the best conversation I've ever had with Claire. These are the kind of conversations I wanted to have with my mother. It felt so normal, so real. It made her feel even more like my mom, and me even more like her daughter. I like feeling like a daughter.

Chapter 6

After weeks of packing and wrapping up my studies at Florida State, we are finally headed *home*. We spent almost two years being exiled from the only place that has felt like home to me since my parents died and my feelings of excitement are finally outweighing my anxiety.

Claire thought ahead with this move and had the moving company come the day before we were actually leaving. They packed up all the furniture and it was delivered to our home in Davidson today. Caroline's mom met them at the house and directed them on where to put everything. Claire thought it would feel more like coming home if our furniture was already there.

Will and I drove together to Savannah yesterday with the caravan of the rest of our family hovering around us. Will said he was tempted to play *let's see if we can lose Furtick* and then find a place to make out, but decided it would cause too much panic. We didn't leave until later in the afternoon since it would be the short leg of the drive. It was nice to have about four hours alone together. We talked honestly about how difficult this transition may be, not knowing how upset those who have known Will since birth might feel about him deceiving them about his death. Some of those people are still Gregory Meyer supporters, not believing the evidence that has been leaked and on display since Holly ended our suffering on the steps of the courthouse.

Will says he isn't concerned about what people think. He knows what he did was the only option for the safety of his mother and the survival of our relationship.

We also talked about how easy it will be to plan our rescheduled wedding since almost everything was already in place. This got me thinking about dates again so I pulled out my phone and scrolled through the calendar. When I saw that the date I was hoping for falls on a Saturday, I didn't say anything. I wanted to sleep on it to make sure I wanted to live with that date for the rest of my life.

Today, before we embark on our second day of driving and I'm forced to drive back with Claire in her car as we did when we left Davidson, I decide to tell Will the new wedding date I've chosen at breakfast.

"I have to talk to you," I whisper in Will's ear.

"What's up? Do we need to go outside," Will answers, taking his napkin off his lap as he prepares to find a private place for us to talk.

"There's no need. I just wanted to tell you I set a new date for the wedding." I smile at Will knowing he'll be happy that I'm bringing this to him instead of him hounding me like he had to last time. Will spreads a face splitting grin and raises his brows in excited anticipation. "May 25th. That was my parents' anniversary. Is that ok?"

"That is more than ok, babe! I couldn't be more honored than to share the wedding date of the two people who brought you into my life." Will takes my face in his hands and gives me a hard kiss. "I love you so much!"

"Whoa! This is not that kind of restaurant you two!" Wes says laughing at our extreme public display of affection.

"Sorry! Couldn't be helped! Layla just set a new date for the wedding!" Will says, still staring into my eyes with joy.

"Oh, Layla! That's wonderful!" Claire beams. "What did you decide?"

"May 25th," I tell them.

"Your parents' anniversary. I think that's wonderfully fitting," Luke says smiling.

"And so romantic!" Eliana adds. "I'm so happy for you both. And now that things have changed, the entire mood of the day will be even more beautiful." She leans into Wes in a move that tells just how much of a romantic she is. Wes smiles at her and I'm sure we'll be celebrating their wedding someday, too.

"We should call the Gardens soon. That time of year can be very busy," Claire says. "Maybe we can chat about that and other wedding things today?" Claire's excitement for my wedding is wonderfully overwhelming. I'm glad she's so into it, though. After Will and I exchanged vows in the garden that day I really lost all concern for what my official wedding day looks like. I'll need her by my side to make sure the day happens like it's supposed to.

"I'd rather talk about it with Will on the drive today," I pout.

"We've been over this, Layla," Luke says. Will and Eliana aren't leaving Savannah until later this afternoon so they can arrive in Davidson under the covering of night. We can't risk anyone seeing them when they get into town. They're both even wearing baseball hats, of which I'm certain Eliana hasn't done since before Will was born, if ever.

"I'm going to miss you, too, babe, but I'll be there tonight. And since we're staying there, the time between our goodnights and our good mornings will be shorter than ever." Will kisses the top of my head putting me at ease.

We leave Savannah 30 minutes later than planned because I can't tear myself away from Will. It's kind of silly, really. I mean, we're going to see each other again before midnight. It's not like I haven't gone a whole day without seeing him. I think it's just the anxiety of what the coming days and months are going to bring that has me fearful. Remembering the last time I said goodbye to Will isn't helping either.

In a matter of days there will be a press conference and Luke will bring Will and Eliana Meyer back from the dead. He'll have to explain why it was a necessary last resort for saving their lives, with Will giving the majority of the details.

I'm nervous for Will. He's going to have to stand up in front of the press and those whom we deceived and explain why I was worth creating a charade so dramatic. I struggle with finding my own reasons why I was worthy of such a move. As much as I've grown over the last three years I still have to walk myself through all of my redemptive qualities, as well as the truths that have become my mantra in the line of defense against the lies Gram ingrained in me.

My parents' death was not my fault.

I am deserving of good things in my life.

I bring joy to people's lives.

Luke and Claire accept me and love me like my parents did.

Will loves me unconditionally.

Will and I send a steady stream of texts for a few hours until he tells me that he's going to spend some time with his mom. He still hasn't told her about the exes coming to testify on Holly's behalf, or about Erin. Wes never told her because he thought it would be better coming from Will. Things were so busy the last several weeks that Will wanted to wait until they had some uninterrupted time. They're going down to the Riverfront where we went for dinner last night. It's a beautiful historic area and Will thought the long walk along the river would be conducive to the talk he is going to have with her.

I indulge Claire in wedding conversation for a good part of the five-hour drive. We decide to have my dress refitted by Claire's preferred seamstress in Charlotte, and consider having a separate reception in Davidson for everyone who won't be invited to our small garden wedding. It's a nice gesture since Will has known most of these people his whole life, and with him coming back from the dead, I'm sure some of them will want to celebrate his marriage. We also decide to reconsider the flowers since Claire says that we should be able to catch some spring flowers at the end of the season.

Our conversation eventually comes to an appropriate end and I put my ear buds in so I can listen to the latest in my Music 101 lesson from Will. I was happy to get through KISS week having learned that they have a few anthems that I like, and even a couple of love songs, but overall, they are *not* my kind of band.

This week I'm supposed to be learning about R&B. I tried to tell Will that I already knew I didn't like that kind of music but I was swiftly silenced when he started listing artists like Usher, Beyonce, and Alicia Keys. So for the next hour or so I listened dutifully to some songs I already liked, and once again gained some new favorites, thanks to my music-loving fiancé.

The drive is peaceful until we cross into North Carolina. That's when my anxiety begins to rise. I physically tense up and Claire immediately notices.

"Hey…it's ok, Layla. You don't need to worry," Claire says in her soft and soothing voice, patting my leg. "He can't hurt us anymore. You're safe."

"I know. I'm just worried about Will. He deceived a whole town of people, Mom. Do you think they're going to hate him?" I say, fighting the cry that wants to consume me. The idea of anyone hating Will, especially for having done something so amazing for me, breaks my heart. "I couldn't bare it if they turned their backs on him."

"I don't know how everyone is going to react. What I do know is that there are enough people who have seen the evidence and understand. There may be some people who don't, but I'm confident that we'll have more supporters than not," Claire says confidently.

"What about Tyler and Chris' dads? They're partners in the firm. How do you think they're going to respond to Will, to you and Luke?" Mr. Fincher and Mr. Marks worked alongside Will's father longer than Luke. I never heard that they subscribed to his philosophy of life, but I never heard that they were incredibly trustworthy either. Chris and Tyler were the anomalies in their families. Their older brothers were success-driven like their fathers…maybe even just like Gregory Meyer.

"I don't know. Luke and I didn't know them outside of work. They may not understand, Layla, but that's ok. They always knew how Will felt about his father's ideas on life and success, but they never kept Chris or Tyler away from Will," she says. "You need to be prepared for a less than warm response from some people in the firm, but I don't suspect that you'll be faced with that too much. I know Luke and Will won't let you alone with anyone they're not absolutely sure is on our side."

I'm put at ease by my conversation with Claire. I know it won't be easy, but we live in a Gregory Meyer-free world now, and the town that was once monopolized by him is now a place of peace. There will always be those who don't understand why Will did what he did, but they've clearly never been loved the way Will loves me.

By the time we pull into the circular driveway of our house in Davidson, the sun is beginning to set. There's a gorgeous red and orange glow to the sky and I'm suddenly overtaken with the urge to get a full view of the sunset from the dock.

I get out of the car and stand, remembering the last time I saw this house. I never told Will about the memorial we had for him out on the dock. It was a beautiful time, but I didn't want him to feel badly about how emotional we all were, especially Tyler.

I begin to walk to the side of the house, intent on walking through the gate to get to the flagstone path that will take me to my favorite place on the planet, but Claire stops me.

"I know you're itching to get out to the lake but we need to at least get a few things inside first," she says. "We're back for good so you'll have plenty of time out there soon." Claire smiles and I know she's right. If I can just hold off until Will gets here tonight, going back out there with him for the first time since graduation will mean even more.

I grab a few bags from the back of the car that hold all those last minute things like toiletries and pantry items and make my way up the steps to the front door. I remember so clearly the first time I stood on this porch with Luke and Claire. I was nervous and excited all at once. I knew my life was changing, even if it was just in leaving behind my life in Orlando for a new one here. Thankfully it turned out to be an even more magnificent change than that. My life was turned upside down when my parents died, and regardless of the turmoil we've been through, my life was turned right side up when I came here.

Luke opens the door and motions for me to enter, which is strange because he always ushers Claire in first. I think he's just trying to give me some privacy as I enter this sacred space, but I'm quickly shown how wrong I am as Tyler, Caroline, Chris, and Gwen yell "Welcome home!"

"Oh my gosh!" I scream and drop my bags, barely noticing the tube of toothpaste and bottle of mouthwash that get thrown from one bag as they all fall.

"Welcome home, darlin'! Caroline says, wrapping her arms around me.

"What are you guys doing here?" I ask as I make my way to each of them, hugging one more fiercely than the next.

"Claire called and said you needed a Welcome Home party. How could we say no to that?" Tyler explains as he lifts me off the ground in a bear hug. "This is a big weekend and she knew you'd want all of us together again," he whispers in my ear. We'll finally be able to tell Chris and Gwen about Will and the whole gang will be back together!

"I've missed you," Gwen says sweetly. Her hug is warm and sisterly and I feel terribly about not having kept up with her as I should have. My heart is happy, though, as her embrace tells me that I didn't ruin anything through my irresponsibility.

"I've missed you, too, Gwen. I'm glad you're here," I tell her. We smile at each other and I know that moving forward my relationship with Gwen is going to be even better.

"Are you two still hot and heavy?" I say to Chris wrapping one arm around his neck while still holding on to Gwen.

"You know it!" he says squeezing around my waist.

"What about you? Let me see this ring! You have to tell us all about this John guy. Caroline and Tyler said he's great and that we're just going to love him." Gwen grabs my hand and inspects my engagement ring. "Whoa! He did good!"

"It was Claire's grandmother's ring," I tell her. "And yes, I know for a *fact* that you two are going to love him. He won't get in until later tonight, but you guys can stick around if you want." I immediately start thinking of ways to surprise them and consider what we'll tell them so they know they have to keep this secret for a few days.

"That'd be awesome! Let's order Chinese and play Monopoly until he gets here!" Tyler is more excited than a kid getting a puppy for Christmas. He was so overwhelmed with emotion when he and Will were reunited, and he's just as excited now that we're all going to be together again.

"You're lucky I still have everyone's order in a note on my phone! I'll order and you unload the truck!" Claire says heading to the kitchen.

Everyone else files out of the living room and through the front door while I text Will to tell him that our friends are here and the veil of secrecy is going to be completely lifted. I instruct him to text me when they arrive so I can make sure Chris and Gwen get the same surprise treatment as we gave Caroline and Tyler…well, I guess the reveal with Tyler was more of a surprise for Will. Just the same, Chris and Gwen are in for the surprise of their lives!

I stand next to the couch and wingback chairs and it's like we never left. The table, the china cabinet, the couch and chairs…everything is in the exact same spot it was in before. I take a deep breath, savoring this moment, not letting it slip away. I thought that first day in July when I stumbled into this room was my fresh start, but I was wrong. Because Gregory Meyer no longer exists to destroy everything I have worked so hard to have, *today* is my fresh start. I look around the room again and know just how right Claire was. It definitely feels like we've come home.

Chapter 7

Will and Eliana have just arrived and I'm giddy with excitement to give Will back to Chris and Gwen. I went back and forth with a few ideas of how to surprise Chris and Gwen, but considering how late it is, I think simple is the best way to go.

"Oh, you know what?" I say to the group. "I left something in the car. I'll be right back." I give Caroline a look and she knows exactly what I'm doing.

I specifically made Chris and Gwen sit with their backs to the kitchen door. When I come back in, Will, Eliana, and I are as quiet as possible. It's not too difficult to stay below the noise level of our four friends, especially when hostile takeovers are being brashly negotiated.

After positioning Will in the entryway, I make as loud a declaration as I can. "Hey! Look what I found!"

Everyone looks to me and Chris literally falls out of his chair when he realizes that he's not dreaming. That Will is really standing there.

The big reveal to Gwen and Chris is just as spectacular as I anticipated. There are tears and laughter, and Chris throws lots of punches at both Will and Tyler for keeping this from him. Gwen is just so overwhelmed that Will is alive and we're all back together that all she can do is cry and hug us both.

When we explain the whole story to them, from Will's disappearance to how I discovered him and his mother, to all the reasons why they did what they did, our friends understand completely. When we make Gwen and Chris swear not to mention a word of it to anyone, they agree without question. Knowing that it will only be a few days was helpful.

I ask Chris and Tyler how their dads are doing with Meyer's death and I am totally surprised by the answer. Apparently they're not all that broken up about it. I never got to know them before we were exiled, but I always assumed Luke was the only lawyer there with a conscience, especially the way Chris and Tyler talked about their dads. They seemed almost as success-driven as Will's father. I'm glad to find out I was wrong.

By the time we finish telling Gwen and Chris everything, laughing, crying, reminiscing, and even playing an epic game of monopoly it's after three in the morning. We shuffle everyone out with arms flying everywhere from all the hugging. Claire sends Luke, Wes, and me outside to get the overnight bags as well as the box with the bed linens, while Will and Eliana clean up after the tornado of fun that swept through the kitchen.

I call to Claire when I come back in with the box of linens. Following her voice toward their bedroom I find her in a room across from the room that had been their office, which is being turned into a bedroom now that we've added three more residents.

"Hey...I got the sheets," I say as I put the box down by the door. "I've never been in here. What did this room used to be?" I open the box and pull out a set of sheets. Each set is folded perfectly and contained in a pillowcase of the set. Claire said she saw Martha Stewart do this and thought it was genius. I have to agree.

"This was Penny's room," she says softly.

"I'm sorry. I should have known." Of course this would have been Penny's room. Luke and Claire's room is just down the hall, and the office is across from here. I'm such an idiot.

"Don't be sorry, Layla. You didn't know. Really, it's ok. Here, help me with this," she says throwing the fitted sheet across the bed. I walk to the other side and pull the elasticized corner over the mattress.

"So...did you and Luke, you know, want more kids?" I ask tentatively. I don't want to stir up any heartache in Claire, but I'm genuinely curious. Two people as loving and incredible as Luke and Claire...I can't see why they wouldn't want another baby.

"We were going to. We thought we were ready...*I* was ready...but Luke had a change of heart. He said he would feel like he was trying to replace

Penny, and that he didn't know if he would ever be able to look at another child without thinking they were only here to make up for what we had lost. I didn't see it that way, but…if both partners aren't on board, it's a no-go. We were consumed by the whole partnership thing after that, and well…" she says.

I remember Claire telling me about the brass ring Gregory Meyer held out for them as the youngest attorneys in the history of the firm to be up for partnership. That's when they shut everything out and pursued their careers hard core. So much so that they didn't even know Gram died until too late, which was their wake-up call.

"I'm sorry about that," I say softly. It's all I can say really. They should have had more kids. They're two of the best people I've ever known and it seems unfair that they didn't bring another one just like them into the world.

"We got our second chance with you." Claire smiles her sweet, loving, motherly smile at me and I know how she feels because I got my second chance with them, too.

Luke and Wes stumble down the hall with more than just the overnight bags Claire requested. Each of them has at least three pieces of luggage on them and they're both laughing as they rumble through the hall like two pack mules.

"Hey babe," Luke says passing us and going straight to their bedroom followed by Wes. "I'm just going to toss these in here for now, ok?" he calls.

"That's fine," she calls back to him. "Hey," she says to Luke when he enters the room.

"Hey." Luke kisses Claire's temple and slides his arm around her waist. "You doing ok in here?"

"Yeah, I'm good, thanks." Claire wraps both arms around Luke's waist and rests her head on his chest. It's not until this moment that I realize Claire probably hasn't been in this room in a very long time. Even when we moved to Florida, Caroline's mom must have handled this room.

"Thank you, both, so much. It means a lot to me that you're opening this room to Eliana." Technically it's for Eliana and Wes, but Will doesn't like to talk about that. He says he'd feel better if, as he put it, Wes "put a ring on it."

"Of course, Layla," Luke says. Claire sighs and it seems to be a cue for Luke to move things along. "You know what? It's late. Let's divvy up these sheets and get everyone to bed."

I find Will and Eliana in the kitchen cleaning up the game and Chinese food remnants. I'm surprised there was anything left considering we were feeding Will, Tyler and Chris. Those boys can each down an entire large pizza and a two-liter of soda on their own. They'll all be spending more time here in the coming days as everyone soaks in as much Will time as they can before the big announcement. Once that happens, the potential for media craziness is imminent and we've told them that they'll have to keep their distance for their own good. We don't want them having to answer questions from the press.

"Luke says it's time for bed," I say as I wet a paper towel and wipe down the counters. I'll have to remember to put cleaning supplies on the list for what to pull out of the boxes first tomorrow.

"You ready, babe?" Wes asks Eliana as he enters the kitchen just a moment behind me. He kisses Eliana sweetly and Will cringes just slightly, but then smiles as he shakes his head. I can imagine it's weird to see your mom like that, but at the core he's really happy that she's found with Wes what she had been denied for so long. Wes treats her like gold and that's what matters most to Will.

"We've got the rest of this. You two go to bed," I tell them. Will doesn't look up from his garbage-gathering task. He's trying, but sometimes trying means that you're containing what would be your natural reaction. He knows that Wes is good for his mom, but he's just really protective of her, especially now that we're back in Davidson. He doesn't want anyone to think poorly of her because she's moved on and in a new relationship.

"If you're sure," Eliana says. I nod and she and Wes make their way to the door. "William?" Will turns around and looks at his mother. Eliana looks like she's not sure exactly what to say; just that she wants to say something. We're headed into a media firestorm and Will is carrying so much of the responsibility for how it goes. Eliana may make a statement, but Will is the one who will field all the questions. "Get some good rest, sweetheart. We've got some big days ahead of us." Will just nods again and smiles sweetly.

It only takes us another five minutes to get the kitchen tidied. With the kitchen boxes still packed in the garage there are no actual dishes to tend to. Ours was a mission of trash pick-up.

"C'mon. Your turn." I grab Will's hand and escort him to his new room. Wes and Eliana's door is now closed and the box of sheets is in the hallway. I grab a set from the box and begin undoing the perfection of its folding and drop them on Will's bed. Will is quiet as I shake the fitted sheet out and begin adjusting it on the mattress. "You want to talk about it?"

"Talk about what?" he says. He doesn't make eye contact with me as he grabs the pillows and begins to fit them with their cases.

"Why are you acting like I don't know you? I know when you're deep in thought, when you're worried." I stop what I'm doing and take the pillow from him. "Talk to me, Will."

"It's…a lot." His eyes are tired and I know he's been running through infinite scenarios of the upcoming days.

"I know. I also know that you can do this." I take Will's hands in mine hold them tight. "You've already come this far. I believe in you."

"I'm glad *someone* thinks I can pull this off."

"Will, what you have to do this week is nothing compared to what you had to pull off to get away from your father. You and Luke coordinated your

65

disappearance and faked your death, which proves you're brave. You can't let having to explain all of that to the press scare you."

"I'm not worried about me, Layla. I'm worried about you, my mom, my family in Hickory…oh, my gosh! What are my grandparents going to think?" Will sits down on the side of the bed and puts his face in his hands.

"They're going to understand, Will. They knew what your father was like. They're just going to be happy to have you back, and they're going to be thrilled to finally have the kind of relationship with you they always wanted." I sit next to Will and put my arm around his back. It's so small compared to his athletically strong body, and doesn't compare to the blanket-like feeling his arms have when they wrap around me. "What's your mom said about it?"

"She hasn't. I haven't asked her about it. It was enough to tell her about the ex-wives, Loretta, and Erin." Will's answer is muffled but audible through his hands.

"How did she take that news?" I ask.

"She feels terribly for them, especially Loretta. She's the only one who knew my dad before the switch got flipped. My mom, and I'm sure the others, can look back and see how my dad manipulated her. Not Loretta. She got to know my dad as a person with a heart who cared about her, cared about their baby. She got blindsided and there was no hindsight. Mom was more concerned with how I felt about Erin." Will stands and takes the pillow to finish getting the bed ready. I follow his lead and grab the sheet.

"How *do* you feel about Erin?" I ask, getting back to the task of making Will's bed.

"Better than I did before. I can't do anything about how she feels about me but…I think I'd really like to get to know her her…if she wants to get to know me. What do you think she wants?" Will looks at me and I can see the frightened little boy in him. After years of his father's rejection I don't think he could take any more. If his father had allowed it, Will would have loved to have had a relationship with Marcus when they were younger, but Will didn't find out that Marcus was his brother until their father had already done too much damage to both of them.

"I think she wants to know you. From everything Luke has said about Loretta, Erin's experience growing up was the polar opposite of Marcus'. She didn't spend her life hearing about how evil Gregory Meyer was. Her mother left because she wanted a better life for Erin, not because she was forced out. And…Erin is, like, 40 years old, Will. I'd like to think she's adult enough to know not to hold you responsible for your father's choices." I know this isn't always the case, but my gut tells me Erin's motives are good.

Will breathes a heavy sigh and helps me straighten the blanket onto the bed. He hands me a pillow and we place both of them against the headboard. When we're done making his bed, Will grabs another set of sheets from the hall, takes my hand, and leads me up the stairs to my room. He's silent so I know he's digesting and thinking.

I take a moment at the top of the stairs recalling the first time I made this trip. I scan the room and it's like we never left. I remember being in awe of the wall of books that became a source of salvation for me. I glance at the couch and then at Will and we both smile remembering our day of nothing, the day that I knew what it felt like to be absolutely consumed with passion. My eyes lift to the wall of windows and I'm overwhelmed with anticipation for tomorrow, knowing that Will and I will be able to walk the familiar path down the flagstone to the dock and take our rightful places by the lake.

"You got quiet," I say as I begin the same bed-making routine that we just finished.

"I'm just thinking. I'm sure you're right about Erin. I guess…I just never factored in any of the other stuff. I didn't think about how my mom's family was going to feel. I was just so obsessed with coming home…getting back what should never have been taken away from us…giving you the life

67

I've wanted to give you from the moment I knew you loved me as much as I loved you." Will takes my hand and I sit on the side of the bed with him. "I may be a really crappy fiancé until all of this is settled. Please don't think that I don't want you or want to marry you or build our life together or…"

"I get it. You're ridiculously in love with me and nothing, not even the complications involved with coming back from the dead, is going to keep us from being together," I smile, grateful that Will is aware and communicating with me about the possibility of me feeling shut out as he deals with everything in front of us. "I love you, too, Will. I know it's going to be crazy and frustrating and scary until everything is out in the open, but we have been through and conquered worse."

"Well…since we both agree that it's going to be pretty crazy around here for a while, and that I'm ridiculously in love with you, *and* our time together may be limited, I should probably go ahead and do this before it's too late." Will leans in and kisses my neck before I even have a chance to respond.

"Oh, wow, um…" I stutter as my head hits the bed and Will's body is pressed against mine. "Yeah, I think you're right," I say as Will continues to kiss the spot behind my ear that we both discovered drives me crazy. "Ah….I'm glad you're feeling better. I was starting to worry about you."

"Layla?" Will stops kissing me and I'm afraid this is it for the night. "Shut up."

"Right. Shutting up now." I smile and grab the back of Will's head, crushing our lips together.

Will's hand travels the length of my body and hitches my knee up to his waist. We can't seem to get enough of each other. We both let ourselves go farther than we normally would have, but not so far that we compromise the boundary that we've abided by since day one. I think we're both just so nervous about the days to come. There are confrontations, revelations, and unknowns out there. Our solace comes from each other and right now we need as much solace as we can get.

Chapter 8

I've tried not to, but I've been thinking a lot about the surveillance photos I found of the night my parents died. I replay the night I found them, flipping through each horrific picture in my mind, and remembering how painful it was to relive that night. After Luke and Claire found me in a huddled mess on the office floor Luke promised he would explain them when Gregory Meyer's trial was over. Since there is no longer a Gregory Meyer trial, I'm hoping Luke will make good on his promise and tell me who took the pictures, and why Meyer had them.

Eliana is helping Claire unpack the kitchen boxes and Will is in the loft going over the statement he and Luke wrote. Luke said he can just read it, but Will really wants to memorize it. He wants to look the press in the eyes when he tells them the truth. He said that a real man looks people in the eyes when he makes a confession.

With everyone else occupied I find Luke in his and Claire's bedroom. There's a sitting area as part of the room that they're making into their office area now that we've expanded our family. Wes is with him and they're sorting through some file boxes.

"Hey, Dad," I say.

"Hey, Layla. What's up?" Luke looks at me long enough to smile and goes back to his files.

"I need to talk to you…about the surveillance photos." I don't even care that Wes is there. I learned a lot time ago not to worry about what I say in front of him since he already knows everything, and if he doesn't he's a steel trap for information he gains.

"I'll leave you two to talk." Wes starts toward the door when Luke stops him.

"You need to stay, Wes. There are things only you can explain," Luke says, putting the file in his hands back in the box.

"Where are the pictures?" I ask. "I want to see them."

"No you don't. That was the most horrific night of your life. Looking at them again is the last thing you need to do," Luke says. He's being stern, but the look in his eyes tells me that the idea of me reliving that night again pains him as much as it pained me that night on the office floor.

"Are you going to tell me why those pictures were in with the Meyer evidence?" My heart is racing and my breathing is on the shallow side. I'm not sure if I really want to know the answer or if I'm just being my stubborn self and demanding answers for the sake of being in the loop. Part of me is saying that I have a right to know, while the other part is telling me to move on. My parents are dead and there is nothing anyone can do about it.

"Are you sure you want to know? You know the answer to any question that involves Gregory Meyer is never good." Luke is stoic and fearful. "I won't be able to undo this once you know."

"I'm sure," I say as I sit on the other side of Luke's desk. Wes sits in the chair next to me and even though I'm about to hear something that I'm sure is going to change things forever, I feel warm and loved. Sitting with me are two of the three men I trust most in this world. I know, without a shadow of a doubt, that I'm both physically and emotionally safe.

"Ok. Well..." Luke takes a deep breath which seems fitting since he's about to dive into a pretty deep story. "A few years after Penny died Claire and I felt like we were ready to have another baby. I wasn't as sure as Claire, but I knew that she wouldn't be complete without another child, and I wanted to give that to her. But...our lives at the firm were busier than they ever had been. We threw ourselves into our work as a way to self-medicate the pain of losing Penny, and we became even more important to firm. I didn't talk with Claire about it first, but I decided I would let Greg know that we were going to try for another baby, and that I felt it would better if we left Meyer, Fincher, and Marks. There were less demanding firms in Charlotte that would allow me to practice and still be there for Claire, who I knew would want to stay home with the baby this time.

"The day I decided to talk with Greg I walked into his office after two quick knocks as I frequently did. This particular day I walked in on him and a female client in a compromising position. Flustered and embarrassed, I immediately left the room. After she put her top back on and left, I went back in to see Greg. I apologized for intruding and he waved his hand, dismissing the whole thing like it was no big deal. He asked what I needed so I told him about Claire and I wanting another baby and that I knew she would want to stay home. He was great about it. He was happy for us, really. I don't think the idea of Claire leaving bothered him. He always erred on the side of chauvinism. Then I told him how I thought it would be better for our family if *I* left the firm for a less prominent one that would allow more time for me to spend with Claire and the baby. That's when things started going downhill."

"What do you mean? How could things go downhill because you wanted to leave, and what could it possibly have to do with my parents?" I'm already confused but I have a feeling my confusion is about to escalate.

"No one quits Meyer, Fincher, and Marks. You leave the firm because you're dead or you've been dismissed. I knew this but thought that because of the reasons why I was leaving, and because I thought I had a different relationship with him, that Greg would understand. Greg told me I was too valuable to the firm and his particular secrets that he couldn't risk me leaving. I stressed my position, assuring him I took attorney/client confidentiality very seriously and he had nothing to worry about. When he emphasized that there was no way in hell I was leaving and that he'd make sure I never practiced law in North Carolina or any states we have reciprocity with, I did something stupid."

"What did you do?" I ask. My eyes are wide and by the looks on their faces it must be clear to both Luke and Wes that I'm shocked that Luke would think he could ever do something stupid. Irresponsibility is not in his repertoire.

"I threatened him." I've never seen this look on Luke's face before. He's sad and embarrassed and angry all at once.

"How?" I ask softly.

"That day wasn't the first time I caught him being *inappropriate* with a female client. I told him I was obligated to report him to the ethics board, but that I could overlook his indiscretions for an uncomplicated release from the firm as well as a stellar letter of recommendation. He complimented my style, took credit for the influence, and asked me to give him one month, reiterating my importance to the firm and the mess redistribution of cases can be. I thanked him, apologized for my brash behavior, and went back to work. Two weeks later your parents were dead."

"I don't understand." My confusion has definitely reached a new level. "What does your job have to do with my parents' death?"

"I wouldn't have connected the dots either, but Greg never could stand to let his mastermind go unnoticed. When Claire and I returned from the funeral, I had a meeting with Greg. We were going to go over some current cases, and I was going to talk with him again about us leaving. I was even more determined to simplify our lives after I lost John and Elisabeth, and almost you. But Greg cut our meeting short before I could get to it, excusing me so he could make some calls. Before I left the room, though, he told me how sorry he was about my brother's death and that perhaps next time I would believe him when he tells me that no one leaves the firm until he says they can. He wanted to make sure I understood the extent of his powerful reach."

"Are you saying Gregory Meyer had my parents killed just because you wanted to quit? How is that even possible? There was a torrential down pour that night! And we only went out because I begged my parents! A car hydroplaned into us! This doesn't make any sense!" I'm sitting on the edge of my seat, trying to convince Luke that he's wrong.

"It wasn't just because I wanted to leave. It was because I challenged him. I threatened him and he retaliated." Luke leans back in his chair, sad and defeated. "This is where Wes comes in. He knows more about how Greg made things happen than I'll ever understand." Luke nods to Wes as if finally giving permission to tell me the secret they've both been keeping.

"Were you involved in this?" I ask fearfully.

"No! And no one you know was. When Greg wanted something done he found experts to do it. You couldn't have just a little bit of experience with something for Greg to use you. You needed to be *the* go-to person for it. So, when he needed a car accident, he went to a former stunt man he had on the payroll," Wes explains. His tone is soft and forthcoming. "The guy was apparently facing some pretty serious blackmail charges from some Hollywood royalty and Greg got everything dropped. A stunt man is the kind of guy you want around when you need to make something look like an accident."

"How do you *arrange* a car accident?" I ask.

"Do you remember when I told you that Greg doesn't do anything himself because he doesn't have the patience to sit his ass in a car for hours and watch someone?" Wes asks. I nod immediately remembering that as one of the first conversations Wes and I ever had. "Your house was bugged and your parents' cars were tagged with GPS so Greg's guys would know when and where you were going at all times. After the bugs and GPS were set, they guys just had to be patient. The storm that night was the perfect condition for a car accident, and when it was clear you were leaving your house, the guys moved. They knew where you were going and with the GPS knew exactly the route you'd take. Greg always had pictures taken in case he needed some leverage with an overconfident *henchman*." Wes gives Luke a look, as Luke is the one who has referred to the men on Gregory Meyer's secret payroll as henchmen.

"How do you know all this?" I ask Wes. If he wasn't there, how could he possibly know all the details?

"We *henchmen* were a fraternity of sorts. We didn't have anyone else to talk to. We were the only ones who knew what it was like to be controlled by Meyer that way. I had just been brought in and a few of the guys were showing me the ropes, giving me Gregory Meyer's Ten Commandments. Well, one of the guys was giving me some 101 on how Greg likes things done. He started explaining the technical side to one of his last jobs...how he did the bugging and tagging and another guy drove the car."

"I want to meet the driver," I say blankly. "I have a right to face him."

"You can't, Layla," Luke says.

"Why not? If neither he nor Meyer is going to pay for what they did, then he deserves a tongue lashing from me at the very least!"

"Because he's dead. He was just the driver and was told what his mark was. The objective was to send a message about what Meyer was capable of. If that ended in his mark dying, fine. If not, the message would still be clear. When he realized you were in car, too, he freaked. The thought that he could have killed a child tormented him for weeks. He went to Meyer and told him about there being a kid in the car and asked to be released from his duties, but Meyer didn't care." Wes sighs. "They found him dead in his car, closed up in his garage with the engine running. He left a note laying it all out but there were too many cops on Meyer's payroll for it to find its way into evidence." Wes's delivery features his usual cool and calm cadence. He knows how to communicate terrible information without letting the awful details deter him from his objective.

"How could you stand working for him after that? He killed my father...your brother," I say to Luke. I'm trying not to cry as I think about the insanity of it all.

75

"I was scared, Layla. I had to stay. He had made his point, and his point was that I was not immune to his rules. I knew exactly what he was capable of. I don't know what he would have done, who else he would have hurt, if I followed through with my threat to turn him into the ethics board," Luke says, his face strained and his voice faltering as he relives the pain he went through.

"That's why you changed your mind about having another baby. You were afraid of what he might do to them." The pieces of this impossible puzzle are coming together and I can't believe the picture that is being revealed.

"And why even five years later I convinced Claire that having you live with us would be too difficult for her. I hated that I had kept her from being a mother again. I felt like the more people there were in my life that I loved, the more targets there were in his twisted game. But…when I saw you standing there in the kitchen after the funeral, so afraid that you were about to be abandoned…I couldn't deny you or Claire the opportunity to have the family you needed. It wouldn't have been fair to either of you. That's when I vowed to spend every second of my time at the firm collecting even more evidence to one day take Greg down."

Wes and Luke wait silently while I absorb everything. This is not what I was expecting, not that I knew what to expect. I've heard about, witnessed, and personally experienced the wrath of Gregory Meyer, but the lengths that man would go to prove a point or send a message is now frighteningly clear.

I consider everything that Will and I have been through over the past three years and see how lucky we really are. After Will raised his voice at his father that night at dinner, and then my refusal to back down at his *House Call*, I could have easily had an *accident* and never been seen again.

The accident.

"Oh my God," I whisper, realization spreading across my face.

"What is it?" Luke asks, taking me by the shoulders in concern.

"Didn't Meyer's response to Will's interest in me always seem extreme? I mean he had no idea where things would go with us. We could have dated a few months and then fizzled out. But right from the beginning he was adamant that I stay away from Will," I say.

"Everything Greg did was to the extreme. What are you getting at?" Luke says.

"Don't you get it? I existed in Will's world because of Gregory Meyer." Wes and Luke look as confused as two people can.

"If Meyer hadn't gone after my parents to prove a point to you, I would never have ended up in Davidson. It's because of him that my parents died, I went to live with Gram and Gramps, and ended up here with you."

I sit on the couch and put my face in my hands. My body begins to shake and Luke is at my side in an attempt to console me. I can't hold back any longer and before I know it I'm laughing uncontrollably. It's that crazy kind of laugh that one does when the choices are either to laugh or to cry hysterically.

"Layla?" Luke pulls me up so I'm sitting against the back of the couch and he can see the weird spectacle I'm making. "What...what are you doing?"

"Don't you see?" I say in between laughs. "He did this to himself! All of it! Everything he's had to *fix* has been because *he* broke it!" I'm trying to stop laughing but it's difficult. "Had he not shoved Holly and Marcus' mother to the curb the way he did, there may not have been a Holly to deal with, and if he hadn't been so cruel to them I doubt she would have shot him on the steps of the courthouse! If he had let Eliana take Will back to Hickory with her, I would never have met Will.

"His culpability was so much deeper than him doing what he had to do to get what he wanted. Everything that threatened his blueprint for success for Will was brought about by his own hand. That's why he was so intent on getting rid of me, of Holly. Will once told me that he used to date girls his father didn't approve of. His father never made any of *them* disappear. When I met Meyer, he had no idea how serious Will and I were, or would become, but he had to cut off the potential relationship because he knew the only reason I was here was because of him, and he couldn't risk me being cut from the same cloth as my activist parents or ethical uncle."

"I'm so sorry, Layla," Luke says, shaking his head.

"Why are you sorry?" I ask, calming down and focusing on Luke's evident pain.

"I should never have pressed him. If I hadn't pushed things, he would have never gone after John and Elisabeth." I can see the weight of our world resting on Luke's shoulders.

"You could have never known he would do what he did. And now that we know about his and Loretta's story, his response makes even more sense. It's not your fault, Dad!" I throw my arms around Luke and hold him tight like the night in Ashville he made sure I knew my parents' death was not my fault. Now it's my turn.

"I knew what he was capable of…I just never thought I'd be on the receiving end," Luke says through soft sobs.

"Dad…"

"Would you have still come to live with us if you knew all this from the beginning?" he asks, wiping the tears that have escaped his eyes.

I think for a moment, not sure how to answer this loaded question. "I don't know if I would or not. It all sounds so farfetched that I don't think I would have believed you if you told me. What I *do* know is that I'm not the same person I was three years ago, and I wouldn't be *this* girl if you and Claire hadn't become my parents." I sit on the couch, still reeling from what Luke and Wes have explained, and the realizations I've come to. "Claire doesn't know any of this?"

"No, and I don't want her to, so please don't say anything to her," Luke pleads.

"I won't say anything, but I think you should tell her. She needs to know why you changed your mind about having another baby," I tell him. For almost eight years Claire has lived under the assumption that Luke couldn't stand to have some kind of replacement child. If she knew that he changed his mind in order to protect her, the pain she's lived with might just go away.

"I can't, Layla. I don't think I could look her in the eyes and tell her I lied to her about the thing that meant the most to her in this world." Luke hangs his head, the weight of all he's carried for so long shifting along his shoulders.

"She'll understand if you tell her it was to protect her, to protect your potential baby. It won't be easy for you to say, or her to hear, but she needs to know. Believe me…I know. The day I found out about my father and the explosion, the hardest part was having been lied to. And today…you kept the real cause of my parents' death from me to protect me. I don't like being lied to, but now that I know and understand, I actually feel pretty loved."

"I'll…I'll think about it. But I'm not making any promises."

"Well," Wes begins. "It's over now, and despite his efforts to the otherwise, Gregory Meyer made us all stronger. Because of him, there is nothing we can't handle. So our next move is to get Will and Eliana ready for the press conference."

"Yes, of course," Luke says, collecting himself. "The press conference is in two days. Layla are you planning on being there?"

"Why wouldn't I be?" I'm perplexed. Why would my attendance even be a question?

"Will wasn't sure if he wanted you there or not. Only because the press can be, well, the press. He's just trying to protect you," Luke explains preemptively before I get frustrated at the thought of being left out of something again.

"I know, but I'm going to be there to support Will," I tell him. "He thinks he has to do everything on his own in some show of Braveheartesque

79

manliness. We're a team and I'm not letting him walk out there into a hungry den of media lions to be eaten alive."

Luke sighs, clearly not wanting me to go either. But, by now they all know better than to fight me on this. "Ok. Then let's get your statement to the press ready."

Chapter 9

We worked on my statement to the press for hours last night. Will and Luke are going to do everything they can to keep me from having to speak, but thought it best to have something prepared anyway. It's a general statement about how I didn't know that Will was faking his death, and that my move to Tallahassee to go to Florida State had been predetermined before I even moved to Davidson and met Will. While I'm glad to be prepared, I hope to God I don't have to say a word.

"Hey babe," Will says as he finds me in the loft in my big green chair. I've missed this spot and could cozy up here all day. I won't stay here all day, though, because Will and I are going to take a slow, deliberate walk down the flagstone path out to the lake. I'm more excited than I can bear and am so glad Will finally finished working on his statement so we can go.

"Hey! I thought you'd never finish! How is it? Are you feeling good about it?" I ask.

"As good as one can feel about a statement designed to confess to having lied to an entire community about my death. But...I can't worry about it too much. I know that what Mom and I did was for the best for us, and my future with you." Will kisses the top of my head and takes my hand, pulling me from my comfy spot.

"I'm proud of you, Will. I know this isn't going to be easy, but you're handling it so well."

"Like I said before, I'm not as concerned about me as I am you and Mom. Regardless of the truths about my father that have come to light, there are some real jerks out there that are going to try and twist things for a good story. I'm hoping it won't come to it, but if it does, just stick with your statement. Don't go rogue on me, ok?"

"Me? Go rogue? I have no idea what you're talking about!" I giggle and take Will's hand as we move to the stairs.

"You know," Will begins, stopping us at the railing and eying the oversized couch. "Since I live here now, I'm thinking we could probably arrange a prom-night-revisit. What do you think?"

"That would be awesome," I say, remembering the beautiful, non-sex filled night we spent together after prom. It was a dream come true to spend the night in Will's arms, waking up with him beside me. I stop myself before I continue to the memories because it wasn't long after that night that the nightmare of Will's disappearance began.

"C'mon. The lake is waiting for us." Will smiles and all the craziness that awaits us in the days to come seems to fade away. I want to relish these moments when our lives seem normal because I don't know how long it will take for the dust to settle and our lives become our own again.

We're about to walk through the French doors in the kitchen that will take us to the dock when Wes comes charging in.

"We have a problem. You two need to come here," he demands. He doesn't even wait for a response, but turns with an expectation that we'll follow him. Which we do.

"What's going on?" I ask as we enter Luke and Claire's bedroom. The TV is on and everyone is huddled around it like they're watching aliens invade. I hear a woman's voice, full of emotion, and she's talking about Holly.

"My daughter acted bravely in the face of a tyrant. Gregory Meyer was a cruel and abusive man, and when it was clear that he was manipulating the jury, she just couldn't stand the thought that he might go free..." the southern voice declares.

"Who is this?" I ask.

"That's Holly's mother, Marlene Harris," Luke replies.

"Harris?" I question.

"Yeah, she went back to her maiden name after Meyer divorced her and never changed it when she married Reynolds," Luke answers.

"Wait. *She's* Holly's mother?" Will says, stunned. "This isn't good."

"Are you saying you dated a girl and never knew who her parents were?" For someone as old school and chivalrous as Will, this strikes me as odd.

"Her mom was never there when I picked her up. I only met her dad," Will says, still staring at the TV.

"Ok…so I still don't get why this is a problem. It sounds like everything she's saying is true," I say, listening to the woman's soft sobs as she recounts the abuse and manipulation Gregory Meyer was known for among his wives.

"Because she's completely unreliable," Claire says. I see a look of frustration on her face, which is strange. Claire doesn't get frustrated. She finds solutions.

"Yes. She spent years, off and on, after their divorce spreading rumors and making false accusations about Gregory, the firm, its clients and me. None of it was true and Gregory almost sued her for libel and defamation of character. Someone at the firm was able to persuade him that doing so would just add fuel to her fire. So, he made a convincing statement to the press and she was laughed out of town. For her to come forward now is going to make it hard for our statements to be credible," Eliana explains.

"I *specifically* told her to wait. Geez!" Luke gruffs as he runs his hands through his hair. "We're going to have to go down there now. Wes, call Steven and tell him we're coming. I'll have to do some damage control and get Will to make his statement now. Are you ok with that?" he asks Will in the midst of his directions.

"I guess so. I don't really have a choice. I can't let her ruin what chance we have of the community believing us. Give me ten minutes." Will takes my hand and leads me to the dock. We walk faster than I had hoped we would upon our return to our favorite place. I wanted to savor every step, but time is not on our side right now. "This is it, Layla. Are you ready?" Will takes both my hands in his and holds them tight. He stares into my eyes as if he's searching for my answer before I speak.

"I'm as ready as I'll ever be," I tell him.

"I'm sorry that this is our first time back down to the dock and we aren't able to enjoy it. I just didn't know where else to take you. I wanted to be sure to have a least a few minutes with you before all the mayhem." Will shakes his head, seeming to try and collect his thoughts.

"It's going to be ok. It'll be crazy for a little while, but it's nothing we can't handle. It's not like we have to hide anymore after today, right?" I say, smiling at him, hoping to convey with my eyes all the hope that fills me.

"I love you," Will says, pulling me to his chest and wrapping his arms around me.

"Not nearly as much as I love you."

*****

We pull up to the backside of the Mecklenburg County Courthouse and park at a meter. Wes pops eight quarters into the meter buying a couple of hours. There's no one around on this side of the courthouse, not that anyone in Charlotte would necessarily recognize Will or his mother. It's only in Davidson that they were local royalty. There are, however, a half a dozen news station vans on the street which tells me that Marlene is either still ranting or Wes' call to whoever Steven is kept them waiting for us.

As we walk down the street and round the corner we immediately see the flock of reporters milling around the podium set up in the shade next to the Government Building where Marlene Harris is talking with a man and a woman, both dressed sharply in suits. It seems she commanded all the attention she can and is hovering around for whatever reason. You'd think she'd leave and go across the street to the jail to see Holly.

Luke's contact, Steven, approaches and exchanges just a few words with Luke and Wes before returning to the media pool. He says something to a few reporters with pads of paper and pens in hand when they look over his should with wide eyes. He corrals them back into the group and connects with a woman who appears to be an on-air reporter by the fact that she's holding a microphone and is pretty well put together.

"Ok," Luke says as he stops us a few yards from the podium. "I'm going to start by giving a short summary of the events, then I'll introduce Will. Will, you'll speak for both you and Eliana unless they want to hear directly from her. Eliana, do you have your statement?" Eliana nods and Wes takes her hand in his and kisses her knuckles. "Will? You good?"

"Yeah, I'm good. What about you, babe?" he asks me.

"I'm good. As long as we're together, we've got this, right?" I say to Will.

"It's you and me against the world." Will gives me on hard kiss and we're all on our way toward the podium.

Luke whispers something to Steven and steps up to the podium. There are four or five microphones attached to the stand like a metallic creature reaching out for him. He's composed and assured of himself. Luke is a pro at standing before a group of people and delivering a statement that some may or may not believe.

"Thank you all for sticking around today after Ms. Harris spoke to you. I had planned on calling this press conference for tomorrow afternoon, but seeing as you were all already here, I thought I'd save you a trip and some money on the parking meters," Luke begins. The reporters laugh and one of them says "Thanks, Luke!" He's got a rapport with the media that I had no clue about. It's almost magical.

I see Ms. Harris taking note of our presence and see her eyes widen when she finds Will and Eliana standing with us, alive and well. She begins speaking animatedly to the man and woman she had been talking to when we walked up. She's upset, angry even. *Have we taken her spotlight?* I wonder to myself as I consider the small backstory I received on her earlier.

"As you know," Luke continues. "I am representing Holly Reynolds in the murder trial of Gregory Meyer. Many of us watched that day as Mr. Meyer was shot on the steps of the federal courthouse not far from here. Ms. Reynolds was arrested on the scene and taken into custody. My job is to make sure Ms. Reynolds is afforded her due process and receives a fair trial. I will be presenting a defense of mental anguish and bringing in testimony that will support our position. Today you'll be getting a bit of a preview of the testimonies we're prepared to present to the jury." Luke turns and gives Will a nod, letting him know he's about to be up.

"Almost two years ago Gregory Meyer's wife and son disappeared. Shortly after that, it was reported that their bodies were found in the fiery wreckage of a car accident near Interstate Forty in Hickory. Today, we are here to tell you that Will and Eliana Meyer are alive." Luke has to stop talking because the questions from the media immediately begin to fire off like rockets at Will. He pulls me closer to him and I do everything I can to let him know that I'm not going anywhere.

"Why would you fake your deaths?"

"Who orchestrated the façade?"

"Where have you been all this time?"

"Whose idea was it?"

"Ok, ok…please, guys, please…save your questions until the end. Will Meyer is here and he's going to speak on his and Eliana's behalf. I ask that you please listen to his statement before you ask any questions." Luke steps aside for Will to take his place at the podium.

Will squeezes my hand and I give them the same look I've seen Luke and Claire give each other hundreds of time. It's the look that tells him I believe in him, that I know he can do this, and that everything is going to be ok.

"Thank…" Will begins but then clears his throat. "Thank you all for being here today. I know you have a lot of questions, so I appreciate you allowing me to give my statement first. I promise I'll answer as many of your questions as I can." Will takes a few deep breaths and I wonder if he's wishing he brought his written statement with him. "What I have to tell you today isn't easy, and some of you may not believe our reasons for doing what we did. My only goal today is to set the record straight so that my mother and I can reclaim our lives in Davidson." Will looks at me and I nod a gesture of encouragement to him. He gives me a faint, tight-lipped smile and returns his attention to the microphone monster before him.

"Without going in to too many details, because, quite frankly, the *details* are no one's business, my mother and I endured years of mental and emotional abuse by my father. It's hard to explain to someone what mental and emotional abuse looks like to another person. The best way I can try to help you understand is to ask you to think about the one person in the world who you love the most. Think about all the things they do to show you they love you. Do they complement you? Do they spend time with you? Do they support or encourage you? Do they tell you they love you? Now think about what life would be like if they didn't do any of those things. Even after you begged them, they had no interest in you.

"Now imagine that there wasn't just an *absence* of those things, but a *deliberate antithesis* to them. That instead of complementing you, they put you down. Instead of spending time with you, they ignored you. Instead of supporting or encouraging you, they manipulated you into thinking that you couldn't achieve your dreams. Instead of telling you they loved you, they used you for their own selfish gain. This is what life with Gregory Meyer was like. He played the part of upstanding citizen well. In reality, he was a conniving, backstabbing, manipulative, controlling man who did whatever he had to, including destroying people's lives, to get what he wanted.

"Almost three years ago I met a girl who changed my life." Will holds out his hand to me and I step forward and take it. "This is Layla Weston and she's not just *a* girl, she's *the* girl. When we met I was scared out of my mind to fall in love with her because I was afraid of what might happen to her. You see, the year prior I was romantically involved with Holly Reynolds. When my father found out, he didn't approve. Instead of having a civilized conversation with me about his disapproval, he went to her family, threatened them, and then paid them to leave Davidson. I don't mean to disrespect Ms. Harris or her husband. I don't blame them for taking the deal my father offered them. To reject the offer would have put their lives at risk. This isn't about them…it's about the power my father wielded and our need to come out from under his reign.

"When Layla and I made our relationship public, my father disapproved and began a similar path to break us apart. Now, it might seem like high school popularity games when I say that my father worked to break us up. I wish it had been that benign. He threatened her life as well as the lives of both her uncle and aunt. They were forced to leave town or suffer the consequences. It was the last straw for my mother and me. We took action and plotted to disappear and then fake our deaths. It was the only way to escape the power and control he crushed us with on a regular basis." Will pauses for a moment realizing that he's actually telling the world not only the secret we've been keeping about them faking their deaths, but the family secrets Will has kept under lock and key his whole life.

"I know you have questions, and I'm going to answer them. But first, I want to apologize to the people of the Town of Davidson. You were what made my life there so wonderful. You're a kind and generous town and I hope you'll be able to forgive me for having deceived you. My mother and

I…we want nothing more than to be a part of your special community again, and we hope you'll take us back."

Will releases the grip he's had on my hand and puts his arm around my waist, drawing me closer to him. Luke comes and stands on the other side of me and I'm guarded by two of my favorite men. Luke directs the reporters to ask any questions they'd like, but that not all questions may be answered.

"Will, where have you been all this time?" a scruffy reporter with a bad comb-over asks.

"We've been living in Tallahassee, Florida," Will answers curtly.

"Why fake your deaths? Why not just disappear and change your names?" another, younger, more put-together male reporter asks.

"My father would never have stopped having Layla's family monitored unless my mother and I were dead. He was suspicious of everyone, as suspicious people usually are."

"How did you fake your deaths?"

"This isn't an instructional seminar, Reggie," Luke says to the reporter he's obviously familiar with. It doesn't seem to bother Reggie since he laughs at Luke's response. "Next question."

"Miss Weston, did you know Will was going to fake his death for you?" a female reporter asks, catching me off guard.

"Oh, uh…no. I wasn't aware of anything until after they revealed themselves to me. I was just as shocked at their deaths, and mourned with the rest of the community." *Whew!* I smile infinitesimally with pride that I actually remembered part of my statement!

"I have a question," a woman's voice calls from the side of the crowd. "What makes you so special that Will Meyer would fake his death for you?" Heads turn trying to see who would raise such a brash and insensitive question. Marlene Harris is standing there with her Kristin Chenoweth pocketsize frame, hand on her hip, staring at me.

"Now is not the time or the place, Marlene," Claire says from behind us.

"Oh, I beg to differ," she says, echoing a Meyerism that I'm confident she heard on a semi-regular basis. With all of her conniving and game playing, I'm sure it turned into a mantra for Meyer with her. I remember how unnerved Luke and Claire were when I told them Marcus had said it to me, and how it confirmed to Will that we were telling him the truth about Marcus being his brother. It seems Gregory Meyer may not have been the only one to repeat this phrase to Marcus.

"Thank you, everyone, for your time today. We hope that you'll respect Will and Eliana's privacy as they adjust to life back in Davidson and the Charlotte area. If you have further questions, please contact me directly. I believe you all have that information. Thank you, again." With that, Luke steps away from the podium, taking Will and me by the elbows to lead us away.

"Leaving so soon?" Marlene asks. She slithers the same way Gregory Meyer did. I'm amazed that he didn't keep her around. She's beautiful with long, blonde, full-bodied hair, and the arm-candy stance that is the prerequisite for any woman who stood at his side.

"What do you want, Marlene? And why did you call this press conference today? I told you to wait," Luke chastises.

"I'm simply here to support my baby girl," she says with feigned concern. "And since when do you get to tell me what to do?"

"Since I'm representing your daughter pro bono," Luke says cold-faced.

"So you're *the* Layla Weston. You're not as pretty as Marcus made you out to be. But, I never could count on him to get anything right so…"

"You need to back off," Will tells her. "Do you have any idea what he did to Layla?"

"My son was an idiot and it got him killed. What do you want me to do about it?" she says so nonchalantly.

I think I might actually throw up. I can't believe the way she's talking about her own son. When Holly told me that she repeatedly made Marcus beg his biological father to take him in I thought maybe it was a slight exaggeration of the truth. But standing before this poor excuse for a human being, I believe it all.

"I'm sorry for your loss, Ms. Harris," I say. "Not that you have a clue what you lost. Despite your pathetic excuse for parenting, Marcus was a great guy. Knowing Gregory Meyer as I did, I used to think that Marcus took after you. But, he was smart and funny, and he cared about people, so…I guess he paved his own path. I'm sorry that Will didn't fight for Holly the way he did for me. Maybe the idea of being saddled to a family that would take any offer Gregory Meyer presented them wasn't so appealing."

"You little…" she begins in retort but I don't flinch.

"We're leaving now. I hope you got your fill of the spotlight you were looking for because it's not about you anymore. It's about Holly, and if you screw this up for her, she'll never forgive you." I take Will's hand and walk briskly back toward the car.

"I can't believe you just did that," Will says to me, smiling from shock.

"I know enough about that woman that I don't have to exchange false pleasantries with her. We're so close to having everything we've ever wanted. I'm not going to let that miniature Barbie ruin anything."

"I thought you weren't going to go rogue on me," Will says with a smirk.

"You told me not to go rogue with the media. You didn't say anything about the witchy mother of your ex-girlfriend."

Chapter 10

We walk back through the door of the house and file into the kitchen. Silent. We're all silent, at a loss for what to say or what to do with ourselves next. Of course Holly's trial is still going to consume much of our time and conversation, but without looming threats or the need to hide something, we seem to have entered a new reality.

"So…" I say to no one in particular.

"Yeah," Will says.

"Is it me or does it seem wonderfully weird to stand here in complete and total freedom?" I recall the day we stood in this kitchen when Will's father presented the dirt he'd dug up on my family, and laid out his seedy offers. That day was clouded by the revelation of lies and the manipulation of a mad man. Today, the sun is shining and the world is ours.

"It is wonderful, isn't it?" Eliana says. She, more than all of us, is relishing in the freedom we all now enjoy. I can't imagine how different her life is going to be now, and I hope that as she walks down the streets of town that she'll be welcomed and embraced.

"I have something for the two of you," Luke says to Will and Eliana with a smile. He lays his attaché case on the counter and pulls out a large envelope. From it he pulls two standard size envelopes.

Will opens his envelope first and takes out the contents, laying them on the counter for us to see. Spread out in a neat row is his driver's license, social security card, debit and credit cards, all with the name William Gregory Meyer.

"I guess I don't need these anymore," Will says, pulling the same cards out of his wallet that bear my father's first and my mother's maiden name.

"Huh. I called you by this name for two years, yet it seems so out of place now," I say, examining the ID's side-by-side. "I was so honored that you took my dad's name, but I'm so glad I have Will Meyer back."

"And Will Meyer is glad to be back," Will says with a relieved smile.

"Eliana?" Claire prompts. "We made the change you requested."

"Oh, yes, of course," she says hesitantly. Eliana takes the same cards from her envelope and sets them in a neat row, just like Will's. "Oh, my. It's odd, seeing my name like that again. I hope you don't mind, William."

Will and I look at her new identification cards and see that she's changed her name back to her maiden name of Hufford. Will stares at her driver's license, picking it up and examining it...letting the name roll around in his head for a long moment.

"I needed a fresh start, darling. I just...I couldn't be attached to that man in name any longer," Eliana tells him.

"Are you going to look at me with regret now? A casualty of the mistake you made in marrying my father?" Will's voice is soft and reflecting the conflict he's experiencing.

"Oh, no, no, no." Eliana glides to Will and embraces him. "You are the very best of everything your father had to offer and I will never regret marrying him. Of all the things he ever gave me *none* of it compares to what he gave me when I had you. Please don't think terribly of me. I need a fresh start, William. Part of that is reclaiming myself by going back to my maiden name. Part of that, well, part of that includes Wesley."

"I'm happy for you, Mom. I really am. I'm sorry. It just struck me. I didn't know you were doing this and it caught me off guard." Will reciprocates his mother's embrace and we all stand there and watch as more Gregory Meyer-induced wounds are healed.

"If it makes any difference," Wes begins. "I'm hoping her name won't be Hufford for too much longer."

I knew it! It's so obvious to watch Wes and Eliana together just how in love they are.

"Really?" Will says to his mother.

"Well, we've only talked about it briefly…and there hasn't been any formal proposal. But, this is good, William. I love Wesley, and he loves me in a way I've never been loved before. I need to know that you're alright with this."

Will thinks for a minute before speaking. It's one of the things I admire about him. More often than not, he's slow to respond, which means he actually thinks about what he's going to say before he says it.

"I'm great with it. I trust Wes and I believe he really does love you. I'm happy for your fresh start, Mom, really." Will hugs his mom and shakes Wes' hand. "I think you and I need to have a conversation soon, though," he says to Wes.

"Of course," Wes says.

I'm not sure if Wes thinks it's cute that Eliana's son wants to have a sit down with him, or if he realizes that there's a lot that Will needs him to know before he takes such a huge step with her. Either way, they're respecting the other as men and don't seem to be letting egos get in the way of what's best for Eliana.

"You want to take that slow, deliberate walk with me to the dock now?" Will asks me.

"I thought you'd never ask!"

I lace my fingers through Will's and we walk slower than we ever have before down the flagstone path to the lake. The weather is warm but the breeze whipping through the trees provides just enough coolness to my skin. I brush the loose locks of hair that escaped my ponytail from my face and tuck them behind my ear in vain. Twigs snap beneath our feet and those little spiked balls fall from the trees. It's a perfect day.

We near the end of the path and slow our pace to almost a halt. We hadn't taken the time earlier today to enjoy the moment of our reunion with this place, but we're here now and plan on making up for that.

"It's just as beautiful as I remember," I say softly.

"I can hardly believe this is happening," Will says. "It's almost surreal."

"Your mom's got the right idea, Will. It's time for a fresh start for all of us. We can live the life here that we were meant to have. It'll be crazy for a little bit, but after a while the novelty of the story will die down and it'll be like it was supposed to be all along."

"I know you're right. It's just that, well, now that I'm back and free, there are some things I have to do. Some wrongs I have to right," he says, tugging me to the edge of the dock.

"What do you mean?" I can't imagine what wrong Will would have to right.

"I need to connect with my mom's family. It's not right how we left, and I'm not sure if she's even contacted them yet." Will sits and rolls up the legs of his khakis and takes off his shoes. I follow suit and take my sandals off, being careful not to let my skirt fly up as I sit.

"I'm sure they're going to understand, Will. They know what kind of a man your father was, don't they?"

"I suppose so. Still, it feels like we should have told them what we were doing," he says, rubbing his eyes.

"What else is going on, Will?" I ask, reading his eyes.

"I'm going to see Holly," he says softly.

"What?" I whisper.

"I *need* to see her, Layla. I feel responsible for what's happening. It was *my* father who tore her family apart." Will's eyes are filled with compassion for Holly, not knowing that everything that happened between them was part of her mother's scheming.

"Well, we'll go see her together then," I say. I want to be there to make sure she doesn't lie to him any more than she already has.

"I need to do this on my own." Will tucks those loose locks behind my ear again and brushes my cheek with his fingers. "Can you understand that?"

It takes me a moment but I finally agree. "I understand, Will." What else am I going to say? I can't tell him the truth about what Holly told me. *She* has to tell him. If I tell him I'll just look like a silly, jealous fiancée who doesn't want her guy seeing his ex. Actually…that's exactly what it is. But, considering the circumstances, how can I deny him. I mean the girl is standing trial for murdering his father.

"You really are so great," he says, pulling me to him and wrapping his arms around me. "I love you."

"I love you more," I say, tightening my arms around his waist. "You should probably wait a few days, though. I mean, with your press conference today, and all the media swarming the court house and the jail…"

"Yeah…I'll give it a couple of days before I go. I'll see if Luke or Wes can arrange a more discrete visit. Thanks for understanding, Layla."

"Of course." Of course I'm going to see Holly before he does. Now that Will is coming back from the dead, she's going to tell him every detail she laid out to Claire and me about their relationship. From her mother's conniving to her insincere pursuit of Will and whatever lies she told him about how she felt about him. She's going to tell him, or I will. I won't let Will spend the rest of his life thinking Holly Reynolds was an innocent victim. He has to know that she was a willing pawn in her mother's game to destroy the Meyer family.

"So…now what?" I ask.

"Now…we live."

"That sounds wonderful. What should we do first?" I sit up and decide it's time to fix my ponytail as a whole.

"We could talk about wedding stuff," he says sweetly. "It's less than a year away now."

"Yeah, by like, a week! You're such a romantic." I lean into Will's chest and kiss him softly.

"Or, we could do this," he says grabbing the nape of my neck and bringing me back to him and kissing me deeply.

"That's an idea," I manage in between kisses. "Actually, we should probably talk about that. Now that you live here we'll have to be extra careful. Seeing you from sun up to sun down is going to make me feel very much like we're married...minus the sex."

"We *are* married, remember?" Will murmurs as he moves to kiss my neck.

"I'm serious, Will! And when did you get so impatient?" It's not like him to be like this. I spent years being flustered every time Will pulled away from any passion we were sharing and now he can't get enough?

"I'm sorry. I don't know what got into me. I just feel so free. Like I can do anything, be anything, and there aren't consequences for being me. When I'm with you...I'm everything I was meant to be. Now that there's nothing threatening our existence together, well, I may find it harder to contain myself." Will cups my cheek and I lean into the comfort of his hand.

I know exactly what he's saying. I've never felt as free as I have when I'm with Will. You hear love stories about couples that just knew they were supposed to be together...that with one look they knew the other person was designed just for them, perfectly ordained since the beginning of time. That's Will and me.

"Well then maybe we should discuss an earlier wedding date," I smile.

"Oh, babe, no. May 25th is your parents' anniversary. It's a date that means something. I don't want to take that from you."

"We already said our vows in the same place my parents did. It's ok, Will. I don't think either one of us is going to be able to wait another year. And we've come this far in showing a ridiculous amount of self-control, I'd hate to ruin that record because we got impatient," I tell him.

"If you're sure, then let's pull the calendar out and see what the Gardens have available. But only if you're sure!" he demands.

"I'm sure, but there is one other thing," I begin. I twist my mouth in an effort to tease and make him think I've got bad news. The reality is that what I'm about to tell him is going to make his day. "I want to get married in a church, here in Davidson."

"What? Really? Oh, babe! Why?" Will is stunned just as I hoped he would be.

"Well, you already gave me a private ceremony in the Gardens. Now I want to give you the bells and whistles wedding you want." I smile at Will knowing that this could quite possibly be the best wedding gift I could have ever given him. It had been so important to him that we have a big church wedding with a gazillion people, but he gave that up for me. The day we said our vows in the Gardens really is all the memory I need of the intimate wedding of my dreams.

"Just when I think that you've reach the pinnacle of awesomeness, you do something like this. I totally don't deserve you, but I'm going to give you the best wedding ever. More than that, we're going to have the best *life* ever."

Chapter 11

As much as I want our normal life to start immediately, Holly's trial is going to dominate our time for a while longer. This means that Luke and Claire have Will helping Eliana get through prepping for her testimony. The trial is still months away, but it's not going to be easy, recounting all the ways Gregory Meyer treated her so poorly like the soulless monster he was. Luke doesn't think the prosecuting attorney is going to try to discredit her, especially with the other ex-wives testifying, but he still wants her to be prepared. It's interesting how *right* she has to get it. The *right* amount of strength. The *right* amount of emotion. The *right* amount of both anger and gratitude toward Holly. I always thought witnesses just got up there and told their side of the story. I had no idea it was so well orchestrated. Wes is working on some security things, which I don't understand since we're no longer under any threat. But…Luke keeps him around and it really doesn't matter why. Since Luke got upgraded to Dad, Wes got an upgrade himself from bonus uncle to just uncle. Then I realized just this morning that Wes will get another upgrade. After Will and I are married and he marries Eliana, he'll be my father-in-law.

It does seem that my life just keeps getting better.

With everyone occupied, now is my chance to go see Holly and make sure she tells Will the truth. Now that Meyer is dead, and Will has come face to face with Holly's mother, I don't see why he can't know the truth, so I'm anticipating this being an easy conversation. I just have to keep myself in check and not let my hatred for what she did to Will in the first place influence my approach. My mom used to say "You catch more flies with honey than with vinegar." She was very wise that way.

I park a few blocks away in a residential area and walk up McDowell Street to Jail Central on Fourth Street. It's a crowded time of day, early lunchtime, and I can't decide if that's good or bad. Will anyone recognize me from the press conference the other day? Or will I shuffle in with the other nameless, faceless people on the street? I'm hoping the latter is the case, and when I round the corner onto Fourth Street to the entrance of Jail Central I can see that I should be in the clear. There are no reporters camped out, no one holding signs to release Holly Reynolds and thank her for her service to our community. The coast is clear.

I approach the security checkpoint, taking my sunglasses off and stuffing them into my purse along with my keys. I keep my head down because the last thing I need is for a mouthy security guard to call the media and tell them I'm here, all for a little extra green in his pocket. They'd be all over me, asking me why I was here, what I said to Holly, what she said to me, and how I felt about Will having been romantically involved with the woman who ended up killing his father.

Apparently I didn't warrant much more than a once over from the security guards and I pass through with ease. Collecting my purse I follow the signage that takes me to the visitor check-in.

I didn't think I'd be this nervous, but I am. The last time I saw Holly she came to say goodbye after identifying Marcus' body. I think about how she tried to talk Marcus down from the ledge that day, how her call bought Luke and Wes time in getting to me before Marcus…

I shake my head to clear the memory of that awful day from my mind. I need to stay focused on my objective to convince Holly that telling Will the truth about their relationship is the right thing to do.

I sign in and wait uncomfortably for Holly to be brought to her side of our windowed desk area. When she appears she's surprised to see me, but smiles. I smile back at her tentatively and we both pick up the payphone-looking receivers on our sides of the glass. For a second I feel like I'm in an episode of Law and Order.

"Layla," she says. "I'm surprised to see you."

"Hi, Holly. How are you?" I ask.

"I'm ok, I guess. I'd be doing worse if not for Luke."

"I think everyone who knows him feels that way." I look down, searching for how to begin this conversation. I remind myself not to let my anger with her lead, but to be practical about it, and let her know that Will is going to understand.

"I saw the press conference. I'm really happy for you. What he did for you…that's really something," she says softly.

"Yes. It was amazing." I don't know how to read her. I don't remember her as being one who shows a lot of emotion when she speaks, but something seems off.

"My mother said she met you the other day," Holly tells me. "I'm sorry if she was rude to you."

"Did she tell you what she said?" I ask.

"No, but she told me what you said. I can only imagine what she did to get that kind of response from *you*. She can be, well…I've already told you how she can be."

I consider telling her what her mother said about Marcus but decide against it. Holly only gets 30 minutes to visit and I don't want to waste time discussing her mother any further.

"I want to ask you to do something for me, Holly," I begin. She looks at me with an understandably quizzical expression. "Will is coming to see you soon, and I want you to tell him the truth about your relationship."

Holly is silent and emotionless.

"Please, Holly. He's coming to apologize to you. He feels responsible for what his father did to your family. He needs to know what really happened," I plead. I try hard not to let my voice give too much of my desperation away. In some, sad way, I have to maintain the upper hand.

"I can't do that," she says.

"Yes, you can," I respond, not hiding my irritation at her immediate refusal. "He needs to know, and he'll understand. So, when he gets here, before he can begin even one word of apology to you, cut him off…tell him about your mother's plot…tell him that you felt like you had no choice…explain that…"

"Layla, Will's already apologized to me."

"What? When?" I feel my face contort into a squishy mess of confusion and I hate that I've shown my emotions this clearly.

"Will came to see me a few weeks before he disappeared. He told me things were going to change for him and he wanted to make sure he apologized while he had the chance." Her delivery continues to be emotionless.

"That can't be true. Will…Will would have told me," I stammer. I hate that she has so obviously caught me off guard, but unlike her in this moment, I can't lie.

"So he didn't tell you. Huh." At first her face reveals nothing of what she's thinking. I search her eyes in hopes of seeing something, but…nothing. And then…she smiles almost sinisterly. "I believe he said he had just been at prom with you the night before."

"Did you tell him then that your relationship was a fraud?" I ask, not addressing the creepy display of her smile. I work to push away the thoughts that are infiltrating my mind that Holly was not an innocent pawn in her mother's game, but an agreeable part of the plan. It's difficult when her face is finally showing emotion, and that emotion is disturbing.

"Why would I do that? What Will and I had was…amazing." She closes her eyes for a moment as if reliving these *amazing* times.

"This isn't exactly the same story I got from you in Tallahassee," I challenge.

"Will was dead. I wasn't going to flaunt our passion in front of his grieving girlfriend. I'm not *that* big of a bitch." And there it is: the thing that wasn't sitting right with me. The apple doesn't fall far from the tree, and I see now just what a co-conspirator she was with her mother. The same slithering tone that I got from her mother is the same one she's giving to me now. It was all a front and I fell for it.

"Passion?" I can't squeeze out more than one word right now for fear I might start crying.

"Will's too much of a gentleman to tell you about his past conquest, I'm sure. It was...*incredible*. But then Will got all chivalrous and I missed my chance to have a Meyer baby."

"You...slept with Will?" I stutter. *Meyer baby?* She was going to *try* to get pregnant?

"I'm guessing by your question that he's still playing the white knight. Don't worry. He'll be worth the wait," she smirks. She's loving every minute of torturing me with her lies.

That's it! *Get out of your head, Layla, and deal with her! Stop letting her lies distract you.*

"You know...I liked you. I thought after everything you told me about your mother that it was by some miracle that you and Marcus escaped relatively unscathed. But I was wrong. You were in on the whole plan to deceive Will from the start, weren't you?"

"Gregory Meyer screwed over my mother, and then my brother. We deserved every penny we got from him!" Holly raises her voice and gets a stern look from one of the guards.

"Why involve Will? He never did anything to you! He genuinely cared about you."

"Will...Will was a casualty of war. In another life, he and I could have been good together. But, our mission to take down the Meyer Empire came first. Gregory Meyer kicked his other wives to the curb. What made Eliana and Will so special?" The real Holly has emerged. Her face has twisted into an expression of hatred and disgust. I have to give it to her. She put on a pretty good show in Tallahassee.

"It wasn't their decision to be kept any more than it was your mother's decision to be left," I say in defense of Will and Eliana.

"C'mon now, Layla. Let's not fight. I've done you a favor. In fact, I've done you a few favors. My call to Marcus is just what was needed to buy Luke and Furtick time to get to you. And now, Gregory Meyer is dead and you've got your happily ever after. Most of the people in Davidson think I'm a hero, and chances are the judge is so happy to not be in Meyer's back pocket anymore that I'm going to be charged with manslaughter and serve less than five years. It'll be worth it, though. Will feels so bad for all the exes that we're all getting a piece of the Meyer fortune. Luke's already discussed it with him, and Will thinks five million dollars to each ex will be more than fair compensation."

"That's what this is about? Money? I still have no clue why Meyer cut your mother loose. She is just like him, and apparently so are you. Greedy and soulless." I'm so disgusted by her that I can hardly stand to look at her. The once attractive woman is now revolting, having shown what she's really made of. "I don't care what Will does with the money, but I'll be damned if you're going to see a penny of it."

"I don't think you have any say in that, dear."

"See this ring?" I say holding up my left hand. "It says *I do*. By the time your trial comes and goes Will and I will be married."

"You better check your pre-nup on that."

"Times up," a guard says to Holly.

"Gotta go. It's been fun. You *will* drop by again, won't you, Layla?" Her expression is so sadistically flat that I feel the pain of unquenchable rage welling up in me.

Pre-nup. I hadn't thought of that. What if Will wants me to sign a pre-nup? I don't really care, at least I didn't until now, and that's only because I want to have some control over keeping Holly and her mother from getting their dirty hands on a single penny of Will's money.

"Of course I'll come back...with Will."

"No you won't. And you won't tell him a word of this either because you don't want to hurt him or for him to know just how used he was. It would kill him and you would never do anything to hurt him. Beside, everything he knows about me is going to make anything *you* tell him look like the desperate pleas of a jealous fiancée," she says smugly.

"Jealous...of his ex-girlfriend...who's in jail. Yeah."

"I'll always be in his head. The girl who got run off by his manipulative father. The girl he'd still be with. His *first*."

"I could never be jealous of you. All you are is a memory. And I don't believe for one second that you slept with Will. His standards are too high for him to even consider giving himself to someone like you." I start to hang up the phone when I realize I have one more thing to say. "Oh, and just so we're clear, you *are* that big of a bitch." I slam the phone down and make my way out of the building the same way I came in.

With every step I take I question every word that I just said to Holly. Maybe Will did sleep with Holly. He told me he hasn't been with anyone, but that was in response to my question about the girls his father made him entertain. Perhaps I should have been more specific in my questioning.

I don't think about the possibility of reporters or news trucks as I did when I arrived, but I wish I had. It would seem that my assumption about one of the guards making a quick buck by ratting me out to the press wasn't totally off base. As I push through the door out into the courtyard, I'm bombarded by flashing lights and microphones and people shouting questions at me. I manage to turn around go back into the building where the security guards seem unfazed by my predicament.

"Thanks," I snort out to them. They just shrug their shoulders like they have no idea what I'm talking about. I pull out my cell phone and call the only person I know who can get me out of this mess safe and sound: Wes.

*****

"You need to tell them, Layla," Wes says after I relay my conversation with Holly. "They need to know, especially Will."

"I know, but how do I tell him without it sounding like the crazed fiancée? I already went to see her without telling him." My head is in my hands and I feel so hopeless.

"Suck it up," he says brashly.

"What?"

"Suck. It. Up. He needs to know what she's claiming…and it sounds like you need to know if it's true.

"Where did you tell them you were going?" I ask, shifting the subject as we pull into the residential area where I left my car. I don't want to talk about my need to know if Will did or did not have sex with Holly. Despite my statement to her about not believing it, I haven't been able to stop entertaining the idea that she may have been telling the truth.

"I told them I was coming to get you," he says directly.

"What? Wes!" I whine in protest.

"Don't worry. I said you got a flat tire. Will offered to come but I told him he needed to stay with Eliana."

"Thanks, Wes. I'd be lost without you." I lean across the console of Wes' jeep and give him a quick kiss on the cheek. "I might make a stop on my way home…I just need some more time to figure this out. Can you tell them I went shopping or something?"

"Sure," he says with a pat on my leg. "You can do this."

"I know. I'm just ready for the drama to be over," I say with a sigh.

"We all are."

Chapter 12

I drive around for over an hour just trying to clear my head, trying to make sense of everything Holly said. There was a time I wouldn't have thought she would lie to me, but I've learned in the past several years that sometimes people do things just because they're evil.

I can't shake one thing she said to me, though. When she told me Will went to see her, she said that it was after prom night. I suppose she could have picked that as an arbitrary event that Will and I would have attended together. If Will hadn't left me that morning, telling me he had some things to take care of and would be out of pocket for a while, of course I'd believe she was lying. But it's more than coincidence. The only way I'm going to know is for Will to explain himself.

The skies open up and rain starts to pour just as I pull into the driveway. I scurry inside and go straight to my room. In the 15 seconds it took me to get from the car to the porch I got nearly soaked. I pull my hair into a messy bun on top of my head and decide to take another shower, letting the hot water wash away the nastiness of the real Holly Reynolds.

Warm, dry, and in a fresh set of pajamas as my standard rainy-day uniform, I settle into the big green chair in the loft and watch the rain, waiting for the best time to confront Will. Every fear and insecurity I've ever had is doing its best to claw its way to the top of my heart, shoving down all the progress I've made over these last three years. I want to believe Holly is lying about everything. That Will didn't go see her, and that he never gave to her what he promised was meant for me, but I'm afraid that as disturbing as she was in her delivery, she's wasn't lying.

"Hey, babe! When did you get home?" Will asks, finding me in the loft.

"Oh…about an hour ago," I tell him with a stone face.

"Hey, what's wrong? Wes said you got a flat tire. Did it blow out on you? That happened to me once and I was pretty shaken for a while after." Will is tender and sweet. He sits next to me in the oversized chair, almost enveloping me with his body.

"I didn't have a flat tire, Will," I say softly. I'm now struck with guilt that I made Wes lie for me.

"I don't understand."

I take a moment and decide that it's now or never. There's no easy way to enter this conversation, so I just blurt out the first question of many that is rumbling through my mind. "Did you go see Holly the day after prom?" I ask. I don't look at him because if he's going to lie to me, I don't want him to have to do it to my face.

"What…why would you ask that?" Will stands and moves to the other side of the couch, essentially as far as he can go without reaching the stairs.

"Just answer me, please," I say. I stand and face him. We're on opposite sides of the couch now and it seems like a canyon of distance.

Will takes a deep breath in and looks down. "You went and saw Holly today, didn't you?"

"You still haven't answered me." His avoidance is answer enough.

"Yes. I went to see Holly the day after prom." He doesn't move from his spot. He just watches me for my reaction.

"Why did you tell me you never knew where she was?"

"I told you that after they left town I didn't know where she was. I never said…"

"Please don't get into semantics, Will. You lied to me then and you lied to me yesterday. You said you had to go see her now because you needed to apologize, but you already apologized to her." I'm holding up better than I thought I would, although I'm not sure how long it's going to last. I still haven't asked him about sleeping with her.

"Why are you so upset? Seeing her then or seeing her now, it's all the same thing," he says in his defense.

"You're kidding, right? The morning after the most amazing night I've ever experienced, your first thought is to go see your ex-girlfriend!" I've raised my voice and now I know that I'm not going to be able to hold it together. He's clueless. "Did you sleep with her?"

"What?" He's genuinely shocked at my question.

"Did. You. Sleep with her?" I emphasize each word letting Will know just how angry and hurt I've become.

"No…technically, no," he stammers.

"Technically. I can't believe you…" I've officially lost it. I manage to get to the stairs before Will knows what's happening and race down toward the door. Will follows after me quickly and slams the door shut just as I open it.

"Let me go, Will!" I shout at him.

"NO! I'm not letting you go. And I'm not going to let you close another door behind me either!" He matches my volume and I'm taken back for a second. We've never yelled at each other before.

"What's going on in here?" Luke says rushing in.

"She talked to Holly today," Will tells him.

"Oh, ok," Luke says then goes back to where he came from.

"What the hell?" I say in astonishment. Luke has always had my back and now he just walks away?

"He knows everything," Will says.

"Everything?"

"Yes. I told you early on that I was going to do everything I had to do to make sure I had Luke's trust." Will is staring, boring his beautiful blue eyes into me.

"So you told Luke all about your past but not me? That's awesome." I cross my arms in an immature stance of stubbornness. "Go away, Will. I don't want to talk to you right now."

"Like hell, I'm going away. We're going to sit down and talk about this like two people so in love they would do anything to make their relationship work. You can either walk to the chair or I can carry you. Either way, we're talking this out."

I want to stay mad at him but it's hard to argue with his logic. We *are* two people in love and we have already done so much to make our relationship work. I'm just so hurt and frustrated right now that it's hard to see through the pain so I don't budge.

"Ok, have it your way." Will bends down and begins to put me over his shoulder to carry me to the chair.

"Put me down! I'll walk! I'll walk!" I shout. Will puts me down and looks at me with anticipation.

"Well?" he says when I don't move.

"Fine." I walk slowly to one of the wing back chairs in front of the window and plop myself down. Will paces in front of me and I can see that he's sorting through the details, not sure of where to start. "Why didn't you tell me you went to see Holly? I mean, after we were settled in Florida," I say in an attempt to be rational.

"I never thought we were coming back here, and certainly never thought I'd have anything to do with Holly again. I just…I couldn't leave without her knowing how sorry I was about what my father did to her family." He's stopped pacing and is facing me now. His expression is serious.

"And…the other thing?" I ask. I start to look away, uncomfortable that I'm asking him about his sexual relationship with another girl, but rid myself of that as my desire to know the truth is outweighing my embarrassment.

Will kneels in front of me. I reluctantly let him take my hands in his. His face is pained and I can see that he's devastated at the hurt he's caused me.

"I'm...I'm not like other guys, Layla. You know that. Chris, even Tyler, would talk about the girls they've slept with. It never appealed to me...I mean, it *appeals* to me...it's hard to explain." Will closes his eyes, frustrated with his inability to convey what he's feeling.

"Please try," I plead softly. I have to understand this. I have to understand how he was able to share something with Holly that he's refused me time and again.

"One night, about a month after Holly and I started dating, things got...out of hand. We were making out and she started getting really aggressive and forward, taking my shirt off and moving my hands to touch her. At first I thought, 'Hey this is great...she thinks I'm hot and wants me, and...'"

"I get it."

"Sorry. Um...well...clothes started coming off and...we got as close as two people can get to having sex without doing it." He looks at me and then looks away as if suddenly struck by the embarrassment of it.

"You saw her naked."

"Yes."

"She saw you naked."

"Yes."

I lean back in the chair, defeated and overwhelmed. Tears begin to sting my eyes and I can't help it when they begin to flow down my cheeks.

"Stop. Stop it right now. I know what you're thinking and you need to look at me. Look at me, Layla," he gently commands. I manage to lift my face and Will begins to wipe away the wet trails of pain. "Don't you want to know why I stopped?"

"Does it matter? You came close enough, Will," I say through my tears.

"It *does* matter." Will takes my face in his hands and locks our eyes. "I couldn't do it because I knew it was unfair. I hadn't even met you yet and I knew that I was taking something from you. In my heart I knew Holly

111

wasn't the one. And even in the heat of that moment I knew that if I gave myself to her, I'd be robbing you, robbing me, of something special. I can only give myself away for the first time once, and I couldn't see that with Holly. I didn't want to trade what I wanted most for what I wanted in the moment because the moment is fleeting. I know it's not *manly* or *cool* for a guy to wait until he's married, but…it's who I am and why I couldn't go through with it with Holly."

"We've been engaged for over a year, but you still don't want me," I say through my soft sobs.

"You want to just go have sex? Is that what you want? We'll just start sleeping together and then we'll get married and *nothing* will be different. We'll have nothing to look forward to. Is that what you want?" His tone is changing and I can tell he's irritated, having been through this with me too many times to count.

"No, that's not what I'm saying," I murmur.

"Why is it so important to you that we have sex? Is that the only way you're going to understand the fullness of my love for you?"

"No, that's not it. I don't know…I spent so long being stifled in my ability to show love. When Gram was alive, I had this tiny window when Gramps and I were allowed to love each other. Where he could cuddle me and I could love on him. After she died and I became Gramps' caretaker, I went into automatic mode of school, housework, Gramps. Some people tried to tell me that I was showing love by taking care of him. I suppose they were right, but that wasn't how I felt.

"When I moved here, I felt like I could be me, be my age, and my world opened up. And when I met you, so did my heart. I've had all these emotions flooding my heart that all I've wanted to do is be as close to you as possible, to show you how incredibly deep my love for you is. I got on board with the waiting thing, Will. Really, I did. And, honestly, it *isn't* that important to me. But when I hear how you might as well have done it with Holly…"

"Getting that close to it with Holly was the worst mistake I ever made. I regret every second of it and wish I could scrub my mind of the memory. But…this is me, my life, my past. I'm sorry I didn't tell you before. I should have. I want to share my life with you…crappy parts and all. Will you share my crap with me, Layla?" He smirks.

"Lightening the mood with humor is my move," I say taking his hands in mine. "I will. I will share your crap with you, as long as you'll share mine."

"I love your crap." Will leans in and kisses me sweetly before pulling me to stand and hugging me fiercely. "I am *really* sorry I didn't tell you. You had a right to know."

"Thank you for telling me now," I say.

"So are you going to tell me why you went to see Holly?" he asks with a bit of chastisement in his tone.

"I went to convince her to tell you the truth about your relationship," I say, not knowing how he's going to react.

"You mean about how her mom used her to get to me as another way of getting to my father?" he answers.

"Uh, yeah. You knew?"

"Luke told me. When Holly was arrested and it was clear we were coming back to Davidson, Luke told me what she told you and Claire. I didn't believe him at first, but Luke has no reason to lie to me, so… There's more to it, isn't there?" he asks, observing my facial expression. I can't hide my disgust for her, and my disappointment in myself for having believed her lies when she came to Florida to get Marcus. How could I not believe her story, especially after she helped us?

"I'm not sure if I should tell you. I…I think it's going to hurt you and I don't want you to be hurt. And…I don't want you to think I'm some crazed fiancée," I tell him hesitantly.

"You went to see my ex-girlfriend in jail. You're teetering on the line between normal and crazed," he smirks. "Just tell me Layla."

"Ok. It wasn't her mom's manipulation. She was in on it, too. She was actually pretty mad when you closed the door on sex. She said she missed her chance at having a Meyer baby," I tell him.

"Are you kidding me? She was going to *try* and get pregnant? Unbelievable. I feel like such an idiot!" Will stands and moves around the room, searching his mind for what to say or do next. "Luke!" he shouts. It's a good rule of thumb to call for Luke when you don't know what to do.

"What's up? Did you two settle things?" he asks me directly.

"Yes, and why are you looking at me like I may have slightly over reacted? Don't answer that." Luke smiles at me, squeezing my arm as he walks by to Will.

"You were right. She is definitely her mother's daughter," he says straight-faced to Luke.

"You knew, too?" I ask.

"No, but Luke had his reservations. She's been too calm," Will answers.

"She thinks she's going to get manslaughter and serve less than five years," I tell them.

"Right now that's definitely how it's looking. The prosecuting attorney isn't slacking, but he isn't pressing the maximum like he would if this were any other case," Luke says.

"And what's this about five million dollars to each of the exes?" I ask.

"She was just *full* of information for you today, wasn't she?" Will laughs.

"Well, she was working pretty hard to make me feel like crap, so she was pulling out all the stops," I tell him.

"Well, I thought about what you said. You know, to give some of the money away to people my dad screwed over. His ex-wives seemed like a natural choice."

"It's nice to know you listen to me every now and then," I jest. "But, Holly thinks she's going to have a share of the five million dollars of sympathy money her mom is going to get," I tell Will.

"Well, I guess she would. Her mom can do whatever she wants with her share," Will says. "Now that I know the truth about her, I don't want her to see any of that money, but I can't do anything about what her mother chooses to do with it."

"Maybe not, but…" Luke starts.

"But what? I see the wheels turning. What's going on in that head of yours?" I ask Luke.

"I have an idea. I'll need to do a little research and run some numbers, but I think we can make sure Marlene and Holly get every penny they're *entitled*."

Chapter 13

It's been a week since the press conference that announced Will and Eliana's return from the dead. The number of reporters camped outside our house has dwindled over the days, but there are a few committed guys left. I'm not sure what they're hoping for. So far they've watched us go to the grocery store, order Chinese food, and they've said hello to our friends that have come to visit. Today, though, they're in for a real treat because Will and I are going over to the college to get registered, and then we're going out for lunch.

They've kept their distance, and have actually been pretty helpful at times. A few of them even helped take some boxes of donations out to the road. But, as nice as they have been, Will is growing tired of their constant presence and decides to address them directly.

"Hey Will! Where are you going?" one of them asks.

"Hi Tom…guys. Gather 'round boys," he says to them. There are six of them in all. Will knows all of their names, but I haven't bothered to try since I'm itching for them to leave and never be seen again. "Can any of you tell me exactly what it is your boss wants you to get from us?"

"Well, uh…" one of them, not Tom, responds.

"That's what I thought. How about this: you guys leave, let us get back to our boring life, and you six can have exclusive statements from me when the trial is underway. Contact Wes Furtick and he'll make sure you've got all the access you need. Sound good?" Will is kind and generous with them. He knows they're just doing their jobs, and since they've really been great and respectful, it's hard to shove them aside cruelly.

"That's awesome! Thanks, Will!" several of them say.

"Great. So, no camping out, no hounding us if you see us out, and no pictures," Will says to clearly define the parameters.

"You're a good, guy, Will," Tom says, reaching out to shake Will's hand. "For what it's worth, we're glad you're back," he says motioning to the other reporters.

I can imagine what the atmosphere of the local media was like with Gregory Meyer manipulating everything. All you ever hear from real reporters is that they have this unexplainable drive to seek out and report the truth they believe the public has a right to know. When Will's father was alive, that was impossible. I'm sure they're all pretty grateful that the ban on truth has been lifted.

"Thanks, Tom. We appreciate how great you guys have been. Now, if you can clear out, that'd be even greater." Will smiles his directive and the guys nod their receipt.

Will opens the passenger door to his car and lets me in. By the time he's buckled and Fleetwood Mac is playing on the satellite radio, all six of the reporters are nowhere to be seen.

"Well done, babe," I say as I give Will's leg a squeeze. "You were so diplomatic. What's Luke going to think about you giving away exclusivity to them?"

"He'll be fine. We don't really care who covers what. The probability for an absolutely true and fair report from *any* media source is slim, so we just don't worry about it," he says.

"Does this feel strange to you? Being back here, driving around like nothing changed?" I ask as we exit the second roundabout that leads to Main Street.

"Yeah, it does. I'm nervous," he says honestly.

"I'm nervous, too, but we can do this. We're together and we've got this, right?"

"Right," he smiles.

By some miracle we find a parking space next to the library. As we exit the car and I turn to see the Green, my mind is flooded with memories. I'm taken back to my first Concert on the Green and the night I first laid eyes on Will. I remember how kind he seemed, reaching out and acknowledging everyone around him regardless of their station in life. I smile as I look across the Green to the coffee shop where I ran into Will, and I blush as I think of how embarrassed I was when I turned his Coke into an icy puddle on the sidewalk. As I scan the shops and businesses along Main Street, I also remember the day I met Marcus in the bookstore, and my mood changes from happy reminiscing to sad.

"You ok?" Will asks, putting his arm around my waist.

"Yeah, I'm ok," I tell him.

"Memories?"

I nod, for fear of crying.

"I know you miss him." Will kisses the top of my head and leaves it at that.

I do miss Marcus. I miss the Marcus I met in the bookstore that warm August day. I miss the Marcus who helped me survive trigonometry and chemistry. I miss the Marcus who made amends with me before I moved to Florida, who comforted me when Will was missing. I miss *that* Marcus and the resentment I feel toward Holly and her mother begins to rise to the surface.

Marcus had a chance at a real life. He was brilliant and could have done anything, been anything. Instead of nurturing that in him, his mother spent her life feeding him the sour medicine of her hate. She bullied him into subjecting himself to repeated rejection. She knew Meyer would never accept Marcus, but she didn't care. It wasn't about him. It was about her and her desire to make sure Gregory Meyer never forgot them or what he did to her. As if he cared.

As we step onto the Davidson College campus I breathe a sigh of relief that we're on the threshold of nothing but a normal life. The admissions office is actually on Main Street, so we could have walked the sidewalk all the way there, but the campus is just too pretty to pass up the chance to walk it. A smile crosses my face as I think about the times Will and I walked the campus in anonymity.

"I still don't understand why you're going to Davidson and not the Ivy League school of your choice," I say to Will. "I mean, Davidson is an amazing school, totally top notch, but you could go anywhere."

"Have you forgotten that we're getting married?" He smiles and then kisses my hand that he is now holding.

"Oh, no, I didn't forget. I just want to make sure that you know you don't have to do this for me. Lots of husbands commute for their jobs between states. I'm just saying that if you want to go to some ridiculously amazing school, you can."

"Layla," he says turning to face me as we stop. "There is nothing that will ever be as important to me as being with you. I don't care where we live or where we go to school. All that matters is that we're there together."

"Well, since you put it that way…" I reach my arms up and around Will's neck and draw him to me. "I suppose I should say thank you." With that I press my lips to Will's in a long, sweet kiss.

"Best. Thank you. Ever," he says breathlessly.

We cross Main Street and enter Grey House, which is the Admissions Office of Davidson College. Everything seems to be going fine. We meet with the admissions counselor who has our paperwork. We asked that the same counselor handle the admissions procedures for both of us since we'll be married soon, to which they've been very accommodating. I'm sure we're not the first couple to ask this. Since Davidson doesn't have a Business major, Will is going to switch to Economics, and I'll be sticking with Psychology. We weren't that far along at FSU, so all of our general education classes are switching over.

"Well that should do it. You're both all registered for classes, so I'm sure you're glad to have that out of the way," the admissions counselor says.

Her nameplate reads Rebekah Woodfin, but she told us that everyone calls her Bekah. She's young…probably not out of college herself more than a year or two. She's a lovely girl with long light brown hair and eyes to match. "When are you getting married?" she asks.

"We haven't set a date yet, but…" I begin.

"It'll be before Christmas," Will finishes. I look at him with stunned eyes.

"Sounds like you two have some things to iron out," Bekah says with a chuckle.

"I guess so!" I say, echoing her laugh.

"Um…I hope you don't mind me saying, but…I just want you to know that, as a community, we're so glad you're back." Bekah smiles at Will, addressing the elephant in the room. She's been so polite and incredibly professional. It was kind of her to wait until we had resolved the academic issues before mentioning anything.

"Thank you, Bekah. It feels wonderful to be home." Will smiles and nods, and it seems we have made contact with our first ally since being home. I hope what she's said about the community being glad Will's back is as true as she believes it to be.

We exit the building and stroll up Main Street as if we didn't have a care in the world. Not much has changed since we left. The Soda Shop still has metal tables and chairs outside and its Specials board propped up by the front door. The bridal shop is a chic woman's boutique now, but it looks as beautiful as it always did.

When we approach Main Street Books, I feel a twinge of sadness again as I think of Marcus. I don't want to, but I can't help it. I look down and turn my head so I can't even catch a glimpse of the store in my periphery.

"Don't," Will says.

"What?"

"Don't pretend like you're not thinking about him. It's ok, Layla," he tells me.

"It just doesn't seem fair to be so consumed with thoughts of him," I say softly. It feels like I'm being disrespectful to Will.

"Layla, baby…Marcus played a big part in your life and I would never want you to pretend he didn't. I hate what you went through with him in Tallahassee, but we know that wasn't the real Marcus. I'm…well, I'm actually kind of jealous of you. You got to know the Marcus that was a nice guy. I never knew him like that. I wish he and I could have known each other…*really* known each other. It would have been nice to know I wasn't alone." Will looks sad now, too, but his sadness comes from the thoughts of knowing he lost a brother before he ever had a chance to know him.

"I'm sorry you never got to know him. There was a time he really was a wonderful guy," I say to Will, brushing his longer hair from his eyes. "I suppose we're both finding the family we've needed."

"Come with me. I want to show you something," he says, smiling big and taking my hand.

We cross the street and walk up the main entrance to Davidson College Presbyterian Church. The front doors are unlocked so Will leads me in. I'm in awe and feel like I should genuflect, but I'm pretty sure it's not that kind of church. The sanctuary is beautiful and grand, and the white pews and walls make the room so bright…a much different feeling than the last time I was here for Will's funeral.

"What do you think?" Will asks excitedly.

"I think it's beautiful," I tell him quietly.

Will walks us up the aisle quickly and stands where a groom would. He smiles at me, so happy and excited about the plans he has for our bells and whistles wedding.

"I can almost picture it. Luke walking you down the aisle. You, looking stunningly beautiful. I'll try not to cry, but I can't make any promises," he says with a sweet smile.

"I can't get married in this church, Will." I'm overwhelmed. I can hardly breathe as I turn and make my way back down the aisle.

"Layla, wait! I thought you said you wanted a church wedding. What it is?" Will catches up with me, taking me by the shoulders.

"I do want a church wedding now, but not here. I buried you here, Will. This is where your funeral was. I can't...I can't be here." I fall into Will's chest and am immediately covered by his arms. I cry softly at the memory of the day I felt my life come to an end.

"Oh, babe, I'm so sorry. I didn't even think of that. I'm so, so sorry!" Will strokes my hair, comforting me with his touch and his words.

"Everything ok in here, Will?" I hear a man's voice say.

"Pastor Bishop...yes, we're, um," Will stammers.

"I'm fine. I'm sorry if we disturbed you," I say. I remember what a lovely job Pastor Bishop did at Will's funeral. "I'm Layla Weston," I say by way of introduction since I'm sure he doesn't remember our brief meeting.

"You haven't disturbed anything. You're not the first to shed a tear in here. That's part of what the church is for," he says. "Michael Bishop, and I remember you, Layla. Can I help with anything?" he asks as we shake hands.

"Can you pray away my stupidity?" Will says with a small laugh.

"If I could do that, that's all I'd do *all* day. I'd have people lined up around the block!" Now we're all laughing.

"I brought Layla here, excited to show her where I thought we'd be married," Will tells him sheepishly.

"You brought your fiancée to the church where your funeral was held? Where she said goodbye to you? William Gregory Meyer...I thought you knew better!" Pastor Bishop punches Will in the arm in manly playfulness.

"Don't you think Lingle Chapel would be a better alternative to the main sanctuary?" he offers.

"Of course," he says with his palm to his forehead.

"Where is Lingle Chapel?" I ask.

"It's here, just across the courtyard," Pastor Bishop answers. "I do hope you'll allow me perform the ceremony."

"As if there were anyone else I'd *let* do it," Will says to him. They have a familiarity that I wasn't aware of and make a note to ask Will about it later.

Will takes my hand and leads me outside and down the walkway to the smaller of the sanctuaries, Lingle Chapel.

"Do over?" Will says as we approach the aisle.

"Do over," I smile. "It's beautiful, and really, much more my speed. The main sanctuary is massive. This is one just right." I wrap my arms around Will's middle and feel his arms cover me. I can picture our wedding here…our friends barely filling a few pews. "We'll have to tell people to sit wherever they want so my side doesn't look all sad and pathetic."

"What are you talking about? Don't be silly!" he says.

"Who is going to sit on my side, Will? Gwen and Caroline will be standing with me. I'll have Luke and Claire, and I guess maybe Caroline's parents will sit with them. Oh gosh, now that I've said it out loud, it really is going to be pathetic."

"You'll have Finn and his latest, and Dana, and Jason and Lisa will be here," he says in an effort to make me feel better. It's sweet of him.

"They said they'd come, but that was when we were still getting married at the Gardens. They're not going to come all the way up here, Will. It's an expensive trip."

"They'll be here," he says, reassuringly.

"That's sweet, Will, but…"

"I'll make sure *all* of them are here," he says a bit more strongly. I furrow my brow in question. "I don't care how much it costs. My bride wants seats filled with her friends, and I'm going to make it happen."

"Should I even *try* to argue?" I say smiling in awe of his love.

"You're the one who told me to do something good with the money. Well, I can't think of anything better to do with it than making my future wife happy."

"You're too wonderful for words. You know that, don't you?" I beam.

"Yes, yes, I know," he says teasingly before he kisses my cheek and leading me out to the car.

Chapter 14

"Layla? Is that you?" I hear Luke call as we walk through the door.

"Yes. It's us. We're back," I reply.

"Great! Will, Wes has some things he could use your help with in the garage. Do you mind?" Luke asks.

"Of course not," Will kisses me quickly then makes his way to meet Wes.

"Layla, I need to talk with you." Luke's face and tone are serious. It always worries me when Luke is this serious. I've learned not to let my imagination run wild on scenarios since the number of them is countless. I simply follow him into the office in their bedroom and take a seat.

"What's up, Dad?" I ask.

"There have been some new developments with the witnesses we're planning on calling," he says.

"What kind of developments?" I ask, tilting my head in query. "And why are you telling me? Wouldn't it be better if Will were a part of this conversation, too?" I remember how left out I felt when Luke and Will were having private conversations after Holly shot Will's father. I'd better make sure I at least vocalize the fairness in Will needing to be here.

"Well, that's one of the things I wanted to talk to you about. What I'm going to tell you...I think you should be the one to tell Will," Luke tells me.

"Oh...well...ok then. What's going on?" I'm beyond curious. What could possibly be happening that Luke thinks *I'm* the best person to tell Will?

"We've discovered something that is going to, well, it's going to change everything Will knows about his life," Luke says solemnly.

"That's a pretty bold statement, Dad. Will has been through quite a bit. What could possibly be so huge that it's going to alter his life so much?"

Before the words have left my mouth Luke is sliding a file folder across his desk to me.

"Open it," he commands.

I'm confident that I won't understand what I'm reading, but appreciate Luke's confidence that I will. There are several forms in the file. All of them are titled Witness Information Form. I read the first form and see that it contains Loretta's name and pertinent information: address, date of birth, marriages, as well as a place for the names of any children that might be related to the victim, as in Gregory Meyer. Erin's name is listed and it all seems pretty standard procedure, for all I know about the law. I flip to the next page and see another woman's name, Victoria Meadows, and it becomes clear that this is the file of the ex-wives that will be giving testimony on Holly's behalf. I scan her form and my heart stops.

Child(ren): Michael Aaron Meadows.

"Oh my gosh." I cover my mouth with my hand for fear that I may say something too loudly.

"Keep going," Luke instructs.

No. No, it can't be. Yes, it can, and it is. As I pass through each page the names are there…on every single page.

Cheryl Brinkley- Child(ren): Sarah Brinkley Moore

Marlene Harris- Child(ren): Marcus Andrew Reynolds

Eliana Hufford- Child(ren): William Gregory Meyer

I look at the dates of their marriages to Gregory Meyer and the dates their children were born. I see the pattern immediately and am disgusted.

Each child was born either the year they divorced or the year after, which means he divorced them *while* they were pregnant.

"I don't even know what to say," I whisper.

"To be honest…neither do I." Luke moves from behind his desk to the chair next to mine, scooting it closer to me. "When we stumbled across Loretta and she told me their story, I felt like I could explain that to Will and Eliana with some ease as it was almost 40 years ago and gave us some insight as to why Greg was the way he was. And we had already dealt with the Marcus situation. But this…I just don't have a clue how to tell Will that he actually had *four* siblings." Luke rubs his hand across his forehead attempting to relieve the stress of the situation we now find ourselves in.

"Did Meyer know they were pregnant? I mean, we know Loretta and Erin's story, and we know what Holly told us about Marcus but…what about Victoria and Cheryl? Did he know about them? Was he supporting all of them? Did he instruct any of *them* to have abortions like he did with Marlene?"

My mind is racing. I can't believe that Gregory Meyer fathered five children, disregarding all of them but Will. I don't know how to tell Will. Luke is right: this is going to change his life. He has done so well moving past feelings of guilt since finding out about Erin. Now to hear there are two more siblings, a brother and another sister, who were tossed aside? Understanding Erin's story is one thing. It's the story of the moment the switch got flipped with Meyer. But…what about the others? I just can't wrap my brain around it.

I don't know how I'll tell him, but I know the only place I can tell him is on the dock.

"I don't know if Eliana knows about the children, but the other ex-wives do. Marlene tried to rally the troops at one point, but I don't think she was able to get close enough to Eliana. Cheryl…she's the tricky one," Luke says, shaking his head.

"What do you mean she's the tricky one?"

"Cheryl doesn't want to testify," he says.

"Do we need her? We've got the others, right?" I say.

"I suppose not, but from everything we've gathered, hers is one of the most compelling testimonies about Greg's abuse. As Holly's lawyer, I feel it would be most helpful for her case. As the soon-to-be father-in-law of the guy she's trying screw over, I'm thinking we can pass on it. She'd only be coming to speak on Holly's behalf. It's not like she's a material witness to Holly's case." Luke smirks and for a moment I feel ok.

The moment passes quickly, though, as I'm brought back to the reality that I am still being charged with telling my fiancé that, not only does he have a sister he never knew about, he actually has two sisters and another brother. By the time all is said and done, he'll have gone from thinking he was an only child, to discovering that he has two sisters and two brothers.

"What about Eliana?" I can't imagine how Eliana is going to feel. Will carried such guilt for being the kid Meyer kept. I wonder if Eliana feels any of the same guilt for being the wife that didn't get kicked to the curb.

"Wes is going to tell her," Luke says.

I sigh a heavy I-don't-know-what-to-do sigh. "I'm going to take a shower. I do my best thinking in the steam. If Will comes in from the garage before I'm out can you distract him from coming upstairs? I may need a few minutes to collect myself before I dive into trying to explain all of this. I'm going to need this folder, too. There's no way I'm going to remember all the names and dates."

"You got it. Thank you, Layla. I would tell him, but, you know...I just think he'll process it better with you," Luke says to me with a hug.

I move quickly out of the room and up the stairs in case Will is coming in. I can't have him catching me now. He'll know something is up and I won't be able to hide it from him, and then it'll come out all wrong. I have to think of the best angle to approach this. I don't know what that is yet, but I'm going to let the steam speak to me for as long as I can.

As the water rushes over me I consider the different conversations Will and I have had about family. I recall early talks about what it was like and how we felt about being only children. Memories of Will's pain for having been kept from knowing about Marcus all those years, brings tears to my eyes. That makes me think about Penny and how I wish I had at least known about her before she died. That at least knowing would have helped me to not feel so alone in our family.

I get dressed and brush my hair from the messy mop I put it in before the shower. I braid it and let the rope of hair rest over my shoulder before I move quietly into the loft. I don't know where Will is, just that he isn't up here as Luke promised he'd make sure of.

I search the house and find Will with Wes and Luke in the office. I don't hear what they're talking about, but for the first time in a while it actually sounds like casual, non-legal, conversation. They sound like a bunch of guys just shooting the breeze.

"Hey, men!" I say cheerfully as I enter the room. "Mind if I steal my favorite guy away for a bit?"

"Ok, but I really can't be gone long," Wes says moving toward the door laughing.

"Very funny, Uncle Wes! I'm going to take my fiancé with me and let you and Dad duke it out for who takes second and third place." I kiss Wes on the cheek, and take Will's hand. I decide not to take the file folder as it would be too obvious that I had something serious to talk with him about.

"Take a walk with me?" I ask when we're halfway down the hall.

"I'd go anywhere with you, babe," he says, kissing my hand.

We walk out the back door and begin the path to the dock. He asks how I'm coming along with unpacking and if the strangeness of being back is wearing off. I tell him that the only strange thing about being home is the freedom we now have. I had worried about the media hounding us, but since Will is Mr. Congeniality with them, I don't worry about them at all. We talk about braving it and going to the next Concert on the Green and both agree that we should tell the event coordinators that we plan on going. We don't want to take anything away from whoever is performing, but it's time for us to reconnect with our community.

"Have you thought any more about Luke's invitation for us to live with them after we're married?" I ask as we sit at the edge of the dock.

"I have. You?" he replies.

"Yes. It's weird to be torn on the issue. On the one hand, who wants to live with their parents after they get married? I mean there will be lots of *married stuff* going on." I blush and smile coyly at Will and he raises his eyebrows and smiles at me. "But, on the other hand...I still feel like a baby in this new family of mine. I just got Luke and Claire three years ago. After not having any family for so long, I have to admit, it's hard to want to leave."

"I understand. I...have...an idea though. I'm not sure how you're going to respond to it, but if you don't like it at all, we can ditch it and come up with a new one, ok?" I nod and feel my face squish together in confusion. "How would you feel about us moving into my old house?"

"The big, stately, White House replica?" I ask a little shocked.

"Yeah," he says slowly.

"I don't know, Will. It seems like it would be weird to move into the master bedroom your parents shared, don't you think?" I'm creeped out at just the thought.

"That's just it. We wouldn't have to. There are five suites in the house. We can choose any of them. We can remodel the whole place, and even turn their old room into something other than a bedroom if you want," he says. He's nervously excited about this. He must have a slew of plans and ideas to revamp the house to look nothing like Gregory Meyer. "The real bonus would be that we'd be super close to Luke and Claire."

"Can I think about it? I'm not saying no. I just need some time to consider it. And…maybe it would help if we walked through the house and talked about the changes we would make?"

"That sounds fair," he says smiling.

"So," I begin. I need to start this conversation about all the exes and their children before we run out of time. Wes may have already told Eliana and I know Will's going to need to process some of this with her. "I was thinking about something you said."

"What's that?" he asks, stroking the inside of my arm sweetly as we let our legs dangle from the dock.

"Do you really wish you had gotten to know Marcus?" I ask softly.

"Yeah…well, the Marcus that *you* knew. Not the Marcus that got twisted by his mom and our dad," he says.

"You really think you wouldn't have felt so alone? It's not like you would have been raised in the same house, or even in some co-parented manner," I say, trying to fully understand where he's coming from.

"Maybe not, but I can't help but feel like just knowing him in a brotherly capacity, that the simple biological connection, would have counted for something. I've thought a lot about that. It's why I'm actually looking forward to meeting Erin now."

This is when I tell him.

I tell him about Victoria and Cheryl. I tell him about Michael and Sarah. I give him as many details as I can remember about who knows what about whom. I also tell him about the pattern of the children being born the same or following year as his father divorced their mothers. I explain to Will that he actually has four siblings. Including Marcus, he has two brothers and two sisters.

I do my best to explain how Cheryl doesn't want to testify. I also tell him that not only does Erin want to meet him, but that everything indicates Michael does, too.

Will is quiet as he processes what I'm telling him. A few tears escape his eyes, but other than that he shows little emotion. I can't imagine what he must be feeling. To have been so desperate for so long to not be all by himself and now to find out that his desperation and grief could have been healed by knowing he wasn't alone after all. It must be devastating.

"Will?" I prompt.

Will says nothing, only starting to shake his head.

"Baby?" I begin to rub Will's back in an attempt to comfort him.

"It's not fair," he whispers. "It's just not fair."

The tears begin to fall in huge drops for both of us. Will, for the pain his father caused him by keeping him from his siblings and for me, the pain of watching Will grieve. It's a devastating feeling to watch the person you love most in the world wrench with pain and not be able to fix it.

Chapter 15

After an hour of alternating between tears and rage, Will is starting to ask questions. Many of them I know the answers to since they're just a recap of what I've already told him. He wants to know names and ages, but as he begins to ask deeper questions for which I don't have the answers I suggest we see Luke. Some of the answers Will is looking for may be found in the file Luke showed me earlier. I didn't read everything on each form so I'm hoping that we'll find the answers there.

We find Luke and Wes in the office and Will immediately checks on his mother through a question to Wes.

"Did you tell my mother?" he asks Wes.

"Yes, but…" Wes begins, knowing that Will is asking if his mother has been told about the other children…Will's siblings.

"But what?" Will's face is hard. When it comes to his mom he's even more protective of her than he is of me. It's been difficult for him to let go and let Wes take care of her.

"Well…Luke and I didn't know this, but…she already knew." Wes' delivery is straightforward, the only appropriate approach for this scenario.

"What?" Will doesn't wait for a response. He moves from the bedroom and immediately starts calling for his mother. His face is actually turning red and I know that he's more hurt by her secrecy than his father's. I immediately follow him, feeling like Luke and Wes are on my heels, almost tripping on me, since I'm having trouble keeping up with my short legs.

"William? What it is? Are you ok?" Eliana rushes from the kitchen into the Great Room.

"No, I'm not ok," he says sternly. I've never heard him use this tone with her. "You knew! You knew and you never told me!" Eliana looks at Wes and he gives her a tight-lipped nod.

"Oh, William, it's not what you think," she says in defense.

"Really? Because what I think is that you knew I had brothers and sisters and you never told me. What I think is that you faked your way through our whole conversation about Loretta and Erin, acting like it was all news to you," Will shouts.

"C'mon, Will, settle down. Let's just calm down and talk about this," Wes tells him.

"Back off, Wes! This doesn't concern you." Will's tone and volume are just as aggressive with Wes and now I *know* just how angry Will is. "How could you do that to me? All the times I cried to you, telling you how much I wished I had a brother or a sister. How could you not tell me? All those years you told me I didn't have any siblings because I was special. Lies!"

"You were special. You *are* special!" she pleads with him. I've never seen Eliana look this pained. Even when she watched her husband get shot, or when he died. "By the time I had you I knew I was going to spend the better part of my life walking on egg shells with your father, fearful that he would take you away from me." She pauses, collecting her thoughts. Wes comes to her side, draping a comforting arm around her. "Marlene came to see me one day when you were almost two. I think Marcus would have been close to four then. I knew who she was, remembering when she and Gregory came to my family's store in Hickory. She told me about how she couldn't go through with the abortion Gregory told her to have, and that he had been supporting her since Marcus' birth.

"She came to tell me how unfair her life was…how hard Gregory had been on her, leaving her with so little compared to what he could have afforded. And then she told me about his other ex-wives and their children. How cruel he had been to them, especially Cheryl, leaving all of them to take care of themselves. She came there to warn me that if I wasn't careful, I'd be out next. The thing was, when she left, all I felt was envy. I *envied* those women. They thought they were kicked aside like garbage, but I knew they had really been set free. Life with Gregory was a prison sentence. I had any material thing I wanted, but I didn't have freedom. I couldn't come and go as I pleased. I couldn't dress as I wanted. I couldn't eat the food I liked. I couldn't even watch television or see the movies I wanted. I lived for the times your father was out of town for even just a day or two just so I could go to a movie! I couldn't even be the mother to my son I wanted to be." Eliana is trying her best to explain, but Will is so distraught over finding out that his mother knew everything all along that I'm not sure if what she's telling him is really sinking in.

"You knew how *alone* I felt. You knew how badly I wanted a brother or a sister," Will pleads softly.

"William, the age difference between you and the others was so great that it never occurred to me to try and connect you with them. When I tried to arrange a play date for you and Marcus, your father found out and forbade me from ever communicating with Marlene again," she says.

"But…when I was older, and I understood who my father really was…" Will is trying desperately to understand why something so important was kept from him. He's reaching out with questions, but no answer is going to satisfy him.

"I was scared. Any time I defied your father in any way he threatened to take you from me. So every decision I made, every secret I kept…everything I did, I did so I wouldn't lose you. I would rather have lived in that hell with him as long as I had you, than to have been set free like the others and never see you again." Eliana reaches out for Will but he pulls away, causing a different kind of sadness to wash over her.

With nothing left to say, Will walks away and upstairs to the loft.

"Please help him understand," Eliana begs of me.

"I'll try," I tell her.

Leaving Eliana in the comforting arms of Wes, I go upstairs to find Will in our oversized chair. He looks sad and small, like a broken little boy.

"Hey," I say softly, squishing my body against his in the chair.

"I know what you're going to say," he says.

"You do, do you?" I run my fingers through Will's hair.

"You're going to tell me what I told you the day you found out about your father and the explosion. You're going to tell me that sometimes not knowing something protects you from something worse. That I need to see my mom as she was all those years, protecting me at the cost of her own freedom."

"Wow, I'm good," I say with a smirk.

"I know all of those things, Layla. And I know my mom spent years doing everything she could to protect me." Will turns his body to face me. I swing my legs over his lap to make us both more comfortable. "But why wouldn't she tell me later, after we left him, after we were free?"

"You still couldn't have done anything about it, Will."

"But just to *know*. When we got to Florida, if she had told me why she couldn't tell me before, I would have understood. She knew Luke was going to call the exes as witnesses, and when I told her about Loretta, she acted shocked. I just don't understand," he says. His voice is faltering, like he's holding back tears.

"Honey, you have to give her some time. It's not as easy for her to shake some of the old habits. She spent almost 20 years pretending to be someone she wasn't, hiding things from people, from you. She's just learning how to be genuine again. It never occurred to her to volunteer this information to you. She didn't keep it from you to hurt you. She initially kept it from you to *save* you. And now, well, she's figuring out how that she has to be aware and intentional about opening up. It's not second nature to her, Will."

I understand where both Will and Eliana are coming from. Information is his coping mechanism. He needs information to make him feel like he's functioning with full knowledge so he can make decisions based on all the facts. I get that. I was devastated when I found out that everyone had hidden the truth about my father's link to an eccoterrorist group. I felt like I had been living a lie all those years.

I also understand Eliana's propensity for keeping thoughts, feelings, and even information to herself. I stuffed so much down during those years with Gram. When I came to live with Luke and Claire it was a daily decision to share things with them, to trust them. It was hard to tell them how difficult life had been, especially the years I took care of Gramps. I didn't want them to think poorly of Gramps, or think I was ungrateful to Gram and Gramps for taking me in. I also remember how hard it was to share certain things about my parents with Will. I never wanted to paint them in a way that misrepresented them.

Will has to process through his feelings. I can't do that for him. I know he'll come to the right place with them. I just hope it doesn't take too long because I know Eliana's heart is breaking with every minute that passes before Will reconciles with her on this.

"She loves you, Will. And you know that everything she did, she did to protect you." I run my fingers around his ear and down his jawline. Taking his face in my hand, I give him one kiss and leave him to his thoughts.

When I appear back in the Great Room, Eliana is nestled at Wes' side on the loveseat. Her face is stained with tears, and Wes is rubbing her arm, telling her it's going to all work out. I love watching them together.

"Oh, Layla…is William coming down? Were you able to reach him?" Eliana asks, sitting up when she sees me.

"He's going to need a bit to really come to terms with everything, but he'll get there. He knows you were only trying to protect him. It doesn't make it hurt much less, but it matters," I tell her.

"Can I talk to you for a minute?" Wes asks me. I nod and he gets up and moves to the kitchen.

"What's up?" I ask him.

"I need to share this with you because I can't share it with Will right now. He's too emotional and I'm too pissed," Wes begins. "I understand that Will was upset, but, if he ever talks to Eliana that way again, he and I are going to have a problem."

"I understand. But you need to understand something, too. There are going to be things between Will and Eliana that they have to handle. It's not that they don't concern you, because Will knows that when you love someone, *everything* about them concerns you," I tell him. "You're going to have to pull back at times, and you're going to have to let them figure some things out on their own. Eliana needs that. She needs to be able to stand on her own two feet. Yes, riding in on your white horse is wonderful, but she needs to fight her own battles and make her own decisions. If you don't let her do that, her life won't be that much different with you than it was with Meyer."

"I don't agree," Wes says. He's protective of her, and that's wonderful. What he doesn't understand is that, despite the way Will just interacted with her, Will is even more protective of Eliana.

"I do." Eliana is standing in the kitchen doorway. She moves toward Wes and he meets her half way across the room. "Thank you for wanting to protect me. I love that about you, Wesley, and I would never want that to change. But Layla is right. William and I will have to handle some things on our own. It doesn't mean that you can't have your say. It just means that we're all learning a new way of life…one that isn't controlled by Gregory. We need to give each other some room to grow. Can you do that?"

Wes puts his hands on her hips. "For years I watched how Meyer treated you. I never want you to feel that our relationship is remotely like that. I love you and I just want the best for you. So, as hard it is may be at times…yes, I can do that. I may need some reminding, though."

Eliana wraps her arms around Wes' waist and lays her head on his chest. "Thank you."

"I...um..." we hear Will begin. He's standing in the kitchen doorway where Eliana stood only moments ago. I wonder if he heard any of our exchange. "I owe you an apology, Mom. If I had stopped to really think about it before I came after you, I would have come to all the conclusions that you gave as reasons why you kept everything from me."

"I was only trying to protect you," Eliana says moving from Wes' arms to Will's.

"I know you were, really, and I'm grateful. It's just...hard. But, I can get through it. I have this ridiculously amazing family, so I'm pretty sure I can handle anything." Will smiles at me and I hear everything he's saying.

"I should apologize to you, too, Wes." Will sticks out his hand the two do that shaking hands into a manly hug thing that guys do.

"Water under the bridge. It's a tense time and we all need to extend some latitude to each other. Let's just keep the yelling at the woman I love down to a minimum though, ok?" Wes says with a smirk. He's partly joking, but mostly serious. Wes loves Eliana the way Will loves me, so I know just how powerful that is.

"Well, I guess the only thing left for me to do is somehow prepare myself to meet my brother and sisters," Will says with a pleasant smile. It's been an emotional roller coaster, but Will has reached a point of acceptance, and maybe even a little excitement.

"You've got some time, William. They won't be here until the week of the trial," Eliana says.

"Not everyone," Wes corrects.

Chapter 16

After a meeting with Luke, Will has the complete overview of every ex-wife and Meyer child. Will examined each date of marriage and divorce, as well as the exact number of days between the date of divorce and the birth of a child. After each one he would just shake his head. Sometimes he would mumble something. I usually couldn't make it out, but it sounded pretty close to *bastard*.

Luke explained that Cheryl has been the least forthcoming with information, so Wes has had to dig much harder to get the scoop on her. All she told Luke was that Gregory Meyer was an abusive man and a part of her past she wasn't going to revisit, not even if he was dead.

"I don't understand something. Loretta and Victoria got hefty sums in the divorce. No alimony, just one lump payment. Marlene is the only one who received anything monthly, but we know why that is. But…Cheryl's single payment is *considerably* less than the others, even if you take into account the difference in years." Will rubs his forehead. He's a numbers guy so he would notice any discrepancies.

"I noticed that, too," Luke says shifting the file folder so he can review the numbers again. "It doesn't matter. She's not coming to testify anyway."

"What is it, Will?" I ask, noticing his unwavering concern for the inconsistency that is spread across his face.

"Where is she now?" Will takes the file from Luke and shuffles through the papers until he finds Cheryl's form. "Virginia Beach. You up for a road trip?" he says to me.

"Now hold on here, Will. You're not going to Virginia," Luke contests.

"There's more to this, Luke, and I've got to find out what it is." Will is emphatic about wanting to investigate this. I can't blame him. He's just trying to put the pieces of the puzzle of his life together. I know what that feels like.

"Dad...what harm could it do. I mean, she barely spoke to you...maybe she'll tell Will more because he's Meyer's son," I say. I think Will has a right to search this woman out and fill in some of the gaps.

"Why does it matter?" Luke asks.

"Luke...I'm finding out more and more about my father, and I need to fill in as many of the gaps as possible. You don't think that as soon as the others get here I'm not going to beg for information? I need to know who my father really was, because, according to Loretta's story, he wasn't always a sorry son of a bitch." Will sighs. "Look...I just need to know. There has to be a reason why her settlement was so much less than the others. He wouldn't have given her less than the others without a good reason. I need to know what that reason was."

"Luke, you need to let him do this," Claire says entering the office from their adjacent bedroom. "It's important to him, and it's not like you can stop him." Claire smiles at Luke with that smile that makes him putty in her hands.

"Is it *really* that important to you?" Luke asks Will.

"Yeah, it is," Will tells him.

"Ok. Then you should go, but...I don't know how comfortable I am with Layla going with you," Luke says with a warning tone that has nothing to do with us confronting Cheryl.

"She has to come with me, Luke. She's a part of everything in my life and I can't do this without her." Will puts his arm around my waist and draws me to him, kissing the top of my head.

"I want to go, Dad. I need to go," I say.

"I don't know..." Luke begins and I think he's beginning to wonder just how much longer Will and I can hold out on the sex thing. I'm sure the idea of his little girl going on an overnight trip with her fiancé doesn't scream sexual purity, even though we all know Will is going to insist upon separate rooms.

"What if Caroline came with us? She'll be back from California tomorrow night…we can leave in a few days. And her boyfriend, Ryan, will be with her so there will be four of us. Safety in numbers, right?"

"How do you even know Caroline is going to want to make this trek? And what about Ryan?" Luke asks skeptically.

"I know Caroline and she'll love the idea! And if Ryan wants to keep Caroline, he'll be on board, too." I haven't told Luke or Claire that Caroline and I have already talked about a girls' weekend in Hendersonville. Caroline has been dying to get back to this amazing bed and breakfast she's raved about for years. It was going to be a last hurrah of sorts before Will and I get married. It won't be the same as a girls' weekend, but we can still get to that before I change my name.

"You really feel like you need to do this, Will?" he asks again. I can hear the nervousness in Luke's voice. It's wonderful actually. It's the kind of nervousness I hear when he's concerned about me. The kind of nervousness you feel when your child is about to do something that might get them hurt. Luke loves Will like a son and that makes my heart swell.

"I do, Luke."

"Ok then. I won't insist on the stipulation that Caroline and Ryan go, but you should know I'd feel a lot better if they were there." Luke puts his hand on Will's shoulder.

"Thanks, Dad," I say moving out from Will's arm and into Luke's. "He needs to fill in the missing pieces. He needs to understand. He needs this for closure," I whisper in Luke's ear as I hug him. I want him to really understand why this is so important to Will. Luke smiles at me softly and I know he's got it.

*****

It took all of five seconds to get a squealing yes out of Caroline. After I gave her the rundown of all the despicable details we had on Will's father, she was absolutely on board with road-tripping it with us to Virginia Beach so Will can really start putting all of this to rest.

"You're sure Ryan is up for this?" I ask as we load our overnight bags into the back of Will's new Prius V.

"Oh please! He's so laid back, he's up for anything!" she says as Ryan approaches.

"Yeah, I'm up for anything…as long as Caroline is there." Ryan saddles up to Caroline and kisses her cheek. He really is so sweet with her, and I'm looking forward to getting to know him better. Although, every time he speaks, I'm expecting the last word of his statement to be "dude." He's *that* much of a Californian.

Claire kisses us all goodbye and we're on our way after Will confirms Cheryl's location with Luke and gets the information for the hotel where Wes made a reservation. When I asked Will why Wes made the reservation he just said that Wes was adamant about where we should stay. Something about it being right up Will's ally.

"So…" Caroline says, breaking the silence after about an hour. "What are you going to say to her?" I knew Caroline wouldn't be surprised by the whole story from Loretta to Eliana. She was a solid source of comfort and understanding when things were rough between Will and me early on. Caroline is the only other person I know who personally faced Gregory Meyer's wary eye and survived.

"I'm not sure. I figure I've got about 20 hours to sort that out," Will says as he stares out onto the highway.

"Did you really fake your death, man?" Ryan boldly asks.

"Ryan!" Caroline chastises him, slapping him across his arm.

"It's ok, Care," Will says. "Yeah, I did."

"He must really love you," Ryan says to me.

"Yeah, he does," I say.

It was about noon when we left, so we should get to Virginia Beach by dinnertime. We'll check into the hotel and hopefully get a good night's sleep. Right now the plan is to just show up at Cheryl's home after breakfast. Will was afraid she'd refuse him if he told her we were coming, or that she might take off before we got there. Caroline and Ryan are going to find out what the latest hotspot is from some locals and go exploring while Will and I invade Cheryl Brinkley's personal life.

We drive in silence about half way until I take over driving. Between driving and running through scenarios of what to say or how this might go, I don't think Will can concentrate on anything else. The good part about it is that I've had complete control of the satellite radio this entire time, which never happens since Will is always working to expose me to new music.

"Do you know anything about this hotel Wes said we just *had* to stay at?" I ask quietly. Caroline and Ryan are asleep. Caroline is curled up at his side, both with earbuds in their ears and iPhones clutched in their hands.

"He didn't say much, just that it's an old-timey place with music from our next lesson," Will says.

"Wes knows what my next lesson is before I do? Sounds like you're cozying up to him a little more," I say.

"Yeah, well…he's not going anywhere so I think I'd better. Not that I want him to go anywhere. He's great to my mom, and she's crazy about him. I've never seen her so happy. She deserves to be happy and I'm on board with whatever it takes to keep her that way." Will's tone is soft and I can hear the real love he has for how happy Eliana is. I hope we're going to find that Cheryl has found that same kind of happiness, too.

It's 6:30 pm on the dot when we pull into the parking lot of the Old Virginian Hotel. It's huge and ornate, reminding me of The Plaza Hotel in

New York that I've seen in movies and the *Eloise* books my mom used to read to me when I was little. When we check in, the stately gentleman behind the counter tells us that the rooms have already been paid for.

"I told Luke not to do that," Will says.

"Deal with it. Arguing with him about money is like me arguing with you about money," I tell him followed by a quick kiss on his cheek. "You've got to know when to pick your battles!"

Will makes a 7:45 pm dinner reservation for the four of us in the hotel restaurant. I don't know that I'll ever get used to the life that Luke and Claire brought me into. The fancy cars and homes, the luxury hotels and unlimited funding. If they weren't so nonchalant about it, I don't think I could handle it at all. As it is, I'm still learning to let go and let them all take care of me.

Caroline and I request a small nap and time to freshen up before dinner, although she and Ryan slept practically the whole way here. We kiss our men and send them to their room across the hall. Ryan gives a boisterous "Dude!" as he walks into their room first. Will raises an eyebrow at me and chuckles as he closes the door.

"I wish I was a fly on *that* wall!" Caroline says, making us both laugh.

"Between both of your accents, you've got your own foreign language at times," I say, still laughing.

"Why, I don't know *what* you're talkin' about!" she says with her most southern drawl.

"So, *makes you want to jump up and slap your mamma* is common vernacular?" Of all the southernisms Caroline has ever said, this one sent me rolling the most!

"They were *really* good pancakes!"

We throw ourselves onto our beds and spread out. The queen-size beds are gorgeous with dark, cherry wood head and footboards. The bedding and all of the décor in the room is burgundy and gold and I can't help but feel a tad bit like royalty.

I've never stayed anywhere this beautiful before. I used to feel guilty about loving this new life I've been growing into. Guilty because I wouldn't have any of it if my parents hadn't died. I used to think I had to either be happy or sad about my situation and if I was sad about my parents' death then I couldn't be happy about my new life. If I was happy about my new life, I wasn't sad enough about my parents' death. It took a long time, but I finally came to realize that I could feel both emotions. I can be sad about my parents' death and happy about my new life – they don't cancel each other out. It's about accepting my past and being grateful for my future.

"Can I ask you a question?" I say to Caroline.

"Since when have you needed permission to ask me a question?" Caroline scrunches her nose at me.

"Because I want to ask you something personal…and embarrassing," I tell her.

"Oh, this should be good! Spill it, girl!" Caroline is way too excited about this and I don't know if I'll be able to get it out.

"Well…um…uh…have you and Ryan…you know…" I stutter.

"Have we what?"

"You know…had…you know…" I'm so embarrassed at my asking this question that I roll onto my side, leaving Caroline to stare at my back.

"I'm just givin' you a hard time!" she giggles. "You want to know if Ryan and I have had sex?"

"You suck! You know how I am about that kind of stuff!" I toss an accent pillow at her and it misses her by an inch.

"Ok, ok! Yes, we have," she tells me.

"Was he your first?" I ask.

Caroline hesitates for a moment before answering. "No. Chris was my first."

"I keep forgetting you guys dated for, like, a year," I say. "Um…"

"What was it like?" she asks, reading my mind. "Well…to be honest…the first time it wasn't that great. It was kind of awkward, really. Neither one of us knew what we were doing. I mean, we knew what we were doing, we just weren't doing very well."

"What do you mean?" I ask. "Not that I want all the gross details, I'm just curious as to what makes it so awkward. I thought that when two people had sex because they really loved each other that everything just fell into place. Eww…that didn't sound right."

"It's not a Julia Roberts movie, Layla! *No one* knows how to do it the first time. You might know what goes where, but the mechanics of getting there can be weird. You don't know what to do with your hands, or where to put your arm. And as the girl, you spend half your time trying to be all sexy that your head isn't in it. It wasn't until we had done it a few times that Chris and I got into a groove," she explains. I have always appreciated how forthcoming Caroline is.

"What about you and Ryan?" I ask hesitantly. I'm usually not this intrusive, but since the reality that Will and I are getting married in less than six months started sinking in last week, I've been thinking about this a lot.

"With Ryan it was different. We weren't each other's first. But…we did have to give each other some time to understand the other one," she says. I sigh, frustrated at my lack of knowledge on the topic. "Don't worry, Layla."

"It feels like a double-edged sword, you know? On the one hand, I'm glad I've waited, and that Will is going to be my first, and me his. On the other hand, I feel like I'm not bringing any experience to the table…or the bed. As much as I don't like to think about it, at least Will's *done stuff* with other girls and has some idea of what he's doing. Will has been my first *everything*."

"It won't matter how many girls Will has *done stuff* with, or even if he ever had sex with anyone before you. It'll be his first time with the woman he's madly in love with. The woman he's gone through hell and high water to be with. The woman he's going to spend the rest of his life with. It'll be all new, because it's you." Caroline moves from her bed to mine.

"Thanks." I wrap my arms around her and hold her close. She's used her logic and love to once again talk me down off the ledge. "I'm so glad I have you."

Chapter 17

Caroline and I exit the elevator in the lobby and make our way toward the hotel restaurant and I hear music crooning. It's old and melodic, different than the current popular stuff made now. It's lovely…and familiar.

Will and Ryan are waiting for us outside the restaurant with huge smiles across their faces. Caroline teasingly questions them about what they talked about during our little rest time and I feel my face flush at the thought that they might have had a similar conversation to Caroline and me. I get over it quickly knowing that Will isn't that free with information about us, and he barely knows Ryan. That, and Ryan says they had a *"whose woman is better"* contest. Will says they went back and forth for a while and decided to call it a draw.

I take Will's hand and we all begin to move into the restaurant when I realize the origins of the familiar music I heard just moments ago. The memory is brought rushing back into my mind when the signage announcing tonight's music will be a tribute to Nat King Cole. *Orange Colored Sky* is beginning to play and I immediately stop and turn around, making a beeline for the front door to get some fresh air.

I'm outside only seconds before I hear Will calling my name. I'm starting to hyperventilate when I feel Will's arms cover me.

"Layla? Honey? What's the matter? Are you sick? Do you want me to take you back to your room? I can have them bring up some soup or something. Maybe some ginger ale and crackers?" He's so attentive that I hate to tell him that this episode has nothing to do with being physically ill. Although, in the past, the memories flooding my mind have made me want to throw up.

"I'm not sick, Will," I tell him as I begin to calm. I take a few deep breaths to regain control of my lungs. "The music…" I begin.

"Yeah, it's our next music lesson. I happened to mention it to Wes and he said he knew of this great hotel that has a restaurant where they frequently do tributes to the Greats. He checked and they happened to be doing Nat King Cole tonight. It's perfect timing, don't you think?" Will's idea of perfect timing and mine are proving to be two different things in this situation.

"I can't go in there, Will," I say.

"Why not?" Will is obviously confused by my refusal, and rightly so. Who can't go into a restaurant playing music by the great Nat King Cole?

"I…I can't listen to Nat King Cole."

"That's the weirdest thing you've ever said to me. Why on earth can you not listen to Nat King Cole? He's one of the greatest artists in history! In fact, I want *L-O-V-E* to be the song we walk back down the aisle to at our wedding," he tells me.

It takes me a moment but I gather myself, and the words to tell him, "*Orange Colored Sky* was playing on the radio the night of the accident…the moment of the accident." I close my eyes, thinking of that tragic night, remembering things I haven't thought of in a really long time. "I don't just hear Nat King Cole…I hear tires screeching and horns blaring and my mother screaming. I can't go in there. I'm sorry."

Will looks at me, his eyes confused, then softening, and then seeming to resolve. "Yes…you can…and you will."

"I can't, Will. The memory is too much. I hear his music, any of it, and all I want to do is cry," I say.

"We're not running from our past anymore. Neither of us! We have to go back in there so you can create a new memory to go with the greatness of this music. We won't let it be the sad symphony to that tragic scene in the movie of your life. We'll turn it into something new." Will has my hands in his and I want to believe what he's telling me is possible. I want to believe that I can create a new memory, but I just don't know how. "Let's make it the soundtrack to the night we settled on our honeymoon, or talked about how many kids we want and what we want to name them. *Anything* that is about our future and not our past."

"You've thought about how many kids we're going to have?" I ask softly after a moment of letting his words begin to sink in. I haven't even thought about that. Then again, I'm just now really used to the idea that I'm going to have a future that includes a husband and a family who would literally do *anything* for me.

"Of course I have," he says, smiling. He looks a little surprised, too, realizing that I haven't. "I think about our future all the time."

"That's really wonderful, Will, but..." I begin.

"No buts, Layla. We're going back in there. I'm not going to let this control you. I love you too much to let this continue to hurt you, and keep us from something that is so special about our relationship."

I don't want to go back in there and listen to the last music my parents heard before they died. I want to avoid it like the plague. I want to pretend that Nat King Cole never existed. But...I can't pretend that Will isn't right, which is why I'm so happy to have him. He's shed a shining light on all the things I've kept in the dark, all the things I haven't wanted to face. Now it seems like the last thing I've been afraid of, the last thing I've been hiding from Will, is finally being unearthed.

"I want to, Will, really," I say, unsure of my ability to connect what I want with what I'm capable of doing.

"Why didn't you tell me? I mean we've been doing music lessons since we met. You had to have thought that this was going to come up," Will says. He's confused and I can't blame him. I'd be confused, too.

"I thought about telling you but...the more time went by, and the more you helped me heal from all that pain, the less I thought about it. The less I thought about a lot of the painful memories from that night. I stopped seeing red and blue flashing lights every night when I closed my eyes. I stopped hearing sirens in my dreams. I stopped hearing my mother's scream.

"I'm just as surprised at my response tonight as you are. It wasn't like he was their favorite singer, or that it was even their favorite song. It just happened to be playing when my mom turned the radio on to this old station they liked to listen to sometimes. It could have been Buddy Holly or Etta James playing…it wouldn't have mattered. It just feels like, well, kind of like what you said. As much as I've healed, that night can still play through my head like a movie. I haven't heard that song since that night."

Will takes my face in his hands, stroking my cheek with his thumb. "Then let's make a new movie. A new *epic* movie about *us*. We'll take all the music we love and give it new meaning in our movie. This is *our* life, Layla, and we can't let the tragedy of our past determine a miserable future for us. We're on the brink of filling in the pieces of the legacy my father left me so I can be certain I never become him. Dealing with your past and uncovering the deepest truths about my father are the catalyst to start re-writing our future." Will's eyes are glowing with hope. I see everything that I've ever wanted in them and know that he's right. I know that even though it seems like we've conquered our past it's always going to be there. The only thing we can do is try to understand it…try to understand the purpose for it right now.

"I've been figuring something out lately," Will says. "You know, as we've been sorting through our past. I figured out that no matter what has happened, it has all worked together to bring us to this very moment, and that this is the moment we can choose to make everything new. I'm ready to make everything new," Will says. He smiles so sweetly that I have to refrain from kissing him. I'm afraid if I start I won't be able to stop, and now is not the time. "Are you ready to make things new, Layla?"

"I am," I tell him. "Thank you. So…starting new…let's start with this whole *how many kids we're going to have and what we're going to name them* thing. Don't you think I should be consulted on this?" I smirk.

"Yeah, I suppose I should chat with you about that, huh?" he chuckles. "But, I figured once we're married you'll be even more enamored with me that you'll find it impossible to say no to anything that I suggest." Now Will is smirking and I can't help but kiss him. It's a great kiss, too. "And if you kiss me like that after we're married, there's no doubt we're going to have at least three kids."

"Three? You want three kids?" I ask, pretending to be shocked.

"I said *at least* three," he says, wrapping his arms around my waist and pulling me to him. *At least three*? Ok…I'm not sure if I'm ready to talk about this after all.

"Um…" I say, feeling a little nervous. "Can we jump back for a minute…maybe talk about the honeymoon first?"

"Talk about the two weeks I'm going to have you all to myself? I can do that!" Will smiles and then kisses me hard. "I know where I want to take you, but if you want to go somewhere else, please tell me. I want it to be a dream honeymoon for you."

"Well I want it to be the same for you," I say.

"Babe, the fact that I'm marrying you makes anywhere we go a dream honeymoon."

"Stop saying things that make me want to kiss you. We'll never get through this conversation and I'm sure Caroline is about to send out a search party." I kiss him anyway because there's no way I couldn't after what he just said. "You may speak now."

"Well…I thought we'd do two different things. One week in Bali and another week in Ireland. What do you think? You can decide where we are which week. It doesn't matter to me." Tears begin to fill my eyes. I try to hold them back, try not to let any escape, but the emotions are too strong and overwhelming that they begin to cascade down my face like a waterfall. "What's the matter?" Will asks as he wipes every tear that falls.

"Never in my wildest dreams did I ever think I'd get to go to places like that. Once, I did a paper on Ireland for school. I looked up all the exotic details and wrote about how wonderful it would be to visit there some day. Gram found me working on it at the kitchen table. She read it and told me I'd never deserve such an incredible trip. That people like me didn't go to wonderful places like that. Sometimes I can't believe this is my life." I don't even try to hold back the tears with Will any more. He's my safety zone. The one solid place I know I am free and not judged for anything. Will told me on our very first date that I could laugh, cry, scream at the top of my lungs, or sit silently with him any time. It's comforting to see him stay true to his word over and over again.

"Then it's settled. I'm going to take my *wife* to the island of Bali and the green pastures of Ireland, because she is the *most* deserving person I have ever known. I love you, Layla, and you need to be prepared for some big changes in your life. I don't ever want to hear you say anything about how I spend our money on you. You've done your tour of duty living with the lie that you're not worth anything special. *I'm* taking care of you now and *I* say you're more special and worth more than you'll ever know, and I'm going to spend the rest of my life driving that through that thick skull of yours!" Will doesn't kiss me, but holds me tight to him. It's not a moment for the passionate love he has for me, but the protective love. The kind of love that makes me feel cared for and safe. The kind of love that tells me that these are the arms that will hold me forever.

"Are you ready to go in there and face this?" Will asks, releasing me from his arms. I'm sad for a moment, as I am the first moments I'm ever out of Will's arms.

"I hope so. No matter what happens, I know I can get through it because you're with me," I tell him.

I take Will's hand in mine and we walk purposefully back into the hotel. When we approach the restaurant I can hear a couple singing *Unforgettable*. It's a beautiful song that makes me think of Will. So, I focus on that. I focus on this moment, right now. I close my eyes and think about Will and me, here together…creating a new life, new memories. I think about Bali and Ireland. I even think about three kids…and smile.

"You ok?" Will asks. He rubs his thumb over mine in a small, comforting motion.

I take a deep breath and surprise myself when I can answer him honestly. "Yeah. I'm good," I tell him. "Let's go in. I'm starved."

Will chuckles and kisses the top of my head just as we begin to move into the restaurant. Caroline and Ryan are seated in a circular booth facing the small stage and dance floor. They're cozied up together enjoying the music. I hope once things settle down that we'll be able to get to know Ryan better. Caroline seems really happy with him, and I can see that he's over the moon for her.

"There you are! Are you ok?" Caroline asks, scooting Ryan over so I can move into the booth next to her.

"Yeah, I'm ok. The past likes to creep up at the most interesting times," I tell her. There's no need to go into all of it again, not now at least. Maybe we'll chat about it later tonight when we're in our room. "Have you two ordered yet?" I pick up a menu and immediately get sticker shock.

"Order whatever you want, Layla. Pretend the prices aren't there," Will says noticing my wide eyes.

"What's going on with you," I whisper to him. "You've got this ridiculous honeymoon planned…you told me to get ready for change and not to argue about how much money you spend on me…and now you're telling me to order whatever I want when half of the things on here say Market Price. I don't even know what Market Price means!"

"I took the money," he says.

"I know, but I thought you were going to disperse it to the exes and to some charities."

"Well, I thought about what you said, and I talked with Luke and my mom, and I decided that you were right. It doesn't matter so much how he earned it. It matters what *I* do with it. Yes, I'm going to give a lot of it away, and Luke is helping me invest quite a bit of it, too. But, what good is having an insane amount of money if I can't splurge once in a while, especially when it comes to you." Will smiles at me and I can see how at peace he is with his decision.

"I won't argue with you because I know it will be futile." I kiss Will softly and then hold his gaze so he really hears me. "I won't ever take advantage of you. I don't care about the money. I think you know that. I'll even sign a pre-nup if you want me to."

"We're not having a pre-nup, Layla. Pre-nups are for people who go into a marriage thinking there's a chance it could end. We're forever. What's mine is yours. I don't care about any of it. I only care that you're going to be my wife. Any thoughts on when that's going to happen? I mean you *are* the one who suggested we move the wedding date up." Will tucks my hair behind my ear and sends a shiver across my body as his hand grazes my skin and I recall the day on the dock when I told Will about wanting a church wedding in Davidson.

"It just so happens that I have. How does October 25th sound? I was thinking that the weather could be really nice, and the leaves would be changing," I tell him.

"It's perfect. You're perfect, and I love you." Will leans in for another kiss but Caroline stops him.

"Alright you two! Calm down! I would tell you to get a room, but you know…" Caroline winks at me and I feel the heat of my embarrassment from our earlier conversation rush to my cheeks.

"Ok, ok…" Will says. "Let's just spend the evening enjoying some great food and great music. Tonight, we're not on a mission. Tonight, Ryan and I are two incredibly lucky guys out with our gorgeous women."

We all smile and settle in for a night of normalcy. I'm glad to see Will so relaxed right now. We have no idea what tomorrow is going to bring. We could walk away with every question answered, or we could discover that we drove six and a half hours only to come up empty. Whatever happens tomorrow, Will and I are in this together.

Chapter 18

Will picks at his breakfast, barely consuming anything but a cup of coffee. He's been staring at this file with Cheryl's name and address on it for the last 15 minutes. I know he's nervous so I leave him to his quiet contemplation. He may be considering backing out, but I won't let him. Just like he told me last night, I'm not going to let him run away from this. He felt strongly about coming to Virginia to talk with Cheryl and I can't let him forget that.

"I'm going to check on Caroline. She said they were going to have a rental car delivered so we didn't have to take them anywhere," I say. I begin to stand but Will grabs my arm.

"Please don't leave," he says softly. His eyes are dark and I can read the stress on his face.

"I know you're nervous Will, and that's ok." I sit down, scooting my chair closer to Will in the process. "The worst thing she's going to do is tell you she doesn't want to talk to you, and then we'll be no worse off than we are right now. Have you thought about what you're going to ask her? How you're going to find out why there was such a discrepancy between her settlement and the others?"

"The best I can think to do is to tell her the truth. I'm going to compensate the ex-wives and I want to be fair. Based on her payout she should get more than the others, but I just want to know if there's an error or what the reason behind the difference is." Will puts his face in his hands and slumps over. I don't think I've ever seen him like this before. It's disconcerting.

"That sounds reasonable," I say. "There's something else, though. You're more nervous than I think you were expecting to be. What it is?"

"I'm afraid she's going to describe the man I could become. A man just like my father."

"That could never happen, Will," I say reassuringly.

"You don't know that, Layla. Look at how Marcus turned out…and he wasn't even raised by our father! What if learning more about my father from Cheryl and the others just makes me see how much I'm like him…what I've really been fighting? What if I can't fight it forever? What if…"

"Will, stop it. You are *nothing* like your father. You have a heart beating inside your chest, and blood running through your veins. Look at everything you did for me, for us! Your father never loved anyone the way you love me. You are *not* him, and you never will be. You said it yourself last night: filling in the pieces of this puzzle only ensures you don't become him."

"I hope you're right." Will twists his body and we embrace each other. I knew this was going to be hard, but I didn't think it was going to take this kind of toll on Will.

Before I can get up, Caroline finds us in the restaurant. She tells us the rental car is already there and they are heading out.

"I thought you had be 25 to drive a rental car?" I ask.

"Wes took care of it," she says with a smile. Of course he did. That's Wes' specialty. He takes care of things.

We say our goodbyes for the day and Caroline gives Will an extra-long hug. She whispers something in his ear and I can only assume it is words of encouragement from a dear friend.

Will and I take a silent ride up the elevator to our rooms to make sure we have everything we need. I take a few extra minutes in the mirror making sure I'm fully composed. I've been strong for Will about all this, but in reality, I'm scared out of my mind. I have no idea if we're going to find another angry and bitter ex like Marlene, or not. I'm just concerned for Will. He's been through so much. It seems that once we digest one piece of startling information, another, bigger piece emerges. It was one thing to find out Marcus was his brother, but since then Will has had to deal with the discovery of three more siblings, the knowledge of which his mother kept from him.

I know he's scared. He wants nothing more than to be the antithesis of his father. I see that he is succeeding, but I think Will is pulling apart every minute flaw he has and examining it for origins in his father. I don't know what we'll find today, but anything we find out about Gregory Meyer is going to prove that Will is on the right path to becoming a man of his own.

"Are you ready?" I ask Will as I find him in the lobby of the hotel. He's pacing and I know I've got a long road ahead of me in talking him off this particular ledge.

"Yeah, as ready as a person can be when they're about to ambush one of their father's ex-wives. I just said *one of*." Will takes a cleansing breath and then my hand and we're making our way through the parking lot to his car.

We follow the GPS to the address in Cheryl's file. After a while I think we have the wrong address or are lost because we're driving down a very long, dusty road. There are pastures on either side of the narrow road and I can help but yell "cow!" when I see a heard of storybook looking black and white cows grazing.

We make another turn and the GPS voice tells us that we've reached our destination. Will and I look at each other, both with puzzled faces. Our ignorance about Virginia Beach is blaring. Having never been here before, I think we both assumed we'd find Cheryl in a comfortable suburb or near the beach…certainly not in the country on a farm.

The dirt road to our destination ends and we're facing a beautiful farmhouse. It's picturesque, painted white with brown shutters. It reminds me of our home in Davidson, but this home has a huge wrap-around porch with white rocking chairs everywhere. The view from any angle is breath taking. It's easy to see why there are so many.

"You're sure you put the right address in?" Will asks, putting the car in park.

"I'm sure. This is it, babe." I take Will's hand and squeeze my support into it.

We get out of the car and start walking toward the house. I don't think Will's ever walked slower. As I take his hand I notice a huge barn to the rear of the house. It's only now that I see the fenced in pasture to the side and rear of the house along with the horses majestically existing in the fields. I remember Will's father saying that he grew up on a farm and wonder if Cheryl's love for that life initially drew him to her. Then I remember that by the time he got to Cheryl he had already been through two wives, so I put away any thought that it was anything but her beauty that would have attracted Meyer.

Before we're anywhere near the front steps to the house a younger woman appears from the side of the house. She's everything a good cowgirl should be: jeans, yellow plaid shirt, cowboy hat and boots. She's beautiful and I immediately know that this is Cheryl's daughter, Sarah...Will's sister.

"Can I help y'all with something?" she asks cordially. "Folks don't usually come 'round her unannounced unless they're lost."

I wait for Will to speak, but I think he's too stunned.

"We're not lost," I say kindly. "We're looking for Cheryl Brinkley. Is she here?"

"Who wants to know?" the woman responds. She's short and protective of her mother and that actually makes me smile. I'm glad to know that Cheryl has someone the way Eliana has Will.

"I'm Will Meyer. I just wanted to ask her a few questions...about my father," Will says breaking his silence.

It takes her a moment to speak, move, breathe, and I wonder if Will's name means anything to her. A smile breaks across her face and she motions us to follow her. Up the steps to the house and then across the threshold Will is squeezing my hand so tight that I think he might break it.

"Can I get y'all somethin' to drink? Water? Lemonade? Sweet tea so sweet it'll give you a cavity?" she asks with a little laugh.

"Lemonade would be lovely, thank you," I say. Will nods indicating he'd like the same.

I stand there silently with Will, not sure if there's anything I can say in this moment to ease his nerves. There are moments he's actually shaking, and that's when I wrap my arm around his and hold him tightly to my side.

"I'm sorry for being so rude. I realize I haven't introduced myself to you. I'm Sarah. Cheryl is my momma," she says returning to the front room where she left us. She sets a tray of glasses filled with lemonade on the coffee table and sits. We follow her lead and sit next to each other on the couch.

"I'm Layla Weston, Will's fiancée," I tell her.

"I know," she replies. We give her quizzical looks and she fills in the blanks for us. "I knew who you were when I saw you standin' like dear in headlights out in front of the house. And since you came lookin' for us, I can only assume that you knew who I was, too."

"I don't understand," Will says. "How could you know who we are?"

"Before you meet Momma, you need to understand a few things. She doesn't know that I know about her past. She worked real hard my whole life to keep me from knowin' about my, well, *our*, father. Once I met him, I knew why." Sarah hands us our lemonade and sits back in her chair. It's like she's been waiting for this moment and she's relishing in it.

"You met him? When?" Will asks a bit excitedly.

"Four years ago I was sortin' through Momma's things, purging what needed to go, sortin' things into new files. It was a mess up there! Well, I came across an envelope I'd never seen before. It wasn't sealed so I pulled everything out so I could sort through it like all the rest. Inside were her divorce papers and the settlement agreement from Gregory Meyer. I knew she didn't want me to see them. I asked a few times when I was a kid about who my daddy was and all she would tell me is that he was a bad man we had to stay away from. I never even knew his name until I found those papers. She treated his name as if it were a curse if uttered.

"I let her words of caution sit for a long while, mullin' them over and over again in my head for years. I just couldn't believe that my momma would ever be involved with someone we had to stay away from *forever*. I thought maybe that was just somethin' she said to me when I was a kid. Now that I'm an adult, married and all, I thought I could actually meet him. So, about a year after I found those divorce papers my husband and I took a little weekend trip to Davidson. We told Momma we were going to Asheville for a romantic getaway 'cause we knew she'd never question that. I didn't want to upset her by tellin' her what we were doin'. Austin, that's my husband…he's always been real supportive." She takes a sip of her lemonade and Will takes the opportunity to say something.

"I still don't understand how you knew who we were," he says.

"Well, we drove into town and right into the middle of some kind of concert, right there in the town square! I had looked Meyer up online and printed out a picture. I thought maybe if I showed it around town someone could point me in the right direction. It seemed like he was some big wig around there. When we found ourselves in the middle of what looked like the whole town millin' around I thought we'd hit the jackpot. We started walking and the first person I showed his picture to knew who he was immediately and pointed him out. When I asked, they were even kind enough to tell me who you were, Will…along with your momma."

"So how did you know who *I* was?" I ask. What she's describing could be one of a dozen nights at the Concert on the Green. Where do I come in?

"I saw Will watchin' you. The way he was lookin' at you? It was clear he was smitten. Austin and I followed Will to the coffee shop thinkin' I might be able to talk to him, but by the time we got there you two were hoverin' over a puddle of somethin' on the ground, just laughin'." *Oh my gosh! She was there the night Will and I met!*

"So what did you do? I mean, did you talk to my…our…father?" Will stumbles over his words. I don't think we ever imagined that Sarah would have a clue about who we were, let alone be so hospitable about it. She actually seems pretty excited that we're here.

"I didn't talk to him. I did come face to face with him though. The concert was over and the crowd was movin' out. I made a beeline for him, plannin' on tellin' him who I was, but…" Sarah pauses as she recalls the moment she faced the Devil. Having had my own run-ins with him, I know what's running through her head right now. "All it took was one look in his eyes to know that Momma was right. His eyes were dark, almost dead, and frightenin'. I knew there was nothin' in him that I wanted, so I pardoned myself like I was just another person tryin' to get out of the crowd, and we left."

"I wish you had introduced yourself to me," Will says softly. He's having a hard time holding in his emotions. Knowing that he was so close to meeting his sister is difficult for him.

"You know…I've worked with animals my whole life, and when you work with them the way I do you have to be able to read them. You work with them long enough and you figure out how to read people, too. One look at the two of you standin' there on the sidewalk and my gut told me that the timing wasn't right. I could see somethin' was startin' with you and I had to let it be. I knew if I told you then who I was, I was gonna disrupt whatever was gettin' started. It wasn't my time, but I knew my time would come…and here you are," Sarah smiles.

"So you've just been sitting on this knowledge for three years?" Will asks. He looks confused and I know exactly why. As soon as Will found out about his siblings he acted. There was no way he could have sat on this for three years. I think we're both shocked that Sarah was able to contain herself, considering how happy she is that he's here right now.

"All my life I felt like somethin' was missin'. Not the "*I don't have a daddy*" thing, but somethin' else. The day I looked at you and knew who you were…that you were my brother, the hole in my heart seemed to fill. Just the knowledge of you was enough for me because I knew, eventually, this day would come. I didn't know when or even how, but I knew it would come." Sarah chuckles and smiles. "I used to think about what you were doin'…imagine you were the star of the football team or class president…how you two were doin', hopin' it was all workin' out 'cause I'd never seen a brighter spark between two people. It was just comfortin' to know that you were out there."

"Sarah!" a woman's voice calls.

"Here she comes," Sarah whispers. "Y'all ready?"

Chapter 19

Entering the living room where we've been talking with Sarah is a lovely woman in her mid-50s. She has shoulder-length brown hair and her skin has seen its fair share of the sun. She's dressed similarly to Sarah in working-ranch garb, from cowboy hat to boots.

"Oh, I'm sorry...I didn't realize you had company," she says to Sarah. "I'm Cheryl Brinkley, Sarah's momma." Cheryl extends her hand like a respectable and hospitable southerner does, and Will and I both stand as we reciprocate.

"They're actually here to see you, Momma," Sarah tells her as she also stands. "This is Will Meyer and his fiancée, Layla."

The smile fades quickly from Cheryl's face. She takes her hat off and runs her fingers through her hair to give it a fluff. She clears her throat and gives all three of us the once-over. I imagine Sarah will hear about this as soon as we leave, but for now she's maintaining a level of cordiality.

"I already told that lawyer that I wasn't testifying," she says curtly. "So I'm afraid you came all the way out here for nothin'."

"Actually, ma'am, I'm not here to convince you to testify," Will tells her. He's soft in his speech, not wanting to upset her.

"Then what is it that I can do for you?" I suppose Cheryl's immediate reaction to a Meyer standing in her living room would be one of defense. I never thought about the feelings we might unearth by just showing up here, although I'm pretty sure Luke started the digging when he contacted her about testifying.

"I just wondered if I could ask you a few questions about my father," Will asks softly.

"I have no desire to talk about that man. And what on earth could you possibly want to know about him?" Cheryl is polite in her delivery, but it's clear the mere thought of Gregory Meyer pinches her with a tiny bit of pain.

"I'm just trying to put some pieces of this puzzle together. You see, I'm about to marry this incredible woman and I just found out some things about my father…some things that make him even more terrible than I knew he was. I thought if I could find out more about him then I'd be certain not to become him." Will is holding back tears. This is more emotional for him than he thought it would be. Having such a sweet and candid conversation with Sarah, and now being face to face with someone other than his mother who can answer questions about his father…it's overwhelming.

"Son, the fact that you just said that is all the proof you need that you'll never be like that man." Cheryl's face softens and a small smile appears, lightening the stress level in the room. "But…I suppose since you came all this way, and I can see that your intentions are good," Cheryl says as she sits in a chair facing the couch. "What would you like to know?"

"Thank you. I appreciate it more than you know," Will says as we sit. "Well, to be honest, the thing that sparked my interest in coming out here to see you has to do with your divorce settlement. It seems that you received a much smaller settlement than the other ex-wives. I was just wondering if you knew why. I mean, it just seems odd…ma'am."

It takes Cheryl a moment to speak, and when she does, she isn't speaking to Will or me. "Sarah, I think you need to sit down. It's time you knew the whole truth." She takes a deep breath as she prepares herself to talk about something she hasn't dared to utter in over 20 years. "You'll hear the same story from all of us. Gregory was charming and inviting when we first met him. He was serious but kind and he promised us the world. The more he worked, though, the harder he became, and his need to control things…to control me…became unstoppable. He was…physical, at times. But the more money he made, the less he felt the need to keep me in line with a slap or shove. He controlled every penny we had and eventually used that as his sole form of manipulation.

"I wasn't allowed to work, but Gregory worked from sun up to sun down. I was given an allowance in an account…the only account I had access to. Sometimes he'd go months without putting anything in it, so I had to watch where I went so I wouldn't run out of gas. If I did, and anyone saw me? Well, let's just say it took running out of gas once to know that I never wanted to run out of gas again. I rationed the food in the house, too. He ate out with the firm daily, but I had to make sure I set aside food he liked so I could make it on the weekend. One time I thought for sure I had two steaks in the freezer. When I went to pull them out, I only had one. He had steak, potato, and asparagus that night. I had rice and beans."

"Why did you stay with him?" Will asks. This is the "elephant in the room" question all five women will be asked. I don't think we'll hear much discrepancy in their answers.

"I was scared to leave. He had his nice moments, but after about six or seven months those moments became few and far between. He was erratic and I never knew which Gregory I was going to get at the end of the day. I just always held out hope that things would get better. When I told him I was pregnant I was delusional enough to think it would make a difference." She turns to face Sarah. "I know you know about some of this, and I appreciate you keepin' it to between you and Austin. I wasn't ready to talk about it before, but I think you should know how things really were between your father and me."

"It's ok, Momma. You don't have to tell me. Honestly, I'm just happy to know Will. And I'm not mad at you for keepin' the truth from me. I know you had your reasons," Sarah tells her.

"Will wants to know, and I think you deserve to know. It's not pretty, but it's the truth, and you wanted the truth," she says. "I was about ten weeks pregnant and we had some fancy charity event to go to in Charlotte. I put on a dress that Gregory let me buy specifically for that night about a month prior. I wasn't thinking when I bought it that a month would go by in my pregnancy and that my body would be changing. When I put it on and it didn't look or fit right, Gregory was livid. He said several mean and hateful things to me that I *will not* repeat, and grabbed me by the arm to take me back upstairs to find something that wouldn't embarrass him. I shouldn't have, but all the way up the stairs I fought him, twisting my arm, trying to get away from him. Well, I did…I got away from him, but it was at the top of the stairs and I fell. I stumbled and rolled all the way down until I hit the bottom with a thud so loud I thought that something else had fallen with me.

"I was immediately sore and too bruised up to go, so Gregory left me there on the floor at the bottom of the stairs and went to the event without me. I pulled myself together, took a shower, and went to bed. Sometime in the night before Gregory got home I knew something was wrong. I started cramping and then there was a lot of blood. I called 911 and an ambulance came to get me. I could barely walk I was in so much pain. The hospital called Gregory but he didn't show up until ten the next morning. When I told him I had a miscarriage he told me that I couldn't even be pregnant right…and then he literally tossed our divorce papers on the hospital bed and left. That was the last time I laid eyes on him. When I got home two days later all of my things were packed and there was an envelope with some cash and the access information for the account my settlement was in."

"Momma, why did you tell him you had a miscarriage?" Sarah asks with confused eyes.

"Because I did. It wasn't until the next morning in the hospital when they examined me that they found you. I had been pregnant with twins. That's why my settlement wasn't as big as any of the others. On the divorce papers the payout was explained in line items. Under the child line it showed what I would have received if Gregory and I had a child together."

"Why didn't you tell him you were still pregnant?" I ask before Sarah can say anything. "He would have paid out what you deserved."

"Darlin' I was *done*. I just wanted to walk away. I didn't know if he'd come back for something if he knew about Sarah. I had enough money from him to buy this ranch, and even hire some ranch hands for a while. I never remarried and I'm fine with that. I have friends and family, and a grandbaby on the way," she says, smiling sweetly at Sarah. "We've done ok for ourselves out here. Even now that he's dead, I don't regret not telling him." Cheryl smiles contently and I know she means every word she's said. She's happy here. She's happy with how her life has turned out and I hope Will finds some peace in that.

"Was there anything…good…in my father?" Will asks hesitantly.

"Will," Cheryl leans forward and stares Will square in the eyes. "All you need to know is that no matter who your father was, no matter who raised you…you are your *own* man. *You* decide what your future looks like. *You* determine your path. You don't have to be a slave to what you're afraid your destiny might be, 'cause *you* decide your destiny."

"Thank you," Will says quietly as he works to digest everything he's just been told. "I, um, have an inheritance, and I want to make sure that you and the others are…helped. I know what my father put you through was worth more than what you got in the end."

"I don't want your money." Cheryl's expression turns flat as she stands. We all follow her lead and stand with her.

"I'm sorry…I didn't mean to insult you. It's not meant as anything other than something to let you know how sorry I am," Will stammers. I guess after Marlene's bid for every dime in the Meyer fortune we were at least expecting the other exes to be fine with receiving a little extra in the way of compensation.

"You didn't insult me, Will. I just don't want anything else from that man. I've said my peace and told you what you wanted to know. Now I've got some horses to feed. It was real nice to meet you both. I don't think you have anything to worry about," she says. "Sarah will see you out."

We shake Cheryl's hand and watch as she leaves the room. I think we're both shocked at the story we just heard. We knew Will's father was a hard man, but I didn't realize he had been physically violent. I wonder if he was ever physical with Eliana. If Will finds out that was happening to his mom he's going to blow his top. And I can't imagine what Wes will do. Right now, though, we're left standing in a living room with Will's sister. *His sister.* She expressed all the same feelings Will did when we talked about his wish to have at least known he had siblings. I watch the two of them looking at each other and suddenly feel like I'm intruding. There have to be things they want to talk about…things they want to know about each other. Do they like the same foods? What about taste in movies? And what about all those childhood experiences? Sarah is going to have a stream of experiences entirely different to what Will had. Growing up on a working ranch is far different than the posh suburbs Will knew. I'm also certain Will wants to express how he feels about his mom not being kicked to the curb, and about being the kid that got kept.

I pull the car keys from Will's pocket and my phone off the coffee table. "I'm going to get some fresh air and call Caroline. I want to make sure she's not lost and arrange a time to meet for dinner. Thank you for your hospitality, Sarah. I know we sort of ambushed you here, so thank you for being gracious." I try to shake Sarah's hand but she won't have it. Before I know it I'm being held in a sweet embrace and a thought enters my mind that surprises me. *This woman is going to be my sister-in-law…and I'm excited about that.*

I smile at Sarah as I leave her arms, and kiss Will quickly before I walk outside. The sun is hot and the weather is dry. I'm glad for my standard summer uniform of shorts, a t-shirt, and sandals.

I'm walking toward the car so I can charge my phone and get the air started when a man rounds the corner of the house. As he approaches I realize that I've seen more cowboy hats and boots in the last hour than I have in my entire life.

"You must be Layla," the cowboy says. He's ruggedly handsome with a surprisingly huge smile.

"And you must be Austin," I reply, extending my hand.

"I am," he says as he actually tips his hat. I'm waiting for John Wayne and some tumbleweed to come into the scene. "Thank you for comin' today. She's been waitin' a long time for this."

"I'm sure you're talking about Sarah because I think Cheryl would have been happy to go her entire life without ever meeting Will or me," I tell him with some sarcasm.

"Cheryl's a private person, but I suppose you learn how to be private when you've lived the life she has lived," Austin says.

"I think Sarah's going to have a lot to share with you later."

"I heard. I was in the kitchen. Sarah asked me to stay close in case things got hairy. I'd say she and Cheryl handled things pretty well," he says, dusting off his hat and placing it back on his head in true cowboy fashion.

"Congratulations on the baby," I say. "That's exciting."

"Yeah…we're excited. It's gonna be a big change, though." Austin's eyes are wide with excitement and it's easy to see how in love he already is with being a father.

"We'd still really like for y'all to have the money," I say, chuckling to myself. Between my time with Caroline and an afternoon with Sarah and Cheryl, I'm morphing into a regular southern bell.

"Cheryl won't take it. She's a stubborn woman. There ain't no way she'll accept it," he says.

"What if we give it to you?" I propose.

"Oh, no, ma'am…we can't take that money. It's not right," Austin refuses. He looks surprised that I would even suggest that we give it to them.

"I wouldn't know how to explain that to Cheryl, and I wouldn't feel right lyin' to her."

"I understand. How about this," I begin. I know Will is determined to make sure some restitution is made for the sins of his father, so I decide to strike up a deal with Austin. "When is your baby due?"

"Not for another seven months," he says, tilting his head as he tries to figure out where I'm going.

"What if we put the money in a trust for the baby? He or she can access it when they graduate from high school, but only for college expenses, and then have full access to it after they graduate from college. Would that be acceptable?" I ask, hoping he agrees.

"Why, I don't know what to say." Austin looks down, humbled by our gift, and I can't help but feel a sense of satisfaction knowing that Gregory Meyer would roll over in his grave if he knew how philanthropic Will and I were being with his money.

"Say yes because I'm just going to stand here and continue to come up with ideas to make sure your family gets this money," I say with a wide smile.

"Ok," Austin agrees after a moment. "That's incredibly generous of you. I'll wait to tell Sarah until all the paperwork is done. That way she won't be able to say no."

We're both laughing when Sarah and Will walk out of the house and down the front steps. They have smiles spread across their faces and I feel my heart flutter with happiness for them both. They've waited so long to have the kind of connection one can only have with a sibling. I feel a twinge of jealousy but only for a moment. I would sacrifice having a hundred siblings if it meant Will's happiness with his.

Will puts his arm around Sarah's shoulder as they approach the car. I see a sparkle in his eye and know that he's found what he was looking for. He whispers something in her ear and she lets out a loud guffaw. It appears that they've known each other for just a short time and they already have their own inside joke. Good for them.

"So you'll send us an invitation, right?" Sarah prompts Will as they meet Austin and me at Will's car. "I'll be as big as a house, but wouldn't miss your weddin' for the world."

"Yes, of course," Will tells her. "We won't meet Erin and Michael until after the wedding, but I hope they feel the same way you do about knowing me."

"It's their loss if they don't!" she says with some offense. "It was so wonderful to meet you, Layla. I'm really lookin' forward to gettin' to know you. Is it ok if I email, and maybe call sometimes?"

"Definitely," I tell her.

"That's good, because since you're marrying my brother, that's going to make you my sister. I don't believe in the whole *half-brother* or *in-law* thing. Family is family, right babe," she turns and says to Austin.

"It's true. She calls my folks Mom and Dad," Austin says as he puts his arm around her, drawing her to his side. "You're family, Will."

We exchange hugs and goodbyes and promises to call, text, email, write…anything just as long as it's soon.

"So…how are you feeling?" I ask Will as we make our way back down the dirt road driveway to the main road. I want to leave it open for him. We heard a lot from Cheryl and Sarah and I'm sure he's just trying to process everything.

"I feel…I'm not sure how I feel," he says.

"Well, I feel great. It was great how welcoming Sarah was, don't you think?" I prompt.

"I don't really want to talk about it right now…if that's ok." Will reaches over and takes my hand in his. He just needs some time in the quiet of his mind to sort through the day. I'm sure once we get home we'll settle in the big chair in the loft and talk.

"That's totally ok," I tell him.

As Will and I drive back out to the main road I'm struck with the reality of the last few hours. We discovered more about Will's father than I think we had anticipated, and gained a sister in the deepest sense of the word. I certainly hadn't expected to end this day feeling this way. The longer we drive, and the more I think about it, the more I see how right Sarah was. When your family comes into view, it's unmistakable, and that little hollow piece of your heart that's been crying out for something suddenly fills and you don't feel so lonely anymore.

Chapter 20

Will is quiet on the drive back to Davidson. Not as quiet as on the way
to Virginia, but quiet still. Except for telling Will about the deal I struck up
with Austin to make sure their family gets the money Will wants to give
them, we haven't really talked about our meeting with Cheryl and Sarah. He
agreed that setting up a trust for the baby was the best compromise and
that's all he's said. We don't offer information about our day except to tell
Caroline that I thought it went really well when she asked. I know Caroline
will want the low down later so I'll make sure we have some time alone to
give her my perspective.

Caroline and Ryan don't sleep on the way home like they did on the
drive up. Apparently they had quite the morning and Caroline is intent on
filling us in. They played a round of golf, walked on the beach, and Caroline
fit it some shopping, of course.

It's almost ten when we get home. The porch light is on, but most of the
rest of the lights are out. Caroline and Ryan grab their bags and head back to
Caroline's right away. Ryan just about flipped when Caroline told him she's
never seen any James Bond movies so he's determined to start her
indoctrination of "the greatest movies ever" with *Dr. No* tonight.

"Are we going to talk about today," I ask as we enter the house and
close the door quietly behind us.

Will doesn't answer, going directly to his room. He opens the door
quickly and I see a manila folder lying in the center of his bed. He picks it
up, thumbs through it quickly and tosses it back down. Then he empties his
overnight back, replacing the contents with new clothes.

"What are you doing?" I ask him. Again, he doesn't answer but
continues to re-pack. "Will! What's going on?" This time, instead of being

ignored, I take the jeans out of Will's hand and throw them on the bed, forcing him to give me his attention.

"I need some time, Layla. I've got to sort through everything," he says. He tries to pull his hands from mine but I hold tight.

"What are you talking about?" I'm more confused now than I ever have been. "What happened to us doing this together? What happened to not running anymore?"

"I'm not running. I'm standing still, trying to figure out where I come from and who I am. I sat in that living room today and listened to a woman tell me that my father served her with divorce papers while she lay in a hospital bed after losing their baby! What kind of a man does that? I have to understand everything about who he was so that I never become him. I'm so scared, Layla. I'm so scared that without knowing it, I'm going to turn into him!"

"You're not! You never could! I won't let you!" I'm trying not to raise my voice. It's getting late and I don't want to disturb anyone. "Didn't you hear *everything* she said? She knew within five minutes of meeting you that you could *never* be like him. Please...please don't leave me," I cry.

"C'mere," Will says, pulling me into his arms. "Shh...it's ok, it's ok. I just...I just need a few days..."

"A few days to do what?" I pull out of what used to be the safety of Will's arms.

"Wes gave me a copy of the other exes statements. I've got to read them, see if there are any patterns, behaviors...anything that I can see in myself..."

"Will, you are *nothing* like your father. I'm not worried for a single second that you're ever going to treat me the way he treated any of his wives!" I can't believe that Will is entertaining the thought that he could in any way ever be like Gregory Meyer.

"Oh no? What about Halloween? I was filled with rage, Layla! I was angry with you for siding with him. I could have literally killed Marcus that night!"

"That was different! We both know what Marcus was doing. He was trying to provoke you," I say, reminding him of the truth of the event.

"How about the night that Eli showed up?" he asks, recalling the night Eli Briggs posed as a reporter for the school paper only to reveal that he was on a hunt for information to take Gregory Meyer down for the death of his father. Will is reaching, searching for any moment he was absolutely perfect to me as some kind of indication of the evil DNA that lives in him.

That's not the kind of behavior Cheryl described at all! Will, those were *events*, not a description of our life together. Please, Will…" I plead.

"Please, Layla. I have to do this. I'm overjoyed at your confidence in me, really, but…I don't have the same confidence in myself. I'm just going to spend a few days at my parents' house, so I'll be close," he tells me.

"I'll come with you. We can read the statements together…I can help you. I know you better than anyone! I can…."

"Layla. No. I have to do this. Alone."

"Will…"

"I love you. I love you so much that I have to do this. I saw the look of pain in Cheryl's eyes when she talked about how my father treated her. I saw that same look in my mother's eyes for years." Will pauses and stares his distractingly blue eyes into mine. "I saw the pain in your eyes, the pain *I* caused, that night at Halloween…the night Eli came and I was so mean to you. I never want to see that look in your eyes again, and I'm going to do whatever I have to do to ensure that."

"Is there anything I can say to change your mind?" I ask, defeated.

"Just tell me you love me," he says softly.

"I love you."

178

Will kisses me and I cling to him, hoping in vein that he never stops. When he does, tears start to roll down my face. Will wipes them and kisses my forehead sweetly, and then he grabs his bag and the file folder and walks me silently to the front door.

"I thought you weren't going to let me close another door behind you again," I say.

"I promised I would do whatever I had to do to keep you safe. I have to know that you being with me is the safest place for you." Words are leaving Will's mouth but I'm still in a daze, not understanding how we ended up here.

"How can you say that?" I feel my face contort from how confused I am.

"Everything is going to work out exactly as it should." Will kisses me softly and opens the door. He walks through it and down the steps to his car, leaving me to close the door behind him, which I think is completely unfair.

I watch Will drive away and all I can do is cry. When I've stood in the doorway, crying out into the emptiness of the night for what feels like forever, I do the only thing a girl can do.

"Mom!"

*****

I haven't seen Will for 36 hours. At the 24-hour mark I called Tyler and sent him over to Will's house. I didn't care that it was 10:30 at night. Will hadn't replied to any of my texts or calls and I just couldn't take not knowing if he was ok or not. At my insistence, Tyler called as soon as he left Will. Apparently they had quite a conversation since it was one in the morning when my phone rang. Tyler said he promised Will he wouldn't tell me what they talked about, but Tyler also made Will promise that he would tell me everything himself. As much as I wanted to beg Tyler for information I had to respect their brotherhood and trust that Tyler would make sure Will didn't leave me in the dark for too much longer.

After Will left and I cried for over an hour on their bed, Claire spent the next hour convincing me that Will would be back before I knew it. That I had to take him at his word and give him the time he's asked for to sort through everything. After Will disappeared on me, it's hard for me to let him be so radio silent. I know Will is an internal processing kind of guy, but I can't stand that he's cut me out of this all together.

I feel like we've come so far that for him to start getting scared now just seems crazy. He's done nothing but prove to me over and over again how *not* like his father he is. He's loved and respected me. He's let me make my own decisions and been there to catch me when I've fallen. Will has a heart. He's compassionate. He thinks of others before himself. He's more of a man than Gregory Meyer ever was.

Caroline and Gwen walk into the kitchen as I'm putting my coffee cup in the dishwasher. Like the true friends they are, I called and they came right away. I've missed them and want to really enjoy the weeks we have together this summer.

"What was so urgent?" Gwen asks.

"Yeah...has Will called?" Caroline asks.

"No, he hasn't called. But just because he's processing doesn't mean the wedding planning stops. We're getting married October 25th and my maid of honor and bridesmaid don't have their dresses yet! Claire is taking care of booking the church and the reception site today, so I told her we'd get your dresses settled," I tell them.

"So everything is still on?" Caroline asks with a huge smile.

"Definitely! In four months, I *will* be Layla Meyer! We haven't been through all seven layers of Dante's Inferno for nothing. Now, let's get our shopping on!"

Gwen is absolutely giddy! Before we went to Florida I was just getting used to the idea of being a real girl with all the shopping and caring about what I looked like. She's thrilled to see me in full-on girl mode, not because I have to be, but because I want to be.

I still don't know where to shop so I let Gwen and Caroline lead the way. Since it's just the two of them standing with me they take me to a gorgeous boutique in Charlotte called The Bride's Head. We walk in and I feel like I just entered a fairy tale. There are whimsical lights and music, and the décor is light and airy. It's just about the prettiest store I've ever been in. Gwen insisted that we were sure to find the perfect dresses here.

I browse the racks of dresses, looking specifically for yellow. Almost any shade of pale yellow will work. It's funny how I never really thought about my wedding before Will actually proposed. Even though I knew it was going to happen one day, it didn't become real until that unbelievable night by the water at our home in Tallahassee.

Caroline and Gwen come skipping through the shop, each with three dresses in tow. They hold them up and my heart starts to flutter.

"I love all of them," I say. "How am I supposed to decide?"

"That's the great part! You don't have to get it down to one dress. We can each wear a different dress in the same color!" Gwen squeals.

"You can do that?" I ask. I've never heard of that. I always thought that bridesmaids all wore the same dress that the bride picked out, regardless if it looked good on them or not. Although, I'm determined to make sure the dresses the girls wear in the wedding make them look as stunning as they do every day.

"Yes! People are breaking those old wedding rules all over the place! Didn't you see that YouTube video of that couple that danced everyone in? You can do whatever you want, Layla!" Caroline says as she holds up all three of her dresses, shaking the hangers in excitement.

"Well…if you say so! Try them on and let's get you two *bridesmaided* up!"

Gwen and Caroline each take their own dressing room, leaving me sitting in the waiting area in front of their doors. I watch their feet as they disrobe and slink into the first dresses. I hear both of them *ooh* and *ahh* at themselves and I can hardly wait to see what they look like. Caroline shouts to Gwen to see if she's ready to come out. When Gwen says she is Caroline tells her to come out on the count of three. As Caroline counts down I feel my heart flutter and tears start to well up in my eyes even before I see them.

In the midst of Will's emotional crisis, I'm here, still planning our wedding. But…it occurs to me that, despite my silver linings approach to this, despite my stubbornness in dragging my best friends out to look for bridesmaids dresses, despite my surety that Will could never become his father…Will *could* come back to me filled with even more fear after reading all the exes statements.

The girls reveal themselves and I start to cry. I wish they were tears of joy at seeing my beautiful friends dressed in what could be their dresses for my wedding, but they're not. They're tears of fear and sadness. I'm losing Will. After everything we've been through, I'm losing him.

"Darlin'?" Caroline comes to my side, kneeling down so she can put her arm around my now hunched over body. She knows my break down has nothing to do with the dresses. They look lovely…what I saw of them. "It's gonna work out. You know it is." Caroline rubs my back, making me feel only slightly better.

"She's right. Will is going to read through all of those statements and know beyond a shadow of a doubt that he's not his father, and he never will be," Gwen says. "When you two were apart, he was so miserable. He was the walking dead. I mean that figuratively and slightly literally, too. You're his heart, Layla. Will doesn't know how to live without you. And it's not like he's broken up with you."

"It's good to hear he was so miserable without me," I chuckle. "He needs to remember that."

"You know what? He does. He does need to remember that, and we're going to help him remember," Caroline says to Gwen. "When we're done here, we're dropping you off and going straight to his house to make sure he remembers what a mess he was without you, and that nothing that any of those exes says about who his father was is going to change who Will is!"

"Really? You two would do that?" I say quietly as I recover from my crying.

"Honey, we're going to knock some sense into that man. There's never been a couple more meant for each other than you and Will. We can't let this fear overtake him. He's stronger than that," Caroline says as she stands, straightening out her dress. "Now, look at us and tell us how beautiful we are in these dresses."

Gwen and Caroline both look stunning. Both pale yellow dresses are knee-length and flowing, like my dress. Gwen's is strapless and Caroline's has two soft straps over her shoulders that cross in the back. I love them in both dresses.

"Wow," I say, wiping the tears from my face. "You both look really beautiful. It's going to be hard to decide." I sit up straight and pull myself together, knowing that they're both right. Will would never really let me go. He loves me too much. I have to let him do this. Part of being in a relationship with someone…part of being married…is knowing when to let the other person do what they have to do to get to the end of their crisis. As much as I want to be next to him for every second of this, I have to let him go through this process. It's all going to work out, just like Will said it would. "I think I'm going to have to see the other four dresses! And, you know, you each might need to try on the other's dresses. We could be here a while." I smile, grateful for such amazing friends who aren't going to let Will and me fall apart.

Chapter 21

I decide to give Will another three days to do what he has to do. If it takes the whole three days that will make seven days that I haven't seen Will. I occupy my time with wedding planning and living in a constant state of hope.

Caroline is in California for a few days with Ryan, and Gwen and Chris are off doing their thing. Gwen and Caroline have been by my side for days since Will lost his mind, so I don't want to call on Gwen right now. She deserves to have uninterrupted, non-depressing time with Chris. They've done enough already by going over to Will's in an effort to talk some sense into him. Unfortunately he wouldn't see them. I suppose he knew exactly why they were there.

I'm sitting on the dock, going through the music on my iPhone, trying to create a playlist of songs I think we should have at the wedding, when Tyler finds me. He's really a sight for sore eyes. I don't know where I'd be without him.

"Hey, beautiful," Tyler calls to me as he makes his way down the dock to me.

"Hey there, yourself," I call back. "What are you doing here? Surely you have something better to do than hang out with my depressing self."

"Are you kidding me? I live for it!" Tyler sits at the end of the dock with me, taking my phone from my hand. "Besides, you're listening to happy music, how depressed could you be?"

"Well, since it's music for the wedding I'm not sure is still happening, it's kinda sad. But," I say taking the phone back from him, "I could use a break, so thanks for coming by." I shove my phone into the back pocket of my shorts and rest against the post of the dock. "Have you talked to Will?"

"Yeah, a couple of days ago," Tyler tells me.

"How is he? Is he any closer to coming to his senses?" I ask, hoping to gain a little insight into how close I am to getting my Will back. "He still won't answer my calls or respond to my texts.

"He's good…just hanging out in that huge house of his…pouring over every single word of those statements over and over and over again." Tyler looks at me like I should know what he's getting at, but then I think it's just me being silly.

"Well…thanks for checking on him. At least I know he's ok," I say.

"That's it? At least you know he's ok? You're just going to sit around and wait for him to eventually come to his senses and get off his ass?"

"What else am I supposed to do, Ty," I say. "I'm trying to give him all the space he needs."

"Really? You're just going to give him *all the space he needs*?"

"Yeah. I mean, that's the best I can do," I reply.

"That's the worst plan I've ever heard of," Tyler challenges with an investigative look.

"What?"

"You're just giving up? I can't believe, after everything you two have been through, you're just giving up," Tyler scolds.

"I'm not giving up, Ty. I'm giving him…"

"…the space he needs, yeah, I know." Tyler rolls his eye and I give his leg a little kick.

"I don't want to argue with you Ty. Do you want to do something with me today?" I ask. "I need to get out of here and the girls are otherwise occupied."

"Sure…what'd you have in mind?"

"I don't know. Let's just start driving and figure it out later," I tell him. I don't really have a particular place in mind, but just the need to get out. "I'll drive!"

ANNALISA GRANT

We pull out of the driveway and I intentionally take the long way out of the neighborhood so I can drive by Will's house.

"Yeah…this isn't stalker-creepy at all, Layla." Despite the fact that it was about me, I still love Tyler's sarcasm.

"What are those cars doing there? Do you know whose they are?" I ask Tyler.

"Nope. Never seen them," he says.

"Hmmm…." I keep driving, deciding to let my curiosity fester inside me. *He doesn't want to see me, but he's got some random visitors?*

"You're not stopping?" Tyler asks, surprised.

"No, Ty. I'm giving him space and time. I'm not going to barge in there like some crazed girlfriend," I tell him.

"You're not some crazed girlfriend, Layla. You're his fiancée. There's a difference."

Tyler is right, but I still feel like I need to respect his wishes. He's processing through a lot and I have to appreciate that what he's trying to understand is a big deal. He's doing it for us and I have to let him.

I don't respond to Tyler but continue driving. I make my way to the highway and decide to go a few exits up to what I refer to as the "real people mall." This is the mall with an Old Navy and Borders Books – places real people shop. There's also a movie theater and I think it'll be great to catch a movie today, too.

As I wind through the parking lot, looking for a choice parking space, I notice a black sedan following us. At first I think it's one of those coincidences when someone is behind you for a while and it feels like they're following you, when really they just happen to be going your same direction. Only this guy doesn't keep going after I turn down a parking aisle. He follows me, turn after turn, regardless of where I go. I find a space between the theater and shopping areas and put the car in park. Black Sedan

186

Guy parks behind me a few spaces over, having backed in so the nose of the car is pointing out.

"Do you see that guy?" I ask Tyler, gesturing to the sedan and its driver. He's wearing sunglasses but I can see that he's got light brown hair, and by the looks of his shoulders, seems to have a fit build.

"Yeah...did he follow us all the way here?" Tyler responds without looking too obviously at Black Sedan Guy.

"I don't know...he got behind me somewhere close to the exit off the highway," I say.

"Do you think he's a reporter?"

"If he is, he's not part of the group that Will knows. He made a deal with them to leave us alone in exchange for exclusivity on coverage once Holly's trial starts." I look at Black Sedan Guy and see that he's holding something up to his face. "Are those binoculars or a camera?"

"Looks like a camera," Tyler says.

"Great!"

"Let him take pictures. What's the big deal?"

"Will has already stood in front of the press and told them that I was one of the reasons why he faked his death. How's it going to look that I'm out with you? They'll twist it and it'll show up in tomorrow's paper causing Will even more stress!" This is the last thing we need and I have no idea how to curb it.

"Don't worry about it. I'll text Will right now and tell him what's up. That way he'll know. Besides, he knows there's nothing going on with us. He's the one who sends me to check on you, remember?" Tyler smiles and pulls out his cell phone. I watch him text Will and wait for Will's response. When it comes it's just a simple "OK."

I was hoping he'd have more to say. Maybe something about telling Tyler to take good care of me, or even telling Tyler to tell me hello or that he loves me. Nothing.

"OK…let's go. I need to walk," I say, almost storming out of the car.

Tyler and I walk around for a while, browsing Old Navy and Borders not seeing Black Sedan Guy anywhere else. I walk through the section of Borders remembering the afternoon I literally stumbled into Will. That was the day I met Tyler and the others and our friendship began. I closed out that day with Will, seeing the view of the lake from the dock for the first time at night. That's also the night I knew I had been sucked into the vortex of being compelled to know Will Meyer. And now here I am, engaged to Will, hoping that there's still going to be a wedding in four months.

My stomach growls loudly, jolting me out of my daydreaming and making Tyler and I both laugh. It's the first time the tension of the day has lifted, which makes me happy.

We stop into what became one of my favorite places to eat before we left for Florida, and as we are seated I realize just how much I missed it. It's the kind of place I could come to with anyone and it was perfect.

"Do you want to see a movie after we eat?" Tyler asks, not looking at me but scanning the menu.

"Yeah, that'd be fun," I tell him.

"Anything in particular you want to see?" he asks.

"Oh, yeah…uh…there's that one with the guy who was in that other movie with the girl who did that TV show." I look at Tyler, eyebrows raised at him like he should clearly know which movie I'm talking about.

"Sure! Then maybe we can see the one with the guy who does that thing and the grifter who scams that girl and then they fall in love." Ok, so Tyler has no idea what movie I'm talking about and now he's making fun of me.

"Ok, ok! I get it!" I giggle.

"I'll look up what's playing and give you your options. Maybe one of the titles will ring a bell?" he laughs.

"So what's the skinny on your love life, Ty?" I ask as I tear the paper from my straw while Tyler scrolls through the screen on his phone. "It's got to be better than mine right now."

"Oh please...you and Will are going to work everything out like you always do. You're Will and Layla. It's what you do," he says, putting his phone down. We'll get to the movie selection later.

"I seriously can't talk about Will right now, Tyler. Please...can we talk about you? I want to know how many girls I have to make sure are treating you right!" I give a small laugh.

"None," Tyler says straight-faced.

"None. No, seriously, Ty. We're halfway through college. Surely there are at least a few girls!" The idea that Tyler wouldn't have any girls waiting in the wings seems preposterous. Next to Will, Tyler is the best guy I know. He's smart and funny, and he's really cute. I can't imagine there not being any girls lined up for him.

"Well...there have been a few girls, but no one that I saw more than two or three times."

"Really? I didn't realize you were so picky!" I say a little surprised.

"It's hard to find the right girl when...no...forget it," he says, picking up his menu.

"What is it? It's hard to find the right girl when what?" I ask.

Tyler looks at me for a long minute before he sighs heavily and then speaks. "It's hard to find the right girl when all I do is compare them to you."

"What? Why would you compare other girls to me?" I squish my face in confusion.

"You have no idea the impact you make on people, do you?"

"What are you talking about?"

"Do you remember when we said goodbye the day you left for Florida?" I nod. How could I forget? It was one of the saddest days of my life. "When

189

I told you that if I had seen you first I would have made you mine, I wasn't just being sweet. It was one of the truest statements I've ever made. Don't worry…I'm not suggesting anything. I'm not trying to tell you I have feelings for you. You and Will are my best friends. I'm just saying that sometimes I wonder what would have happened if I had moved faster that day on the Green."

"What do you mean *move faster*?"

"Will saw you sitting there with your aunt and uncle and pointed you out to me. I don't know how long he had been watching you, but together we watched you for a while. We saw how you interacted with Luke and Claire…how you responded to the music…how you smiled and your eyes lit up as you watched people with their kids. As those minutes passed we knew you weren't like any girl we had ever known. Before I knew it Will was uttering the words *I've got to meet her*."

"So, what, that's like the gentlemen's way of calling dibs?" I chuckle.

"Sort of." Tyler takes a long draw from the straw of his drink as he thinks. "I mean, it wasn't like Will was free to date who he wanted. He always knew his father's view of love as a distraction. There was just something so different about you. And once we met you, got to know you…it was hard to not want to be around you all the time. Will struggled with that for a long time…wanting to be with you but knowing his father would make it difficult."

"Yeah…he ran hot and cold a lot," I say, recalling the times I caught Will smiling at me, only to watch the smile fade right before my eyes.

"You can't blame the guy. If you had any idea…you'd understand." Tyler looks intently into my eyes. I don't think I've ever seen him like this. "All I'm saying is that the pickings are slim for a guy who's already met the perfect girl when said girl is taken by his best friend."

"That's very sweet of you to say, Tyler. You are an *amazing* guy, and chances are good had I met you first, I wouldn't have said no to you. But life happens the way it does for a reason. I've learned to accept that. You just have to give some other girls a chance. It's not fair to compare them to anyone...especially me," I tell him. "I'm so jacked up with baggage...consider yourself lucky that you didn't have to navigate through all of my crap like Will did...does."

"I doubt that!"

"No, really! I'm sure Will's at least given you an idea of some of the junk I've had to wade through. I've had some serious stuff to deal with, but Will has been there every step of the way. Sometimes it was really hard. And when I didn't want to talk about it, Will made me. He never let me go through any of it alone," I say with a smile as I think about just how steadfast Will has been.

"But...you're just going to let him wade through this crap with the exes statements all by himself." It's not a question, but a challenge.

"This is different, Ty," I reply.

"How is it different?"

"It's different because...because...I don't know how this is different. Oh, geez, Ty! What the hell have I been doing?" I cover my face with my hands, embarrassed that I didn't fight to keep Will from doing this all alone. I shouldn't have cared that he said he needed to do this by himself. I should have insisted on going with him or refused to let him go. I should have fought harder and now I've spent the last four days without him. Worse than that, Will has spent the last four days wallowing in the grunge of his father's treacherous past. I am the worst fiancée ever!

"It's settled then. We'll eat, skip the movie, and go get Will off his ass!"

Chapter 22

We pull up to Will's house and I sit frozen in the driver's seat, staring at the cars that are still there. I was focused earlier on the two cars I didn't recognize that I don't know if I missed Wes' before or if it wasn't there then.

So maybe Wes came to talk some sense into Will, too. Wes being Wes Will wouldn't tell him to go away. Having both Wes and Tyler here with me, I feel even more confident in my position that I'm not going to let Will walk through this alone any longer. I can't believe how stupid I was!

"So…are we going to sit and play name that car or are we going in?" Tyler says.

"We're going in," I reply, ignoring Tyler's sarcasm. I get out of the car and shove my phone in my back pocket.

As we approach the door I'm not sure if I should knock or just go in. Will *did* offer this house to me as our home when we get married, so I kind of feel like I have a right to just walk in. I think about it for another 30 seconds and decide that I do, indeed, have a right to just walk in without knocking.

"Aren't you coming with me?" I ask Tyler as he steps away from the door.

"Nope. You've got to do this on your own." Tyler kisses my cheek and leaves me there with my hand on the door. I give him a thankful smile and watch him until he drives away in my car. It's a good thing I live close. If things end poorly I'll be walking home.

I open the door slowly and walk into the grand foyer. The home has a very different feel now that the Devil doesn't occupy it. Even though the foyer still greets you with those huge marble pillars, and the house is still filled with the relics of Gregory Meyer, it almost seems warm and inviting.

I hear the laughter of a group of people coming from the back of the house where the kitchen and Great Room are. I'm sure that there hasn't been that much laughter in this house, well, ever.

I cross the threshold into the Great Room and see Will, Wes, and Eliana engaged in lively conversation with an older couple and a man who looks to be about Luke's age. They're gathered around each other closely on the leather furniture. The older woman is laughing sweetly, patting Will on his knee. When I've just about decided that coming here was a terrible idea, the older woman sees me.

"Oh my! You must be Layla!" she says as loud as her old voice will go.

"Layla!" Will says, shocked at my presence.

"Don't be rude, now, William. It's time I meet this young lady, don't you think?" the old woman says.

"Yes, of course, Nana." Will walks toward me as I stand like a statue. This is Will's grandmother. *Grandmother*. I'm instantaneously nervous. My stomach begins to flip and I feel my heart in my throat.

"Hey…what are you doing here?" he asks softly.

"I…uh…I came to talk to you, but I can see it's a bad time. I'm sorry." I turn around and start to walk back to the front door when Will stops me.

"Layla…please don't go." I feel Will's hand on my arm, but I don't turn around. I have a myriad of feelings streaming through me that I'm not sure I know what to do with. Seeing Will there with his mom and Wes, and his grandparents…it stirs a sorrow in me I didn't know I still had.

"Will," I begin as I turn to him. "You *left* me."

"I know."

"Why would you do that? You convinced me that you had to sort through everything alone. What happened to us being a team? What happened to me being part of everything in your life?" I'm speaking softly. I don't want Eliana or his grandparents to hear me.

193

"I thought I had to do this on my own. I didn't know what I was going to find and I was afraid that if you read what the exes said my father was like that you'd get scared. Hell, I was terrified of what I was going to find!"

"I've never been more sure of anything than I am of the *fact* that you are *never* going to treat me the way your father treated his wives. After everything we've been through, Will!" My voice is slightly louder now and I notice the conversation in the Great Room quiets. "I should go. We can talk about this later. I didn't mean to interrupt your time with your family."

"*Your* family, dear," I hear Nana say from behind Will. "If you're going to marry my grandson, then we're *your* family, too."

Nana is a sweet looking older woman with mostly grey hair. There are highlights of red and brown streaking beautifully throughout, and I can see that this is where Eliana got her gorgeous locks. Nana is short compared to everyone else in the room, possibly even me. There's nothing trendy about what she's wearing, and she has soft, kind eyes. Her smile is warm and inviting and I realize that everything about her reminds me of the heart of Will.

"Oh…that's very nice of you to say. Um…I'll leave you all to your visit." I tell her.

"Pish posh! Get in here so I can get to know my grandson's fiancée!" Nana grabs my arm and pulls me back into the Great Room where Eliana is smiling widely. "Now, come sit down. I have a few things to say to you. You may not like what I have to say, but that's too bad because I'm going to say it anyway."

I sit down as instructed and brace myself. Nana has been very kind to indicate that I'm a part of their family now, but…the last time a grandmother sat me down to tell me like it is, I was told not to speak of my parents ever again. Is Nana angry with me for being the catalyst to the pain they experienced when Will and Eliana "died?" Is she going to analyze me to determine my worthiness? I mean, just because she's acknowledged that Will is marrying me doesn't mean she thinks I deserve him?

I run through these scenarios knowing in my logical mind that she's probably just going to actually try to get to know me as she said. But the fear of the unknown is taking over and I stupidly decide to cut her off at the pass with a preemptive apology.

"I'm so sorry, Mrs. Hufford! I know the pain you went through thinking Will and Eliana were dead. If I had known they were going to do something like that I would never have let them. I'm so sorry!" I blurt out.

"Hush, dear! What are you talking about?" she scolds.

"I just…I know that I was part of the reason why they did that and I just wanted you to know how sorry I am." I say quickly before she can cut me off.

"Layla, you don't honestly think I blame you for what they did, do you? Now listen…I've already told my grandson he's a knucklehead for sequestering himself in this big house, leaving you out in the cold to wait for him to come to his senses. And I'll tell you what I told him. I haven't managed to stay married to Pop for 50 years by trying to do *anything* on my own. Once you find the person who makes even the worst part of life better, you don't leave them. You work things out…*together*. When life stinks like a cow pie in the middle of summer, at least you have someone to swat the flies off of you!

"And no more of this Mrs. Hufford nonsense! You can call me Nana or Nana Grace, I answer to either! William has told me all about what brought you to him and I'm here to tell you that as long as I'm around you will never feel that way again. Grandmas are for baking cookies and giving their grandchildren loud toys and sending them home all sugared up! You're my granddaughter now too, and I won't take no for an answer!"

Nana smiles sweetly and I think I've entered another universe. There's something about this beautiful old woman that in this moment she's somehow started replacing all the terrible grandmother memories I had with new ones, starting with this one. It's almost magical and I'm not sure I know how to respond. Most kids grow up with their grandparents and know how to receive the kind gestures of hugs and hard candy, but not me. I mean, I know how to reciprocate kindness, but this is different.

"Thank you, Mrs....uh...Nana. That means more to me than you'll ever know," I say feeling the sting of tears in my eyes. "I don't mean to be rude, but can you please excuse me for a moment?" I say.

I wait only long enough for Nana to give a nod and then I'm walking swiftly to the foyer and out the front door. I hear Will call my name and I make it all the way to my car before the tears start falling.

"Layla!" Will calls as he jogs from the door to my car.

"Will," I say as I fall into his arms. We stand there while he holds me tight in his embrace.

"Are you ok?" he asks, not letting go.

"I'm sorry. I had no idea meeting your grandmother was going to affect me like this," I tell him in muffled speech because my face is half pressed to his chest.

"It's ok...it's ok," he tells me. "I understand. It's a process. I don't talk about it, but sometimes it's hard to be around Luke. He's everything a father should be and sometimes it makes me sad for what I didn't have."

"Really?" I pull my face from Will's body and look up at him. His eyes are glowing and I think about just how much I've missed looking into them over these last days.

"Yeah...but then I think about what I've got now. Luke is more of a father to me than my dad ever was. And I've got Wes now, too. I've got role models coming out of the woodwork!" he laughs.

"Why didn't you ever tell me about how great Nana Grace is?" I ask.

"I don't know. You never asked and...I guess I didn't want to rub it in your face that my grandmother is one of the greatest people ever. I didn't want you to feel bad. Don't take this the wrong way, but…you remind me of her." Will squints his eyes, afraid of seeing my reaction to being compared to a grandma.

"Um…thank you?"

"I know it sounds weird, but you always have. You're both spirited women who, when their mind is made up, are forces to be reckoned with!" he says with a wide grin.

"I suppose that's not so bad of a comparison. I do already like her a lot. I mean, she called you a knucklehead so clearly she's got excellent judgment," I tease.

"Yeah…about these last four days…I've been miserable. I've been scouring through the statements and they all read pretty much the same," he says.

"Did you find anything that concerns you?" I ask, mentally preparing how to reiterate my solid belief that Will could never turn into his father and treat me so poorly.

"Not really. I mean…it's made me think about the times I haven't been as respectful of you as I should have, but…no, there's nothing there that makes me concerned," he tells me.

"Good, because *we* are not going anywhere. *We* are forever. And *we* are getting married in four months. Things aren't always going to be perfect. I'm going to think you're a jerk sometimes, and, on occasion, I might be a little difficult," I smirk. "But it's like Nana said. We have to *stink* together. So this is it. Live together or die alone."

"I'm sorry I hurt you. I should never have left you like that. I didn't know what I was going to find, and I was scared that there might be something in there that, if you saw it…you would be afraid of me. I don't want you to be afraid of me, Layla." Will's eyes are scared like they were the night Marcus died. This is the terrified feeling Claire told me about.

"I could *never* be afraid of you, and I am *never* going to leave you," I tell him with all the love and seriousness one person can muster. "I've already made my vows to you, and I'm pretty sure God takes those seriously even if we aren't legally married. And I'm sorry, too. I should never have let you go. I should have fought harder."

"You're not the only one who can be a little difficult sometimes. Nana passed down her stubborn gene to me," Will says. He takes a deep, cleansing breath and smiles. "Thanks for not giving up on me."

"Never." I throw my arms around Will's neck, hugging him tightly as he lifts me off the ground. When he puts me down I stumble a moment and spin around as I steady myself. "Oh my gosh! He's here now, too?"

"Who?" Will asks.

"Black Sedan Guy. He followed Tyler and me to the mall today. I think he was taking pictures, too," I tell him.

"Is that when Ty texted me that you two were hanging out today?" Will asks.

"Yeah. I thought maybe this guy might be taking pictures to make it look like I was cheating on you or something," I explain.

"Wait here. I'll take care of this." Will steps away from me and begins a determined gait toward Black Sedan Guy, but as his foot hits the street the car pulls away faster than Will can get to him.

"Do you think it's one of the reporter guys from the house? Maybe he was there before you struck the deal with Tom?" I suggest.

"I don't know...maybe. He doesn't look familiar. I'll call Tom tomorrow and see if he knows anything. In the meantime, let's go back inside. Nana monopolized all your time and you still haven't officially met Pop or my Uncle Andrew." Will takes me by the hand and leads me back into the house. I feel only slightly hesitant, a little embarrassed that I bolted out of there the way I did.

When I re-enter the Great Room, Pop is the first to greet me with a kiss on the cheek and a warm embrace. He immediately reminds me of Gramps and I'm filled with so much happiness that I return Pop's hug a little too emphatically, although he doesn't seem to mind. When I finally let him go, he calls Will over to us, still holding onto me with one arm. Pop is tall, like Will, with balding white hair. He's shaved most of it, rather than having one of those embarrassingly thin comb-overs. When I look into his eyes I see where Will got his beautiful blues.

"She's had her say, now I'm going to give you my two cents," he says quietly to us in our little huddle. "You think I held onto that doll for over 50 years by accident? Every man in my family has stayed married to his first wife until death. That's how we do things. I've looked at Grace every day since I met her and thought, *damn, I am the luckiest man alive.* So I treat her like I know how lost I would be without her." Pop looks at Will, commanding his attention. "You want to know what kind of a man, a husband and father, you'll be? You want to know what's in your blood? *That* is what's in your blood. You've got Hufford blood running through your veins and *that's* how I know you two have a long life ahead of you."

I smile at Pop, and then at Will, who is tearing up again. Relief is overflowing from him. He's spent his life doing everything he can to not be like his father. What a gift to know that generation upon generation of Hufford men have never given up on their marriages, never let the worst of life tear them apart from the love of their life. What a joy to know that Will can embrace this part of his lineage and know that the odds are more than in our favor.

Chapter 23

The past three months have been a like a dream. Pop and Nana Grace's pep talk were just what Will and I needed. We've been moving forward with the wedding plans, not letting anything get in our way.

Pop, Nana Grace, and Uncle Andrew have been to visit several times, but not always together. Their furniture business in Hickory is doing really well so one of them has to be there as often as possible. They're closed on Mondays so they try to come for an overnight on Sunday as much as possible.

We've been to visit them as well. It was wonderful seeing where Eliana grew up, and getting to know my future in-law family. They've shared stories about Eliana and Andrew as kids, and I even got the scoop on where Eliana's name came from. It turns out Nana Grace was really into this international soap opera when she was pregnant, and when she heard it she just knew that her baby was going to be a girl and that her name had to be Eliana. She didn't even have a boy name picked out!

I've watched Will with Pop and seen exactly what Eliana was talking about when she told me that Will's natural inclination for working with his hands is inherited. Pop has put him to work a few times and to see what Will has made just from the picture in his head has been amazing. Will is so happy when he's working. It's like letting a caged bird fly. It's what he was meant to do.

I feel like I've spent the last three years filling the vacant spaces in my heart. First, Luke and Claire took over the emptiness left by my parents' death. Then Will filled a hole in my heart that only he could fill. And now I have a new set of grandparents who are fulfilling every hope and dream I ever had for what having grandparents could be like. Grace is doting and loving with a healthy dose of meddling. Pop is sweet and kind and, just like Gramps, adores his wife. I know the day may come when they need our help, but I'm not afraid because I know that it won't be just me, sacrificing my life for theirs. It will be Will and me helping Eliana and Wes, a village of people joining together for the love of those who have built a legacy we embrace with gladness.

Will has gone to see Holly a few times with Luke. I told him I wasn't comfortable with him going to see her by himself and he was totally fine with that. While he wouldn't have been alone with her, he didn't like the idea of him going to see her without some kind of backup. She's asked him to come without Luke, but Luke told her that it could be bad press if the media catches him coming to see her alone. They're playing it cool, not letting on that they know about her involvement in her mother's scheming. And, if they do what I think they're going to do, Holly and Marlene are going to get *exactly* what's coming to them.

Holly's trial date has been set for November 17th. Will and I will have just gotten back from our honeymoon, but that's ok. It'll mean more when I sit next to Will in the courtroom and prove to Holly that Will and I are a team and stronger than ever. It makes my blood boil to think of how she played me, played all of us. I would hate the idea of Will playing nice with her if I didn't know it meant that she was going to get a taste of her own medicine in the end.

We've seen Black Sedan Guy a few times. There are no plates on his car to run, but Will hasn't given up on trying to find out what he wants. We hit kind of a dead end when Tom told Will he had no idea who he was, though. Tom wouldn't mess up his chances for the exclusive that Will promised, so we feel pretty confident that he's being honest. We got a better look at him on an overcast day when he wasn't wearing sunglasses. He seems pretty tall by the way he sits in the driver's seat, and I think he has brown eyes, but I'm not sure. They're dark, though.

None of the pictures he's been taking have shown up in any newspaper we're aware of, so either his editor realized how boring we are and isn't going to print them, or it just hasn't gone to press yet. Whatever happens, I know Will and Luke and Wes will take care of it.

The most exciting thing we've done, besides wedding planning, is go back to the Concert on the Green. We weren't sure what to expect, not having been out and about during a crowded town event yet, but it was really wonderful. Chris and Tyler's families were there, as well as Caroline and Gwen's. It was amazing to see how blurry the line between the "haves and the have nots" has become since Meyer died. It's shocking to realize just how much influence he had over everyone. There are still socialites who park their picnics to the right of center stage, but it was incredible to see just how many people made the move to sitting wherever they wanted and getting to know the regular folks of this amazing town.

When we walked around the corner and onto the Green you would have thought the President had arrived. The crown erupted in applause! I even turned around to see who they were applauding before Will leaned over and whispered, "I think that's for us." Everyone was warm and hospitable and seemed genuinely excited that Will was back. That made me happier than anything. I had been so nervous, so scared, that the community would be so hurt by Will and Eliana's lie that they wouldn't embrace his return. I'm so glad that I was worried for nothing.

"Layla, please don't forget that we have your final fitting today at three," Claire says, reminding me. I haven't been a typical bride. Caroline, Gwen, and Claire have had to remind me on more than one occasion about deadlines and appointments. Left to my own devices I would probably have missed every scheduled appointment I've had.

"I won't forget. I'm on my way to meet Will at the other house but I should be back by two," I tell her. I stopped calling it Will's parents' house months ago. It just felt weird. I haven't agreed to it being our house yet either, so I found a term more appropriate and started referring to the house that Will grew up in as *the other house*.

"It's almost one now, so you better get going so you're back by 2:15, ok?" Claire gives me a little nudge, knowing that the sooner I get to Will the more likely I'll be back in time to get to the seamstress in Charlotte.

"If I'm not back in time, at least you'll know where to find me?" I tease as I scurry from the kitchen and out the front door.

It takes only minutes before I'm pulling into the circular driveway of the huge, White House replica of a home. It's so ostentatious that I can hardly stomach it, but Will said he's been having a few things remodeled and wants me to check it out.

Will is emerging from the front door as I get out of the car. He looks like he's been working and it reminds me of the year it took him and Luke to finish the basement as my 18th birthday present. Will is a hard worker and he loves to get his hands dirty. It's one of the things I admire most about him.

"Right on time!" Will says as he greets me with a kiss.

"Hey, babe!"

"So I know you haven't made up your mind yet on where we're going to live, but I've made a few adjustments to the house that I wanted you to see. If you don't like them, I can always sell the house. It's not a big deal, ok?" Will tells me. "But…we are getting married in a month so we should probably get this figured out sooner than later."

"I know, I know! Let's go in! I'm in suspense!" I say.

As we walk to the front door I think about some things that Will could have changed. The furniture throughout the house was a bit too ornate for my taste, even though most of it was made by Eliana's family's business. The antiques could go, too. I think Will and I have much simpler taste than all that. The furniture in his parents' bedroom will have to be burned. There is no way I could even relocate it to another room in the house.

"Are you ready?" Will asks with bated breath.

"I'm ready, Will. I mean…seriously, I think I can handle seeing new furniture and a new coat of paint," I say with some sarcasm. I don't know why he's making such a big deal about this…until he opens the door.

The door swings open and I feel like Dorothy coming out of her house in Oz. I am not in the same house I was in three months ago. This house isn't posh and ornate. It isn't filled with antiques or lavish furniture. This house looks warm and inviting like a cottage or a lodge.

The two huge, marble pillars that flanked the curved stairs are now boxed with rich wood from the floor to the two-story ceiling, and there are framed pictures of Will and me on all four sides of each. The marble flooring has been replaced with warm hardwood, and the brass railing that used to run along the stairs is now a wood and wrought iron bannister.

The new warmth of the decor continues into the Great Room and dining area. There's still a table that seats ten, but it looks more like barn chic than high society, and the set in the Great Room is neutral with floral accent pillows. There are coordinating afghans thrown over the sofa and loveseat making it look like the perfect place to cozy up with Will and watch a movie on the ridiculously huge TV mounted on the wall over the fireplace.

Everything, everywhere, looks entirely different than it did before. There are no traces of Gregory and Eliana Meyer to be found anywhere. Will has transformed this home into a place that holds no reminders of the haunting memories that used to reside here.

He's turned this house into a home…for us.

"Oh, Will," I say, covering my mouth in awe.

"Do you like it?" he asks hesitantly.

"Of course, I love it!" I do a three-sixty turn, taking it all in. "You have a pool?" I ask, noticing the backyard for the first time. I've only been in this home twice. The first time I was subject to the Meyer Inquisition. The second time, just three months ago, I was focused on Pop and Nana Grace.

Both times I was far too distracted to even think to look out the back windows.

"Yeah…and a pool house there," he says pointing to a cottage-looking house on the other side of the pool. It's a beautiful, picturesque house with trellises and climbing vines. It's way too big though. It actually doesn't look much smaller than Gram and Gramps' house. "I suggested to Mom that maybe we could remodel it and she and Wes could move in there after they get married, but she said no. She wouldn't feel right living here in any capacity."

"I can't believe you did this! How did you do this so fast?" I'm amazed. It seems to me that a project of this size would take years not just a few months.

"I hired the best and told them my deadline. I needed the entire project done in ten weeks so that I could either give it to my bride or sell it. So…am I giving it to my bride or am I selling it?" Will looks at me hopefully. I believe him when he tells me he'd sell the house if I just couldn't live here, but I know he's hoping we can create a new life here. A legacy so opposite of what used to fill these spaces.

"I think…this will make a wonderful first home for us. Thank you, Will."

I lean into him and let his arms fold around me as I continue to take in the wonder that is now *my* home. Never in my wildest dreams did I imagine that this cold and bitter place could be magically turned into something so warm and inviting.

"Will, honey, are you crying?" I ask, feeling a tear land on my face.

"You have no idea how happy you make me. It means so much to me that we reinvent this place. There were terrible, terrible memories here. Memories I still haven't told you about. I didn't know if I could exorcise them with a simple remodel. But when I saw the finished work, I thought, maybe, just maybe it could work and we could build a new life here. And then…for you to stand here and see what I see…Layla…I think it's actually really hitting me that this is happening. After everything we've been through. Over three years of highs and lows and struggles and moving heaven and earth…it's happening. In four short weeks you're going to be my wife, and we're going to officially start our lives together. I love you more than I could ever fully express."

Will pulls me back into his arms and we hold each other there for a long time. My phone buzzes in my pocket and I know it is Claire calling to find out why I'm not back in time to leave for my fitting, but I don't care. In this moment nothing else matters but Will and me and the re-creation of a place that will be the start of our life together. And…even though I thought it would be a good first home for us, I have a feeling that I could really build a *life* here with Will. A place we can raise our children…and a place we can grow old together.

*****

Claire forgives me when I tell her about the miraculous changes Will made to the other house and how I'll be referring to it as Will's and my house from now on. She winces for just a second with sadness that Will and I are not going to take them up on their invitation to live with them after the wedding.

"Mom, we'll literally be walking distance from you and Dad. It's the next best thing to living with you," I tell her as I stroke her arm. "We can take after dinner walks, and maybe actually start that Couch to 5k running plan. It'll make the time we have together even more special."

"I understand, Layla. I guess I just thought we'd have a daughter at home for a little bit longer." She sighs and replaces her frowned face with a bright smile. "Well, we have a month left and we're going to fill it with all the wonderful things mothers and daughters do when preparing for a wedding."

"Are we picking Caroline up?" I ask as we pull into her driveway.

"Yes. I was going to have you just run in and get her, but Carol asked me to pop in," she says.

I ring the doorbell and Caroline answers before the chime is done echoing. "Hey! I didn't know you were coming with us today. This will be even more fun! Do you think Gwen wants to come, too?" I give Caroline a hug. I'm excited to tell her all about the house, and the 45 minute drive into Charlotte will give us plenty of time. I watch our mothers disappear in the direction of the kitchen and guess that Caroline's mom is showing Claire some great new kitchen gadget. Claire has fully embraced the role of chef and is always looking for ideas and tools to make cooking easier.

"Gwen's got something going on today. C'mere for a minute. I want to show you something," she says, hooking her arm through mine.

We walk to the back of the house and through the Great Room to the doors to the patio. When Caroline opens them I'm greeted with cheers of "Surprise!"

"What? What's going on?" I stutter out, stunned.

"This is your bridal shower, girl!" Caroline squeals.

I'm shocked! If someone had asked me to make a list for a bridal shower I could have come up with seven names, maybe ten. There are definitely more than ten people here and my heart stops as I scan the garden and see Dana and Lisa…and Finn! I'm filled with excitement and trepidation. They don't know about Will being Will. How on earth am I going to explain this?

Before I can faint from fear all three of them are rushing to me, throwing all six of their arms around me.

"Congratulations, darlin'!" I hear Dana's sweet southern drawl say.

"Oh my gosh! I can't believe you're here! I…I have to explain something to you," I begin.

"No need. John…uh…Will called and told us everything. It's pretty amazing what he did, what you two have been through," Finn says. "I'm only slightly mad at you for not telling me, but I suppose I understand." Finn's arms are around me again and this time I'm hugging him back with all my strength. My worlds have not collided, but merged and I'm elated.

"Lisa, is Jason here?" I ask.

"No, he had to work. But Finn made him promise to take extra time off before the wedding for J-…Will's bachelor party," she chuckles. "I think it might take me a bit to get used to calling him Will!"

"Oh you did, did you?" I tease Finn.

"Well, when Will told me everything, he gave me Jason and Dana's numbers and told me to call them. He thought we might need someone to talk to after he dropped that bomb on us. Jason and I got talking and hit it off. He's becoming a pretty great friend." Finn smiles and my heart flutters. I didn't realize until now how much I missed that smile.

"I can't believe you!" I say to Claire, giving her a huge hug. "How did you pull this off?"

"It wasn't that hard. You have been impossible about remembering your appointments so I knew I could tell you that you had one today and you'd just go along," she says beaming.

"I look awful! Had I known I was coming to my bridal shower I would have worn something else!" I'm dressed for ease of taking my clothes off since I thought I was headed to my fitting.

"I've got that covered!" Caroline says. She takes me by the arm and leads me upstairs to her room. Laid out on her bed are three new dresses, all so perfectly me.

"Where did these come from?" I pick up one of the dresses, a blue and white polka dot with a flared skirt.

"Claire brought them over yesterday. She knew you wouldn't be dressed for the shower so she wanted you to have something to change into," Caroline tells me. "Now pick one of those darlin' dresses and get downstairs! You've got gifts to open…most of which I'm sure will embarrass the crap out of you. I know my gift to you will!"

Caroline laughs in that adorable laugh of hers and closes the door behind her. I change into a light pink dress with brown trim and a pair of brown wedge sandals. Claire thought of everything. I check myself in the mirror and begin to make my way back out to the garden when Finn meets me at the bottom of the stairs.

"I can't believe you're here! Don't you know that bridal showers are for girls only? Unless of course you're here to make me a chai tea latte!" I say as he takes my hand and helps me off the last step.

"I think the rule is actually that you have to be into guys to be welcomed at a bridal shower," he laughs.

"Oh, well, then I guess you're good then!"

We take a few steps toward the back of the house, my hand still in Finn's. I'm so happy that he's here…Lisa and Dana, too. I was afraid that I wouldn't get to really see them when they came up for the wedding. Things are going to be so busy, and there will be a lot to keep me from just sitting and enjoying their company.

"I'm glad you're ok," Finn says as he stops us. He's serious now. More serious than I think I've ever seen him. "I wish you had told me about everything. It's terrible to go through what you did and not have anyone to talk to. I would have kept your secret."

"I wanted to tell you…so many times. But…it wasn't just my secret to tell. It was Luke and Claire's, and Will and his mom's. You looked out for me with the whole Marcus thing, and I feel bad that I kept things from you when that situation could have hurt you, too. I mean, if Marcus knew I told you anything about him…I don't want to think about what his twisted mind would have done." I take Finn's hand in both of mine. "I hope you can understand."

"I do." Finn lifts my hands with his and kisses them. "We're friends for life, Layla. Things can only get more awesome from here, right?"

"Right. And lucky you…you get to go to both the bridal shower *and* the bachelor party! Now, c'mon. I understand there's a table full of embarrassing gifts awaiting me!"

"I don't know what you're talking about. I got you a blender," Finn says with a smirk.

"No you didn't."

"You're right. Just make sure you've always got some AA batteries on hand!"

"Finn! You didn't!" I say, wide eyed as Finn laughs hysterically.

"I'm just kidding…maybe!"

We teasingly push and hip bump each other all the way to the doors that lead to the garden. With a final bump and kiss to my cheek, Finn opens the door. Once again, I'm greeted by smiling faces of women who are here to enjoy this long awaited celebration.

Everyone I would have expected to be here is here. Gwen and her mother are here along with Eliana and Nana Grace. Even Sarah made it down from Virginia, which is so amazing. We've been growing closer over the months and my heart swells with joy that she's come.

There are some faces that surprise me like Mrs. Whitman from Heyward Prep, a few I recognize from the law firm retreat, and Chris and Tyler's moms who I never really got to know. Their presence here warms my heart and reminds me of the silent support Will and I have had from so many.

I scan their faces and am overwhelmed at the outpouring of love. Every time I turn around I'm being amazed by yet another piece of evidence pointing to the fact that I'm no longer alone in this world, and I can't help but feel like the champion of a fight I wouldn't wish on my worst enemy.

Chapter 24

Will has been a busy bee getting our little love nest ready. Luke suggested he move out into the new house once it was ready. I wasn't jazzed about it but thought that it would build some wonderful wedding night anticipation to have to say goodbye to Will again every night.

With the wedding just three weeks away, I thought I should start packing. It actually didn't occur to me until Will showed me the closet in what will be our bedroom and told me I could start bringing my things over any time I wanted. I won't have any furniture to bring, so really it's just my clothes and books and whatnot.

Packing...again.

It's not the same this time. I'm still nervous, and a little scared. I'm still headed into so much unknown. I'm still packing up one life to move to another. But this time it's totally different. This time it's all about my future, my happiness. Will and I have worked harder and overcome more than two people should have to in order to be together. We couldn't have done any of it without Luke and Claire, and to be honest that is the one thing that makes me sad about leaving this place.

Luke and Claire gave me a life I thought had long disappeared the night I moved in with Gram and Gramps. Any thoughts or dreams I had about my future were shoved aside and ignored like an inconvenience. I couldn't afford to even look at them for fear I might start dreaming again. When friends at school talked about boys or college or careers, I had to turn a deaf ear to the conversation. How could I think about the future when I didn't know how I was going to get through the day?

It wasn't until Gram died that I allowed myself to think about any of that, but only for a moment here or there. I'd look at Gramps, sitting quietly in his favorite chair and wonder what it might be like to find someone who would love me as unconditionally as he loved Gram. I'd let myself dream about finding someone who would grow old with me. Thanks to Will and Luke and Claire, I don't have to wonder anymore.

Now I'm packing to leave the place that breathed life back into this lifeless existence of mine. Even though I've only been with Luke and Claire for three short years, and we'll be living just a few streets over, it seems a little strange to be leaving. This has been the most *home* I've had since before my parents died. It's a bittersweet feeling, I suppose. I'm excited to start my life with Will in our home, but a little sad to be leaving Luke and Claire.

Will has been spending all of his time making sure our house is more than ready by October 25th. He said he wants to come home from our honeymoon and not have a single detail to worry about. Since we opted to wait until next semester to get back to school, he's had more than enough time.

Today, though, he's made me promise to keep my distance as he's shopping for gifts for the guys, and me. I told him I didn't need a wedding gift. Marrying Will is the only gift I need. I told him he's already gone overboard with the remodel of the house and our honeymoon to Ireland and Bali but he doesn't care. The problem is that I have no idea what to get him. I think about options like monogrammed cufflinks because that sounds like one of those fancy gifts rich people give each other as a wedding gift, but shake my head as I realize I just put myself in the "rich people" category. I suppose I am, or will be since I'll be married to Will and he refused to have me sign a prenuptial agreement even though I offered.

Maybe Eliana or Pop or Nana Grace will have an idea. I'll have to wait until Sunday night to ask them. Eliana and Wes are in Hickory until then. Pop said that if Wes was going to be part of their family, he had to understand the family business, which was fine with Wes. He's a lot like Luke and Will. He loves working with his hands like that and from what Claire said about Eliana's texts, he has a real knack for it.

That's it! I know exactly what I'm going to give Will! *Oh, my gosh! It's perfect!* He's not the only one who can remodel and build a gift from the ground up!

"How's the packing coming along?" Luke asks, gently knocking on the doorframe to my room.

"Fine, I guess. There's really not that much to pack. It's mainly just clothes and books," I say as I resume sorting clothes and packing. "I haven't heard an update lately. Any word from Wes on which of Meyer's guys took care of those two jurors?"

Once Meyer died all of his current henchmen disbanded. I imagine they're all just trying to start over somewhere new with a clean slate. Wes had always been able to contact them, but has had a hard time finding a few of them since they all disappeared into thin air. So far none of the guys has admitted doing either job, and the ones Wes has connected with don't know where the others are. Luke even got Agent Croft and his team involved. Since jury tampering was shuffled in amongst all the charges against Meyer it wasn't a stretch for them to take on the investigation.

"Nothing yet," Luke tells me.

"It's not right. If we could just find the second juror's body, his family would at least have some closure. Has Wes told the other guys that? Do you think they're covering for whoever did it? I feel so bad for his family. I remember how unsettling every day was when I thought Will was missing and didn't know where he was," I say. "What was his name? I feel awful calling him juror number four all the time."

"His name was Albert Blasi. I'm sure Wes has expressed that our intention is to help the family find some peace. Wes said that the guys know he wouldn't be looking for whoever did it to get him in trouble. He'll keep looking. You know how relentless Wes is," Luke says with a small smile. "And Agent Croft said his best agent is leading the team on this. Agent Lassiter is apparently the best of the best."

"Well, that's good. Oh, hey…I need your help with something. Do you know who Will used to remodel the house?" I ask excitedly as I think about the plans brewing in my mind.

"Yeah…the same designer who helped with the basement, and a contractor friend of ours. Why?"

"Do you think they can give me a blueprint for a project by the end of the week?"

"What's going on, Layla?" Luke asks curiously.

"I have an idea for Will's wedding gift, but I'm going to need your help while we're gone. Can you help me? Please?" I won't be able to pull this off without Luke's help.

"Of course. I'll get you their numbers," he says.

"Thank you so much! I'll fill you in after I've spoken with them. I have to make sure they can do it first. Oh, it's going to be so great!" I'm giddy with excitement as I consider my plan. Will is going to flip and I'll finally get to be on the giving end of a ridiculously over-the-top gift!

"You have ten times as many clothes as when you first got here…thanks to my wife no doubt!" Luke chuckles. He moves a box from the bed to the floor and sits in its place. "Are you…are you sure you're ready for this, Layla?" Luke asks. He looks nervous and a little sad.

"Why would you ask me that?" I ask. I know Luke isn't questioning if marrying Will is the right thing, but it's the first time he's raised a question like this.

"Well, you two are still really young and there's no reason to rush into anything," he says softly. I look in his eyes and see that his questioning is not about my age or how long Will and I have been together. It's about letting me go.

I've seen this look in Claire's eyes several times over the last few months. With every wedding-related appointment or conversation she's become a little emotional. She's given me another letter she wrote to Penny, and one she wrote to me. Because of her direct involvement in the wedding planning, I think Claire has had a little more time to ease into the idea of me leaving. Luke has not been eased into anything and I think he's just realizing it now.

I sit next to him on the bed and take his hand in mine. "I'm going to miss you, too."

"Thank you for not letting us send you to that stupid boarding school." Luke wraps his arms around me and I hear the sniffing of him trying not to cry. "When I think of what I would have missed out on…"

"Oh, yeah…it's been a grand time of being forced out of your job and moving out of state to protect me, faking deaths, getting kidnapped, hiring personal security, and defending my fiancé's crazy ex-girlfriend for killing his father. Good times," I say with a little laugh just to keep myself from crying, too.

Luke looks at me and smiles while trying to hold back his tears. "I don't regret a single moment of it. Layla…losing Penny was the worst thing we've ever experienced. When…when you lose a child like that, well, there comes a point when you realize that all the things you were looking forward to are never going to happen. We never helped her learn how to ride a bike, or taught her how to tie her shoes. We never taught her how to read, or even got to potty train her. I never got to yell at her to get off the phone or turn her lights out and go to bed, or kick a boy out when it he had stayed his welcome. There were no slumber parties or science fair projects. There would be no more family meals or the elation of watching her open up Christmas gifts again.

"But then you came to us and…you changed everything. You brought back so much of what we thought was lost forever. And now I'm going to get to walk my daughter down the aisle." Luke can't hold back the tears anymore and they begin to stream down his cheek. "If you had let us ship you off to that boarding school I would never have known this kind of joy.

You are my daughter, Layla, and I would relive every second of these last three years.

"I know you're going to literally be around the corner, but...I'm having to let you go. I'm going to walk you down that aisle and put your hand into Will's and he's going to be responsible for protecting you from that point on. I don't know if I'm capable of letting go again."

I reach up and wipe the tears staining Luke's face. "I've lived the last three years experiencing moments I never thought I'd have. Some of them were because I believed Gram when she told me I wasn't worthy of them, others because I didn't have a dad or a mom to share them with me. This is one of those moments. Here I am, sitting with my dad as he tells me how hard it's going to be to let go of me on my wedding day. Who says we have to let go, though? Why do we have to walk away from each other just because I'm getting married? Yes, Will is going to be my husband and I trust him to take care of me, but...why can't we all just keep taking care of each other? So let's not act like the moment I meet Will at the altar that the life you, Claire and I have as a family is somehow over. Let's savor it as the moment our family gets bigger, because all I know is that the more of us there are, the stronger we become."

I sit there for I don't know how long, being held by my father in his warm and protective embrace. I wonder how long he's been sitting on this, shoving these feelings down. I imagine as a parent there comes that moment when you realize your baby isn't a baby anymore. There are probably lots of these moments actually. The first time you let go of the bike and they ride on their own. The first time you watch her pull out of the driveway in the car alone. The days you watch her walk across the stage at her high school and college graduations. And, of course, the day you walk her down the aisle to the new man in her life. Luke and Claire have only gotten to have one of these big moments with me so far, and now they're getting ready to have a second in three weeks' time.

Perhaps it seems a bit cruel or unfair that they haven't gotten to enjoy more of those moments with me before I get married. Or…maybe…knowing Luke and Claire as I do, they're just grateful that they had any moments to share with me in the first place. I know that's how I feel. I'm grateful for these last three years, however insanely rollercoaster-like they were. I'm grateful because it was during this time that I was able to relinquish the guilt and sorrow and finally be held in loving, caring arms. I was able to lay down the weakness I had accepted for myself and take up a suit of armor made strong through the love of Luke and Claire and Will.

As awful as the last eight years of my life was at times, I know that I am better and stronger for it. We're all stronger than we were three years ago…and I wouldn't change a single thing that made it that way.

"Well," Luke says as he finds a way to release his hold on me. "I suppose I should let you get back to packing." He stands and pats my shoulder before moving toward the door.

"You know, Dad…maybe I could leave my winter and spring clothes here. I mean it's not like I'm going to need them tomorrow or anything. I'll just come back and sort through all that stuff later. Do you think that'd be ok?" I smile.

Luke sighs and smiles back at me. "Yeah, that'd be great."

Chapter 25

It's going to be a chillier weekend than I thought it would be and I feel badly for Gwen and Caroline in their short, strapless bridesmaid dresses. I opted to put them in the same dress even though they both looked stunning in all of the dresses they tried on. This one though…this one just spoke to me. It's the perfect shade of pale yellow. It's gathered in the bust and the chiffon layered skirt is so romantic…and looks glorious next to the grey suits Chris and Tyler are wearing. Putting them in the same dress also seemed like a more traditional move for the traditional bells and whistles wedding Will is giving me.

The rehearsal and rehearsal dinner are tonight and I'm nervous as Will and I park the car and walk toward Lingle Chapel. It all seems so surreal.

"Are you ok?" Will asks as he takes my hand.

"I'm just holding my breath, that's all," I tell him. "We've had so many setbacks…I think I'll believe this is really happening when we walk back down the aisle together."

We approach the doors to the chapel and Will takes both my hands in his. "Believe it, babe. This is it. This is the moment we've been waiting for. Tomorrow you'll wake up as Layla Weston, but go to bed as Layla Meyer."

I shake my head and sigh. "I'm so happy. I want you to know just how truly happy I am."

"We've worked hard for this, Layla. Climbed mountains and fought dragons. And we won. Nothing is going to keep me from marrying you tomorrow. Nothing." Will leans down and kisses me, holding me to his lips by the nape of my neck. It's warm and smooth and my stomach flips as I realize that after today, we'll have no reason to stop. An electric current of excitement shoots through me and causes both Will and I to take a half step back and gasp.

"You felt that?" I ask, biting my lip.

"I did. What was that?" Will's eyes are big and excited.

"That, I guess, was my body responding to the realization that tomorrow…um…well, that tomorrow night is…you know…the night." I blush with slight embarrassment and Will lifts my chin so our eyes meet.

"Are you nervous?" he asks sweetly.

"I have moments," I tell him in the biggest understatement ever.

"If it's any consolation, I'm nervous, too," he says.

"Then I guess we'll be nervous together, which, I think, will make me a lot less nervous," I giggle.

"C'mon…let's go practice for our official wedding," he says taking my hand and opening the door to the chapel.

We're greeted with cheers from our friends and chastisement from our mothers about being late. Before I can even give Will a quick kiss Claire scurries me, Gwen, Caroline, and Luke to the back of the church where we are instructed to wait in the foyer. Claire is a little tense right now. I've never seen her like this, but…her daughter has never gotten married before. It's a good thing I'm going with the flow. I can imagine the clashing between a mom like Claire and bride who is totally involved with all the details of her wedding.

Linda, the wedding director, is a thin woman with shoulder-length brown hair and bangs. She's smiling from ear to ear and it's clear that she loves her job. She situates all of us in order that we'll walk down the aisle. Gwen will go first, followed by Caroline.

"Then we'll close the doors. That way when it's time for you to walk, Jimmy and I will open the doors and it'll be the grandest of entrances!" Linda says. The pianist starts to play and Linda nods to Gwen to start walking. "Not too slow, but not too fast either, dear. Ok, now when you see her get to that pew riiiiiiight there, that's when you go," she says nudging Caroline to start walking.

"How ya holding up, Dad," I say to Luke as he clutches the hand of my arm that is hooked in his.

"I'm a total mess, but it's great," he smiles.

"Mom seems to be doing pretty well." Linda ushers us and centers us behind the doors. She's closed them and seems to be waiting for the first song to finish and the second one to start.

"That's because she's preoccupied with all the wedding planning and coordinating. Come Sunday morning she's going to be a mess, too," he laughs.

"I hope so. It's kind of nice being someone to be missed," I tell him.

The doors open and Luke and I stand there, waiting for just a moment as Linda has instructed. When she cues us, we begin to walk slowly down the aisle to Canon in D. I'm holding this paper plate with ribbons and bows from my bridal shower that Nana Grace made. Apparently it's some kind of tradition to use this adorably sloppy makeshift bouquet at the rehearsal. There are huge bows and long ribbons hanging off of this flimsy plate, and I'm holding a stem of ribbons, trying to keep it up. I stare at it for a few seconds and smile. I love everything about it and think that maybe I'll have this bouquet preserved rather than the one I'm carrying tomorrow.

Everyone is standing at the front of the chapel watching us as we pace ourselves, pew by pew, to the music. "Not too slow, but not too fast", I hear Linda shouting in a whispered voice. Claire is smiling with adoration, looking on as Luke walks his daughter, step by step, down the aisle. And even though this is just the rehearsal, she's beginning to tear up, as are Gwen and Caroline.

I'm glad we chose to have the wedding in the smaller of the sanctuaries. Our official guest list is barely going to fill four or five pews, but since Luke made an unofficial open invitation to the ceremony to the community, we may see 20 or so more romantics who just love a good wedding and happy ending to a story like Will's and mine. It would also take me twice as long to walk the path to Will in the other sanctuary. I watch him standing there next to Pastor Bishop, his hands folded in front of him. He's smiling and I feel a rush of warmth come over me. When Luke and I finally reach Will and the pastor, I feel Luke's grip on me tighten. I squeeze his hand back and smile at him softly, telling him how much I love him.

"This is the part where I ask who gives this woman to be married to this man," Pastor Bishop says to Luke. "Most fathers say *her mother and I do*."

We never talked about it and I didn't know the pastor would ask this, so I don't know what Luke is going to say. He and Claire are my father and mother now, so I'm totally great with him taking the pastor's suggestion.

"So I'll start again, and you can answer however you're going to answer." Pastor Bishop clears his throat and begins again. "Who gives this woman to be married to this man?"

"Her parents do," Luke says.

Tears immediately fill my eyes. I look at Luke and he smiles, keeping his own tears at bay. He's made sure that, in his own special way, my parents are a part of this day. He's not kept them away, pretended that they don't exist. He's acknowledging that I have *four* parents who are giving their blessing to my future with Will. I can feel them with me. Even just in the sentiment of it, they're here, and marrying Will somehow feels absolutely complete.

"Oh, Dad," I say hugging him. "Thank you."

Luke just smiles, afraid he'll cry if he tries to speak. He shakes Will's hand and then joins my hand with his before sitting with Claire.

"You ok?" Will asks, squeezing my hand.

"I'm perfect."

Just as Pastor Bishop is about to begin the run through of what he's going to say during the ceremony, his cell phone rings, surprising all of us because the ring tone is the sound of a baby crying.

"Oh my goodness! I'm so sorry. My wife is *very* pregnant and could go into labor any day now. This is her ring tone. She knows I'm here so it must be important. Excuse me for just one minute." Slightly embarrassed, Pastor Bishop excuses himself to the back of the stage area.

"You're sure you don't want to write our own vows?" Will asks.

"We already did that in the gardens, and I loved that it was totally private. I'm completely happy with the very traditional wedding we have planned for tomorrow. How lucky could one girl be? I got to have two weddings!" I giggle and Will kisses my cheek. "Are you good with not writing our own vows?"

"I'm great. I agree. We had our intimate garden wedding months ago. We're getting the best of both worlds. And in the end, really, all that matters is that you're my wife."

"I'm so sorry about that. Um...my wife is in labor. She's having contractions and her sister is taking her to the hospital. Soooo...Yeah, we're going to need to speed this up." Pastor Bishop looks a little flushed and nervous.

"Is this your first baby?" I ask.

"Yeah...can you tell?" he says.

"It's going to be great! Just give us the Reader's Digest version and I'm sure we can figure out the rest tomorrow," I tell him.

"Ok. Awesome." He takes a deep breath, trying to calm himself and get his bearings "So, I'll say something super spiritual about marriage, talk about how I've known Will forever, and say something sweet and kind about how you're just the best thing that ever happened to him. Then I'll ask if you take each other, you'll both say I do, you'll repeat your vows after me, I'll ask for the rings, with this ring I thee wed, what God has joined together let no man separate, pronounce you husband and wife, and then you can kiss your bride. Any questions?"

"None. Go have a baby," Will tells him laughing, amazed at the precision and speed with which Pastor Bishop was able to give us the run-down of the ceremony.

With that, Pastor Bishop is rushing down the aisle in a blur of nervous excitement.

"That is so going to be you one day," I smirk and nudge Will.

"Oh, we're talking about kids now?" he asks smiling and nudging me back. "I thought you weren't ready to talk about that yet."

"I wasn't then, and I'm not saying let's name them now. I'm just saying that, in about five years, you'll be the one rushing nervously from wherever you are to get to me."

"I won't be rushing anywhere because when you're *that* pregnant I won't let you out of my site. I'm not going to miss a second of that experience with you."

"If you two are done making your birth plan, can we please go eat? I'm starving!" Tyler chuckles as he comes between Will and me, ushering us back down the aisle with his arms draped over our shoulders.

We're having the rehearsal dinner at Luke and Claire's. It seemed silly to go to a restaurant when there are so few people involved in the wedding itself. I wanted to cook because it really just felt like we were having family over, but Claire was firm in her contention that I had to treat it like the special even that it is. So we compromised by having the dinner catered by a personal chef that she knows. Claire brought in extra tables and linens and had the living room transformed into a fall wonderland with rustic centerpieces and cute place card holders made from wedges of thick branches.

"Oh, Mom, it's beautiful," I tell her. "It's overwhelming, really."

"Now aren't you glad I didn't let you cook?" she says pulling me to her side.

"Yes. As usual, you were right." I walk around the tables and see everyone's names written in pretty script on their place card. Name after name echoes in my head and I feel so overjoyed at the family I have gained in three short years.

The chef's staff begins to bring out the first course and we all find our seats. When everyone's plate has been set in front of them in the proper place so as to get the full effect of the presentation of the dish, Luke stands.

Oh no. I'm absolutely about to cry.

"I have to do this tonight because I'm afraid I won't get through it tomorrow. And, I'm not sure I want to share everything that's on my heart right now with more than the special people who are in this room right now." Luke clears his throat and takes a sip of his wine as Claire stands with him. "When Layla came to us three years ago, we were scared and unsure of ourselves in our ability to take on a teenager. We didn't know each other, and the circumstances surrounding the reasons for that were, well, they were less than pleasant. What happened next, though, and what has continued to happen over the last three years, is something pretty remarkable. We grew into a family.

"I remember the first time Layla called me *Uncle Luke*. It was also the first time that she hugged me. And when our arms reached around each other all I could think was how perfectly we fit together, the way family is supposed to," Luke says. I remember that day, too. It was the morning I overheard Luke tell Claire he was just trying to take care of me in a way that would honor my parents.

"Layla became like a daughter to us, and eventually there was no *like* about it," he continues. "Layla is our daughter. And as I prepare to do one of the hardest thing a father can do – put his baby girl's life into the hands of another man – I know that Will is going to love and protect her." Luke starts to get choked up and Claire pats his back before taking over.

"It's no secret what Will and Layla have gone through to be together. It was a very difficult and scary time for all of us, but we couldn't be prouder of how they've both handled themselves. They made difficult choices and never faltered in their quest. So," Claire says as she raises her glass. "…make an extraordinary marriage your quest. Don't settle for less than the best of what each of you has to offer. And enter your marriage knowing that the doors are locked from the outside. You don't quit. You don't give up. You never have before, so there's no reason to ever start."

Luke takes a breath, having fought the emotions and won…for now. "So here's to Will and Layla. May you know all the joy that your life together still has in store for you."

Everyone raises their glasses while I wipe the tears falling down my cheeks. They've done it again. Between Claire's letters and my talk with Luke the other day, they have filled my emotional love bucket up to overflowing.

"I don't know if I even have the vocabulary to express how I'm feeling right now," I say as I stand. "I'm marrying a man I never dreamed could ever be mine, and I'm going to be walked down the aisle by my father…an event that at one time was impossible. I have endured tragedy, and lived under the weight of things that no one should ever live under. I've come out on the other side stronger, and I know that's because of the incredible love I have so undeservingly been given. But I receive it. Oh, my gosh, do I receive it! I would be lost without it. So tomorrow, as I change my name and begin a new life with Will, know that this change, this new life, really started three years ago when two strangers agreed to take me in. Mom, Dad…thank you. You gave me my life back and I will be eternally grateful. I love you."

Luke, Claire, and I all move from our places around the table and find each other in a warm embrace. The kind where arms are moving everywhere, trying to get a better hold on both of the people you're trying to hug. We stand there for a minute, letting the sweet reality of the moment sink in. We are the family we never thought we'd have.

This is real.

This is my life.

This is everything I always wanted.

Chapter 26

The doors open to the chapel and I cling to Luke's arm for dear life. I didn't think I'd be this nervous, but I am, and even more so because it seems that the whole town has accepted Luke's invitation to the ceremony. There are so many people standing that I can't see Gwen or Caroline already in place, or Will. It seems he's just out of sight.

We begin to make our slow, but not too slow, walk down the aisle. Each step calms me, and every time my foot lands in another step I realize that I'm just feet away from having everything I've always wanted. I acknowledge people as I walk by with a small smile. I want them to know how much joy it brings me that they would share this day with us. They all smile back...except for one.

One old woman doesn't smile at all, and as I get closer her whole face becomes clearer and I realize that it's Gram. She looks just as she did most days before she died, wearing a short sleeved, button-down dress, and an apron. She's just staring at me. Then...she's yelling.

"After what you did, you don't deserve this! None of these people would be here if they knew what you did! Will is too good for you! He doesn't really love you!" She yells with the disapproving tone I knew all too well.

"Yes, I do," I call back to her. "And Will loves me! Dad, help me!" I pull on Luke's arm but he doesn't acknowledge me or the yelling that's going on between Gram and me.

"Don't call him that! Your father is dead and you killed him! You don't deserve Luke or Claire as your parents. And you certainly don't deserve to wear your mother's wedding dress!" She points her accusing, boney finger at me and I cower closer to Luke.

I continue to fight back, telling her that I *do* deserve everything I now have. That I've worked hard to forget all the terrible things she made me believe. That for all the years of punishment she gave me, Will is my reward, and Luke and Claire love me like my parents did.

She just keeps yelling. She won't stop. Luke keeps walking like he doesn't see her. He's almost dragging me up to the altar while I'm trying to defend myself against Gram. I keep turning back and trying to combat her, but she *just won't stop.*

When we finally reach the front of the church, Luke takes my hand and puts it in Will's. I can see Gram better now that I'm facing Will. She's relentless in her chanting, continuing to give me the disgusted look she frequently did. I want to, but I can't look away. I run through in my mind all the things I wish I had said to her but was always too afraid to say. Will takes my chin in his hand and turns my face so our eyes meet.

"That's not your life anymore, Layla. She is your past. I am your future. You can let it all go, once and for all. You did it. You became everything she said you never would. You're strong, independent, loved, accepted. You overcame everything she did to you. Every lie. Every manipulation. You threw it to the ground and set it on fire. Stop and listen." Will is calm and soothing and I do as he says.

I close my eyes and listen. Gram is yelling cruel things that used to stab my heart. I feel Will squeeze my hands. As I stop and listen to what Gram is saying I begin to hear Will's voice, too.

"What is the truth, Layla?" he says.

The truth…the truth…the truth is that I had nothing to do with my parents' death. And…if *that* is the truth, then whatever Gram says about it is a lie. I focus on the truth. I focus on all the things Luke, Claire, and Will have told me over the last three years. The way they've made me feel loved, accepted, wanted. *Focus on the truth.*

I'm not responsible for my parents' death.

I deserve love.

I deserve Will.

I deserve Luke and Claire.

I deserve a family.

I chant these things in my head while holding on to Will's hands for dear life. The more I chant the quieter Gram becomes, until she's eventually mute. I turn and look at her. She's still yelling, but there's no volume. I can't hear her anymore. That nagging, sometimes loud voice that has been relentlessly pounding my head with lies is *finally* silent.

I look at Will and beam. He looks at me and, mirroring my expression says, "Now, let's get married."

"Layla? Layla, honey, are you ok?" I hear Claire's voice echoing in my head. Suddenly everything disappears and I'm brought back into reality. "Layla?"

"What…what are you doing?" I ask with a groggy voice that's a little hoarse just from it being morning. I open my eyes and find Claire angled on the bed next to me.

"Your alarm has been going off for ten minutes. You must have been having some dream to sleep through it like that. You've never done that before. What time did you come to bed last night? I told Will he had to be gone before midnight. Bad luck and all," she smiles. It is my wedding day and Claire is a sponge, soaking up all the fun, excitement, nervousness, and joy there is to be had today.

"Yeah…I was having a bad dream, but then it turned good," I tell her. "What time is it?"

"It's 8:30. I'm glad your dream turned good. I'd hate for you to have had a nightmare the night before your wedding. It wasn't about the wedding was it?" Claire says getting up and gathering clothes for me to put on until it's time to get dressed for the wedding.

"Yes, but it's all great now," I say. I don't want to rehash the nastiness of Gram. Just because I had to endure it in my dream doesn't mean Claire should have to deal with it in real life. "What's first on the agenda? I'm the bride. Just tell me where to go and what to do. I'm putty in your hands."

"I'm so glad to hear you say that! Gwen and Caroline should be here in about an hour. The photographer will be here shortly after that. The hair stylist and make-up artist will be here at noon. We're having lunch brought in around one. You *have* to eat before the wedding. The car will be here at 3:30 to take us to the church where the florist will meet us. And then," she sighs. "And then you're getting married at 4:00." Tears well up in Claire's eyes and begin to flow before she has a chance to stop them.

"Mom...c'mon...please don't cry. This is going to be the best day ever because of you," I tell her as I wipe her tears with my blanket.

"I'm not sad, Layla. I'm so incredibly happy for you...for all of us. Luke and I woke up today and are going to do something we never thought we would. Not only do we have a daughter again, but by 5:00 tonight we're going to have a son, too. Life can be hard, but sometimes we don't give life enough credit. Sometimes...sometimes life treats you *so* good." Claire squeezes my hand, letting pure joy ooze from her. "Now...let's get going. Get in the shower. The hair stylist said not to wash your hair though. Just toss it in one of those cute, messy buns you like to do and she'll take it from there."

Claire stands up and begins to leave. "Mom," I call to her and she turns around as she reaches the door. "Thank you for everything. I meant what I said. Today wouldn't be as amazing as it's going to be if it weren't for you."

Claire just smiles sweetly at me and leaves me to begin preparing for my wedding. *My wedding. Oh, my gosh.* I'm actually marrying Will today. I grab my phone, turn it on, and brush my teeth while I wait for it to boot up. As soon as it's up I hear the alert tone that I set for Will. When I check it there is a message from him.

Will Meyer: Good morning, sweetheart. I have the privilege of becoming your husband today. I am the luckiest guy on the planet. See you at the altar.

My heart pounds and does flips and flutters inside my chest like I've never felt before. I look at the ring on my hand that used to belong to Claire's grandmother and feel honored that she would allow it to be mine. I hold my right hand out and look at the ring that used to be Nana Grace's...the first ring Will gave me as a promise that today would become a reality. And as I stare at these rings, I think that *I'm* the lucky one.

Layla Weston: Good morning! Can't wait to say I do. See you at the altar. Don't be late!

I try not to take too long in the shower but I can't help it. I know that as soon as I step foot downstairs the whirlwind of my wedding day is going to begin. I'm not trying to delay it. I'm just trying to enjoy these moments of blissful anticipation of all that is to come. Eventually I let go of the solitude and dress in the outfit Claire has laid out for me. She said to be sure to wear a button-down shirt or they'll end up cutting me out of my shirt when my hair is done.

My foot touches down at the bottom of the stairs and just as I predicted, the wedding day whirlwind begins.

"Layla! Oh, my gosh! It's today! Can you believe it?" Caroline squeals, throwing her arms around me.

"Move over, Caroline!" Gwen demands. "Just wait until you see the jewelry you're going to wear! My mother got her guy at Tiffany's to lend it to you...just like a movie star!" Both of their arms are around me at the same time and I couldn't be happier.

They shuffle me to the dining room where Eliana and Nana Grace are waiting. More arms are thrown around me and more tears are shed before I've had a chance to say anything. When things finally calm down, and Claire has us all gathered in the dining room, I take one, very deep, cleansing breath and smile.

"Alright girls, now I want to be sure that everyone eats. I know the excitement can get to all of us, but we have to make sure no one faints up there today," Claire says as she hands us each a plate. She has set out a beautiful spread of fruit and yogurt, and bagels and about four different kinds of cream cheese from Panera. There's coffee and tea and orange juice, too. As usual, Claire has thought of everything.

"I have something I'd like to say," Eliana begins as we find our seats at the dining room table. "Layla, I want you to know just how happy I am for you and William. I feared he would never find love, but yet here you are. You are a bright and beautiful young woman and I am so excited to watch you two build your life together. And, even though we've gotten to know each other quite a bit over these last two years, I'm looking forward to getting to know you as my *daughter-in-law*."

"Thank you, Eliana," I say, realizing I've got tears welling up in my eyes. "It's hard to believe this day is finally here. Things between my mother and my grandmother were, well, let's just say they weren't good." Claire raises her eyebrows in as if to say *that's the understatement of the century*. She would know, too, just how difficult Gram made life for her sons' wives. "I want you to know that I'm committed to having a wonderful relationship with you. I don't subscribe to the belief that wives can't get along with their mothers-in-law. It's been a long, very rough road to this day. I truly am the luckiest girl ever. I've said I have four parents who love me with all their hearts, but today I can change that number to five."

"Alright, y'all, let's get all the crying done now because we've got to have time to get all the puffiness down before we have our make-up done,"

Caroline says, dabbing her eyes with a napkin. "I can't be lookin' like a raccoon now!"

We all laugh and take that as our cue to let the joy flow, but not the tears. It's going to be an unbelievable day and I'm now so anxious to get it all started.

"So, *Mrs. Meyer*," Gwen says to me, drawing out the Mrs. part. "I hear you're a little nervous about tonight." The girls have both already had their hair done and now Caroline is sitting between Gwen and me as she gets her make-up done and the hairstylist works her magic on me.

"I...uh...Caroline!" I say completely flustered.

"What? We were just talking and...we're girls, what do you want!" she says in her defense.

"C'mon, Layla. It's just the make-up and hair girls and us. You won't say anything, will you girls?" Gwen says in her sweetly sardonic way.

"Honey, please! You wouldn't believe some of the things I hear. A young bride's nervousness about her wedding night is G-rated compared to the other things I've got locked away up here," Alexa, the hairstylist, says tapping on the side of her head.

"My lips are sealed. No worries, darlin'" Gina the make-up girl echoes.

"See...it's all good," Gwen says reaching over and patting my leg.

"You two," I say with a heavy sigh. "Yeah, I guess I'm a bit nervous, but Will and I had a little talk and I feel better about it. He's nervous, too, so we decided that we'd just be nervous together."

"So...do you have something totally hot to wear tonight?" Gwen asks.

"I am *not* discussing the details of my wedding night with you two or anyone for that matter! Now can we please just move on to another topic?" If I we keep talking about this I'm going to have to think about it and thinking about it is what makes me really nervous.

"Leave the poor girl alone, Gwen! Yes, let's talk about something else. What did you decide on for Will's wedding gift?" Caroline asks saving me from the sexy Spanish Inquisition Gwen was about to unleash on me.

"Oh, it's going to be so great! I'm having part of the pool house remodeled. Do *not* tell Will! You can ask Luke all about it when we're gone because he's going to oversee the project. All I can tell you is that Will is going to love it!" Yes, this is much better conversation to get me in a better, less frazzled state of mind before my wedding.

"Ok…you're all done," Alexa says. "You ready to see it?"

I take a deep breath. I have no idea what she has done, except that my hair is pulled back. Claire showed Alexa my dress and the two of them decided on a style they thought would work best. I had one trial run, but didn't want to see it. I wanted to be surprised today. "Yes, I'm ready."

I stand up and Alexa and Caroline turn my chair around to the three-way mirror Alexa brought with her. She and Gina have turned the living room into a full on salon. I close my eyes and Caroline helps me sit again.

"Don't look yet," Caroline says. "Claire! Eliana! Her hair is done! Keep your eyes closed," she says to me. I hear Claire and Eliana come into the room and the breathless *oh my goodness* of both of them. "Ok…ready?"

"Ready."

"Open your eyes, darlin'," Alexa instructs.

My eyes are down when I open them. I lift them slowly, taking myself in from the chest up. I reach my neck and see it is bare. I'm in awe when I finally allow myself to take in the whole picture. I turn my head to see the magic that Alexa has worked. My bangs are softly swept to my right. She's braided my hair loosely along the back of my head from my left ear to my right, and woven an intricate braided bun just behind my right ear. There's a large braid at the center, with smaller, tiny braids winding around it, and there are sparkling silver and gemmed pieces scattered across the bun.

"She's going to put small daisies in it, too," Claire says. My mother wore a crown of daisies on her wedding day and Claire knows that this will make the whole thing absolutely perfect. Alexa puts the flowers in and I know I'm going to cry. "What do you think?"

"I think it's everything I dreamed it would be." I'm trying not to cry, but the perfection of this day is already so overwhelmingly wonderful. "Thank you." I stand and give Alexa and hug, and then Claire and Eliana. I don't have the words to express at this moment so I just smile and say everything I can with my eyes.

"Dry those eyes! It's time for your make-up!" Gina says.

I do as she says and have a seat at her station. It doesn't take her long to make me look like a fresher, brighter version of myself, and when I see my hair and make-up all done together I think I'm going to cry again. I hold it together and take several deep breaths.

The photographer has been taking pictures since she got here...pictures I'd never think of taking. But, I'm glad she's here now because there are shots of Gwen and Caroline and me just talking and lots while we're having our hair and make-up done. There are shots of Claire and Eliana getting dolled up, too. I love the everydayness of the pictures she's taking and don't think I'll be able to whittle down the number of prints I have made from these moments alone.

Alexa and Gina go ahead to the church while Claire and the girls manage to get me into my dress without messing up my hair or make-up. When I'm all buttoned up and my shoes have been securely fastened to my feet, I stand in front of Claire's full-length mirror and stare.

I stare at this girl standing in front of me. She's wearing my mother's wedding dress and white daisies in her hair. Her hazel eyes are bright and full of hope, and her smile is bigger than any I've ever seen her wear. This girl, so opposite of the one I stared at the day of Gramps' funeral, is a woman now. A woman ready to begin a new chapter in her life. A woman who knows that what lies before her is a life filled with love and peace and the knowledge that she is more than she ever thought she could be. A life with the one person who makes her feel like the world would be a sad place without her in it.

I sigh and smile and receive all the goodness that is being given to me because today is the day I put all the pain behind me. The cracks in my heart have been filled and the life waiting for me is better than anything I could have dreamed of for myself.

Claire, Eliana and the girls help me get into the limo ever so gingerly. The soft fabric of my mother's wedding dress is delicate and anything happening to it is the only thing that could ruin this day.

When we arrive at the church everyone gets out of the car first so they can help me out just as carefully as they helped me in. We're ushered into the vestibule of the church where only Luke is standing facing the closed doors to the chapel. As I stand there, waiting for Luke to turn around, the photographer positions herself to get shots of the first moments the father of the bride sees his little girl all dressed in white. When she cues him, he turns around and immediately becomes overwhelmed.

"Hi, Dad. How do I look?" I say to him, smiling and so full of joy.

"You look...you look just like your mother. So beautiful." Luke takes my hands in his. "They would be so happy and proud of you today."

"Thank you...for everything." I lean in and kiss Luke on the cheek. "I'd give you a hug, but I'm under strict orders not to do anything to muss my dress, hair, or make-up," I chuckle.

"It's ok...there will be plenty of time for that at the reception after the ceremony and after the formal pictures are taken. Are you ready for this?" Luke hands me the bouquet the florist just gave him to give me.

"I am *so* ready for this," I tell him with a huge smile.

Luke holds out his arm and I hook mine through it. Settling ourselves to the side of the foyer where no one can see us, Linda opens the doors for

Chris and Tyler who sneak a kiss on my cheek before they escort Claire and Eliana to their seats and then take their places with Will at the front of the chapel. Once Gwen and Caroline have both begun their walk down the aisle, Linda closes the doors and Luke and I get into position.

The music stops and I begin to anticipate Canon in D's first notes. As the piano starts to play, Linda and her assistant Jimmy open both the doors to the chapel and I'm blown away. This part of my dream-turned-nightmare was a premonition. The chapel is packed with people. Luke's invitation for the town to celebrate the ceremony with us was apparently well received. I'm stunned at the amount of support the town is pouring on us and I'm overjoyed for Will. This is his home and what a solid show of understanding from the people.

We walk the aisle at a pace I hope Linda finds satisfactory and soon I'm passing pews filled with friends and family. We only invited about 100 people, 90 of them from Will's side, but every single one of them came.

Will and I lock eyes and that's when I begin to get emotional. He's stunningly handsome in his grey suit and grey tie tucked under his vest. He's wiping tears away as he watches me and I only hope that the photographer is capturing these moments.

"Who gives this woman to be married to this man?" Pastor Bishop asks Luke.

"Her parents do," Luke replies. It has just the same effect on me today as it did last night when Luke first uttered the words.

Pastor Bishop smiles and nods once, indicating that it's time for Luke to actually give me to Will. Luke kisses my cheek sweetly and smiles softly as he releases my hand. He shakes Will's hand and gently places mine in Will's before sitting next to Claire who is already crying.

Will and I step forward and listen to Pastor Bishop say *something spiritual about marriage* as he put it last night. I hand my flowers to Caroline and turn to face Will. The pastor begins a question with "Layla, do you…" and then I get so lost in Will's eyes that I'm only moderately paying attention to what he's saying. Will was right. This really is it. This is the moment we've been waiting for. The dragon has been slayed and we're embarking on our Happily Ever After.

I refocus on what Pastor Bishop is saying when I begin to hear words like better and worse, richer and poorer, sickness and health. My ears perk up, though, when I hear Pastor Bishop say "for as long as you both live." There it is. The words that hold every commitment I'm making to Will.

Will and I are forever and there's nothing else I can say except "I do."

Chapter 27

It didn't take too much convincing for Will to agree that we should have our reception someplace nice, but not super fancy. So, we're having the reception at Campania, the Italian restaurant Will took me to on our Day of Nothing. It's not an over the top elegant restaurant. In fact, it's pretty modest and a little rustic with its exposed brick walls. But, being a family owned, neighborhood restaurant, it kind of represents everything that I love about Davidson. The owners were so wonderful and accommodating to close the restaurant for our private party on a Saturday night that Luke was sure to make it worth their while.

We enter the restaurant and cheers erupt before I can get everyone into focus. Pop and Nana Grace are clapping and Pop puts his fingers in his mouth and whistles louder than I've ever heard someone whistle before. Jason and Lisa, Finn, and Dana are standing by the bar, smiles spread wide across their faces. I'm thrilled beyond words that they're all here, but that joy multiplies when I see Sarah and Austin.

She meant it when she said she didn't believe in *step*families or in-laws. For the months since we met her and Cheryl in Virginia Beach, we have been in almost constant contact. She's kept me up to date on her growing belly, which is looking so adorable on her now that she's close to six months pregnant, and her presence at my bridal shower made the day even more special. She and Will have really grown close. Having eased into a relationship with a long-lost sibling and seeing it developing wonderfully, I think Will is feeling much better prepared for when he meets Erin and Michael next month.

"Hey darlin'! You look beautiful," Sarah says to me as she wraps her arms around me. "Oh, my gosh! Look at that! I'm already so big I can't even get right up on you to give you a real hug!"

"Oh, stop! You look absolutely adorable! How is he doing?" I give her belly a little rub. "Have you decided on a name yet?"

"We're gonna name him Noah. Noah James," Austin answers as he hugs me.

"That's a great name," Will says. "I actually got Layla to talk about kids last night. Can you believe it?"

"I knew she'd come around, but you better give her time, sugar!" Sarah's sweet voice lingers in the air like wisps of cotton candy. "Ok, c'mon Austin, let's go over to the bar. You're drinkin' for two." With a laugh, and little swat to her behind, Austin follows Sarah through the maze of tables and into the crowd.

We dutifully make our way around to everyone. I thank Gwen and Caroline's parents for coming, as well as Chris and Tyler's. There was a time I didn't know how Chris and Tyler's dads were going to respond to the truth about Will's disappearance and death. I had once thought they were Meyer clones, legal sharks making prey of any needy person who had the misfortune of swimming into their open waters, but I have been so pleased to see that I was wrong about them. They've been nothing but kind and warm and completely understanding, so much so that they've offered Luke the senior partner position at the firm. This would change the name of the firm to Weston, Fincher, and Marks. I told Luke he should take it, but he hasn't decided yet, mumbling something about needing to get his daughter married off first before he could think of anything else.

Everything about the night is perfect. We did a fixed menu of four options for dinner: a meatless pasta dish, lasagna, and the two dishes Will and I had on our first date here, chicken piccata and veal saltimbocca. The bar is open for everyone but the bride and groom, and Will found an amazing local band to play so we have live music all night.

When we've made our rounds and actually had a chance to eat, Will takes me by the hand and leads me to the dance floor. The lead singer of the band announces that it's time for the bride and groom's first dance and I feel my stomach flutter with excitement. Will takes me in his arms as the band begins to play *To Get Me to You*. Will played it for me during country week of our music lessons and I just knew it had to be our first dance.

And I don't regret the rain/Or the nights I felt the pain
Or the tears I had to cry some of those times along the way
Every road I had to take/Every time my heart would break
It was just something that I had to get through
To get me to you

"We did it, Mrs. Meyer," Will says as we begin to sway.

"Yes, we did. It's like a dream, Will. I can't believe it," I tell him.

"Believe it, babe, because it only gets better from here. You are my *wife*," he says, drawing me closer.

"And you are my *husband*."

"Always and forever," he says. "You look so beautiful. The seamstress did an amazing job with the dress. It looks like it was made for you."

"Thank you. Yeah, I was amazed, too. It means so much to me that I got to wear my mom's dress. And did you see my hair, see the flowers? Mom wore a crown of daisies," I tell him.

"It's perfect, Layla. Everything about today is just perfect." Will pulls me closer as we move and sway around the dance floor. Sometimes he sings along with the song to me. It's the most magical moment of my life.

The night is filled with all the greatness a wedding reception is supposed to have. The music is loud and the dancing doesn't stop. I even dance with Wes who tells me that he's already asked Will's permission and plans on proposing to Eliana later tonight. I'm so happy for them both and thrilled that Wes will officially become part of my family.

241

Will and I dance with our friends, I throw the bouquet the florist made for the toss, and Will has a grand time taking the garter off my leg. Tyler catches the garter and, as only fate could do, his date Kelly catches the bouquet. I'm happy to see him giving someone a real chance. I only got to chat with her for a few minutes, but she seems really great. She's really pretty with strawberry blonde hair and blue eyes, and she's just as brilliant and funny as she is beautiful. I'm sure we'll have them over for dinner when we're back from Bali and settling into our life as the *new* Meyers.

"Babe, we've got to go," Will whispers in my ear as I'm talking with Mrs. Whitman.

"Really? It seems so early," I say.

"We have a flight to catch and we both need to change," he says

"Congratulations, Will!" Mrs. Whitman cheers, giving Will a hug.

"Thank you, Mrs. Whitman. Thanks so much for coming. I'm afraid I have to steal my wife away from you. We've got a honeymoon to get to," he tells her.

"Of course, of course! I'm so happy for you both!" she beams.

We begin to move toward the back door where our parents and friends are waiting to say goodbye. We stand at the top of the few steps in front of the door and Will puts his arm around my waist as he addresses the crowd.

"Thank you all so much for celebrating with us. Most of you are aware the journey Layla and I have been on to get to this place, which makes the fact that I can now officially call her my wife even more special. I sound like a broken record but, really, I am the luckiest man alive. I get two whole weeks alone with my wife in the green pastures of Ireland and the sandy beaches of Bali. If you need us, well, you're kinda screwed because we will be completely unreachable!" Everyone laughs and Will pulls me closer. "You ready?" he asks.

"More than ready," I say with a huge smile. "Thank you so much, everyone, for coming. This day has been more than I could have ever imagined."

As we start to leave the band begins to play Marvin Gaye's *Let's Get it On* and I see Tyler and Caroline standing next to the guitar player pretending to dance seductively to the music. I feel the blood rush to my face and I swear to myself to kill Caroline when we get home. Will laughs, making me laugh, reminding myself just how much I love Caroline and Tyler, and how much they love me. This little stunt of theirs actually puts me at ease and I grab Will and kiss him. The crowd cheers and Will and I are out the door, followed by more cheering. We turn, wave goodbye, hug and kiss our parents, and climb into the limo.

"So..." Will says, taking my hand in his. "We did it."

"We sure did," I say with a mixture of excitement for all that lies ahead, and nervousness for tonight.

"I love you so much, Layla." Will leans into me and kisses me sweetly.

"I love you, too." I sigh, letting the nervousness slip away and the excitement take over. "So what's the plan? I mean I know we're leaving for two *amazing* weeks together, but I don't know any of the details."

"We'll get changed and go straight to the airport. Our bags are already in the back of the car. Claire said she laid out something for you to wear," he tells me, all the while stroking my arm tenderly.

"Well...it sounds like everything's been taken care of. I really am so excited. I can't believe you're taking me to Ireland. We've been married for four hours and you're already making my dreams come true," I sigh leaning into Will, *my husband*.

"Get used to it, because I'm going to spend the next 70 years making sure every dream you've ever had, and the ones you didn't even know you had, comes true," he says, brushing my cheek with the back of his hand.

"*You* are all the dream-come-true I need." Will kisses me and I kiss him back in a new way. It's like my body knows I'm kissing my husband and is responding differently. It's an indescribable feeling of warmth that is taking over. Thank God we arrive at Luke and Claire's because that kiss had the potential to turn into something much more. Something neither Will nor I wanted it to turn into in the back seat of a limousine.

"Well, Mrs. Meyer, shall we change and get to the honeymooning?" Will says as we enter the house. He takes my hand and we walk upstairs to my room…my old room. I'm glad he's there because my dress is a bit much to navigate up the stairs.

Claire has laid out a pair of dark jeans, a green button down shirt, and a pair of brown boots. The perfect fall outfit for travelling. I turn and face Will and the nervousness begins to creep back in.

"Um…can you, uh…help me with the buttons?" I ask breathlessly. If there were any other way to get out of this dress I would do it.

"Of course," he answers softly.

I turn around and Will begins to undo each button. One by one, each one is released. His hands brush against my skin and goose bumps race across my body. When all the buttons are undone we just stand there, not sure of what to do next. I feel Will's breath on my neck, and then his lips. I close my eyes and take in his passion for only a moment.

I manage to say his name. "Will."

"Yes," he says in between soft kisses to my neck and shoulder.

"You have to stop." I am a crazy person.

"No, see, that's the beauty of being married. We don't have to stop anymore," he says quietly, caressing my bare arms.

I muster the energy to step away and turn around, holding my dress in place. "Will…this is my room…in Luke and Claire's house."

As if coming to from a dream, Will shakes his head and understands what I'm saying. "You're right. This is not...this isn't how I pictured it. I'm sorry."

"Don't be sorry." I step forward and touch his face. "It's going to be so wonderful."

"I'll get changed downstairs. Don't take too long. Our flight leaves in two and a half hours, and it's almost an hour to the airport." I promise I won't take too long and Will kisses me briefly before he leaves me in the quiet of my room.

It takes me a few minutes to figure out how to step out of my dress without stepping on it. Once that hurdled is passed I lay my mother's wedding dress neatly on the bed and take it in for a moment. It was an incredible day. I married the man of my dreams in a chapel in the town that has accepted me as one of their own, with parents and friends standing with us as we embrace the life that we have worked so hard to have.

I dress and check myself in the mirror, realizing that Will and I are going to have a heck of a time pulling all the bobby pins out of my hair. It's so beautiful. I hate to have to take it down. As I give my reflection the once over, I feel a huge smile take over.

"Hello, I'm Layla Meyer. It's nice to meet you," I say to the girl in the mirror. "Layla Meyer. It has a nice ring to it."

I give the room one more look and meet Will down stairs. We grab our coats and the limo driver is closing the door behind us in a flash.

"How long is the flight?" I ask.

"A little less than two hours," Will says.

"Oh, do we have a layover somewhere?" I ask as a follow up.

"Yes, in New York."

"Ok...so how long is the layover?" I feel like I'm fishing.

"Two days," Will smiles.

"Two days? We're going to New York for two days?" I ask excitedly. "I've always wanted to go to New York!"

"I told you I was going to make every dream you've ever had come true." Will puts his arm around me and I nestle into his side.

"Well, *husband*, you're off to a fabulous start. Thank you."

We ride and Will tells me a little about the hotel in Ireland. It's actually not a hotel, and we're actually going to be in two different locations. Will says they're both converted castles and I think I'm going to scream. Just another way that my new husband is making sure my dreams are coming true.

Our flight is quick, only about an hour and a half. A driver is waiting for us in baggage claim with a sign that reads *Mr. & Mrs. W. Meyer*. He's already retrieved our luggage from the baggage carrousel so we walk directly to his town car, which is waiting in a designated area for limos and taxis.

"Don't you want to know where we're staying?" Will asks as we pull away from the curb.

"Nope! I want to be surprised. You told me that I had to start letting you just take care of me. So…this is me just going with the flow and letting you take care of me!" I tell him.

It's a 45-minute drive from JFK to our hotel and I fall asleep as I lean against Will, letting the adrenaline that has been driving me all day finally dissipate. When we pull up to the hotel, Will nudges me gently. After a moment to get my bearings, the driver opens the door and I step out onto the sidewalk. It's dark and the lights from the overhang glow magically in the glass doors.

"Oh, Will. You brought me to the Four Seasons. *The* Four Seasons in New York City. I can't believe it," I say in awe as Will pulls me to his side.

"Nothing but the best for my wife." Will kisses the top of my head and the doorman opens one of the glass doors for us.

"Um…this is going to sound silly, but, can we walk through the revolving door? I've never walked through one before," I say sheepishly.

"Of course," Will says with a huge smile. "You're so cute."

I enter the revolving glass door and push. It takes more effort than I thought it would, but Will is in the section behind me pushing, too, so it gives way quickly. When I exit the turning door I'm greeted with everything that one would expect from the Four Seasons in New York City. The stone floor and walls are regal and the décor is sophisticated and chic. There was a time when I would have been swallowed up in the dichotomy of my existence in this elegant space, but not anymore. This girl is enjoying every second of her first experience in the greatest city on earth.

"Good evening, Mr. and Mr. Meyer. We hope you had a pleasant flight," the girl checking us in says. "Congratulations on your marriage. We're so pleased you've chosen to celebrate part of your honeymoon with us here at the Four Seasons New York. We've got you all set in a premium park-view executive suite on the 48th floor. And, per your request, I've made a dining reservation for you at Per Se for 7:00 tomorrow evening. Is there anything else I can assist you with? Perhaps some theater tickets?"

"No, thank you. It sounds like everything is just right, and I've got the tickets taken care of." Will takes our room keys from the marble counter and leads me to the elevator.

"You have theater tickets already?" I ask, excitement stirring in me.

"My father had season tickets. He had a lot of business here in the city," Will tells me.

"What kind of business? Lawyer business or…" I begin.

"Honey."

"Right. Sorry," I say as I scold myself for bringing up the last topic on earth that should be discussed on one's honeymoon.

"You seem to know your way around the hotel," I say noticing that Will has walked us directly to the elevators without seeming to look for them or ask where they are.

"Yeah…sometimes when my dad had business here he'd bring Mom and me with him. Does it bother you that I've been here before?" he asks as we enter the elevator. I push 48 and wait for the elevator to jolt us upward.

"No, of course not. I've never been anywhere so everyone I know is well travelled compared to me. You may have been here before, but you've never been here with me." I wrap my arms around Will's waist and savor this first of many first experiences with my husband. "Will, where are our bags?" I'm just realizing that we haven't seen our bags since Will tipped the driver as he was taking them out of the car.

"They're in our room," he says. I furrow my brow in curiosity and Will fills in the blanks. "Our room was ready when the hotel sent the driver. So, when we arrived he had the bell service take them directly to our room while we checked in." A satisfied smile spreads across Will's face.

"Oh, well, that makes sense," I say. "Can you tell me what play we're going to see?"

"I thought you wanted to be surprised," he says with a tickled pinch to my waist.

"I'll be surprised right now when you tell me!" I bat my eyes at Will and he just laughs at my cuteness.

"You're too much, you know that! We're going to see Wicked. Is that ok?"

"Oh, my gosh! Yes! Yes! That's totally great! Thank you, Will!" I hug him tightly and kiss him only briefly, afraid that if I get carried away we'll end up very embarrassed should the doors open to awaiting strangers.

We exit the elevator and this time Will does look for some direction to see which way our room is. We find our room at the end of the hall and the nervous butterflies that had once migrated have reappeared. I'm about to walk into a hotel room…with my *husband*.

Will opens the door to our room and looks at me. "So, Mrs. Meyer. Are you ready to officially start our honeymoon?"

"Definitely."

With that Will bends down and scoops me into his arms. "What are you doing?" I squeal in a loud whisper.

"Did you expect me to be any less traditional?" he says with a knowing smile.

"No…I should have fully expected you to do this," I say with a contented sigh. "Ok, Mr. Meyer. Carry your wife over the threshold. Wait. Are you going to do this at every hotel and when we get home?"

"Absolutely."

"Good."

We glide over the threshold and the door shuts behind us as Will sets me down in the entryway of our suite. Will turns a small accent lamp on, takes my hand, and guides me into the living area. The furniture is beautifully simple, elegant, and warm with neutral colors. The huge windows of this corner suite give the most spectacular view of the city and Central Park. The buildings are lit up in an explosion of colors, inviting me to step closer to the window for a better look.

"I can't wait to see this view in the morning," I say to Will. "It's amazing. Thank you." I turn to him and rest my head against his chest, letting his arms cover me. I look to the other side of the suite and see the bed, the big, king-size bed, and my heart starts to race.

"Layla," Will says breathlessly, pulling me from him so our eyes meet. It's the most intense moment I've ever experienced with Will. The heat of anticipation has risen to whatever the kelvin measurement is for the Sun and I don't think either of us can stand it much longer.

"Kiss me, Will. Kiss your wife," I demand.

Will's lips are immediately pressed to mine in a rush of explosive passion. His hands are around my waist, grabbing and pulling me closer to him, touching me places he's never touched me before. My fingers twist through his hair, pulling him closer to me with just as much anticipation.

"Will," I say, managing to pull myself away from him. "I…I want to change…freshen up."

"Yes, of course," he says catching his breath. He runs his fingers through his hair to straighten what I'm mussed.

I kiss him quickly on the lips, grab my overnight bag, and find the bathroom. After a few deep breaths to catch mine I sit on the side of the huge tub and let the gravity of the situation sink in. *This is it, Layla*, I tell myself. *The moment you've been waiting for.*

I open my bag and find the piece of lingerie I planned on for tonight. It's simple, classic, white and flowing, and falls several inches above my knee. I put it on, and as I fold the clothes I just took off I realize I'm taking way too long in here for a girl whose super-hot husband is waiting just outside the door. I leave my hair as it has been all day since I have no idea how long it will take to get it all undone. One last look in the mirror and decide that it's now or never.

When I open the door, Will is seated on the bench at the end of the bed. He's changed, too and is wearing only a pair of black linen pajama pants that hang in the most unbelievably sexy way low on his hips.

"Wow," he says, standing to meet me next to the bed.

"Do you like it?" I ask quietly, a little shy.

"Like is an understatement. You look so beautiful, Layla."

"You were so right, Will," I say.

"I have a feeling I should write this moment down for posterity," he chuckles. "What was I so right about?"

"This moment, right now…there is *no way* that letting ourselves get carried away before would have felt nearly as magical as this. Standing here with you like this is the definition of perfection."

Will takes his fingers and runs them down the length of my arms, letting his blue eyes become one with mine. He reaches behind my ear and begins to pull the bobby pins out of my hair. One by one, he places them on the table next to the bed, his eyes never leaving mine. The bun begins to loosen and my hair starts to fall. Once all the pins are out Will undoes the braid and runs his fingers through my hair, letting the locks cascade over my shoulders.

Will wraps his arms around my waist and I intuitively lift my hands up his arms to his shoulders, and in one flawless, fluid motion, Will presses his lips to mine. As Will kisses me with unbridled passion, I know that my understanding of perfection is about to be redefined.

Chapter 28

It's late when our plane touches down in Charlotte and I can't believe how fast the last two weeks have gone by. We had the most amazing time in New York, doing everything we could pack into two days. We walked through Central Park, which was vibrant with fall colors, saw a Broadway show, ate at one of the best restaurants in the city, and went to a real New York deli. Of course, that was all in between perfecting our perfection.

There are no human words to describe how beautiful Ireland is. The people were kind, the culture was incredible and the castles where we stayed were unbelievable. Our time in Ireland was laid back, filled with our own self-guided tours in our rental car, getting lost not knowing how to read a map because neither of us thought to download an international map app. And since the legal age to drink alcohol in Ireland is 18, I had my first drink. We promised Tyler we'd visit the Guinness Storehouse in Dublin, so it seemed only fitting that I have my first drink there. Truth be told, I didn't like it all that much. It was pretty strong. Will said that I'm probably just a lightweight and I've got a few months before I can try something else at home.

Our week in Bali left us both undeniably more relaxed that we ever have been. After the journey we took to get here, we both agreed that closing out our honeymoon with a week of nothing but lying on the beach was just what the doctor ordered. I feel a little bad about not doing more. I'm sure there were some lovely tours of the island we could have taken, but between sunning ourselves and all the other married things we just didn't make time for anything else.

"Don't be mad," Will says as he puts me down after his fifth time carrying me over the threshold.

"What?" I ask him warily.

"I got an email from Luke and I have to meet him tomorrow morning…to see Holly," he tells me, clearly concerned for my freak-out level.

"Really? Tomorrow? We just got home from our honeymoon and the first thing you're going to do is go see her?" I say, frustrated. I hold back though since I really don't want to have our first fight now, and I certainly don't want it to be about Holly.

"It's not my idea, Layla. Take it up with Luke. Trust me. My plan for tomorrow included barely leaving the bedroom to eat," he says with a seductive smile.

"Don't do that!" I playfully smack his arm as he pulls me to him. "I reserve the right to be upset that you're going to see your ex-girlfriend the day after we get home from our honeymoon. Besides, I was going to give you your wedding present tomorrow," I pout.

"Honey, you didn't have to get me anything. In fact, I'm pretty sure I told you not to get me anything." He's looking down at me over his nose with slight disapproval.

"I believe I told you not to get me anything either, but yet here I stand in a completely remodeled house fresh off a flight from my two week honeymoon," I counter.

"I only made those things your gift because you wouldn't let me do anything else."

"Well…it's already done, so you'll just have to live with it," I tell him with slight indignation.

"I guess we both have to get used to the other one taking care of us, huh? So, about tomorrow…I want you to be there, too. Luke has run all the numbers and drawn up the papers for the settlement for each of the exes. I think you'll enjoy watching Holly and Marlene's response to what they'll be receiving," Will says with a smirk.

"*Another* wedding gift!" I mirror Will's smirk.

Will scoops me up again in his arms and I squeal. "Now that that's settled…on to more important things!"

Will stomps up the stairs with me in his arms and heads straight for our bedroom. When we reach the room, Will drops me with a plop on the bed and jumps on after me. In the last two weeks I've learned that having sex with your husband can be sexy, seductive, sweet, and yes, even silly.

*****

"I had the best dream ever," I yawn, discovering that I'm in the same exact place I was when I fell asleep. My head is on Will's chest and his arm is wrapped around me. "Oh, wait…it wasn't a dream. We're really lying in bed together…in *our* home."

"This is my favorite place for you to be, you know,'' he says stroking my arm.

"I know what you *were* talking about now…when you said you wanted to wake up with me and no one would come looking for us because we would be exactly where we're supposed to be. I love this feeling." I inch myself even closer to Will as his hold on me tightens.

"I told you it'd be worth it," he says. "So…we've got a couple of hours before we have to be at the court house. How about…"

"Good grief, Will!" I shout playfully as I stumble out of bed. "We have to get moving or we'll never get out of here. You get in the shower and I'll make you a latte!" I throw my robe on and escape Will's persuasive kisses to coax me into taking a shower with him and send him to bathe alone. I brush my teeth and go down stairs, passing a table in the foyer that is piled with gifts, including a basket with a mound of envelopes. *We'll have to get to those later, too.* Claire must have brought them by. I'm a little surprised. I figured she would have kept them at their house so I'd have to come there.

I pass through the kitchen, tip toe into the Great Room, and look out the window into the back yard. It's a beautiful fall morning. The trees are almost all barren as the orange and gold leaves scatter and blow around the patio and the pool cover. There doesn't seem to be any sign that anything happened at all while we were gone, but Luke assures me that everything went exactly as planned.

Satisfied that Will's gift won't be spoiled if he comes down and looks out the back windows, I make us two lattes and head back upstairs. My husband is just emerging from the shower, wearing only a towel. *I love being married.*

"Hey! I made us lattes," I say as I hand him his.

I take a sip and realize I got them backwards. Will does not like his sweetened and I just took a too-big sip of bitterness. "Oh! How can you drink it like this?" I say swapping out our cups.

"It's manlier this way," he says, flexing.

"I'm going to take a shower. Can you bring up my bag? I wanted to wear that sweater I got in Dublin today," I tell him.

I turn the shower on and stare at the stall for a moment. It's pretty spectacular. There are four showerheads protruding from the wall making sure every inch of your body is massaged by the jetting streams of steaming water. I step in and think that maybe I should have taken Will up on his offer.

I let the water rush over and around me as I consider the day ahead. I hope our meeting with Holly and Marlene doesn't take too long. I really have no desire to spend a second longer with them than absolutely necessary. I wonder if Claire will be there, too. I'm anxious to see her. It's funny…I have only been apart from Luke and Claire a few times since I've been with them, and those were just for a few nights and not very far. The fact that I haven't seen them in 16 days feels so strange to me.

"What do you think about having everyone over for dinner tonight?" I ask Will as I emerge from the bathroom, wrapping my robe around me and tying the belt.

"Depends. Who is *everyone*?" he replies. He's dressed now and my heart sinks just a little that I missed watching him in that process.

"Just our parents. Luke, Claire, your mom, and Wes...your soon-to-be step-dad!" I giggle. "I can't wait to hear all about the proposal! And it'll be fun to open all the gift and envelopes with them, don't you think?"

"Ok, ok...let's bring the step-father thing down a notch." I can tell he's partly serious. He'll never call Wes *Dad*, even though I know he sees him as a father figure. "Yeah, sure...sounds like fun. We'll have to go to the store. We've got food, but not enough for entertaining."

"Going to the store for groceries...how domestic of us!" I open my suitcase and find the sweater I want to wear, and get a pair of jeans from the closet. It's oddly wonderful how normal it feels to walk around this room and gather *my* things. When we were on our honeymoon, in hotels, it was different. This...this is permanent.

It is 11:00 when we walk through the security check point at Jail Central and meet Luke. He sees me and looks so happy and relieved. Claire isn't here, but that's ok. I'll tell Luke that they're all coming for dinner and gift-opening tonight and she'll be over joyed.

"Hi, Dad!" I say throwing my arms around his neck. It feels so good to hug him. I loved every second of my honeymoon, but I don't think I want to be away from Luke and Claire for that long again anytime soon. "I missed you!"

"Hey!" he says hugging me just as fiercely. "No, you didn't!"

"Well...if I hadn't been having such an incredible time, and actually had a moment to really think about it, I would definitely have missed you and Mom." Luke hugs Will and Will seems to be a little offset. He doesn't look Luke in the eyes. He just greets him and smiles weakly as they embrace.

"Marlene is already here, so we'll just have them moved to the attorney meeting room," Luke says, leading the way.

"What was that about?" I whisper to Will. "Why were you so weird with Luke?"

"It occurred to me as I was facing him that I, well...I've had sex with his daughter. It felt weird to look him in the eyes for some reason," he says quietly.

"Honey, everyone in that restaurant two and a half weeks ago knows you had sex with me. Hell, Tyler and Caroline made an anthem of it! We're married, and Luke knows we waited, so if anything he has mad respect for you. Don't sweat it, ok?" I think it's cute that Will is a tad bit nervous facing my father. It makes me wonder if Luke felt awkward, too.

"Oh, um...I hate to throw something else on you, but...Loretta and Victoria arrived yesterday. Erin and Michael are here, too. They're anxious to meet you, Will," Luke tells us with some hesitation. It's a lot to take in. We've been home less than 24 hours and we're already having to process the possibility of seeing Meyer's first and second wives, along with their children, Will's siblings.

"Let's have them over," I say before Will can respond.

"Layla...I'm not sure I want to do that." Will says. "Don't you think it'd be better to meet at Luke's or even at the court house?"

"They want to meet you, get to know you. The best place to do that is at our home...the one *you* redesigned to reflect who *we* are. I'll make dinner," I say with a comforting smile. "It'll be laid back and wonderful."

"Luke?" Will defers to Luke to get an idea of how he thinks Loretta and the others might respond to our invitation.

"I think it's a great idea, Will. Layla is right. If what they want is to get to know you, having them for dinner at your home is a good place to start." Luke smiles supportively.

Will takes a cleansing breath. "Ok. If you think it's what you really want to do," he says to me. "Let's have them over for dinner."

"Great! Tonight! Tell them to come at seven, ok, Dad?" I say with a jail-appropriate level of excitement. "But can you and Mom, and Eliana and Wes come a little earlier. We haven't seen them and I really want at least a few minutes with them before the others arrive."

"That sounds perfect. Claire will be thrilled to see you," Luke says.

I take Will's hand and squeeze it reassuringly. He's a little lost in thought but comes back to the moment as Luke leads us through another door marked for attorneys and into a room where an officer is standing guard. We walk into an open room with a single table and four chairs. It's not like the protective glass and corded phone set up for one-on-one visits with inmates. Holly is seated at the table, handcuffed to a metal bar fixed to the table.

"Hi, Will," Holly says with a smile, but her smile fades a little when she sees me. "Hello, Layla. I understand congratulations are in order."

"Hello, Holly. Yes, thank you," I say. It's best if I keep any conversation with her or her mother as short as possible.

"Why if it isn't the next in a long line of Meyer wives. Hope your pre-nup is better than mine, honey," Marlene says. Her voice is like nails on a chalkboard to me.

"You don't talk to my wife," Will says bluntly.

Holly's eyes go wide, shocked at his response. Until now Will has been the epitome of honor and respect, but that's only because they thought he was blindly unaware of how they used him as a pawn in their game.

"Will wanted to have all the settlement issues handled before the trial starts in a few days, so we're just here to go over that information. After some consideration, Will and Layla have decided to raise the gift amount from five million to six million. With the amount of money being given, we also wanted all of you to sign documentation that the funds received are a gift, and that you understand any attempt to collect more money will be considered a hostile action of extortion and will be punishable to the fullest extent of the law." I've not seen Luke in full on lawyer mode like this before. It's interesting to see just how cool, calm, and collected he is. "Do you understand?" Luke directs his question to Marlene.

"Yes, I *understand*," she answers with an overly annoyed tone.

"Great. Now if you'll just sign this indicating that you're in agreement, we can get on with this. As an attorney I advise you to read it before you sign it," he warns her.

"I trust you. You folks are all squeaky clean, law-abiding citizens. I'm sure it says exactly what you said it does." I gotta give it to Marlene. What you see is what you get. She doesn't pretend for a second to be anything other than what she is: a scorned, southern woman with a thirst for the almighty dollar.

"Thank you for your confidence," Luke says as he takes the signed document and files it back into his briefcase. "Will…care to explain the distribution of funds?"

"As I considered the gift I wanted to give to each of my father's ex-wives, I couldn't ignore the fact that each of you already received a settlement when your divorce from my father was finalized. So," he says as Luke hands him another legal document of sorts, "considering the settlement you received after the divorce, this is the amount that will be automatically transferred into your account." Will slides the paper across the table where Marlene is sitting beside Holly. They both lean over the table with heightened anticipation at the amount of money they're about to receive. I wonder what they've already bought thinking their credit troubles would be over with the push of a button by a bank official.

"What the hell?" Marlene stands up in a fury, knocking the chair she was sitting in to the floor. "What is this? 600,000? I think you're missing about three zeros here Will!"

"No. Nothing's missing. You, unlike the other ex-wives, managed to squeeze 5.4 million dollars from my father. That's what $25,000 a month over 18 years adds up to. To be generous, I decided not to include what Marcus received from my father on a monthly basis into the calculation. But, I'm sure you've already spent that because Marcus never touched a penny of it." Will counters Marlene's disgust with cool delivery, not flinching once.

"I don't understand why you're doing this, Will," Holly says with her feigned sweetness. "It's not like you to play games like this."

"Cut the sweet act, Holly. You want to talk about playing games? I know everything. Sorry the whole *Meyer Baby* thing didn't work out for you. *That* is reserved for my wife." Will puts his arm around my waist and draws me to his side. I'm not trying to, but I can't help smiling. I had no idea they were working this financial magic. It makes me so happy to see them squirm after the agony Holly caused Will.

"You bitch. You told him," Holly says with astonished disgust.

"Of course she told me! In what world would my *wife* not tell me about how you betrayed me? Oh, yes, that's right...*you're* jacked up world. You know what? We're done here. These are the last words you're ever going to hear from me or my wife." Will rests his palms on the table and leans ever so slightly into Holly. "I cared about you. I thought you were a girl who had the potential to be anything, do anything. But now all I see is a pathetic apple from this shriveled up tree.

"You're lucky Luke is a man of his word. In a few days he's going to defend you and give you the trial you deserve. My mother and the other ex-wives will testify to the horror of a man my father was. And, chances are good you're going to get the charges lowered and serve the next mere five years in prison. I'd take advantage of the degree programs they offer in there because you're going to need a job when you get out. If you think for a second that your mother is going to wait for you, you're fooling yourself. Now that she's only getting a fraction of what she thought she had coming, she's going to take every cent of it and disappear. So, yeah…good luck with that."

To say Holly looks stunned would be an understatement. She's looking at Will and me and then to her mother who is avoiding eye contact with Holly at any cost.

"Mom…aren't you going to say anything?" she asks with fear coating each word. "Aren't you going to tell them that they're liars? That you would never do that to me?"

"Well, honey…" Marlene says after a beat. "You know your father and I…we have some plans…things we're going to do until you're out. Daddy's going to invest some of it, too. It won't be as much as we planned, but…there will probably be something left over for you. Maybe." Marlene is walking beside and behind Holly, pacing and still looking anywhere but at her daughter. Fear floods Holly's eyes and I get a look at the real girl for the first time. She knows her mother and has made the mistake of thinking that she's immune to Marlene's conniving. Had Will given them the full six million, Marlene would have planned on giving Holly a small portion of it. Now that they're working with a fraction of what they were expecting, Holly will never see a penny of it.

Will takes my hand and we walk toward the door.

"Layla," Holly calls to me in desperation. "I helped you with Marcus…"

"So…what…you think that earns you another few million?" I spin around before Will can intercept her comment, furious that she would use Marcus as some kind of last chance card. "You people jacked him up in the first place! If it weren't for the mind games all of you played with him his whole life, I wouldn't have been in that situation! So don't you *dare* use him as some kind of leverage! Marcus was good and kind. Despite everything you did to him he worked hard to separate himself from you. He didn't want to play your games but time after time you shoved him in, head first, into deep, shark-infested water. Take what you're getting and pray your mother saves a few dollars for you."

I walk out of the room, proud that I didn't punch Holly in the face. Of course she would try to use Marcus. I thought she had really come to my rescue in Tallahassee but now I question everything. Had they planned to kill Meyer all along? Was Marcus a distraction? Did they push him and make him believe that I felt the same way about him? The whole thing is just so gross that I think I might be physically ill.

"Babe? You ok?" Will says coming behind me down the hall and out the door into the main waiting area. "You really let her have it."

"I was fine until she brought Marcus into it," I tell him. Leaning into his chest I let his arms cover me and help stop my shaking.

"I know...I know. It's over now. We'll sit in the courtroom and won't have to say a word or interact with her in any way. As soon as the trial is over, we'll never see her face or speak their names again. Ok?" Will rubs circles on my back, soothing me.

I take a deep breath and let it all just float away. "You're right. We've been married for 17 days and this is nowhere in my plan of how to spend the first month of our marriage. Now that we've taken care of all this, let's go be domestic and pick up some groceries for tonight. Ok?"

"Yes ma'am!" Will smiles and with that we walk away from Jail Central forever.

*****

I'm rushing around like a mad woman trying to get all the food put away. I want to have plenty of time to show Will his gift and not be rushed in prepping dinner.

"Hey, where's the fire?" Will says bringing in the last bags. "They're not coming for, like, five hours."

"I just want to get everything put away," I tell him in a slight fib.

"Hey…what's going on?" he asks as he takes the cans of green beans from my hands and puts them on the counter.

"I just really wanted to give you your wedding gift today," I tell him with a sigh. "And I'm afraid there won't be enough time. It's something that you're going to have to explore and I just don't want you to feel rushed."

"Baby, I already explored everything there was to explore in New York, Ireland, and Bali," he says with a seductive smirk.

"I'm not talking about that! C'mon, Will!"

"Ok, ok! Wow, this gift must be pretty incredible. You've built it up and now I'm anxious for it. Give me my gift!" he says with a laugh.

I take Will's hand and lead him outside. It's chilly so I move us quickly across the patio to the pool house. The puzzled look on Will's face is going to make the big reveal even better.

"Why is it in the pool house?" he asks with a scrunched up face.

"Close your eyes," I tell him as we stop at the door. He does as he's told and I lead him through the door. We walk across the living area of the pool house and to a newly erected wall with a single door. Will hears me open the door and pull him through to the other side.

"Did you just open another door? Where *are* we?" He's utterly confused and I love every second of it.

I close the door and position Will against it so he's also in the corner where he can get a full view of the whole room. "Ok. Open your eyes."

"Oh, Layla," Will responds in awe. He takes in the room and sees that I've converted it into a workspace…a small version of the space where Pop designs and builds furniture in Hickory. There's a drafting table where he can design, and state of the art tools in stations around the room. It's a craftsman's dream and Will is just as overwhelmed with it as I hoped he would be.

"Honey, this is amazing." He pulls me into his arms and holds me so tight. "I can't believe you did this for me."

"It came out of the account you added me to. I hope that was ok," I say.

"I added you for a reason. You don't have to ask permission to use it," he says. He looks at me intently as if to drive home the point that he will never control me the way his father controlled his mother.

"So you love it? Luke helped. He connected me with the same designer you used for the remodel of the house, and the same contractor. Pop helped with what tools to have." My heart is racing with excitement right now. I feel such a huge sense of accomplishment in having finally given Will such a wonderful, over-the-top gift.

"I more than love it. It's amazing, honey…you're amazing. You just keep proving to me why I am the luckiest man alive." I'm giddy with excitement that Will loves the space so much.

"We cut down the pool part of the pool house so much. Maybe we should start calling it the workhouse! I hope I haven't created a space where I'm going to lose you. I'm not going to become a workhouse widow am I?"

"I make no promises. These tools are ridiculous! They are seriously the best on the market!" he says picking up tools, turning other machines on.

"Well then I better see some pretty amazing, hand-crafted pieces for the house!"

"I will make you whatever your heart desires." Will glides across the room to me and takes me in his arms in the most fluid of motions. This is by far the best thank you kiss I've ever received. Will moves us through the door and into the living area of the pool house, kissing me with every step and shuffle. Before I know it, we're on the couch, christening the pool house with perfection.

Chapter 29

The doorbell rings at 6:30 and I rush into the foyer with such frenzied excitement that my sock feet slide across the hardwood floors, causing me to almost slam into the front door. When I open it, Luke, Claire, Eliana, and Wes are all standing there like little kids trick-or-treating for the first time, so excited they can hardly stand it.

"Come in! Come in!" I step back and hurry them in so I can throw my arms around all of them. "You're here!"

"Welcome home, sweetheart," Claire says, holding me tight. "We missed you so much!"

"I missed you, too, Mom! Does Eliana have something to tell us?" I whisper in her ear. I know Wes was going to propose, and I know Eliana would say yes, but sometimes you never know how things play out.

"Why don't you ask her yourself?" Claire answers, releasing me into Eliana's arms.

"Are there congratulations in order?" I ask.

"Yes, I believe there are," she says with a huge smile, holding up her hand. The ring Wes has given her is very different than the umpteen karat one Will's father gave her. This one is a simple, solitaire diamond that I'd guess is about two karats. It's perfect and symbolized the beautiful simplicity of their relationship. There are no strings attached and no stipulations, just a simple love between the two of them.

"So, Wes, you're going to make an honest woman of my mother," Will says entering the foyer with an extended hand. "I'm happy for you both…but I'm *not* calling you Dad."

"Oh, dear God, no, don't do that!" Wes says with wide eyes. "Thanks, Will. It means a lot that you're supportive. I'd marry her anyway, but things will go much smoother with you knowing how awesome I am and how ridiculously in love with her I am."

We all have a good laugh and move into the Great Room. I've had a brisket in the oven cooking low and slow for several hours already, so the house smells divine.

"This might be what I miss most about having you living with us," Luke says opening the oven to peak.

"Gee, thanks!" I say giving him a playing smack to the arm.

"Yeah, thanks!" Claire says with a small laugh.

"I'm kidding…sort of," he says. "So let's hear about Ireland and Bali."

"Oh my goodness! They were amazing! Ireland is greener and more beautiful than I could have ever imagined. The people were wonderful and the culture is so rich. We stayed in these two converted castles and it was simply magical. And Bali! Oh, my gosh! I could have gone blind from the reflection of the sun on the water there. It was…it was unbelievable. My husband has spoiled me and now he has to spend the rest of his life living up to standard he set!" I wrap my arms around Will's waist in another show of appreciation for the amazing honeymoon he gave me.

"How was New York?" Eliana asks. "William and I always had the best time when we were there. We shopped and saw matinees of Broadway plays. Did you take her to the deli you always made me go to?" she says with a smile. It's lovely to see her reminisce about her time with Will. Despite the fact that Gregory Meyer most likely took them with him for show, and to have Eliana on his arm at some social function, she and Will made the most out of their time together and that makes me so happy for them.

"It was great! Yes, I took her there, and guess what? Ira is still there and remembered me! We haven't been there in, what, eight years?" Will and his mom share a smile, remembering a moment in their past that was sweet, and not marred by the controlling of Will's father.

"I'm so glad it was everything you hoped it would be," Claire says.

"It was more," I tell her with a smile.

"Well…Loretta and the others should be here any minute," Luke says, breaking the jovial mood. I look at Will and his demeanor changes. He becomes a little tense and apprehensive.

"Hey," I say stroking his arm. "It's going to be great."

As if on cue, the doorbell rings and we all look at each other not quite sure how quickly we should move. I take the first step and Will follows when I take his hand pulling him with me.

"Are you ready?" I ask quietly as we stand in front of the door.

"No, but open it anyway." Will squeezes my hand and then lets it go.

When I open the door, there are three beautiful women and one very handsome man standing in front of me. Erin is obviously the youngest of the three women. She's average height and has long, wavy, dark brown hair that is cascading over one shoulder. I assume the older woman with slightly lighter colored hair is her mother, Loretta, leaving the blonde haired woman to be Victoria, Michael's mother.

"Hello. Thank you so much for coming." I open the door as wide as it will go and motion for them to enter. The ladies enter first with Michael entering last. I close the door and we all seem to stand there, unsure of who should do what first.

"I'm Will," he says, extending his hand.

"Michael." He reciprocates and shakes Will's hand. Michael is not warm and fuzzy. In fact, he's a little on guard. It seems that maybe this wasn't his idea and that he's really just here for his mother. He's tall, like Will, and has classically short dirty blonde hair. His facial features are strong, also like Will, and it's clear to see that these two men are related.

"It's nice to meet you," Will says with a tightlipped smile. He moves his hand to Erin and she looks at him as if to say *I don't do handshakes.*

Then, in a flash, Erin steps forward and throws her arms around Will's neck. Not sure how to respond, it takes Will a moment before he gives in to his emotions and hugs her back, wrapping his arms around her waist. Will buries his face in her shoulder and they both cry softly, so happy to finally meet another part of them.

"Thank you for seeing us," Erin says through stifled crying.

"Are you kidding? Thank you for wanting to see me," Will says as he pulls them apart from each other to look at her. "I'm so sorry." He looks at Erin and Michael, waiting for their response.

"There's nothing to be sorry for," Erin says as she wipes her eyes. "They were *his* choices, not yours."

"Michael?" Victoria prompts.

Michael stands there for a moment before he speaks. "I can't do this." Michael turns and walks back toward the door.

"Wait...please," Will pleads.

"What, Will? We find out we have siblings we never knew about and we're somehow supposed to be all chummy?" Michael sighs and closes his eyes, collecting his thoughts. "Look, I'm not mad at you. Erin is right. Things are the way they are because of the choices he made. But all being victims of his apathy isn't enough for me to jump in head first here." Michael is straight and to the point. He doesn't seem angry, or even upset for that matter. He's just weighed the facts and determined that he's not willing to invest himself in this new relationship with his brother and sister.

"Don't you think it's worth finding out if there's more common ground here? I do, and I think it'd be a shame to walk away before you even give us a chance," Will says to him. It's the first time I've seen Will step up and defend the opportunity to embrace the siblings his father kept from him. This is a huge step for him and I think Erin's vulnerability helped Will open himself up.

"If you two want to come together and bond, that's great. I just don't think I'm ready for that. I'm sorry, Mom." Michael turns and walks out the door, but hopefully not forever.

"It's not you, Will. He hasn't exactly warmed up to me, either," Erin tells him.

"Babe? Are you ok?" I ask Will, taking his hand in mine.

"Yeah…I'm disappointed, but…he has to make his choice, too." Will gives a tightlipped nod and brings himself back into the moment with Erin. "I'm glad you're here," he tells her.

"It's a pleasure to meet you, Will. I'm Loretta," she says, stepping forward and giving Will a small hug. "Thank you for having us," she says to me.

"We're so pleased you could come," I tell her, offering her a hug in return.

"Yes, thank you for having us. It was very kind of you. I'm Victoria. I'm very sorry for Michael's behavior. It's been difficult for him. I think it's a father-son thing, but he's honest about not blaming you, Will. I'm hoping time will help him come around," she says.

"I hope so, too," Will says. "Please, come with us." Will and I lead the women to the back of the house where the Great Room is, and where our parents are waiting. "You've met everyone?" Will asks the women.

"Yes, Claire and Eliana have been very kind," Loretta says.

"Dinner will be ready in a few minutes. Can I get anyone something to drink beforehand?" I offer. There are echoes of *no, thank you* and *I'll just have something with dinner*, so I take a seat next to Will on the couch.

"So, Will…here's the deal," Erin begins. Will's eyes get a little bigger in anticipation of what Erin is about to tell him. After her warm and emotional response, I can't imagine that she would have anything but something kind to say. "I don't want to talk about Gregory Meyer. I only care about him because he gave you and Michael and Sarah to me. I've known about you since, well, since I was your age, so I've had a long time to process and get used to the fact that I have a brother...and I'm thrilled about it. I want to get to know you, Will. I want us to be a part of each other's lives. The question is, do you want the same thing?" Erin's brown eyes are soft and warm. She is so clearly at peace with all of this, and seems genuinely hopeful that Will is going to share her feelings about bonding.

"Any hesitancy I had about meeting you came from being scared that you resented me, resented my mom," Will says.

"We hold no resentment against either of you," Loretta says sweetly. Her voice is soft and smooth and comforting.

"I can see that," Will says smiling with joy. "I spent my whole life wishing for a brother or a sister, thinking that it would make life a little less lonely. When I found out I actually had two brothers and two sisters, it was a shock...especially considering the circumstances. I lost Marcus early on, even before..." Will takes my hand remembering the awful conditions by which Marcus died. "I'm disappointed Michael didn't stay, but I hope once he's had a chance to digest everything that he'll come around. I've already connected with Sarah, which has been better than I ever dreamed. So, yes, I want to get to know you, too, Erin. I can't imagine walking away from you now."

"I'm so happy to hear you say that," she says, moving to the seat on the couch next to Will.

"Will," Victoria says, calling his attention away from Erin. "Michael only found out a few months ago. I wasn't as forthcoming with him as Loretta was with Erin. Had I known he would act this way, I would have told him a long time ago. I'm sorry."

"There was no reason to believe we'd ever be sitting here like this. The only reason I found out about you is because of my father's death. So, please...there's nothing to be sorry about," Will tells her.

"So, let's get started," Erin says to Will with excitement.

"What do you want to know?" Will chuckles.

"How about how you and Layla met?" she asks looking at me.

"Hold that thought! Dinner is ready so let's get everyone to the table and we can start with the barrage of questions. Who's hungry?" I say as I move to the kitchen. I take the meat out of the oven and put everything into serving dishes while everyone finds a place at the dining table.

"Let me help you with those," Eliana says as she enters the kitchen.

"No, Mom, it's fine, I've got it," I tell her. "But...how are you? I mean is it weird sitting here with Loretta and Victoria?" I think I would be totally freaked out.

"Well, I won't lie and say it's perfectly fine. But...we talked yesterday at great length. It was very healing for all of us I think." Eliana smiles and I can see that she's growing into a great place of peace. It's one thing to know about your husband's ex-wives, it's another to sit with them and have a pow-wow about each of your experiences with him. I don't think she'd be able to get through it if it weren't for how strong her relationship with Wes has made her.

Eliana and I bring the food to the table and take our places. We spend the next few hours talking and getting to know each other. We tell them about the night on the Green when Will and I met and I literally knocked his drink out of his hand. Erin tells us how she met her husband, Logan, and shows pictures of her son David, who's 12. We share wedding and honeymoon stories and there are even a few times when we're all laughing so hard that we're crying.

We don't talk about Gregory Meyer. We don't even utter his name. Will has obviously decided not to grill Loretta and Victoria about his father, and I don't think it's just because Eliana is sitting across from them. I think Nana Grace and Pop set him straight after the whole thing when we got back from seeing Cheryl.

There are times as I look around the table that I have to remind myself that we're all here because of him. Then I laugh, because despite his efforts to keep all of these women down and to abandon his children, they all found a way to rise to the top and find each other…and all are better for it.

"Well," Loretta says after taking the last sip of her coffee. "Dinner was delicious, Layla. Thank you. I think we need to get some rest. Luke has spent almost two days preparing us for the trial. I think I'm going to go back to the hotel and go to bed with no intentions of getting up before noon tomorrow," she laughs.

"I think that's an excellent plan," Claire agrees. "And I think Will and Layla are more jet lagged than they're letting on." She may be right. Fatigue is starting to set in.

"We know you're just here for the trial, but maybe we can have some time together before you leave?" Will says hopefully as we walk Loretta, Erin, and Victoria to the door. I'm so happy to see him embracing his sisters, and feel hopeful that Michael will come around and join them.

"That would be wonderful," Erin says. "Thank you for everything." Erin hugs us both, followed by hugs from Loretta and Victoria.

I close the door behind them and we all look to Will to see how he's doing now that the night is over. "So…" I say to him.

"That was remarkable. Once we got talking, it was like we had known each other forever." Will has a look of amazement on his face. I think he had hoped for a congenial relationship. I don't think he ever imagined there would be such a connection from the start. Even with Sarah it took a little while for him to feel as bonded to her as he does.

"I'm so happy for you, babe!" I tell him as I come to his side and put my arm around his waist.

"Yes, William, I'm so happy for you, too. I know this has been something you've been waiting for, and I'm thrilled that it seems to be everything you hoped it would be," Eliana says. "Now come, Wesley, we're going to clear the table."

"What? How did that happen?" Wes says as we all shuffle back to the dining room. It's so funny to see Wes absolute mush around Eliana. He's got it bad.

"Here, Layla, why don't you and Will open up some gifts? You've got to start somewhere." Claire brings in a few small, wrapped boxes and puts them in the chair Will sat in at dinner.

"I don't feel like opening actually gifts because then I have to figure out where to put them. What if we opened cards?" I counter.

"That sounds like a plan," Will says kissing the top of my head. He leaves the dining room and returns a moment later with the basket of cards I noticed early this morning. "You don't have to, like, *read* every card do you?" he asks sarcastically.

"I don't usually, but after that look, I think I might!" I tease. He kisses me on the cheek and we each take a card from the basket. "Ooh! This one says that love is an eternal flame, not to be snuffed out by the distractions of this world." We all laugh at the absurdity and the cheese-factor.

"Ok…I can play that game. *Mine* has a picture of two old people holding hands and walking down a beach," Will says, countering my sappy card with one of his own. "Oh, wait, this one is way better. This one says that through the years we will be challenged to love when we don't feel like loving, to forgive when we don't feel like forgiving, and to listen when we don't feel like listening. At least it has a hundred bucks in it!" We laugh as I reach for another card.

"Ok, ok…I have a feeling this one is going to be even better than that one!" I say as I open the thick envelope in my hand. "This one says…" I stop as I look at the contents of the envelope and my mood and tone both change. "This one says if we want to know where to find juror number four's body, we'll pay him the rest of what Meyer owes him for the job."

Chapter 30

I drop the envelope on the table, spilling its contents. In front of me are a dozen or so photos of me in various places and situations. There are photos of me with Gwen and Caroline the day we picked out their bridesmaid dresses, me with Will walking across the Green on some random day, and me with Tyler the day he convinced me I had been a fool to let Will pour over the ex-wives statements alone. There are even a couple photos of me with Will in New York on our honeymoon. We flip through the pictures, each one making me feel more violated than the next.

"It's Black Sedan Guy, Will. This is why he was taking the pictures. He was never some unknown reporter," I say with shaking hands as I pick up the letter. "This can't be happening."

"It's going to be ok, Layla. I'm going to take care of this," Will says, putting one arm around me and taking the letter from me with the other.

"What else does it say?" Luke asks.

"It says my father owes him $250,000 and that he wants it on Thanksgiving Day. Davidson will have their annual parade and most of the police department will either be in the parade or on duty for it. He expects cash and wants to meet at the North Harbor Club...and he wants Layla to do the exchange." Will's delivery is flat, emotionless.

"Ok, so how do we do this?" I ask directly.

"We don't," Will answers bluntly.

"What do you mean we don't? Is it the money?" I'm confused.

"I don't care about the money, Layla. I'm sorry that the juror's body hasn't been found, but I'm not willing to risk your life to find it." Will looks at me as if this is a no-brainer answer to my questioning.

"His *name* is Albert Blasi and he has a family. What are you going to say to his children when they discover we had the opportunity to find out where their father's body is and didn't take it? How are you going to explain to them that they'll never have closure on his disappearance? We can't do that to them Will. When you were missing, all I wanted was to know where you were. Dead or alive, I just wanted to know because the not knowing was killing me. Albert was someone's husband, someone's father. I know the pain they're experiencing and if we can help them in any way we absolutely have to." I hold Will's gaze, intent on driving home how vital our obligation is here. There's no way I can walk away from the chance to help this man's family.

Will's sighs heavily. "I can't lose you, Layla. This guy, Black Sedan Guy…he's already shown us how close he can get without us even knowing he's there. You going out there alone will be over my dead body."

"I agree," Luke says. "It's too risky, Layla."

"We'll get a team out there, watch for him and take him down when he shows up," Wes says matter-of-factly.

"What is wrong with you? This man's family needs to know where he is! Why do none of you care about that?" I stand in a fury of confusion as to how the most caring group of people I know are blatantly denying a family the chance to finally grieve properly over the loss of their loved one.

"We do care," Claire says. Her tone is soft as it usually is when she's trying to diffuse me. "We just care about you more."

"Are you telling me that Wes and a team of FBI agents can't keep me safe in a situation with one guy?" My tone is intentionally sarcastic, wondering if I might be able to appeal to Wes' sense of pride and kick him into gear.

"I could get a body double for her," Wes says, taking my bait. "We'll put a hat on her, scarf and coat…he'll never know the difference. She'll drop the money where he tells us and then walk away."

"I…uh…*she* can't just walk away. We have to get him to tell us where Blasi is. We can't fake him out on this. I'll just get the information and give

275

him the money. I mean, Wes and Croft's team will have eyes on him and snag him when he walks away, right?"

"This is bigger than you realize, Layla. Agent Croft's team has been investigating the juror situation for months and they keep coming up empty. This guy is *good*, whoever he is. Even Croft's best of the best, Lassiter, has hit a dead end." Luke considers what he's saying, shaking his head at his own realization. "I'm afraid this is the break they've been waiting for. And, as much as I hate to say it, the only way they're going to get this guy is if Layla does this. And the only way Layla is getting in and out of there unscathed is if Croft's team is behind us," Luke says. He's thoughtful in his delivery, making sure not to worry us with the fact that even the FBI hasn't been able to catch this guy.

Honestly? What makes us think that he's just going to give us the location of Blasi and take the money and run? What's to say he isn't going to try and put a bullet in my head? He's smooth enough to make one murder look like a home invasion, and make the other victim just disappear. All I know is that I have to at least try to help this family. I can't stand the idea of them stuck in the pain that I was in when I lost Will.

"We've got two weeks to get everything in place. In the meantime, let's get some rest. It's been a long day and I'm sure Will and Layla are fighting jet lag. I'll give Croft a call in the morning. We'll be able to get everything strategized this week before the trial starts on Monday," Luke continues.

"Everything is going to be just fine," Claire says as I hug her at the door. "You were a lovely host tonight, Layla. I'm so proud of how you handled Erin and the others. And this whole thing…well, you constantly remind me of just how brave…and stubborn…you are. That said…please don't throw yourself in the fire just to save someone else you don't even know. I know you want to help this man's family, but don't forget that you have a family of your own now."

"I know, Mom. I just…if there's any way that I can help eliminate the pain I know they're feeling, I feel like I need to at least try," I tell her. Claire looks at me and smiles knowing that there's nothing she can say that is going to change my mind.

Will and I close the door on our family, hearing Wes and Luke discussing the beginnings of various ideas of how to execute this situation flawlessly. I have faith in them, and Agent Croft's team, and know that it's all going to work out.

Will and I finish cleaning up from dinner in silence. I've attempted to engage him, at first in conversation about how we're going to handle the situation, then on to lighter topics like how great Erin was tonight. In both cases he blatantly ignored me. By the time we get upstairs to get ready for bed, I've had enough of the silent treatment and am about to tell him, when he breaks the silence on his own.

"Why are you doing this?" he says to me, his tone both sad and angry.

"Will, I have to…" I begin.

"No, you *don't* have to! Do you have any idea how this could end? Have you even thought about how I could lose you forever? We have no idea what this guy is capable of doing!" Will shouts.

"I have thought about that! What if it were me, Will? What if something happened to me, and you didn't know where I was? You couldn't have closure. Wouldn't you want someone to help you?" I counter.

"Don't do that, Layla. You can't flip this around and try to make me feel guilty for not wanting my wife of 17 days to commit herself to standing in the line of fire for a complete stranger! But you know what the worst part about this is? The worst part is that I have to go along with it and watch whatever horror may or may not unfold because regardless of what I say you're going to do this anyway!" Will pulls his shirt off in a fury and throws in on the floor, followed by his pants. This had become the highlight of my

277

day but tonight it's certainly not the same as it has been over the last two weeks.

"I'm sorry," I say softly.

"You're only sorry that I don't support this potential suicide mission. And now I have nothing left to say." Will walks into the bathroom and slams the door.

Wow. I thought we'd make it longer than 17 days before we had our first major fight. I've never seen Will so angry with me before. I just need him to understand. I'm not trying to send myself on a suicide mission. I'm trying to help Blasi's family. The night Marcus died Will got a glimpse of the pain I experienced for months. He has no real idea of the emptiness and the grief this family is feeling. Their imaginations are running wild with scenarios of where their father is. His wife is holding out hope that he's going to come home alive. They'll never be able to move on until they know for sure what happened to him. They have to lay him to rest so that they can finally get some themselves.

I change out of my clothes and into a set of pajama pants and a t-shirt and crawl into bed. I turn my back to the bathroom door because I don't want Will to see me crying when he comes out, although since he's been in there so long I'm beginning to wonder if he's made a makeshift bed out of towels in the garden tub.

I don't know how long I lay there, soaking my pillow with tears, before I feel Will slide into bed next to me. At first he just lays there and I resolve that it'll be morning before I hear his voice or, if I'm lucky, feel his touch.

"I can't lose you, Layla." I hear Will sniff and know that he's trying not to cry.

I turn around and find my sweet spot, laying my head on his chest, Will's arm blanketing me. "You're not going to lose me, Will," I tell him. "I'm not going anywhere."

"You don't know that. I understand the reasons why you want to do this, but don't you see that you're totally ignoring my wishes and my feelings about this? How is that supposed to make me feel?" Will turns his body so he's facing me, both of us propping ourselves up on an elbow. "You are consistently doing things whether I'm in agreement or not. It almost got you killed with Marcus, and you let Holly's lies eat away at you until you believed something about me, about us, that wasn't true. I am doing my best to take care of you but you won't let me. You are so damn stubborn!"

He's right. I am stubborn.

I look into Will's eyes in the light the moon is casting through the window. They're grey-blue right now. His eyes are like a mood ring, and this is a mood I've never seen in him.

"I guess I'm failing at the letting you take care of me thing, huh?" I say, running my fingers through Will's hair.

"I'm not sure you're even trying," he says honestly.

I don't know what to say. I can't defend myself because, if I'm honest, the only thing I've let Will do to take care of me is remodel the house and plan the most perfect honeymoon a girl could dream of having. Will's hands were tied for so many of the major hurdles we've had to leap. Being as independent as I am, I just jumped as high as I could, all on my own, taking care of things while Will watched from the shadows.

"Being totally independent is a hard habit to break. I had to work really hard, and make it a conscious choice every day when I first moved in with Luke and Claire. And I think, maybe, I was able to let them take care of me because I was longing for parents. I needed to be a child and they gave that to me." I pause, collecting my thoughts as they rush through my mind. "But now I'm a wife and I don't know what that's supposed to look like or feel like. I *want* you to take care of me Will. It's hard for me to let go, though, because I want to take care of you just as much."

"I *need* you to let me have a say in how this goes down. I can't just sit by and let Luke and Wes lay out *another* plan for you without my involvement. You're my *wife* now, Layla, and I swore to take care of you and protect you. I *need* you to let me do that." Will holds my face with his hand and I can see the desperation in his eyes. He feels so disconnected and it's killing him.

"Of course," I tell him with a small sigh of release. This has to be as active a decision as it was with Luke and Claire. "Tell me what you want to do and I'll do it. I love you and the last thing I want is for you feel like you're not holding up your end of our vows."

Will breathes a huge sigh of relief and pulls me to him. "I'm so sorry I yelled like that. I was just so frustrated," he says as I find my sweet spot again.

"*I'm* sorry. I have to stop being so stubborn," I say putting my arm across his stomach and squeezing. "What do you think we should do?"

"Let's just sleep on it. We've got a little while before we have to have anything laid out. Luke is right, we're both feeling the jet lag and the fatigue is not helping us handle this very well. Things will be clearer in the morning."

"My mom used to say that," I tell him. Will strokes my arm sweetly until I begin to fall asleep. "She was usually right...and I'm sure you are, too."

*****

Morning comes and seems to bring the clarity Will and I were hoping to find. Sleeping for 12 hours probably had a lot to do with just how clear we're seeing things now, too. It was almost noon when we got up. Now that we're showered and dressed, I'm feeling refreshed and ready to leap over this new hurdle with Will's hand in mine.

"I was just reading through his letter again," Will says as I set his lunch in front of him on the counter. He's seated at the bar and has the letter and pictures from Black Sedan Guy spread everywhere.

"Did you discover anything? It seemed pretty straight forward last night," I say.

"Not really." Will shakes his head in defeat. "I just keep wondering why now? I mean he's got whatever my father paid him up front. He could literally just walk away and no one would ever know. Why push it?" We're communicating like a team and asking questions that no one seemed to think of last night.

"It doesn't make sense." I pick up my phone after it pings and see that Luke has just sent me a text. "Luke says that he and Agent Croft are on their way over with Wes. That's good, right? I mean, we can start mapping this out," I say, standing next to Will and resting my arm on the back of his stool.

"Are you going to let me take the lead here?" he asks, putting his arm around my waist.

"Yes. Whatever you think is best, I'll do it," I tell him.

"Thank you." Will's words are thoughtful and I can tell that it truly means a lot to him for me to stop trying to handle everything on my own. I don't want to do this alone. I want to stop feeling like I have to be in control and really let Will do what he's promised to do.

The doorbell rings and we both move to answer it together. Will takes my hand and gives me a smile and a nod before opening it. Standing on our front step are Luke, Wes, and Agent Croft. I haven't seen Croft since the day he told me he had enough evidence to arrest Will's father and charge him with, among other things, conspiracy. I remember him telling me that he would consider it a personal triumph to make sure Gregory Meyer spent the rest of his life in prison. Croft never got to do his victory lap.

"Hello, Layla, or should I say Mrs. Meyer?" Agent Croft says stepping into the foyer. He reaches out his hand but I ignore it and choose to give him a hug.

"Hello, Agent Croft," I say. "It's so good to see you again."

"It's lovely to see you, too. I've heard your entire story from start to finish and all I can say is...remarkable. It's a pleasure to meet you Will," he says shaking Will's hand.

"It's nice to meet you, too. Thank you so much for all you've done and we appreciate you coming today. We're hoping you can help us navigate through this as smoothly as possible," Will tells him.

"I'm going to do my best," Croft answers.

"Um...shouldn't your Agent Lassiter be here? I thought he was leading a team of your people on this?" I ask. It seems strange that the lead agent on this case wouldn't be here to analyze the letter or the photos, or even ask Will and me anything about Black Sedan Guy.

"I got a call from the CSI unit. They think they've been able to pull some new evidence from the DNA they collected off the body of the first juror. Lassiter is a forensics guy and thought he'd be of better use there, so here I am," he says with a smile.

"The CSI unit? That sounds so prime time!" I say with a little chuckle.

"I actually have an old friend from the academy who does consulting for one of those crime shows. They try to make it as accurate as possible. There are too many people like me who would call and tell them they got it wrong!" Agent Croft laughs and I remember why I liked him so much when we met in Florida. He's just so real. "Ok...so let's see this letter."

"Here it is," Will says as we all crowd around the kitchen bar.

"These pictures are good," Wes says. "He knew what he was doing, what he was looking for. He knows that Layla is the mark."

"What do you mean I'm the mark," I ask.

"It means that he knows the way to get Will to do what he wants is through you. He hasn't come right out and said it, but he's threatening you. See how you're just slightly more in focus than anyone or anything else in these pictures?" I nod as Wes shows me what he's talking about. "He's making sure that Will knows just how close he can get to you."

"Do you know who this could be?" I ask Wes. I remember him explaining that Meyer always had someone take picture of his hits in case the henchman got mouthy. I wonder if, now that he's seen how good the pictures are, if Wes thinks he might know who it was.

"It wasn't any of Meyer's guys. Not only are these pictures very good, they're also very personal. The proximity with which he had to be from you is not a mark of one of any of the guys I worked with. They always kept their distance so as to never be seen. This guys has been bold in how close he's gotten, even letting you see him. Besides, even if it was, once Meyer was in the hospital every last one of his guys disappeared. None of us cared about the money so we certainly wouldn't come back months later for it. All we ever wanted was to be free." I can see in Wes' eyes just how true a statement that is for him. Now that he has his freedom, there's nothing that would make him go back to a life chained to anything that had to do with Gregory Meyer...not even $250,000.

"How do we know this guy is even going to tell us where Blasi's body is? How do we know that he's even the guy responsible? What if he's just trying to get an easy quarter million from Will?" I ask in the clarity of the new day. The FBI has to have dealt with this kind of thing before. I mean, what's to stop some crazy person from bilking millions from the wealthy just by saying they have information?

"We don't," Croft answers simply. "That's a risk we're taking. Now, Luke said you're willing and ready to take this on. Are you sure you want to do that?"

"Yes," I say as I take Will's hand. "But Will has the final say in how this goes down."

"I thought we were settled last night?" Luke asks with a quizzical look on his face.

"We were, well, I was. But Will and I talked about it last night and I trust Will to decide what he thinks is best." I smile softly at Will, hoping that his heart is full of joy at my willingness to let go and let him take care of me.

Will smiles back at me and I know I've put him at ease. "I've been thinking about this and there really isn't any other way around the situation but for Layla to do the exchange. But, since he didn't specifically say she was to go alone, I'm going with her." Will's delivery is straight forward and to the point. He's going to go with me so he can do everything he can to make sure I'm kept safe.

"Do you want to get both of you killed?" Luke says. "He said that *Layla* was to do the drop. You really think he's going to discuss the semantics of his instructions with you? We'll have eyes on her at all times, and Croft already suggested a transmitter earpiece so we can talk to her and hear everything on her end. You have no idea how this guy is going to respond if we don't follow his instructions exactly. It could be disastrous."

"I'm not arguing with you, Luke. Layla is my wife and I'm *not* sending her out there to face some psychopath by herself," Will tells Luke directly. This is interesting. I've always seen Will and Luke work together. Will had always been on board with whatever Luke thought was best, but that was when I was Luke's daughter.

Luke looks at Will for a hard minute, processing this uncharted territory. I'm not sure he knows what to do. We certainly never thought we'd be in a situation like this now that Gregory Meyer is dead. It seems I'm not the only one struggling with letting go and letting Will take care of me.

"Agent Croft," Luke begins. I know what he's doing. He's going to try and get Croft to tell Will it's an insane idea to do anything but follow Black Sedan Guy's instructions to a T. "What do you think of Will's idea?"

And there it is: the first pissing match between my husband and my father. I just never thought my father would be the one to start it.

Croft takes a deep, thoughtful breath, seeing exactly what's happening. "Well, he didn't specifically say for Layla to come alone, and he hasn't actually threatened anyone. He's offered information in exchange for money. Other than his claim that he knows where Blasi's body is as an indication that he's likely the one who killed him we have no reason to believe he'll be aggressive. Chances are good he's really just after the money, and Will showing up with Layla may not mean anything to him."

"Luke," Will says. "If I thought for one second that my going with Layla would put her in serious harm, I wouldn't go. She is my *wife*. I can't just send her out there. I need you to understand that. What if it were Claire?"

Luke looks down and seems to be searching himself for that answer. What if it where Claire? What would he do? When he finally realizes that he would do the exact same thing for his wife, he looks to Will and nods. "Ok. But I want all the same precautions on her that I mentioned. She's *my* daughter. Can we at least do that?"

Will extends his hand and shakes Luke's. Luke and I have learned a valuable lesson. Will Meyer is committed to taking care of me and there is nothing that is going to get in his way any longer. Not my father, not the FBI, and certainly not me.

Chapter 31

With the plan laid out by Agent Croft, and approved by my husband, father, and uncle, all that's left to do is wait. Holly's trial starts today, so that should take up a good portion of the ten days until Thanksgiving. Wes has resumed his post as personal security, ensuring our safety between now and when, as he put it, he personally takes down the bastard threatening his family.

We take our seats in the courtroom and wait for Holly to be brought in. We don't sit anywhere near the front row. Will didn't want to be that close to Holly, and I was in full support of that decision. Wes and Eliana sit with us while the other ex-wives, along with Michael and Erin, take up the row in front of us.

"How are you doing?" I ask Eliana.

"Fine, actually," she says. I imagined she would be a ball of nerves, but she's holding together just great. "Luke is calling me last."

"You're going to do great, Mom," Will tells her.

Wes puts his arm around Eliana and smiles. "Yes, she is."

The officers finally bring Holly in and seat her next to Luke. She's dressed nicely in a green, knee-length skirt, white sweater, and tall brown boots. She looks solemn, which is probably how Luke told her to look so the judge will see some level of remorse in her. Her mother is seated on the bench behind her and Luke, dressed in her trademark skin-tight dress and heels so tall I'd break my neck if I tried to walk in them.

"Is that Holly's father?" I whisper in reference to the man sitting next to Marlene.

"Yeah. Gordon Reynolds. Odd couple, aren't they," Will says.

"Very odd." Holly's father looks nothing like Gregory Meyer. He isn't a tall man at all, his head coming just inches above Marlene's. He's also balding and is working a sad bit of a comb over. He's not the angry figure I had in my head. When Marcus and Holly both talked about him, this is not the gambling addicted, stepson ignoring, lawyer I imagined in my head...at all.

"All rise," the bailiff calls. "The Honorable Judge Tabitha Harris presiding." We do as he says and the judge walks in a takes her place at the bench. We are told to sit down and all the official documents of the today's case are read.

The judge asks Holly to stand. "Miss Reynolds, you waived your Miranda rights and have confessed to murder by shooting of Gregory Meyer. Is this correct or would you like to amend your statement?"

"That's correct, your honor," she answers quietly.

"Alright then...does the prosecution have anything to add?" The judge reviews some documents while the prosecuting attorney speaks.

"No, your honor. What you have in front of you are the agreed upon terms. We've agreed to lesser charges should Your Honor agree that today's testimonies help corroborate the defendant's claims of mental anguish." The prosecuting attorney gives Luke a nod, and Luke reciprocates. They've clearly straightened everything out already and today's appearance before a judge is a mere formality.

"Then I guess that leaves it all up to you Mr. Weston." The judge doesn't say anything else, but sits back and lets Luke begin.

"Your honor, today's proceedings are solely to present a defense in Miss Reynolds' case for mental anguish. We're not asking for an acquittal, but are hoping you'll see that Miss Reynolds is not a danger to society. She acted rashly, without premeditation. As she watched the trial of Gregory Meyer – someone who had caused not only her own mother, but four other women, great pain – it was becoming clear to her that Meyer would not be made to pay for the anguish he caused so many. That day, Miss Reynolds heard the news reports of one of the jurors being murdered and, because of her experience with the deceased, truly believed he had something to do with it.

She made a split second decision, found her father's gun, went to the Federal Court House, and shot Gregory Meyer.

"Today I'll be calling first hand witnesses who will testify to the abuse and yes, even terror, that Gregory Meyer was known for among those closest to him. You'll hear similar testimony from all of the witnesses today as they detail the systematic, and often unimaginable, abuse they suffered. It is the defense's hope that this testimony will paint a clear picture of the fear Miss Reynolds had that Gregory Meyer would continue to inflict pain and suffering on others as he did to his ex-wives, including her own mother, and that Your Honor will take this testimony into consideration when determining sentencing. Thank you." Luke sits and waits to be told what to do next. I remember Luke telling me that, in court, you don't do anything unless you have permission to do it. Some judges are sticklers for rules of conduct and will throw a contempt of court charge on you in a heartbeat.

"You may call your first witness then, Mr. Weston," Judge Harris instructs.

"Thank you Your Honor. I'd like to call Loretta Morcos to the stand." Luke turns around as Loretta stands and makes her way to the front of the courtroom. She's not being sworn in since she's not giving testimony to help determine Holly's guilt or innocence, so she takes her seat and waits for Luke to begin. "Mrs. Morcos, would you please tell us your relationship to the deceased?"

"I was his first wife," she answers briefly.

"And can you tell the court the nature and course of your relationship?" Luke asks. He steps aside so that Loretta can speak almost directly to Judge Harris.

"Gregory and I met in college. It was the beginning of our sophomore year. He was pre-law and I was an English major. We had a very normal college sweetheart relationship. We went out when we could afford to go out, and when we actually had time. Most of our *dates* were study dates with

288

pizza and beer. But…we were happy. We had been dating for a year when Gregory asked me to marry him. He proposed in our favorite spot in the park. There was a little pond where we would take a picnic and feed half our sandwich bread to the ducks. He got down on one knee and everything." She gives a small laugh, remembering the good times with her husband.

I look to Eliana to see how she's handling hearing Loretta's story, but recall that she already knows it from both the written statements and then when she met with Loretta and Victoria the night before Will and I returned from our honeymoon.

"Were things always happy, as you put it?" Luke is paving the beginning of the path that is going to lead to hearing about the abuse that Gregory Meyer inflicted on all of his wives.

"Well…we were happy for a long time, I think. We were engaged for a year before we married. We honeymoon in Cape Cod. My parents had some friends with a summer home there. They let us stay there for free, which was good because we were still totally broke college students." She smiles again and I can't help but believe that she'll be the only former Mrs. Meyer that will do that on the stand today. "We had been married about a year and a half when I found out I was pregnant. We were both very excited. I was teaching and Gregory was in in law school. We were busy but, we made it work, and we were confident I'd be able to stay home with the baby, or maybe just teach part time." Loretta sighs and I know she's about to talk about the transition Meyer took from loving husband to control freak.

"Take your time, Mrs. Morcos," Luke says reassuringly.

"I…developed some complications mid-pregnancy and was put on bed rest for a month. Gregory was wonderful during that time. He took me to more doctor appointments, and started coming home early so I wasn't by myself for too long, and also so he could make dinner for me even though he was in a very prestigious internship." *Gregory Meyer knew how to cook? I would have never guessed!* "Eventually all the time he was spending taking me to the doctor and leaving early caught up with him and he was dismissed from his internship. It was at that point that a switch got flipped."

"What do you mean by that?" Luke asks.

"Well, he became very distant from me. He stopped asking how I was doing, or how the baby was. He started drinking more often, and more expensively."

"What was his behavior like when he was drinking?"

"He became physically and verbally abusive. I got on in my pregnancy but moved a little slower as a lot of very pregnant women do. He would shove me into the counter in the kitchen, and he slapped me across the face a few times. Then there were the insults about my weight, telling me I better lose all the baby weight because he couldn't have a fat wife." Loretta pauses to collect her thoughts. I watch her and wonder if it's just as difficult to talk about now as it was then. It seems that the pain of the one person who's supposed to love and support you most speaking to you and treating you so harshly wouldn't go away easily, or ever.

"I finally broke down and told my mother what was happening. She got in the car the next day and drove four hours to come and get me. We packed up all my things and I left. I intentionally left my mother's phone number in the note so that Gregory would have it right there to call me. A week went by before he called, but only to tell me he needed half of the rent. That's when I knew it was absolutely over. I had our daughter Erin three weeks later. My mother called him before we left for the hospital, thinking that maybe he might get there in time if he left right away. She was hopeful but I knew not to expect him. He never showed up.

"I reached out to him several times and he never responded. I sent pictures of Erin, but clearly that didn't mean anything to him. When Erin was almost a year old, and Gregory had not being involved in any way shape or form, I sent him the documents requesting him to relinquish his parental rights. I sent them on a Monday and I had them back by the following Monday."

"Thank you, Mrs. Morcos. I appreciate your time and honesty here today." Luke takes his seat and jots something down on his legal pad. Maybe something he thought of asking Loretta but decided just to wait and pose it to the next witness.

"Thank you, Mrs. Morcos. You may be seated," Judge Harris instructs. "Mr. Weston, you may call your next witness."

"We'd like to call Victoria Meadows to the stand," Luke says, turning and nodding at Victoria. Michael, sitting next to her, doesn't flinch when she gets up from his side and walks to the front of the courtroom. I can't see his face, but I imagine he's completely stoic.

Victoria takes her seat in the witness box and, after stating that she was Gregory Meyer's second wife, Luke poses the same question to her as he did to Loretta about the nature and course of their relationship.

"Gregory was very charming when we first met. I was the receptionist at a law firm and he was opposing counsel on a big case our firm was handling. He was frequently at our office for meetings. He eventually asked me out to dinner. I wanted to say yes, but wasn't sure if it would be a conflict of interest or not. When I mentioned it to him, Gregory said not to worry and that he would take care of it," she explains.

"Did you ever find out what *take care of* it meant?" Luke questions her.

"We started seeing each other and then after the third date or so, I was let go. It wasn't an unpleasant situation, and at the time they didn't say it had anything to do with me seeing Gregory. It wasn't until Gregory and I had been dating for several months that he told me he was behind it. He told me that he wanted to take care of me, which is why he discouraged me from getting a job. He had risen to the top of his firm almost right out of law school…a real power house consistently winning nine out of ten cases. He was doing well enough that I didn't have to work. It was nice to be taken care of by him. I had always worked. I'd had a job since I was 14, and I was 23 when we met.

"We got married about a year after we first met. Things seemed wonderful at first, but I was very lonely. Gregory worked all the time and since I wasn't allowed to work, I didn't have many friends. I told Gregory that I wanted to *do* something, get a part time job, but he wouldn't have it. One night I pushed him to talk with me about why I couldn't get a job. It turned into a huge argument and he eventually slapped me across the face."

"Tell me about your relationship after that first incident," Luke directs. He's got to lead each one of the exes into telling the story of what a maniacal monster Gregory Meyer was. How he charmed his wives and then turned on them in the end.

"He became increasingly cold and distant. Any affection I could get from his was like feeding a starving animal. He barely spoke to me so the only time I could have any connection with him was when we were intimate, but…I use the word intimate loosely," she tells Luke, lowering her head seeming to just realize that she's talking about her sex life in open court. I remember Eliana telling me the same thing about being intimate with Meyer and I can't fathom having to beg Will to be with me. It would be an embarrassing feeling, and a devastating blow to any woman's self-esteem.

"He began rationing our funds in a way that left me with little to work with for food and other necessities, and he became more verbally and physically abusive when I wasn't as compliant as he required," Victoria explains.

"Can you tell us about the day Gregory Meyer served you with divorce papers?" Luke inquires.

"Yes. I told him the day before that I was pregnant. I was nine weeks pregnant and my husband told me he wanted a divorce," she begins.

"Mr. Weston," Judge Harris interrupts. "I understand you intend to call two more ex-wives to give similar testimony of their marriages to Gregory Meyer. Is this correct?"

"Yes, Your Honor," Luke answers with a quizzical tone. I look at Will and furrow my brow, confused.

"Mr. Rossen, will the prosecution stipulate that the rest of the defense's witnesses will give similar testimony as Mrs. Morcos and Mrs. Meadows?" the judge asks. She seems a bit annoyed, but it could be the black robe and pedestal she's seated on.

"For the most part, Your Honor. I would stipulate that the rest of the testimonies to be given resemble Mrs. Meadows' more than Mrs. Morcos'," he answers.

"But you will agree that the remaining testimonies will not provide any information that greatly differs from what we've already heard, including the testimony of the defendant's mother," Judge Harris reiterates, now slightly even more perturbed.

"Yes, Your Honor," Rossen says with the same confused tone as Luke's.

"Excellent. I'm ready to sentence. Will the defendant please stand," she instructs.

We all look at each other, not understanding exactly what is happening. Is this is a good thing? Doesn't she need to hear what all of the ex-wives have to say? If she doesn't let Marlene testify, she'll never know about how Meyer tried to force her into an abortion. If she doesn't let Eliana speak, she'll never hear about how Meyer constantly threatened to take Will away from her if she tried to leave.

Maybe she just feels that the testimonies are an unnecessary formality. Perhaps she had enough dealings with Gregory Meyer to know that, while Holly has to face some consequences for her actions, what she did really was a service to the community. Yes, I'm sure that's it.

"Holly Reynolds, you have pleaded guilty to the murder of Gregory Meyer. You've agreed to a plea of manslaughter and the prosecuting attorney has submitted a sentencing recommendation for five years." Judge Harris pauses, reviewing the documents in front of her. "Based on the heinousness of the crime, I'm hereby sentencing you to the maximum 144 months, or 12 years, including the seven months you have already served. You may be eligible for parole in 72 months, or six years."

The court erupts in gasps and Holly covers her face with her hands. Luke and Mr. Rossen look at each other wide-eyed, confused as to why the judge would hand down such an extreme sentence when Rossen made a clear recommendation for a five-year sentence. I see Holly's body shaking either from crying or sheer shock.

"Your Honor, Mr. Rossen's office has reviewed the evidence and agreed that a five year sentence is truly a fitting punishment for Miss Reynolds. She has no prior charges and is not a threat to her community. I urge you to reconsider..." Luke begins with a respectable fury.

"Counselors, approach the bench," Judge Harris demands.

"What's going on?" I ask Will.

"I don't know. I don't understand why she would give Holly the maximum sentence. At least she didn't change the charges to murder and give her the death penalty," Will says. He's looking at Holly with sad eyes. As angry as we both were with her the last time we saw her, we never wished this on her. We were all so sure that she'd be out in five years like Luke said.

"The judge had to have been totally duped by Meyer," Wes says, leaning across in front to Eliana. "Why else would she give Holly the max? It's almost like she's taken Meyer's death personally."

I watch Holly's parents. Gordon leans over and brushes Holly's back sweetly. Marlene doesn't move an inch and I can't help but wonder if she's relieved. Now Marlene has all the time in the world and won't have to worry a bit about pretending she's going to save any of Will's monetary gift for her.

Luke and the other attorney are dismissed from Judge Harris and take their places at their respective tables. Luke makes it known that he plans on appealing her ruling, to which Judge Harris replies, "Duly noted, Mr. Weston." The judge adjourns court, we all stand, and Holly is escorted from the courtroom back to jail.

The family and ex-wives gather in the hall outside the courtroom while we wait for Luke. I see Agent Croft and wonder if he had been there the whole time.

"Agent Croft," I call to him as I approach. "When did you get here?" I ask him.

"I slipped in right after everything got started. I don't like all the pomp and circumstance," he says with a smirk. "Crazy how things went down in there."

"I know. I'm dying to know what the judge told Luke and the other attorney," I tell him. I can't stop shaking my head in disbelief. "Is Agent Lassiter here?"

"He was, but had a meeting. I was hoping you'd get to meet him. He'll be at the exchange on Thanksgiving, but probably already in place when you and Will arrive."

"I guess we'll just have to connect after, you know, everything," I say awkwardly. I'm not well versed in how to casually discuss things like meeting a possible murderer to give him $250,000 in exchange for information on where to find the person her murdered.

Luke bursts through the doors of the courtroom and finds us immediately while the other attorney takes off down the hall. "We've got a problem," he says. "I don't know what they're relationship was, but Judge Harris and Gregory Meyer *had* to have had something going on."

"What did she say?" Claire asks her slightly frantic husband.

"She lit into us about what an upstanding citizen and outstanding attorney Greg was, and how she couldn't believe that we would even think to charge Holly with anything less than murder," he explains.

"But I thought you said the judge has to sign off on the charges that are being laid against the defendant. If she signed off on them, why would she be so furious?" Eliana asks. Wes is holding her by the waist with her hand in his.

"A judge has the right to reject the sentencing agreement. They're not legally bound to the number of years we've agreed on, even if they sign off on it. But...she didn't sign off on it. Judge Bell was assigned to this case. He had a heart attack last week and has been in the hospital. Just Harris only got the case on Thursday. Had there been enough time, she probably would have rejected the plea agreement. In that case Rossen and I would have worked something else out. Not that it would have mattered." Luke starts moving us as a group down the hall and toward the exit. "Rossen is still in agreement with five years for manslaughter, so at least we're straight there. But I think I'm going to have to do some digging. I don't know Harris well. She was a prosecutor when I was with the firm, but I never had any cases with her. She's a new judge, which makes me think she and Meyer had something going on at some point."

"I'll start working on it," Wes tells Luke.

"So what happens to Holly now?" Will asks.

"Well, Holly's going to be processed and sent to the women's prison in Raleigh. I'll work on her appeal here and try to find a way to get it overturned. We'll have to find something that would have been grounds for Judge Harris to recuse herself from the case in order to make that happen. There was nothing illegal about Holly's sentencing, so we've got to find the smoking gun. It could take *months* to find the proof we need." Luke looks defeated, like he's going to do his best to help Holly, but he's not all that confident that he'll be able to come through for her. "C'mon...the press is waiting."

We step outside and there is a swarm of news reporters with their microphones on and lights flashing. At the center of it all is Holly's mother. The cameras are rolling and she's called action.

"I'm devastated about the sentencing today. I don't know why the judge would rule so harshly, but I must continue to believe in our judicial system and know that she did the best she could with the evidence she was presented. My husband and I must say goodbye to our daughter now. We know we won't see her for some time and want to spend some time with her before she leaves. Thank you for respecting our privacy." Marlene dabs the corners of her eyes with a tissue and walks away with Gordon trailing behind her like a sad puppy dog.

"Luke! Luke! What do you have to say about today's sentencing?" random male voices call out.

"We're disappointed by the sentence today. The prosecuting attorney's office and I reached a plea agreement and Judge Harris, within her legal authority, rejected the terms. We *will* be appealing this sentencing. I have no further comment at this time." Luke delivers his bad news with a stone face and tone. This is a bigger blow to Luke than I thought it would be.

The reporters call out to Will and Eliana for a statement of some kind but they don't answer. Luke makes his way to see Holly while the rest of us walk in a huddled, protected group to our cars. We hug and agree to talk later when we've all had a chance to rest and process how quickly things went sour today.

"How are you?" I ask Will as we drive down the long stretch of highway back to Davidson.

"I was angry at Holly for how she used me, how she deceived all of us. But...she doesn't deserve this," Will says sadly.

"Luke is going to work it all out. Wes will find the evidence they need that Judge Harris and your father were connected somehow, and she'll get another chance." I take Will's hand in mine and graze my thumb across his knuckles. "It may take a while, but it'll work out."

"I hope so. I don't ever want to see Holly again, but I don't want her to suffer an unwarranted punishment," he says, giving me more evidence that my husband is *nothing* like his father.

"Luke will take care of, Will. He always does."

Chapter 32

It is Thanksgiving morning and I should be waking up with excitement and joy in my belly instead of the freaked out butterflies that I can't seem to get calmed down. I curl up next to my husband and we hold each other tightly, knowing what this day is going to bring.

"We need to have a real conversation about today, Will," I say him, keeping my head resting on his bare chest.

"We've had plenty of conversations about today, Layla. There's nothing really to discuss." Will strokes my arm that is laying across his stomach. I close my eyes and savor every pass his fingers make from my shoulder to my fingertips.

"We've talked about logistics and key words and phrases, how to be cooperative without compromising, and how to make sure we get as accurate information as possible. What we haven't talked about is the reality that one or both of us could get seriously hurt...or worse," I say.

"I know. I don't want to go into it thinking the worst. I want to go into this believing that I'm going to sit down to Thanksgiving dinner with my wife and our family in our home tonight. Remember what Croft said. We have to be aware of the negatives but focus on the positives. Focus on how it's going to feel to tell Blasi's family that they can give their husband, their father the proper burial he deserves." Will pulls me tighter to him, making me feel as safe with him as I always have.

"You're right. It's just...It's made me think about something I've been wanting to ask you," I tell him. "The day we first saw Lingle Chapel together, you and Pastor Bishop seemed like you had known each other for years. What was that about?"

"Oh, that, well...my mom used to take me to church when I was kid. My dad *obviously* didn't go, and it was kind of the one thing that my mom was allowed to do with me. We went for years actually. It wasn't until I was about ten that Dad forbade us from going. He ran into one of the other pastors at the coffee shop and he came on a little too strong with Dad about the importance of going to church as a family. He didn't like being made to look bad, so we had to stop going. We just resorted ourselves to going when Dad was out of town. Dad being gone over the weekend didn't happen that often, so we eventually just dropped off the church grid. Pastor Bishop kept in touch, though. He was always so great to us." Will moves to his side so we're facing each other now. "How did all this make you think of that?"

"I don't know…thinking the worst I guess. I was thinking it might be nice to try going to church. I mean, I like Pastor Bishop," I say, not really sure why I feel like we should go. Maybe it's that I'm thinking if we both make it out of this alive, we're going to owe God something. I figure a couple of hours once a week is a small price to pay.

"Sure. We can go," Will says with a smile. "I'm sure Pastor Bishop will be happy to have us."

"I love you, Will."

"I love you, too, Layla. Thank you for saying yes."

"Thank you for asking."

We stare into each other's' eyes and somehow I know Will is feeling the same thing that I am, asking the same questions. *What happens if one or both of us doesn't come home today? What do I want my last memory with Will to be?* As if on cue, we lean into each other, our lips meeting. Will pulls me close to him before moving above me. Yes, this is the last memory I want with my husband. I want to remember the feeling he gives me in these moments of perfection…the love, the peace, and the knowledge that we are everything each other needs. So we spend the early morning hours savoring each other before the unknown of the day takes over.

*****

"This transmitter feels weird in my ear," I say as I shove the small electronic devise into my ear. It makes a little screeching feedback sound and I wince.

"Sorry about that," Agent Croft says. "How's this? Is this better? Testing, testing, one, two, three."

"Yes, that seems better I think. Does Will get one of these?" I ask.

"We're only giving one to you," Agent Croft answers. "We thought it would be too distracting if you both had one. Agent Watts is going over some tactical things with Will right now, so we thought it would also be distracting if he was listening to me talk while he was trying to stay aware of the external situation."

"You mean if Will has to physically defend us," I say, filling in the blanks with layman's terms.

"Yes." Croft nods once.

"Where is everyone else?" I look around the surveillance truck we're in and realize that it's just me, Agent Croft, and another female agent I haven't been introduced to yet.

"Agent Lassiter and his team got in place before you arrived," he says.

"Where's Wes?" I have to know where Wes is. If I know where he is then I can at least feel a wave of ultimate protection coming from his direction.

"I don't know. Luke said Wes was handling this on his own. He assured me that Wes was not going to do anything illegal, so as long as he abides by that, I'm good." I'm put at ease by Agent Croft's openness to Wes doing what Wes does best. I'd be a mess if he tried to restrict how Wes does his job, because Wes is very good at what he does.

"It's time, sir," the female agent whom I still don't know says as Will and the other agent climb into the truck.

Will puts his arm around my waist and pulls me to him. It's a cramped space so it both puts me at ease and helps to create more room.

"Are you ready?" Will asks me.

I take the deepest breath I think I've ever taken and exhale in a rush. "I'm ready to help the Blasi family find closure. Let's do this…for them."

"Alright then. You both remember everything we went over?" Croft asks and we nod. "Agent Duke will be here in the truck monitoring the audio we'll be getting from you earpiece. Watts and I will be in the grassy area to the southeast of the marina and have eyes and ears on you the whole time. My portable transmitter will let me hear what you hear, too. I'll also be able to give you any instructions. If we see anything going down that you can't handle, we'll be there." We start to move out of the truck when Croft stops us. "You can do this."

I give him a tightlipped smile and take the small duffle bag containing the $250,000. Will threads our fingers together and we walk across the parking lot and down the steps that lead to the marina.

We're quiet as we walk, coming up on the sidewalk that runs the length of the marina. We pass the little shops in the building next to the North Harbor Club. Everything is so quiet. The shops are closed and so is the restaurant. There are plenty of boats in the slips, but there's certainly no activity since it's so cold.

"So what do you think we should name our kids?" Will asks as we approach the ramp that will officially put us on the marina docks.

"Will…" I begin.

"We're going to talk about our future, Layla," he says, squeezing my hand for emphasis.

"Will…" I say again, unsure I can focus on anything else.

"Future."

"Ok…um…I don't know. I've never thought about it," I tell him. We make a u-turn from the ramp and onto the wooden dock and continue to walk slowly past the trademark yellow umbrellas of the North Harbor Club.

"How can you have never thought about it? I've thought about it," he smiles. *Oh, he smiles.* The small flash of that unbelievable smile washes a wave of calm over me.

"Oh, really? What, then, do you think we should name our children?" I smile, too, forgetting for a moment that we're not on a lovely mid-morning stroll along a beautiful marina, but on our way to an uncertain encounter with a man claiming to be capable of murder for hire.

"I've always liked Natalie for a girl, and Andrew for a boy," he says.

"I like both of those," I tell him. "Well, that was easy. Now you just have to wait five years to see which we get first."

We stop at the small section of boat slips before the last big one and wait. You can see the highway from here. There aren't a lot of cars passing by, but enough to let you know that it's the holiday.

"Hello, Layla." Will and I turn and finally get a good look at the man who has summoned us here today. "I wasn't expecting you, Will, but, ok." He's arrogant and I find it immediately unsettling.

"It's you," I say, turning to see the elusive man who has been following us and taking pictures of me for months. The man who summoned us here to get the rest of his payoff. He's tall just as I thought he would be. The sunlight shows just how light brown his hair is, almost dirty blonde, and his eyes are a rich, brown color, like chocolate.

"It's me. Now, what was that endearing name you had for me?" he asks with a smirk.

"Black Sedan Guy," I tell him reluctantly. "How did you…" I begin, but before I can finish I hear Agent Croft in my ear.

"Why is Agent Lassiter there? Layla? What's going on? Did you just call him Black Sedan Guy?"

"By now Agent Croft is probably telling you that my name is Agent Lassiter. You can call me Tony, though. Is he doing that thing where he talks slow but loud? I hate that," Lassiter says annoyed.

"I don't really care who you are. We brought the money and now you need to tell us where Blasi's body is." Will is strong and direct in his speech, making me feel like it's all going to be ok.

"Layla, just follow Will's lead here. Lassiter is a forensic agent but he spent four years in the military as a weapons specialist. He knows his way around a gun and has remarkable aim," Croft buzzes in my ear and I flinch and wince at the static.

"That was Croft giving you a snippet of my resume, wasn't it? I don't like to brag but, yeah, I'm the shit, so you should do whatever he tells you to do." Lassiter pulls a gun from behind his back and just holds it at his side, like he just wants us to see it.

"Here," I say as I take a step forward and put the duffle bag down halfway between us. "I suppose this is how Meyer got to you. He waved dollars signs and you just bowed down, didn't you?"

"Layla," Will scolds me softly.

"I like her," Lassiter says to Will. "Feisty! I like you! *Of course* it was about the money. When is it ever *not* about money? Every crime I've ever investigated had money at the center of it. Well, except a few of the murders. They were about sex."

"Tell us where Blasi is." I try to have the same strong and direct tone as Will but I'm afraid I can't muster it.

"Well…here's the thing," he begins, cocking his head to one side. "I don't know *exactly* where the body is."

"What?" I say a little too loudly.

"Layla," Will scolds again. "Just tell us what you *do* know and we can work with that," he says directly to Lassiter. Will's tone is much calmer than mine.

"Watch your tone with him, Layla," Croft warns in my ear at the same time. Being scolded by Will and Agent Croft is not helping me right now.

"Shut up!" I say, pulling the earpiece out and shoving it in my pocket.

"What are you doing, Layla?" Will says as he tries to reach for my pocket and retrieve the annoying thing.

"Stop, Will! I can't listen to Croft and you and Lassiter." I focus my attention on Lassiter now. "What do you mean you don't know where he is?"

Lassiter gestures his hand out to the lake and raises his eyebrows.

"You dumped his body in the lake?" I can feel my temperature rising.

"Yeah, but that was like, seven months ago. With the ebb and flow and tides of the water, who knows where the body actually is now. Then you have to account for decomposition and there are actually some fish in there that might have already started to eat him," he says with complete nonchalance. He doesn't care. Of course he doesn't care. He killed this man on the instructions of Gregory Meyer, the poster child for apathy.

I believed, *truly* believed that we would find out where Blasi was and bring peace and closure to his family. Now all that's left is a stinging feeling, knowing that this family will be in pain forever. Rage begins to rise up in me and I act before I think when I kick the duffle bag off the dock and into the water.

"Layla! What the hell are you doing?" Will yells at me for my rashness. I'm going rogue again when I promised Will I would let him take care of things. *What have I done?*

"See, now you've pissed me off. I don't like to be pissed off. And if you still had your earpiece in, you'd be getting a warning from Agent Croft about what happens when I get pissed off. Looks like I'll just have to show you." Lassiter raises his gun and points it at me.

All I can think in this second is that I wish I could speak and tell Will how sorry I am, how I didn't mean to go rogue. I just couldn't stand the thought that Blasi's family will never know the kind of peace that comes when you know for sure what's happened to someone you love. They'll live forever letting their imaginations run wild with theories about where he is and what happened to him. They may even come up with stories, lies they tell themselves about what happened to him just to feel better. They'll wish they were dead because death would be sweeter than the pain the uncertainty brings.

Lassiter's face twists from the rage I've just caused him. I stand still and wait for the shock of pain to enter me, to blast through me like a cannonball. Lassiter fires his gun and all I see is Will's body rush in front of me.

The shot hits Will in the chest and sends him diving into the cold, November water.

"Nooo!" I scream. "No! No! No! Will!" I fall to my knees, desperately reaching for Will, but it's already too late. His body dove out too far from the dock and went under quickly.

"Get up!" Lassiter shouts at me. "That's one brave guy you had there. Had you not freaked out on me, he might still be alive. As it is, you just cost me a quarter of a million dollars. I hope your daddy has some extra cash put away. I have a feeling he'll pay a lot more than that for you."

"Let me go!" I shout at him as I start to cry. I try to pull free but he's yanking and dragging me down the dock with a firm grip on my arm. I have to go back and search for Will. I can't just let him float away into oblivion.

"I know you're watching, Croft! Keep your distance. You know I'm not afraid to do whatever I feel is necessary!" he shouts out into the chilled air.

As we approach the ramp that will take us back up to the sidewalk I continue to twist my body around, looking back at the place where Will fell in the water after he saved my life. *Oh, my God, he saved my life!* I can't see him though, and the ripples from where he fell are gone. *This can't be happening.*

We're about to make the u-turn onto the ramp when I get shoved down and away from Lassiter. When I look up I see Wes has tackled Lassiter to the ground. Lassiter still has his gun, but Wes is doing an incredible job of keeping it away from himself.

"Go! Layla go find Will!" Wes shouts.

I run back down the dock and hear gunshots. I turn back and see that Wes is holding Lassiter's arm out to the side. The gun has fired rounds into the water. Wes must be trying to empty the clip. Agent Croft and the rest of his team are descending on Wes and Lassiter, their own guns drawn.

I go to where Will fell in the water and begin screaming his name. "Will! Will!" I lie on the dock on my stomach and try to get as close to the water as I can, hoping I can see something. I can't just jump in not knowing where he is. I'll freeze and then we'll both be dead.

"C'mon, baby, where are you? I'm so sorry! Please don't leave me!" I chant as I move around the dock on my belly, thinking maybe Will has drifted under the dock. I'm about to shove my head in the water like an ostrich when I hear coughing. I turn around and see Will at the very end of the dock, trying to pull himself up.

"Oh, my God, Will!" I rush to him and pull him out of the water with all my strength. I pull and twist, trying to get a good grip on him. His clothes are freezing from the almost frigid water, but I manage to get finally get him out, laying him flat on his back. I look back to where Wes and Lassiter were fighting and see that Agent Croft's FBI team has surrounded Lassiter, guns drawn. "Oh, baby! Just lay here. I'll get some help. You're going to be ok!" I tell him as I stroke his face. I look at his shirt and try to find his wound but can't seem to find any blood anywhere. I'm pretty sure I should be applying pressure to it to keep him from bleeding out. Will moves my hands and unbuttons his shirt revealing a bulletproof vest. "What? How did you…" I can't seem to form a complete sentence. I'm just so happy he's really ok.

"L-Luke, W-W-Wes, and I thought it'd be a g-g-good idea. Ch-chances were g-g-good you were g-going to g-go rogue on m-me," Will says through the freeze his body is fighting.

"I'm too happy that you're alive to be mad at you right now! Oh babe! I can't believe you did that!" I throw my body over Will's and get a better idea of just how cold he is as the freezing water soaking his clothes begins to soak mine, too.

I hear the rush of footsteps behind me and see a crew of paramedics headed for us. One of them has one of those silver blanket things I've seen runners use. They get Will's shirt and the bulletproof vest off of him and wrap him in a warm blanket and the silver one.

"Layla?" I turn and see Agent Croft behind me. I'm sitting more to the side now that the paramedics are getting Will's vitals so I stand up and meet him. "How is he?"

"He's going to be fine. I'll be mad at all of you later for not telling me he was wearing a bulletproof vest. But...thank you for that," I tell him with a small smile.

"It wasn't my idea. Take it up with all the other men in your life," Croft smiles. "How are *you*?"

"I'm ok. I just don't understand why Agent Lassiter would do this? I mean, I know that Will's father manipulated people like Wes, but I don't know what the payoff was for Lassiter, or why he'd push for the rest of the money," I say.

"We'll find out when we interrogate him. Do you want to know what he says?" Croft asks. I remember him telling me that because I asked a lot of questions, I might make a good FBI agent one day.

"Yeah. I'm studying psychology. Maybe I'll join the behavioral analysis division of the FBI one day." I smile at Agent Croft and turn back to Will. He's sitting up now and his color is returning.

"His vitals are good. He's going to be fine, but we can take him to the hospital for a more thorough exam if you'd like," the paramedic says.

"No, I'm good. I don't want to go to the hospital. I want to go home. It's Thanksgiving," Will says. He's not shivering anymore, so that's a good sign.

"I'll just take him home. Thank you so much for your help," I tell them.

They leave Will with both blankets and help him stand at his request. It takes Will a moment to get his bearings but then he's fine. Will cuddles himself in the blankets and I wrap my arm around his waist as we walk the length of the dock. By the time we reach the parking lot Agent Croft and his entire team are gone.

"I can't believe you all thought I'd freak out!" I say to Will, Luke, and Wes. "Talk about not trusting a girl!"

"Honey, you *did* freak out," Will says.

"I was so angry. I know how much pain Blasi's family is in. I just wanted to alleviate it." I lean in closer to Will and he rests his head on top of mine.

"It's not over, Layla. If it means that much to you, we can have them drag the lake," Will says. His voice is still a little hoarse from the frigid water and all the coughing.

"That would be awesome, but who knows if Lassiter was even telling the truth? Let's just go home," I say. My clothes are cold and wet from hugging Will, and I need a nice, hot shower to ease the tension of the day. "It's still Thanksgiving and there's still plenty of time to cook the turkey and eat at a reasonable hour."

We send everyone home and try to go about our day like we didn't just face the barrel of a gun on a dock on Thanksgiving morning. Will and I even have time to take a nap. I bundled him under the covers on our bed even though he says his body temperature is just fine.

"I can think of other ways you can raise my body temperature," Will says with a flirtatious tone.

"We'll get to that, Mr. Meyer," I say, just as flirtatiously. "I still can't believe you jumped in front of me like that." I run my fingers through Will's hair as he lies on the bed next to me.

"I don't know why. I told you, Layla…all I've ever wanted to do was protect you. What would you have done if I hadn't been there?" Will turns and faces me, tears welling up in his eyes. "I couldn't bear it if I lost you."

"I'm so sorry." I lean in and wrap my arms around Will's neck and then move into my sweet spot on his chest. "When I thought I had lost *you*…it was so awful." His body is warm now and the fear I felt earlier when I pulled him from the water is gone. I can hear and feel his heart beating and it's the most wonderful sound in the world.

"It's ok, babe. We're here, together, alive and well," Will says, stroking my hair in that comforting way that soothes me to my core.

"I wish we could lie like this all day," I sigh.

"Me, too, but we've got family to take care of today." Will sits us up and locks his beautiful blue eyes on mine.

"Not just today. We've got family to take care of everyday," I tell him.

Epilogue

Five years. I used to hear the term *five years* and cringe. *Five years* would conjure up memories of my grandmother's obsession with making me pay for my parents' death and the years I spent as my grandfather's caretaker. It would bring up the feelings of abandonment, rejection, and sadness with having forgotten who I was becoming before my parents died. *Five years* meant sadness, heartache, and pain.

But…*five years* doesn't have the same meaning to me anymore.

Five years is now the length of time I've been Layla Meyer. I look back and see all that Will and I have accomplished over these years. We graduated from college, having managed to arrange three years of class schedules perfectly. Will got his contracting company off and running and has more business than we ever dreamed he would. He spends time in the workshop I gave him as a wedding gift creating and designing and making us all proud that he's carrying on the Hufford legacy.

I've been so lucky for the last year and a half to work with an agency that helps children who have lost a parent. I help them grieve and walk them through all the feelings I was never allowed to feel. It truly is the most gratifying thing I've ever done.

Knowing how much it meant to me, Will took charge of having the lake dragged and searched until Albert Blasi's body was found. It took almost a year, but Will just kept saying that until the search teams told us every inch of the lake had been searched, we were not going to give up until Blasi was found. At least Agent Lassiter hadn't been lying that Thanksgiving Day at the marina. I could hardly hold back the tears when Agent Croft allowed me to go with him to deliver the news to Blasi's wife and children. They were so thankful that they would be able to give him the proper memorial he deserved. They were even more thankful when we told them Lassiter was convicted of murder and jury tampering and sentenced to life. That was an outstanding day.

Five years means so much for the people I love most, too. Claire and I threw a small, but beautifully elegant wedding for Wes and Eliana three summers ago. We had the ceremony on the dock at Luke and Claire's at sunset. Eliana wore a simple, yet elegant, ivory dress that flowed when the wind blew, making her look like an angel against the orange glow of the sky. I'd never seen Wes so happy. Not only was he marrying the love of his life, but his daughter Anna came to the wedding. At Eliana's urging, Wes reached out to Anna to reconnect and help her understand what happened all those years ago. Anna was reluctant at first, but as Wes explained and Eliana backed up everything that Wes told her, she came to understand more clearly what Wes had done and why. Anna's mother hasn't jumped on board yet, but that's not what's most important to Wes and Eliana. They're building a beautiful relationship with Anna and it's a joy to watch them together.

Anna and Eliana have become so close that at Eliana's graduation from Davidson College, Anna was the first one to break out of the group and rush to embrace her. She practically tackled Eliana to the ground. There's a great picture of the three of them, my favorite in fact, hanging in the foyer of Wes and Eliana's new place. They chose to move out of the neighborhood to another one on the lake. It's so fun to be at Luke and Claire's house and take their new boat across the lake to Wes and Eliana's.

Luke spent the first two of the last five years digging into Judge Harris to find out why she would give Holly the maximum sentence and not the five years that Rossen recommended. It took that long to find any evidence, *anyone* who could give them an idea of what kind of relationship she had with Gregory Meyer. When the gross facts came out, I think I threw up a little bit. It turns out Judge Harris and Meyer had been sleeping together for almost a decade. I don't know what the benefit was to either of them. Luke looked back at all of their cases for the last ten years and nothing overlapped. The only thing Luke could determine was that she was just one more in a long line of women Meyer used for his own selfish gain. That, or in her twisted mind she thought she could one day be the next Mrs. Meyer.

Once the truth about Judge Harris came to light, a new judge reduced Holly's sentence to the five years recommended by Rossen. Unfortunately that wasn't going to mean a whole lot to Holly's family. A year into her sentence Marlene and her husband left town. Wes tracked them to France but Holly told Luke she didn't want to find her. Holly was happy they were gone. Holly broke down with Will, apologizing for the way she behaved. She wanted to speak directly to me, but I told Will her apology to him was enough for me. Apology or not, we have no plans of ever seeing Holly again. She was released a few months ago. Wes and Luke did for Holly what they did for Will and Eliana. She's starting over again with a new identity in Georgia.

There have been five Thanksgivings since Will and I married. As hard as we worked for it not to be, the first was marred by the events with Agent Lassiter. The other four, however, have been full of everything we ever dreamed they would be. But this one, this sixth Thanksgiving is going to be the most spectacular one yet.

"I don't know if I'm going to be able to wait until tomorrow to tell them," I say to Will.

"I know, but it'll be the best Thanksgiving ever. Our moms are going to flip!" he says with wide eyes and an even wider smile.

"Layla Meyer?" the nurse calls as she opens the door to the waiting room. Will and I stand up and follow her to the exam room. "How have you been feeling?" she asks.

"Good. Tired. I've been sick, but only really early in the morning," I tell her.

"Good. That's all very normal." There's a knock at the door and Dr. Kendall comes in, greeting both Will and me with a handshake.

"How are you, Layla? Feeling good? Sick at all?" he asks, reviewing my chart quickly and then washing his hands.

"Yes, good. All the normal stuff," I tell him.

"Ok then…I'm just going to measure you, see how you're doing here." Dr. Kendall feels around on my stomach and I imagine my little kumquat dodging his poking. "Are you certain of the conception time frame?"

I blush at his question because I remember exactly when this baby was conceived. Will had been asking me for months when we were going to start trying for a baby and this was the night I told him I had been off my birth control for a month. He thought I was telling him that I was already pregnant. When I told him I wasn't, he scooped me up in his arms and said that he was going to fix that. We had the most wonderful night of perfection ever.

"I'm certain," I say. Dr. Kendall notices the flush in my skin and blushes a little himself. "How about we do a quick ultrasound?"

"Is there something wrong?" Will asks with obvious concern.

"No, no. You're about eight weeks…we'll take some pictures and measure the baby. It's all good."

The nurse squirts my belly with cold goop and the doctor takes the ultrasound wand and rolls it over my stomach. In a minute we're hearing a rapid sound coming from the machine. Will and I stare at the screen, not sure of what we're looking at, but smiling like fools because we know our baby is somewhere in there.

"How about that?" Dr. Kendall muses.

"What? What are we looking at here? I'm sure our baby is on the screen somewhere, but…" I say with a small laugh.

"Well, this is your baby," he says, circling the cutest blob ever with the keyboard controls on the machine. "And this is your *other* baby."

"I'm sorry…what did you just say?" Will stutters.

"Layla is having twins," the doctor says with a smile.

Will squeezes my hand and I look up into his eyes. Tears are welling up and turning his eyes a brilliant shade of blue, bluer than they've ever been. It was hard to believe we were having a baby in the first place, but now to find out we're having twins!

All Will could say the whole drive home is, "I can't believe this! This is amazing!" And now that we're home, he's added, "Two! Two babies, Layla!"

I lay down on the bed and watch Will pace excitedly around our bedroom, smiling as the love of my life spits out every thought coming to his mind. "Where should we put their room? Maybe they can each have their own room, I mean, especially if we have one of each. I could remodel the house…give them a Jack and Jill bathroom. Or, what if it's two girls? They'll need their own bathrooms, right? Your people need your own bathrooms right?"

Will finally falls on the bed. He lifts my shirt and kisses my belly. "I hope we have two girls, just like you," he says in between kisses.

"I hope we have two boys, just like you," I counter.

"How about this," Will says as he moves to lie next to me. "Let's hope for one of each."

"That's great, but I think we'll be stuck with whatever we get. I guess it's good that you already have two names picked out, huh?" We laugh for a moment before Will kisses me, taking me by my waist and pulling me on top of him. I smile as we kiss, feeling his hands caressing the skin on my back. "Don't tell me you're already afraid? You're not going to hurt me, or the babies, Will" I say.

"Oh, no. I just thought we'd reenact the night we made those two little jelly beans," he says as he unbuttons my shirt. He stops his hands for a moment in between buttons and locks his eyes on mine. "I love you, Layla."

"I love *you*, Will."

I thought the last five years had been the most life changing for me. I can't imagine how life altering the next five will be. What I do know is that the next five years are going to be filled with nothing but love.

Love I longed for.

Loved I earned.

And more love than I could have ever dreamed of.

The End

THE LAKE

Acknowledgements

I continue to be so grateful to you, the readers. I'm blown away by your love and support. You invested your time and emotions into Will and Layla's story and came to love them as much as I do. Thank you, from the bottom of my heart for coming along this journey with us!

Thank you to my editor, Lisa, who fixes all my 'buts.' I'm so grateful for you and our growing friendship, and I'm more than thrilled to be 'stuck with you!'

I'd be lost without my Fab Four: Lisa S., Lisa B., Kelly, and Jenna. Your love, support, encouragement, challenges, and overall pure and undying love for Will and Layla's story has been unbelievable. Thank you for being honest voices. You all hold such a special place in my heart!

To my dear, sweet friend Dana. You believed in me from the beginning, encouraging and cheering me on. Thank you for your constant support. I treasure you and our friendship, and I don't know what I'd do without you.

I'm a go-to-the-source kind of girl, so I'd be remiss if I didn't thank my personal Attorneys On Call, Joe Lackey and Author Robert Whitlow. You helped me iron out the legal details and made sure that Luke knew what he was talking about.

I'm also very grateful to Will Rankine, my friend of 20+ years and my medical resource. Not only did you help me pass high school biology, but you helped me kill Gregory Meyer in a plausible manner. I'm grateful for the way you've always made yourself available to me, but mostly I'm grateful for your genuine friendship.

A huge thank you to Amazon. Thank you for making it possible for independent writers to get their work out there. You've created an outlet that fulfills the creative need in so many and I am eternally grateful! I look forward to many more projects with you!

To my family: my parents, brothers, sisters-in-law, nieces and nephews. I'm always moved to tears when I really consider just what an amazing family we have. We don't adhere to *in-law* stereotypes. We love each other and support each other like no family I've ever known. I'm grateful for all of you and the support you've all given me from day one. Thank you for believing in me.

To my kids, Truman and Claire, who inspire me every day. You are brilliant and beautiful people with the brightest futures ahead of you. Never stop reading. Never stop writing. Never stop dreaming.

Finally, it goes without saying that there is no way I could have could be living this unexpected dream without the most amazing husband on the planet. You never once doubted that *The Lake Trilogy* was going to be a success. You made sure that I was always filled with hope for what these books could become, and you reminded me of that still, small voice and the promises it whispered. There's no way I could make it in this world without you. You are everything, and more, than I could have ever dreamed up for myself. You are my happily ever after. I love you, Donavan.

For more information, visit:

AnnaLisaGrant.com

Facebook.com/AuthorAnnalisaGrant

Author photo by Charlotte Photography

CharlottePhotography.com

Cover art by Derek Wesley Selby/Divine Spark Creative Services

dwselby@gmail.com

THE LAKE

Made in the USA
Charleston, SC
16 April 2014